THE SACRED PAW

Sculpted in black argillite by a Haida Indian artist in
British Columbia, the Bear Mother of the world's
best-known story suckles the infant Bear Son (which, like
all little bears, has sharp teeth and scratchy claws).
Mothered by a human princess and fathered by a bear
chief, the son's divine origin enabled it to instruct
humans in the rituals of the hunt. *British Columbia
Provincial Museum, Victoria, B.C.*

Paul Shepard
and Barry Sanders

THE · SACRED · PAW

The Bear in Nature, Myth,
and Literature

VIKING

VIKING
Viking Penguin Inc., 40 West 23rd Street,
New York, New York 10010, U.S.A.
Penguin Books Ltd, Harmondsworth,
Middlesex, England
Penguin Books Australia Ltd, Ringwood,
Victoria, Australia
Penguin Books Canada Limited, 2801 John Street,
Markham, Ontario, Canada L3R 1B4
Penguin Books (N.Z.) Ltd, 182–190 Wairau Road,
Auckland 10, New Zealand

First published in 1985 by Viking Penguin Inc.
Published simultaneously in Canada

LIBRARY OF CONGRESS CATALOGING IN PUBLICATION DATA
Shepard, Paul, 1925–
The sacred paw.
Includes index.
1. Bears. 2. Bears—Mythology. 3. Bears in literature.
I. Sanders, Barry. II. Title.
QL737.C27S485   1985   599.74'446   83-40692
ISBN 0-670-15133-5

Page 244 constitutes an extension of this copyright page.

Printed in the United States of America by
R.R. Donnelly & Sons Company, Harrisonburg, Virginia
Set in Galliard and Kabel Medium

This book is dedicated to the memory of Isadore and Istvan
—BARRY SANDERS

Who will find peace with the lands? The future of mankind lies waiting for those who will come to understand their lives and take up their responsibilities to all living things. Who will listen to the trees, the animals and birds, the voices of the places of the land?

—Vine Deloria, *God Is Red*

My paw is sacred. All things are sacred.

—Sioux Bear Song

The Turning

I

A bear loped before me
on a narrow, wooded road;
with a sound like a sudden
shifting of ashes, he turned
and plunged into his own blackness.

II

I keep a fire and tell a story:
I was born one winter
in a cave at the foot of a tree.

The wind thawing in a northern
forest opened a leafy road.

As I walked there, I heard
the tall sun burning its dead;
I turned and saw behind me
a charred companion,
my shed life.

—John Haines

Contents

Illustrations: Frontispiece, pages 22, 23,
25, 27, 29, and following page 110

Introduction

From time far older than memory, the bear has been a special being: humanlike, yet close to the animals and hence to the source of life. Like us, the bear stands upright on the soles of his feet, his eyes nearly in a frontal plane. The bear moves his forelimbs freely in their shoulder sockets, sits on his tail end, one leg folded, like an adolescent slouched at the table, worries with moans and sighs, courts with demonstrable affection, produces excrement similar to man's, snores in his sleep, spanks his children, is avid for sweets, and has a moody, gruff, and morose side. The bear is himself a creature in his own right, needing no justifying or compliance with human purpose. Try as we may, however, the bear's independence is hard for us to allow, for we cannot shake off the impression that behind the long muzzle and beneath the furry coat so unlike our naked skin there is a self not so different from us. He is a kind of ideogram of man in the wilderness, as though telling of what we were and perhaps what we have lost: wily, smart, strong, fast, agile, independent in ways that we humans left behind when we took up residence in the city. Moving away from his presence, we also surrendered a world view that held him in reverent esteem. The bear symbolized the harmony of society and nature, a harmony disrupted in the modern world, in a philosophical lurch separating man from his natural origins.

Yet our long association with the bear seems imprinted in daily language, religion, literature, folklore, fairy tales, place names, toys, plant and food names, even surnames. As a stuffed-toy companion, as a family in "Goldilocks," and as the forest ranger "Smokey," the bear remains alive in the popular imagination. Even in the urban doldrums he imparts feelings of vitality and strength, immediacy and exhilaration in the names of athletic teams. In his liveliness we sense a secret power, as though he were the embodiment of our *anima*—spirit, soul, or holy breath.

For us now this all seems to follow from the historical fact: around the northern hemisphere, wherever he migrated, man found the pawprints of the bear. More widely than most other animals, the bear has adapted to different weather and geography, making all places his own. A species of bear can be found in every continent except Australia, from Venezuelan deserts and Malayan jungles to the polar ice fields. Even where the bear has been extirpated he haunts human memory and is brought back, caged, and made to dance his shaggy jig. Where there are no real bears, the name is given to other animals, such as the koala bear, an arboreal Australian marsupial.

The bear strikes a chord in us of fear and caution, curiosity and fascination. In self-absorption we may fool ourselves, forgetting his otherness, and feed him in a national park as if he were a pet dog. Perhaps the impulse is the same, whether we invite the bear to share our food or our folklore: the urge to be reunited with something lost and treasured, seen in the animal that most resembles us. It is almost as though in him we can see how great is our loss of contact with ourselves. Perhaps the bear can still serve as a pilot and messenger.

Versatile in meaning as he is, in his natural state, the bear is many things to men: the stuffed Teddy and Pooh of childhood fantasy, the shambling, morose clown of the circus, the huckster and caricature of cartoons, the terrifying monster of the forest and arctic ice, the prince of game animals, the grandmother in mythic kinship to humans, a constellation marking the passage of the night, the season and the cycle of life, a symbol of the Church, and a powerful spirit who mediates between man and a forest god.

There is far more to know about man and bears than we can tell in this book. Their history together has been rich and primal. The bear has represented fearful evil and, at other times, regenerative power. The bear is not only complex, but ambiguous and contradictory. In literature it is both smart and naïve, forgiving and vicious. Here we may track the bear through its remarkable biology, glimpse a thousand centuries of a shared ecology, and scan its transformation in myth and literature, only to raise questions about our incessant desire to capture it. When he crosses into "our" world, in what sense does he remain a bear? How are we to argue for his presence in a world committed to minimizing risk and cost? When we see him as an old man in a furry coat and speak of him as "elder brother," do we falsify him or acknowledge a shared reality?

For longer and more widely than the record can prove, men have studied the bear track and kept the slain bear's paw as a sacred talisman. In his dark cave, the sleepy bear licks his paw for reasons we do not understand, but only mock when we eat a sweet "bear-claw" pastry. Science now hangs a radio transmitter on the bear's neck to trace his movements, but we may ask who is really lost.

The bear has been an ancient sacred presence since the beginning of European culture. Through folk customs and archaic rites far older than the records of state and empire, European and Mediterranean peoples were linked to traditions of Scandinavia, Russia, the Far East, and pre-Viking North America; before Socrates and Moses, Latin peoples venerated and perhaps even celebrated the bear in performances basically similar to, though differing in detail from, those of northern peoples around the world. The mills of time have scattered the records of those ceremonies, but indirect evidence for the bear's role in the birth of human consciousness is found in archaeological relics, in the residue of belief today in tribal cultures, and in the structure of the language we use.

The Oxford English Dictonary, for example, devotes several pages to the many meanings of "bear." The Teutonic stem word *ber* is the forerunner of *bar,* the German for "bear," and such terms as "bar-row," "burgh," "barn," "barley," "beer," "berth," "bereave," "be-rate," "berseuse" (or lullaby), "berg," "burgher," "bier," "bairn"; such proper names as the cities of Bern, Berlin, and Bergen; and personal names like Bernard, Bertha, Gilbert, Herbert, Robert, and, literally, the Scandinavian name Biorn or Bjorn. Other extensions from the stem syllable produce *pare* and *pero,* or "parent" and "father," which are in turn related to *generare* and *procreare.* A series of connected words, *berusjis, beruseis, bruseis,* tie the Teutonic stem word to the Latin *oursis* or *Ursus* as well as to *orso* and *oso,* "bear" in Italian and Spanish, through *urcsus* to *arctos,* "bear" in Greek. In this way "arctic," as well as personal names such as Arthur, may be seen as bearish in their origins, the latter being the half-legendary king of medieval England, who was said not to be dead but only sleeping on the isle of Avalon. *Ber* is also cognate with *fer* and *ver*. From *fer* comes *ferrum*, the Latin for "iron," as well as "feral," along with "ferry," "fertile," and "ferocious." From *verfortis* is derived the Icelandic word *eofor* for "man," or *eorn* which, as *bjorn*, means "formed," and is also "bear" in Danish. As for the Greek *arktos*, a cognate word is *arkhos* or "chief," with its scores of related words such as "archaic," "archbishop," and "archaeology," all referring to "overarching" primary sources and powers.

Arcturus, the name of the bright star in the constellation of Boötes, the hunter of the bear in the northern sky, comes from the same word. In 1832 an ancient statue of *Artio,* a Celtic bear goddess, was exhumed from beneath the streets of Bern, Switzerland. The source of the name Bridget is in the stem word for "bear"; she is a Celtic fire goddess and Christian saint. Linked to the same word origins are "bright" and "shine," reminding us of Jung's assertion that there is a bear with glowing eyes deep in the human unconscious. *Bruin* means not only "bear," but also "brown," "bright," and "burnish."

The welter of terms that seem at first to have no unifying theme— a slab for carrying the dead, a fermented drink, a grain, a child, a lap, a load, a mountain, a resident of a town, a building—now begin to make sense: all of these fit in with the idea of the parent-creator. Barley is the "bear's grain," incubated underground to make beer. The bear is the prototype of the wild animal, a kind of model of man in the wilderness, whose home is the mountain or "berg," where the bear people live, to whom the bear returns in hibernation and in death.

Such connections cannot be proved. For example, does being bare, or naked, refer to the nearly hairless state of the newborn cub? And, then, to grow hairy and bristly on the face—is that to be *bear*ded, that is, with a beard? Etymologically, there can be no way of knowing. These words could, many centuries ago, have referred to observations of the animal. Indirectly, there is reason to think that such a reference actually was meant, that the life history of the bear was a kind of paradigm for men, a model of human existence— birth and maternal care and many other behaviors, such as hibernation, are echoed in human culture through rebirth rituals associated with caves and the mortuary ceremonies of death, burial, and reincarnation.

"Bury" and "borrow" (as in the old "borrow-mound" graves or the act of "burrowing"), like "bier," speak of the bear's relationship to death, not because the animal was so powerful but because it moved between the underworld of the dead, the land of the living, and the sky home of eternal spirits. Among tribal Scandinavians and Eastern Siberians a human borne to his grave on a bier (sometimes a door taken from its hinges) was, in effect, brought to the grave on or in a bear, wrapped with a bearskin, carried out of the tent or house through a special doorway, just as the hunted, slain bear was brought in by an entrance having no other purpose.

Bruin—"brown" in German—also means "bear," that is, the brown animal, a Teutonic euphemism that, like many others around the world, enables men to speak of a sacred being indirectly. Likewise, the Old English *burlic,* also from *beran,* means "exalted," and we know that the bear is widely associated with a holy mountain in myth and revered as a constellation in the night sky. The German word for "mountain"—*berg*—and the Latin root for "fortress" come from *bherg,* as do a passel of words meaning "to hide" and "to protect."

In these terms we see the bear in cyclical motion: "going away," as in its funeral rites; and, in other linguistic elements, engaged in "carrying in" or "bringing" a message of divine grace. The bear has for thousands of years been the master of souls, bodies, and minds in transition. The syllable from which comes "bear" also produces "basket," "amphora," and, perhaps most important of all, "metaphor," meaning literally to "carry over." Metaphor is the bear's carrying of his poetic and transfiguring messages between the human and the spiritual domains.

Perhaps the most revealing aspect of an animal's name is its use as a verb. Such infinitives as "to duck," "to fox," "to skunk," "to hog," and "to bug" are said to be irreducible verbs; that is, there is no simpler expression of their meaning. "Bear" is one of the richest of such primary words, a synonymy of noun and verb, being and action. "It is one of the basic verbs in the language," says etymologist Charles Ruhl, "whose meaning cannot be formulated in words." It has inherent, general meaning unconsciously understood, a "semantic unity" with an underlying sense of "to carry."

INDO-EUROPEAN ROOTS OF "BEAR"

While the familiar stem word for "bear" is *ber* or *bar* and the verb *gebaren,* there is an even deeper substrate of word roots which may never actually have been spoken as a language. These somewhat hypothetical root terms are like fossil traces that show relationship. Such "semantic unity" as the diverse meanings of bear-related words have may best be understood in their origin. For "bear," these roots are:

bher- words meaning to carry or give birth, Old English *beran, forbearan, bier, bearm, bearwe* ("basket"), "burlic" (ex-alted or borne up), "burly," "burden," "birth," "bairn," and other Old German *bur-*words. *Bher-* with the root *enek-* produces "to reach" and, as *bhrenk,* "to bring," as in the German *bringan.* The Gaulish *berta* means "to shake," the Latin *ferre* means "to carry," and the Greek *pherein* gives us "amphora" and "metaphor." *Bher-* may also undergird the Old English *brun,* producing "bright" and "brown." "Birch" is derived from this source.

bherg- produces the Old English *beorcan,* meaning "to growl or bark," and perhaps "bereave" and "berate."

bhergh- is the root of terms meaning "to hide or protect" and the Old English *byrgan,* "burial" or "to bury." It is also the source of "hill," and "borrow" via "berg," and its inhabitant, a "bergher." "Barn" and "barley" are here, the first being derived from the second as "barley-place" or *bere + n.*

There are, of course, dozens of other permutations from these roots, whose actual connection to bears would be tenuous. The possible inferential terms that grow and change with language are unlimited. Yet those deductive meanings depend on an en-during and inherent idea, on what is said to be the "monosemic" meaning—which may perhaps be traced back to the beginnings of speech and an indelible imprint from real bears.

The Teutonic *ber* is short for the Old High German and Old English word *beran* or, in Latin, *ferre*, "to carry." But the dictionary has much more to say: it gives at least forty-four meanings for the verb "to bear." Many of these tend to be so similar that it is not difficult to group them into the following fourteen categories:

1. to bring forth, give birth, yield, or produce
2. to support, hold up, or carry, to "bear responsibility"
3. to maintain, to "bear the love of"
4. to be susceptible to, to "bear watching"
5. to orient or take direction, to "take bearings"
6. to lean or push steadily, as boats "borne by the current," to forge
7. to refer, to have relevance, to "bear on" a subject
8. to be accountable, to "bear watching"
9. to have fortitude, to tolerate or endure, to "bear misfortune"
10. to convey, transmit, or relate, to "bear tidings"
11. to possess or have a visible quality, to "bear shape"
12. to corroborate or confirm, as when results "bear out" expectations
13. to lend aid, to support, to "bear arms"
14. to remember, to "bear in mind"

And these fourteen can be compressed still further into three distinct categories:

I. NAVIGATION. The bear moves across the terrain like no other animal: a purposeful and methodical transit keyed to the plants and fruits of the seasons, the places where young ungulates are being born, caterpillars are emerging, acorns are ripening, or salmon are running. The bear knows all sources of food and all den sites. He moves through space tuned to the needs and possibilities of the seasons, as deliberate as the celestial rhythms. He departs from the earth into the ground, seeming to know the way and time to enter the underworld, as well as when and how to return from it. Above all, across the northern sky the Great Bear rises according to the season and makes its impeccable circuit of the North Star each night. It guides men on earth to their similar physical needs; it precedes them by example into the realm of death itself and back again to new life; and its perfect movement in the arc of the sky helps men on earth keep oriented and is their clock in the course of the night. The whole vault of the heavens seems almost to revolve in time with the energy of the bear's chase, providing the momentum for the passage not only of the night but of the coming of the sun and, as the days pass, the season of the year.

II. TRANSPORTATION. For centuries men of the northern world have known that the hunt was a holy activity, and that death, far from being tragic, was, in the form of the quarry, the gift that showed men to be in good grace. The body of the slain bear was accepted by them not only as a sumptuous container of meat, fat, healing substances, and fur, but as a communication. To these American and Eurasian tribal peoples the bear is not a mundane food but a special bestowal accompanied by a still-living soul. The bear brings to the people a message of good ecology and good relations between them and the sacred powers that govern the world. When the bear delivers himself by allowing his den location to be known, and the ceremonies and songs of his presence are celebrated—the bear being addressed as a guest at his own feast and sent off with the joyful reverence of his hosts still ringing in his ears—his spirit returns to his mountain home and the domain of the ruling divinities of the forest. He himself has become the message. The flesh and skin of the bear are not part of the ordinary needs of the people, and so, not being daily tender, he is freed to be almost wholly symbolic, to *convey* in the richest sense, to mediate between the world of humans and the world of spirits. He is an emissary in both directions, reporting man's respect and goodwill toward the forest, mountain, or animal gods as well as the continued favor and generosity of the world in providing for men.

III. TRANSFORMATION. The bear knows not only where the salmon and berries are in their season (in a sense bringing them into existence), but how to live without them. As a "she," the bear "knows" about death and how to survive it, both in her self-healing ability and in the little death of her hibernation. She is therefore seen by traditional peoples as a guide to the movement between worlds. The bear is the guardian of the underworld, and yet, since the she-bear comes forth from the earth with babies born deep in the dead of winter, is also a preeminent giver of life. Nurturing the cubs with loving care, licking and educating them, she transforms them into wholeness. When they are old enough, she deliberately sets them on their own, as though formally initiating them into their independence. So the bear mother, constellation, and messenger not only bring new bears into the world, evidenced by the cubs' remaining in the den, but guide the year's ripening, testing man's gratitude, marking the season, and acting as mentor in birthing and dying in the endless cycle of becoming.

What can these diverse terms associated with the stem word *ber* possibly have in common, other than their shared syllable? Is there an underlying theme that relates them to each other and to the image of the bear? Any answer we may give is speculative, since no one can prove that such a family tree of words also expresses a history of related ideas, yet it seems almost as though there were some lost, primal language based on permutations of the idea of the bear. Such an "urtext" of bear images probably never existed, but the various uses of the terms may show the result of a long evolution of word meanings in which, at some stage, the bear provided the most compelling example or even the concrete reality around which a concept was shaped in human thought.

Language supports the evidence from anthropology and archaeology: the figure of the bear looms in the history and prehistory of a large section of mankind, an image around which the electric pulse of thought and expression forms and reforms. Many of the words are themselves resonant with sounds made by bears, as in *brummbar,* a grumbler in German. The action connoted by so many verbs for "to bear" reveals centuries of men pondering the bear in the light of their own thoughts and deeds. The metaphors have grown like twigs on a great, verdant tree. Naturalists today refer to male and female bears as "boar" and "sow," as though the bear were a kind of pig, but the terms were probably first used for bears. "Boar" may be traced to the same origin as "bear," and its Icelandic cognate means "man."

If to us, today, the bear no longer seems to be a transcendent being, we can nonetheless see that, deep in our unconscious, where language "means" in multiple ways, the bear's sacredness is still part of our lives.

·1·
THAT
URSINE QUALITY

Modern science makes quite clear what is an animal and what is a man. In popular imagination, however, bears always seem about to transcend that division. Around the world furry creatures in folktales, legends, and myths, being both human and bear, remind us how alike are their ways and ours—and how fascinating are the differences.

The bear is the only very big omnivore. The omnivores—raccoons, men, coyotes, crows, foxes, pigs, and badgers—are generalized eaters, and the bear is supreme among them in his taste for diversity, from a single acorn or beetle to a whole reindeer or blueberry patch. True to this fellowship of the open mind, its attention to potential food is broad and unrestricted, so that, for bears, the whole world is interesting. Watching them explore their environments, we recognize a consciousness somewhat like our own. We have an uncanny feeling that beneath the fur is a man. Skinned, the corpse of a bear is much like that of a human.

Alive, the bear is burly and clearly more heavily built than we; a long gut for digesting grass makes his body more barrel-shaped than ours. Also, as a solitary hunter unlike pack-hunters such as wolves, the bear must be more powerful than his largest prey. The bear's heavy pelt, padded by several centimeters of fat, adds to the brawn a hulking shape that can be misleading, for bears are neither clumsy, obese, nor slow. The bear is like a macho bullfighter whose grace and precision seem to contradict his somewhat portly appearance. Large bears can outrun a horse in a sprint and kill a musk-ox with a blow. Despite this great strength and size that overshadow those of man, the bear's adroit use of its paws, as well as its excellent senses and cunning mind (smarter than horses or dogs, says the famous founder of the modern circus, Carl Hagenbeck), sounds a sympathetic and creative note in the human imagination.

Like us, bears are mammals and, being mammals, are hot, hairy, and sometimes smelly. They give birth to nearly naked, helpless young who are carefully tended and suckled on their mother's milk, an experience more important to their personality than mere nourishment because of the social imprint of the deep relationship it fosters between mothers and babies (and between one baby and another). Besides having few young who remain with their mother for more than a year (though maternal care lasts as long as three years in some species), and the other mammalian traits already mentioned, the bears share with their kindred mammals a complexly regulated body temperature.

Although they and humans are both in the mammalian order, the bears share their origins with the dog family. The oldest known true bear, *Ursavus elemensis,* the size of a fox terrier, lived in subtropical Europe twenty million years ago, in the Miocene period. The dogs— or canids—and other members of the carnivore order were also present: weasels, cats, and raccoons. But the bears were small and did not come into their own until much later, in the Pliocene era of about six million years ago. Huge, predacious forms then existed in the Old World, but among them was a little bear known today as *Protursus,* which left its bones in Spain, and was to sire the modern line of bears. The first of the genus *Ursus* appeared about two and a half million years ago. *Ursus minimus,* the "little bear," was a 45-kilogram* bear—about the size of the Malay or sun bear of today— and among its descendants was the Etruscan bear, *Ursus etruscus,* which ranged through both Europe and Asia. From it evolved several species of both living and fossil bears, including Denniger's cave bear, a contemporary of *Homo erectus,* the early man who was already

---

*We have used metric weights and measures throughout this book. A conversion table for those who may be more familiar with other units:
    1 meter = 39.3696 inches = 3.2808 feet
    1 centimeter = .3937 inch
    1 kilometer = .62137 mile
    1 kilogram (or kilo) = 1,000 grams = 2.2046 pounds
    1 liter = 1.0567 U.S. quarts

keeping fire 700,000 years ago. The cave bear of Europe, *Ursus spelaeus,* also came from the Etruscan bear and was known to both Neanderthal and modern man. Its thousands of fossil remains span the period from about 300,000 to 10,000 years ago, when it became extinct.

The great cave bear, therefore, lasted in Europe and Russia for two ice ages and the intervening warm period. Reconstruction from the bones shows it to have been huge—400 kilograms for a male— with a great, stout body, long thighs, short, massive shins, and large, strongly inturning feet—all features of a browsing animal rather than one that pursues running prey. Most notable was its broad, domed skull and steep forehead, small eyes, upward-opening nostrils, and reduced anterior premolar teeth, all consistent with its vegetarian diet. The high skull and heavy zygoma, or cheekbones, provided leverage for anchoring the masseter and temporal muscles, indicating a grinding rather than a slashing jaw. The forehead resulting from these muscles and bones gave the bear an intelligent look—a face—so that when a man looked into the eyes of the cave bear, he received a deep impression of manlike consciousness.

Members of the bear family, the Ursidae, have migrated across the Siberia-Alaska land bridges into the New World at least three times. Very early on, the large *Ursavus* bear produced a side-branch, the genus *Indarctos,* some of which spread into and left their bones in North America. Then, about one and a half million years ago, at the beginning of the Pleistocene period, bears from the *minimus* or *etruscus* stage of *Ursus* evolution crossed into North America and moved south, initiating a burst of bear evolution which produced the gigantic short-faced bear, *Arctodus,* in both North and South America, and the Florida cave bear, *Tremarctos floridanus,* which occupied what is now the southern United States from Florida to California. These giant, ice-age animals all died out except for a single descendant species, the spectacled or Andean bear of South America, the survivor, according to paleontologist Björn Kurtén, of "a once-mighty host of American bears."

Meanwhile, in China, other lines from the Etruscan bear produced the black and brown bears. The third migration into America, about 250,000 years ago, brought the brown bear at about the same time it spread west into Europe, where it coexisted with the cave bear. In America its posterity became the Alaskan, Kodiak, and grizzly bears. The polar bear, *Ursus maritimus,* branched off the *Ursus* stock of brown bears about 100,000 years ago—only yesterday in bear history.

It is possible that the black bears, both American and Himalayan, arose from the Etruscan ancestry even before the brown and cave bears; it is not clear when the ancestors of the American black bear went east, although the bear was probably in America early in the Pleistocene era. The remaining Asian bears of today—the sun bear, *Helarctos,* the sloth bear, *Melursus,* and the panda, *Ailuropoda*—have a more obscure kinship to the bears mentioned so far. Perhaps the pandas derive from the "dawn bear," *Ursavus elemensis,* while the others could have the same or a later start with the early *Ursus* bears.

The similarity of the bear family to the animals of other families of the order Carnivora has long been a subject of interest and speculation to scientists as well as to hunters and naturalists. The wolf, raccoon, and bear families are generally regarded as especially close. Their common ancestors belonged to the fossil family Miacidae, all small, climbing flesh-eaters. Members of the three families are sometimes ecological competitors, in their eating of fruit or rodents, for example, or are sometimes members of each other's food chains. Siberian wolves are a major danger to young brown bears. Arctic foxes scavenge the leftovers from polar bear meals, occasionally themselves becoming the meal. Of the use of dogs in Eskimo bear hunts, Nicolas Gubser says that dogs infuriate bears, "so that only the death of the bear or the dog ends the encounter." A special bear hound was developed in Tennessee which is widely used by American black bear hunters. Raccoons are also hunted with dogs, and are similar to bears in many of their habits. Although sometimes killed and eaten by bears, the raccoon is so like a little bear that in northwestern Europe it is the *Wassenbear,* the bear that washes its food.

The most troublesome members of this group of families are the pandas. Anatomically they share traits of both raccoon and bear families while also having special characteristics of their own. In the past some zoologists classified them as bears, others as raccoons, still others as a separate family. The difficulty arises because natural selection can favor dissimilar traits in lines of descent that are actually closely related, as, for instance, in the polar and brown bears. On the other hand, similarities in ecological niche can result in the selection of likeness in animals that come from very distant kinships, such as the true bears and the koala bear, the latter being a marsupial whose nearest common ancestor with placental animals such as the bears lived more than 70 million years ago. The more conservative features of animals, notably at molecular and biochemical levels, are less subject to selection because of niche differences. Using data from protein structure—which is a direct consequence of gene action and a reliable measure of biochemical similarity—some biologists feel that the panda problem has been resolved. Their analysis shows the giant panda to be a true bear whose peculiar anatomy is due to its specialized eating habits. The same analysis indicates the families Mustelidae (weasels) and Pinnipedia (seals and walruses), along with the Procyonidae (raccoons), to be more closely related to the bears than to the canids. According to this study the bears and raccoons developed from a common ancestor 18 million years ago; that bear-coon animal traces from a shared progenitor with the weasels 27 million years ago—a progenitor that itself evolved from a division from the wolves and other canids.

Of course, to a degree, classification is a word game played by taxonomists (from the perspective of molecular evidence, man, go-rilla, and chimpanzee should probably be placed in the same family, but may never be for subjective reasons), but the intent is to follow genetic lines of descent. In this view the koala is only a "bear" because its roundish appearance reminded English settlers in Australia of bears, as other marsupials reminded them of cats, deer, mice, and rabbits. As a pouched animal, its anatomical details leave no doubt, but even if there were uncertainty, a comparison of blood proteins with the true bears provides a measure of its unbearness, just as such studies have shown the giant panda, in spite of its peculiarities, to be a bear.

Although the differences between the living bears and members of the raccoon or canine families are obvious to the casual observer, the details of skull and leg bones are the usual criteria for biologists. The members of the Ursidae are more than 45 kilograms in weight when fully grown, and have stocky bodies with relatively short legs, necks, and tails. They have five toes and walk on the whole foot, with a pigeon-toed inturning of the front feet. They strike, handle, dig, and climb with the forefeet only. They can run swiftly and have long, nonretractable, curved claws. Their forty-two teeth (only forty in the sloth bear) include pointed canines to the rear of the front teeth or incisors, and heavy, crushing molars. The premolar teeth are not specialized for shearing, as they are in canines. Bears can stand up on their hind legs, and frequently do so to reach, fight, or observe, but they do not, in the wild, walk that way. The young of bears—possibly not including all the southern species—are born after three to five months of interrupted development, the actual embryonic growth of all bears taking only about two months. They are extremely small, blind, and sparsely furred, and their juvenile coats are marked with white on the chest.

The different species of bears have characteristic food habits that depend in part on the environment and in part on adaptive food preferences. All bears are omnivorous, but the proportion of meat to plants in their diets varies, not only among different species but seasonally and with availability. As with their eating habits, bears are difficult to characterize in terms of habitat. A species such as the brown bear may occur from alpine meadows to thick riverine forest, from arid barrancas to open parkland. Even individual bears may move through a variety of vegetational or topographic environments; bears need lots of room and normally live in densities of many square kilometers per bear. Each of the eight species occupies a large niche in its habitat and tends to be a generalist rather than a specialist in its demands. The distribution areas of two or even three species overlap in many parts of the northern hemisphere, although when that happens there is separation of habitat preferences, as the different species are not congenial.

Within their home ranges, bears are active in both day and night except where there is heavy human activity, in which case their daytime activity is often reduced to dusk or early morning. In areas where food is abundant and forest cover dense, the bear may move about within a few square miles, but where food is scattered and cover sparse, the home range of the individual may not only be enlarged, but may take on an hourglass shape, with areas of feeding or drinking connected to resting areas by corridors. Such a big, mobile, versatile animal does not live in a tightly partitioned segment of the environment the way a small specialist, such as a rodent, does, making it possible for a dozen species of small mammals to live in a single forest. Nonetheless, the different bear species show emphatic adaptations to vegetation and to the climate in which they live.

Bears are powerful swimmers who enter the sea, rivers, and lakes to travel, escape from pursuers or insect pests, feed, cool off, and perhaps improve their health (bears recovering from the effects of drugs administered by research biologists have been seen to bathe with unusual frequency). They apparently do not swim well enough, however, to have reached Antarctica or Australia. At the other extreme, bears live at desert fringes and do well where there is sufficient woody vegetation, but they have not been known to cross sandy deserts, and thus to spread from their formerly occupied range in northern Africa south across the subequatorial deserts.

Man's keen attention to bears has been mirrored in the bear's own sensitivity to whatever comes into its vicinity. It has an especially keen nose with which it is said to be able to detect a man a mile upwind or the odor of carrion at 16 kilometers. A rock kicked by a man from the top of a talus slope, rolling to the bottom, carries enough human scent to send a bear at the bottom running. Its hearing is also acute. At 300 meters the bear can detect human conversation, and it responds to the click of a camera shutter or a gun being cocked at 50 meters. The vision of bears has a lower reputation among hunters and naturalists; some report its sight to be inferior. But there is evidence of color perception, usually an indicator of a visually keen animal. The bear's activity both in daylight and at night is also a sign of good eyes. Much of the anecdotal information on bear vision assumes that the animal approaches strange objects because it does not see them well at a distance, but crows and coyotes do the same thing and nobody doubts their visual acuity.

Apart from the separate senses, the overall sensitivity and responsiveness of the bear reveals a personality not limited by single-channel specialization. When a bear enters a feeding area where other bears are present—a situation pregnant with explosive tension—the new arrival seems almost heedless of the others, regardless of their various sizes and genders, or of the moods that charge the atmosphere. Yet it is clear from the path he takes, the adjustments in his behavior and demeanor, and the assertiveness of his feeding that he is aware of every bear around him and all postures, movements, odors, and sounds that signal their intentions. This combination of overall awareness and seeming nonchalance is among the bear's most manlike capacities: a taciturn, calculating mixture of knowing and blasé sophistication that can be unnerving to human observers.

Human uncertainty about a bear's next move is in part due to lack of experience. The muzzle and face that seem masklike are, to other bears and practiced bear-watchers, highly expressive. Facial musculature, body movement, and vocalizations reveal the bear's mood and the probability that it will attack—which may vary from unlikely to certain in any given meeting between bears or between bears and people. Typically, bear society has the prickly quality of the interruption of solitude. Like whales, housecats, and orangutans, bears have long been described as loners, especially the old, temperamental males who go their own ways after mating (at least among northern bears). But among all these "solitary" species the exceptions are so numerous that the picture of bears as isolated creatures is changing. Little bears spend the first two or three years of their lives in a highly social setting, with their mother and usually one or more siblings, which means that female bears are in the company of other bears most of their lives. Even after separation from their mother, the sibs may remain together for several more years. The association of adult males and females during mating, which may last for two or more weeks, is well known. Because of the seasonal concentration of certain foods such as berries or fish, bears often find themselves within growling distance of six or a dozen other bears. Moving through their overlapping home ranges, individual bears are continuously aware of the presence of other bears through footmarks, tree scratchings, urinations, and defecations. Pandas even have scent glands for marking. In areas where there are limited first-class denning sites, both polar and brown bears are known to den within a few dozen meters of others of their own species.

If socialization is defined by living in packs or year-round mate association, then bears are solitary. But perhaps the net of bear sociality is cast so wide that primate observers like men, with their poorer senses of smell and hearing, cannot appreciate its subtlety and scale. If bears have in their heads a constantly revised map of the locations of other individual bears, should we not then consider them as truly socially oriented?

Unlike many other mammals, bears exercise all the senses, including excretory messages and the marking of trees by clawing or biting. Sometimes the same tree is used repeatedly over several years, but whether bears stand up and cut the tree to sign it, to shorten or sharpen their claws, or to get to the sap has not been finally settled. If this action does not pass messages to other bears, it certainly produces a puzzle for foresters and bear-watchers, and it elicits predictable outrage from those whose trees are damaged.

A tactile sense of some importance to the education of bears is their tendency to walk in existing footprints. Brown bears lumber along, more or less moving both legs on the same side at once. The individual can place his hind paw in the track of the front, and successive traveling bears match their strides to the steps of the bears ahead. In boggy country, over many generations, the effect is remarkable. Middendorf, a Russian zoologist, has described wet or snowy countrysides with hundreds of miles of trails composed of foot-sized holes resulting from thousands of superimposed pawprints. On harder ground a narrow trail instead of holes develops, so heavily used that Middendorf speaks of the illusion of human footpaths between villages and the impression in remote Siberian forests of a peopled place.

The use of certain trails, like the scratching of certain kinds of trees, is, like much else in bear life, seasonal. Apart from the stages of growth, the principal rhythm of the life cycle of bears is the annual round.

Polar bears follow extensive migratory routes. Himalayan, sloth, and grizzly bears make vertical migrations in the mountains. The human concept of the bear is anchored in this arrival and departure in connection with the shifting location and rise and fall of the food supply and, above all, the trait that has fascinated man for thousands of years—the remarkable winter sleep. The giant panda and the three tropical bears—the sloth, sun, and Andean bears—may retreat to holes, caves, or other secluded places for days at a time, or to bear young, but not for weeks or months as do some populations of the northern species: the polar, brown, moon, and American black. Even among the latter, those in the mild climates may not enter the true physical state of hibernation, but simply sleep in. Many polar bears are active year round.

Hibernation has been studied mostly in three species: the brown, polar, and American black. It is not known whether day length, weather, or food supply—or some combination of these or other factors—triggers the bear's entrance to a secluded place under logs or brush, a dug hole, a cave, or a snow chamber. Nor does it appear that the bear "decides" at the last minute, for in many cases the den is prepared well in advance and, before entering, the bear must be in proper, fat condition, pregnant, or accompanied by cubs of the previous winter.

Until recently, biologists had ceased to use the term *hibernation* to describe bear "dormancy," "lethargy," "physiological diapause," or "sleep," because some physiological details were unlike those of "true" hibernators such as the marmots, bats, and some other mammals. The main difference is that the bear's body temperature does not drop to within a few degrees of the surrounding air, as does that of ground squirrels, which typically curl into a ball and become comatose, waking periodically to excrete but otherwise becoming rigidly passive so long as the burrow temperature does not actually approach freezing.

The bear's temperature drops only about 5 degrees Celsius. In some ways its state is like that of the small mammals, as in certain changes in the component patterns of the heart rhythm, slowed to fewer than ten beats per minute, but in other ways the bears prove to be more complex. While the rodents turn on and off like lights operated by a rheostat, some parts of the bear become dormant while other parts do not. Although its heart rate during nightly sleep in summer is about forty beats per minute, and drops to around eight in winter denning, the animal's oxygen consumption only drops about 50 percent, so that it survives perfectly well in dens in which the temperature is well below freezing. Females give birth, lick, cradle, and suckle cubs, in spite of which they are able to exist entirely on the fluids and foods stored in their bodies. During winter a bear burns about 4,000 calories per day—which is very efficient for such a large animal—while its fat diminishes 20 to 30 percent over the season, providing both water and food through its breakdown. The nitrogenous wastes from normal cell death are degraded and reabsorbed, so that most blood plasma substances, such as urea, remain constant; an accumulation of these would be poisonous. All of this is achieved, in part, by what in diving animals such as whales (but including polar bears) is called brachycardia, the main feature of which is a constricted blood flow to many of the body's muscles while others and the brain receive a normal oxygen supply. Although the bear can appear a little groggy before, during, and just after hibernation, it can become alert in a few minutes and its heartbeat can reach a normal ninety-eight per minute if the animal is disturbed. Unlike many hibernating rodents, bears do not defecate, urinate, or eat while in the winter den. In the southern parts of their range the bears may lie up, come out and eat, and then go back in, in which case it is doubtful that the metabolic changes associated with lowered oxygen consumption take place. The same is true of adult male polar bears.

Among those that will go in for the whole winter, the late summer is marked by hyperphagia—that is, eating as much as 20,000 calories per day, with consequent rapid weight gain and polyurea that produces as much as 16 liters of urine per day. In the last days before denning, brown and black bears may eat nothing or only indigestible materials, with the result that an undigested mass occupies part of the rectum and plugs the anus. The system is controlled by neuroendocrine substances that continue to influence the bear's behavior after it emerges in the spring. In general, the bear survives its fast in the den better than it does the early weeks after waking if, like some of the grizzlies, it emerges into two feet of snow where food is scarce and the bodies of winter-killed sheep or deer are a principal food resource not always easy to find.

Many questions remain to be answered; it is clear, however, that the bear is not only a hibernator but that some of its finely tuned metabolic adjustments are more elegant than those of the smaller hibernators. Females generally dig bigger dens, make leafier nests in them, and enter the dens earlier and stay longer than do males. Non-denning bears do not show the heavy fat layer that denning bears have, which, in the brown bears of Asia, may be as much as 13 centimeters thick and make up a third of the animal's weight. Bears are fond of certain tender green herbs that come up at the edge of the spring snowmelt, such as skunk cabbage, and will travel some distance to find them, probably for their purgative or tonic effect.

The degree of care in winter den-making in the subarctic and temperate climate habitats depends partly on the severity of the climate. Denning behavior is further elaborated by the use of summer dens or resting sites, some used only once, others regularly. Even the daybeds may be lined with moss and lichens. Such polar bear daybeds are, "by personal experience, delightfully comfortable," says one bear researcher. Himalayan and sun bears make "nests" in trees, where they "bask," and the former is said to dry out carefully in such a platform before retiring to an earth or rock den. The sloth bear does not make a den but, true to its name, naps regularly and snores loudly. The spectacled bear also makes its sleeping "nests" high in the trees.

Among the northern bears the birth of young takes place during winter sleep. Although mating occurs in midsummer, the blastocyst or hollow ball of cells resulting from growth of the fertilized ovum "free-floats" in the female reproductive tract for as many as five months, its development halted. Then it implants in the wall of the uterus, and the gestation period of about three months follows. Such delayed implantation also occurs in the mink and bat families— in all of these animals it is probably adaptive to the seasonal round. Its biological service in bears may be to accommodate mating early in summer, while avoiding the penalty of having the young born just as winter begins. It is not obvious why mating could not take place in the fall, followed by a more typical mammalian development. Possibly there is some advantage to the whole population in keeping courtship and mating—perhaps with its side effects of competition and territoriality—as early as possible in the season, or maybe early pregnancy has some physical effects on the mother that give her needed preparation for the combined demands of a long fast and the burdens of bearing and suckling babies.

Among the denning bears there is no further participation of the male in family life (nor is there a bond bringing the same bears together again later on, although since they are long-lived and highly individualized, there is no reason to doubt that bears know each other as individuals, or that two bears who had been mates would recognize each other as former partners). The tropical bears, however, appear to do things differently, although the evidence is scanty. Big, old male bears have been seen in the company of a sow and cubs, but nobody knows how long or for what purpose that relationship lasts.

The tininess of bear newborns relative to adults is one of the most surprising facts of bear life. An infant grizzly weighs about 1/625th as much as its mother; that is, 255 grams compared to 135 kilograms. A newborn human child's weight is about 1/25th that of its mother. Pinkish, hairless (except for polar bears), and blind for several weeks, the little bears are virtually helpless. The mother licks them and, lying on her side, cuddles them between her front and hind legs. Although the figures vary from species to species, the cubs are about twelve weeks old and weigh about four pounds when they come out of the den with the mother. At first they nurse at her abdominal nipples, but later stand to nurse at her anterior teats as she sits.

Life is hazardous for little bears in their first year. The baby bears' rule, the same as that for tourists, is "no strange bear is a safe bear." Whether this rule applies to Himalayan bears, with their continued association of the parent couple through successive litters, is not known. But among brown bears concentrated at a salmon river, the dominance hierarchy is formed with big, lone males at the top, mothers with cubs next, then single, subadult males, followed by all younger bears. Because of this, bear mothers are cautious around big bears, aggressive toward people and other creatures smaller than themselves if they perceive danger to their cubs, and stern with the cubs themselves. When the latter do not scramble up a tree fast enough, they may get spanked. They also respond to her vocal signals to "stay there" and "come down," or risk a cuffing. The cubs continue to suckle for more than a year, although, like human babies, they sample a variety of foods as they get older. Little bears are the sine qua non of baby animals, perhaps because they act so much like human children. They play alone and with each other and with their mother. Their expressive faces and cries, infectious moods, rascally personalities, and manipulative approach to the world seem at once familiar to us, even on seeing a cub for the first time.

As the end of their first year approaches, young black, brown, and polar bears den up with their mother. Brown bear young will spend still another winter after that with the mother before separating from her. In their second or third summer, juvenile bears go or are sent off on their own. This is the most perilous time of their lives. Without familiar space of their own, not yet fully grown, and with much to learn, they are subject to many lethal dangers, especially bigger bears, dogs and men, wolves, and the accidents that may result from bad judgment. Conspicuous and assiduous foragers, bears go where the seasonal food supply is, from fish to greens, berries, corn, apples, or mast. Sometimes this brings them together with touchy adults who are working out their pecking orders, and the subadults are always at the bottom.

By the time it is five years old, a bear is likely to have some scars, but has become big and experienced enough to have better than an 80-percent chance of living another year—up from only about 60 percent for the preceding four years. Some species reach sexual maturity by age two, others not until four or five. Since the young remain with the mother for more than a year, she does not reproduce more often than every two years. Among brown bears the interval is more often three years, or sometimes four. The variables that affect reproduction are population density and food supply, the production of little bears picking up where densities are low or food resources good.

Over many hundreds of centuries, eating habits and other ecological relationships are central to the evolution of the physical differences among bear species. Head shape and size, for instance, are influenced by dentition and jaw muscles. Polar bears bite to kill their prey and eat more meat than other bears, and therefore have holding, chopping, slashing jaws and a skull shaped to anchor the appropriate muscles. Brown bears may bite or maul, but they kill or fight by swatting with their forelegs. A large part of their eating requires grinding and crunching. The subtropical bears are still more vegetarian and insectivorous, and the spectacled bear is more frugivorous than its northern relatives. The termite-eating sloth bear has little need for heavy grinding or slashing teeth. The more arboreal bears, particularly the sun bears and spectacled bears, are smaller and more nimble than others, even though the first is a short-haired, tropical animal and the second a shaggy inhabitant of the Andes. The northern bears can climb, but adult brown bears, like adult gorillas, don't climb much and are careful to step only on big limbs. Less of their food comes from trees, so that most of their climbing is done as cubs to reach safety from enemies. The black bear, as befits its middle distribution, is intermediate in its tree use. The Himalayan and grizzly races of the brown are adroit rock climbers, and the polar bear travels rapidly across the extremely rough pressure ridges of ice fields and glacial landscapes. When a biologist once attempted to define the uniqueness of man as the only animal who could walk or run many miles, swim a river, and then climb a tree, he overlooked the bears, who can do all of these faster and with more endurance than man, not to mention digging a fifteen-foot-deep hole or killing a horse with a blow of the forepaws. On the run, a bear is about

50 percent faster than a man, and all bears seem to like water, although the polar bear is the exemplar. Brown bears spend weeks in and out of the water at salmon-fishing time, and the evidence from zoos is that all bears like to cool off in water during hot periods.

As for the annual cycle, much less is known about the three southern bears. A typical round among the more northerly brown bears begins with a light grazing on early greens after emerging from winter dens, focuses for a few weeks on fish, shifts to a sequence of blueberries, crowberries, rowanberries, and currants as they become available, and works toward the meat of the young and old of mammals as opportunities present them and the season of reproduction makes them vulnerable. Both brown and polar bears have been known to kill reindeer, caribou, and musk-ox. For the polar bear, the ringed seal is a mainstay, but it also eats plants from the arctic tundra, a salad to which may be added a touch of lemming or bird eggs, interspersed with gorging on a beached whale.

Black, brown, and Himalayan bears eat livestock too, but much depends on individual circumstances and taste. The scavenging habits of bears draw them naturally to garbage dumps, campgrounds, and storehouses. The black bear, living in areas ranging from Louisiana swamps to prairies, hardwood forests, and evergreen forests, is also a denizen of rural landscapes and logged-off woods, and has a diverse diet to match its range. It is perhaps best known for looting and panhandling, which leads it to situations such as staring into automobile windows, being stuck in chimneys, crashing through cabin roofs, lunging into tents, rifling knapsacks, and solving problems presented to it in the form of tree-hung caches. In retreat, it may be covered with molasses, honey, maple syrup, grease, flour, or feathers.

When hunting large game, bears may stalk catlike, then run the prey down with a sudden spurt and kill it with blows of the forepaws and bites through the neck. In hunting seals on ice floes, polar bears slither on their stomachs, pause when the seal looks up and cover their black noses with their paws, then rush the seal from fifteen or twenty feet. When ringed seal pups are born in chambers three feet down in ice, the bear digs and smashes his way to them; grizzlies move great masses of earth to get marmots or ground squirrels.

Writing of the "cognitive complexity" of the grizzly, Lance Olsen has observed the bear's apparent consciousness of self-concealment, both in eluding and ambushing its pursuers. The grizzly seems to be aware of its own track-making, jumping twenty feet to one side to confuse a tracker, stepping in its own prints when backtracking, avoiding muddy spots, or going into a winter den during a heavy snowfall, with the result that its tracks are covered within minutes.

Like all wild animals, bears have both internal and external parasites, about eighty kinds of which are known. These range from bacteria and protozoa to trematodes (such as intestinal and bile-duct flukes), cestodes (like tapeworms), nematodes (roundworms, typically *Ascaris* and hookworm), and external forms such as lice, fleas, and ticks. Some of the intestinal parasites probably starve to death during the bear's hibernation. The nematode *Trichinella* may cause serious and prolonged illness in people who eat bear meat. Several strains are known, the most severe in man being those from the polar and brown bears. About three-quarters of the grizzlies are believed to be infected. Thorough cooking kills *Trichinella,* but when bear meat is eaten raw or when it is smoked or insufficiently cooked, the worms are liberated. They reproduce in the human gut and the offspring migrate via the blood to various parts of the body (just as they do in bears after the bear has eaten a rodent that has been infected by eating plants contaminated with bear droppings) and encyst there, usually in the muscles. If they lodge in the heart or brain, the effect can be deadly. Like other mammals, bears are also bothered by midges, flies, and mosquitoes, and go into the water or to high, windy places to escape them.

In general, the ecology of bears is that of a "top animal," a large predator who catches, plucks, and gleans from every level in the pyramid of life, from delicate tubers and ants to the meat of other large mammals. As such, the bear is not likely to be an important factor in the abundance of any other species, nor is it, in turn, overly dependent on the success of any particular plant or animal. As an occasional competitor with other large mammals, the bear sometimes faces off with tigers, leopards, lions, or wolves. Among the closest associations of any known between bears and other mammals is that between the polar bear and the arctic fox, one or more of the latter accompanying the great bear like pilot fish around sharks, haunting the fringes of the action for leftovers. Black and brown bears sometimes kill the trees they bite and claw—for the tonic sap, the taste of cambium, to make a mark, or whatever the purpose—

and are condemned and killed for doing so. Man himself is roughly a "same-size" predator, and for many thousands of years has been both a competitor and a danger to bears.

In spite of his size and rarity, the bear does experience some risks in addition to the presence of man. The cubs are especially vulnerable, but even large bears can be killed by the big cats, die of starvation because of a broken jaw, or from an infected gut wound received in a moment of carelessness from the horns or hooves of a cornered moose, reindeer, caribou, musk-ox, or other prey. Killer whales and large bull walruses are a peril to the polar bear, as are, presumably, poisonous snakes to the southern bears. Although little is known about the natural history of bear mortality, probably the most universal and ancient danger to the bear (besides man) are members of a closely related family, the canids. Wolves and wild dogs are known to harass and kill bears in much of their range. Man is the other bear-killer of note, and the combination of man and dog has marked the reduction of bears of all kinds almost everywhere. As a hunted animal, the bear is cautious and elusive, and among traditional tribal peoples it was usually, but not always, killed in or at its den. Modern men using firearms do not kill many bears without the help of dogs.

For most of the world's bears, man has been a relatively small factor in its natural history until lately—recent centuries in some places, decades in others. For polar bears the combination of rifle and helicopter has proved deadly, but in general bear deaths are due not so much to hunting as to the increase in human population and the clearing and cultivation of the land. The bear needs ample space. Wherever it lives, it uses whatever resources it can find, be they wild foods or those grown and tended by man. In this competition, whether for seals in the arctic, for barley in the tropics, or for honey in temperate zones, it usually suffers.

Each of the wild animals whose lives are increasingly dominated by this potential conflict with men—the whale, the tiger, and the wolf—has been watched and admired by men for thousands of years. Each means something very different in the human imagination. More than the others, the bear seems to us to be manlike in his habits and appearance. He is our natural haunt and cousin, and we discover in his natural history much that stimulates our wonder and admiration.

THE BEAR TEACHER

There was once a man who lived deep in the forest where he was perfectly content. Everything he wanted was at hand, and he had only to reach out for all the fruits the forest had to offer. He was safe and comfortable. He noticed the other animals hardly at all, but they too seemed to lack nothing.

But slowly things changed. The forest became sparse and the foods more scattered and hidden. The weather shifted, turning seasonal. Danger appeared, so that nothing was so simple and easy as it had been. The man had many needs—foods of all kinds, herbs for his health, healing substances, materials for his bed, and so on. As an omnivorous, traveling animal, his needs were flexible yet demanding, and it was hard work just to learn everything he had to know to survive. Gradually he saw with a growing sense of respect how the other animals succeeded, each in some particular way beyond his own ability: the wolf pursued prey with supreme endurance, the horse was strong and swift, the caterpillar wove and the marmot dug expertly, the otter was a master of swimming and the squirrel of climbing; and it dawned on him that he might learn from them. So he studied them all, admiring each for its gift and revering the wisdom that such skills showed. It was as though every animal was a piece of the whole of nature, and at the same time a tutor or teacher to the man. He saw that each was an aspect of himself, the beaver reflecting one thing, the snake another, and he learned from them all.

But one problem remained: how to put all the skills together as parts of himself in proper proportion, and to use each in its right moment in the course of the day or the year. Keeping the different talents tuned to the seasonal rhythm was the most difficult task of all, and the man wondered who, like himself, had so many things to remember. At first there seemed to be no animal who had mastered this. Then he noticed that the bear looked a little like himself and attended all things. The bear could swim and climb and dig; it could play and make love and make a bed on which to sleep; it knew where to find the early spring greens and when the salmon would come; it knew not only the habits of the elk but when to look for the grouse's nest and when the acorns would be ready. The bear was brave and strong, yet also a tender mother. It seemed to know even more than the man could learn—to sense the coming season and to understand the art of living underground without eating.

So the bear became the man's special guide in shaping all the separate acts of life into a harmonious whole, fostering in the man's mind the idea of coherence and sequence and even transcendence. Further, in its assured and solitary way the bear seemed to know something that was not enacted, perhaps to have a secret. The man watched the bear for many years and finally he understood: the bear, knowing what was to come from what was, was himself the eye of the future watching the present. His gift of revelation, unlike those skills which man could learn from the other animals once and for all, was continuous. His message was the health of the wilderness, which was always changing. The bear was the voice of the earth itself. Then the man, remembering that the bear was his mentor, realized that he himself had that voice, if only he could learn to sing as sweetly as the bear.

·2·
THE KINDS
OF BEARS

In all the world there are but eight species of bears. They are enough alike that all are easily recognizable as bears, yet so variable in the details of size, color, and habits that zoologists of the nineteenth century gave species names to dozens of geographical races that are now regarded as only local variants. In most of their range, most of the time, adult bears are dispersed, long-lived, and highly adaptable, so that even bears who look alike and are members of the same species may behave differently because of the weather, shifts in the food supply, or the effects of human activity. All of these factors make it difficult to generalize about bears. This flexibility in their natural history is echoed in their role in human culture, in which they are many things—a source of meat and fur, a metaphysical symbol, a cuddly infant, and an ogre whose next move is fearsomely unpredictable. This chapter is about the biological differences among the bears, all of whom share a common ancestor.

The Brown Bear

The brown bear, *Ursus arctos,* is the heartwood of the family tree. Its home is much of the northern hemisphere, south as far as Spain and Persia, including North Africa until Roman times, north into Norway, and from there east over Asia and from Italy east to Syria and northern Afghanistan, into China, Japan, and Manchuria, across Alaska and western North America south into Mexico.

The brown is shaggy, high-foreheaded, humpbacked, the most widely known and most diverse in size and color of all bears. On Alaskan islands and in Siberia the brown bear vies with the polar bear as the largest predatory land mammal, nearly three meters long and weighing as much as 800 kilograms. The grizzly, a parkland, steppe, and chaparral race of North America, is but half that size in its arctic form but, as the golden bear of California, can reach 680 kilograms. The Syrian brown bear, found northeast of the Mediterranean, weighs only one-fourth as much as the Siberian, and the races of Europe and other parts of Asia fall between. Brown bears are blue-black in Tibet, shimmering silver-tipped in America, reddish in China, and running to yellow, tan, buff, and chocolate in different parts of the world. Its summer molt seems to lighten its color.

The concave or dish-face of the brown bear is associated with a long muzzle and a steeply rising forehead, and the head is large in proportion, giving the animal a babyish or teddy-bear-like appearance. The claws are longer and narrower than those of other bears, sometimes looking ivory on grizzlies. Above all, the brown bear's forte is a capacity for protracted winter denning, although in the Balkans and probably in other southern limits of its range, some male bears do not den.

Typically, in September the bear scouts out and digs its den. The preferred site is in dry earth, well up from the valley floor on slopes of about 30 degrees. In the Ural Mountains of Central Russia, most of the dens face south. Whether tradition or adjustment to local climate determines which direction the den faces is not clear. The browns of northern Alaska also prefer a southern exposure, while those of the Alaska peninsula have dens that usually face eastward, and the Kodiak Island bears choose north-facing slopes. In the Urals, sometimes as many as ten bears dig in within one or two square kilometers, but this is more likely due to a limit on high-quality den sites than to sociability. In wet years the same bears forsake any excavation and look for natural rock grottoes and caves. The bears of wet forest regions, as in the Alaskan islands, often prefer to den under fallen logs. When dug, the den is usually placed under a large boulder or the roots of a big tree. The interior dimensions vary with the race of bear—in the Lake Baikal region of Russia, just north of Mongolia, the sleeping chambers are about 150 centimeters long, 100 wide, and 75 high. Pregnant or cub-accompanied females make

The *Iyomande* or "sending home" ceremony of the slain bear was practiced as late as the 1930s by the Ainu of Hokkaido, Japan. The rearing and sacrifice of the divine bear was central to the religion of the Ainu, who saw the bear as an intermediary between them and a mountain god. To the god, the bear spirit returned to report the scrupulousness of his captivity and the death rite. *Courtesy The Brooklyn Museum*

bigger dens and nests than do solitary bears. Like those of the Urals to the west, these bears congregate in the best areas, up to six or eight in a square kilometer. Some dens are reused in successive years, although not necessarily by the same bear. By contrast, in the Brooks Range of northern Alaska there is too much rainfall and not enough tree root to hold the earth against the summer thaw, and most of the dens collapse. The bears that do not den are usually males experiencing a year of poor food supply. In Eurasia these individuals may nestle into haystacks or brush or under fallen trees for periods, emerging occasionally to forage. In such years a severe winter can kill those insufficiently protected by fat.

The biggest browns may have 15 centimeters of fat just under the skin at the start of hibernation. The fat serves both as insulation and reserve food. The bear enters its den during an October snowstorm and therefore leaves no tracks. The tunnel varies in length, but can be as long as four meters. The bear has prepared a bed by raking pine needles, leaves, mosses, and grasses into the sleeping chamber. This bed is 20 centimeters thick, although in the coldest regions it may be 30 centimeters deep, with a rim piled up to 47 centimeters. Once inside, some bears shove some vegetation into the den entrance, partly closing it. During this early part of the denning and the weeks just prior to it, the bear is secretive and skittish about the den's location. Human intruders, especially on motorized vehicles, may frighten the bear so that it abandons the den, runs off, and starts over. During hibernation the bear does not eat, drink, urinate, or defecate, although it may give birth, lactate, lick its paws or cubs, or just change position. In the Balkans the bear may sun at the den entrance as early as February, but the great majority are comatose. Such is the extraordinary adaptation of a large, demanding omnivore in a world where food is abundant for half the year and scarce the other half.

When the bears come out in April they appear drowsy or groggy for a week or two. Leaner individuals emerge first, mothers with new cubs last. Breaking their long fast seems to require a tonic. Their alimentary tracts have been plugged at the anus with a ball of hardened plant materials, nutshells, hair of hoofed animals, and other undigested materials from their last pre-denning meals. Even as they begin to munch such tender greens as serve the purpose, they continue to lose weight for a week or two. Perhaps the delicate

American black bear

Grizzly bear

Polar bear

CHARLES W.
SCHWARTZ

green herbs and grasses tune the system. Then, digging under the snow, the bears find frozen bilberries, rose hips, or other berries or fruit remaining from the previous fall. They also seek a meat meal in the carcasses of winter-killed deer or reindeer, hibernating ground squirrels, or, along beaches and strands, the carrion of dead fish or sea mammals. The availability of meat early in the season is thought by some naturalists to affect the bear's reproductive capability during the coming months. Among all bears, only the polar eats more meat (or spends more time in the water) than the brown.

When they have risen to the full rhythm of daily activity, brown bears, through most of their range, enter a pattern of movement dictated by the seasonal round of food ripening or readiness. This pattern varies depending on local topography, but is most often played out in migrations from the denning areas down to the valleys or to coastal areas for the new shoots of grasses, sedges, and herbs. Then, following the greening up the mountain, the bear widens its diet as summer comes on, to include ants and other insects, small mammals, the eggs of birds and invertebrates, and the first berries of the middle slopes. In Alaska and Siberia the bears then go back down to the rivers to gorge on salmon for three or four weeks. They usually stand in the river to fish, the dominant bears choosing the best spots just below waterfalls. When fishing is good, the bears may not pause to eat, but only bite off the tails of the prey so they cannot flop back into the water, and continue fishing. As they become satiated, the bears may eat only the salmon's reproductive organs, which they obtain by a delicate filleting stroke of a claw, and leave the rest for young or lower-ranking bears, or gulls and other scavengers. As summer progresses they once again go up the mountain, higher still, seeking berries, mushrooms, pine nuts, or the calves of elk or deer, and ending the summer on subalpine meadows, digging out marmots, mice, roots, corms, and bulbs. In southwest Asia they also eat corn and oats which, on game preserves, are planted for the bears.

As elsewhere, the newly emerged bears of the Carpathian Mountains of Czechoslovakia eat very little at first, then get the laxative bilberries and seek the flesh of wild pigs and deer. Thereafter their diet embraces willow and aspen shoots, birch leaves, dock, sorrel, and spring fungi. In early summer they go up the mountains to strip spruce and fir trees and lap the sap, feast on whortleberries, and raid

Sloth bear

Spectacled bear

Sun bear

gardens and orchards. A diet of various berries continues in autumn, along with fruit, beechnuts, and sometimes horsemeat. In Kazakhstan, in the south-central USSR, the brown bear inhabits a wide range of forest communities—coniferous, deciduous, aspen-birch, and juniper-apple-walnut communities—yet it depends heavily on berries of dogrose, honeysuckle, raspberry, currant, and barberry.

Brown bears with access to the seashore may tarry there through the summer, scrounging algae, shrimp, crabs, mollusks, and the washed-up bodies of larger fish. Inland, where the bears have neither mountains nor seacoast, they may still seek spawning fish, as at the Lake Baikal tributaries, where they catch bullheads. But even in mountainless country their six months of foraging are nonetheless strategically adjusted to the calendar of food readiness and location, and to the physiological needs of the bear in the schedule of emergence, breeding and foraging, and pre-denning fattening. Bears probably learn, beginning as cubs, where to expect to find the in-season food, but no two years are the same, so the animal must work its range, varying the basic routine in most of its wandering up and down the mountain.* Although carnivorous, brown bears seldom kill healthy, adult, wild hoofed animals, such as caribou, deer, or elk, but they do prey on the weak, sick, and injured. They are probably a major factor in removing the ungulates wounded by human hunters. More often they eat the young of these antlered forms, which they deliberately seek during the calving season. The remains of a carcass too big to eat in a single meal may be buried and later exhumed and finished. Salmon are also stored in this way. Generally, meat (including insects, birds, small mammals, reptiles and amphibians) constitutes about 20 percent of the bear's total food intake. The proportion of flesh-eating differs in different ecologies. Among Russian bears, for example, those of the taiga (the northern coniferous forests and tundra edges) eat more meat than those near the Caspian Sea. Those who eat less red flesh get more of their protein from insects and plant seeds. In Japan, bears regularly kill and eat livestock, in contrast to those of the Balkans (in central

---

*In the popular song, the refrain "The bear went over the mountain/ To see what he could see" makes sense in terms of its seasonal movements up, down, and then back up the slopes. But the following verse, which claims that "All he saw was the other side," betrays the view of those who watch from a fixed position. What the bear could see, of course, was a likely place to smell out a good taste of something.

Himalayan bear

Giant Panda

Bulgaria), who live peacefully in the precincts of men and their animals except in years of food shortage, when they may kill sheep, pigs, or calves.

Overlaying the seasonal phenology, or ripening schedule, the bear's own reproduction and growth influence its movements. Three-year-olds, newly separated from their mothers, may wander widely in a random subadult dispersal. Although parted forever from their mothers, the littermates may remain together for as many as three more years. Adult females in estrus may attract adult males from a distance of many kilometers. Bears in the state of Chihuahua, Mexico, in parts of Iraq, and in other arid places may have to adjust their seasonal movement patterns to the distribution of water to wallow in or drink.

Bear experts concur, broadly, that bears have a home range but not a proper territory. That is, they spend most of their time within a certain area, but do not attempt to exclude all other bears from it. Where their home ranges overlap, their truculence seems to keep them at a distance from each other. The mean size of the home range varies in different parts of the northern hemisphere. In Siberia it is 100 square kilometers, in Alaska 115, on Kodiak Island 24. In Yellowstone National Park the average is 160 square kilometers, but is complicated by some of the bears having a different range in late summer from that of early summer, the two being connected by a corridor. These figures can be misleading, since the range of females is much smaller than that of males. For example, in the Yukon territory males range over 414 square kilometers, but females stay within 73. The male bear's home range normally overlaps those of his neighbors, and several male territories extend into that of each female.

On the whole, bears avoid direct encounters in these generous spaces except during the weeks of mating in early summer, when the males may fight fiercely. Females not accompanied by cubs are in estrus for about three weeks in late May and early June, although some have been known to mate as late as July. Most of that time is spent with an individual mate, but she may breed with subordinate bears at the beginning or end of that period.

A female is likely to be six or seven years old before she mates successfully. Thereafter she will mate every third or fourth year, depending on her health, her age, and probably the density of bears and the amount of human disturbance. Litter size, as well as the interval between them, is also influenced by these factors. So, in ways not yet entirely clear, the bear reproductive rate adjusts to both food supply and population. By the time a female is fifteen, she is not likely to continue to reproduce successfully, so that the bear may have only three litters in a lifetime. During February, two or three (the mean is 1.8 to 2.5) tiny cubs are born, weighing about 2.2 kilograms for grizzlies and up to 5 kilograms among big Russian bears. The newborns are lightly furred and their eyes will not open for about four weeks. Emerging from the den with their mother in April, they remain nearby for several days. The mother is still lethargic. She eats snow or digs a few roots while the cubs nurse, or slide on nearby ice. Sometimes the mother makes leafy daybeds not more than a few meters from the den.

At the end of the first summer the cubs hibernate with their mother, passing their first birthday under the winter snow. At sixteen months, during their second summer, the activity period of grizzlies is about fourteen hours a day in spring and summer, increasing to seventeen or twenty hours in the fall, as they put on fat. Ninety percent of the day is spent foraging—grazing, rooting, browsing, digging. The cubs nurse about four times each day for five minutes at a time, or about one percent of the time. The cubs play, sometimes with mother, for about four minutes, ten times a day. One-half percent of the time is spent traveling and the rest grooming, scratching, defecating, or resting. The cubs will continue to play-fight, even after separation from their mother, until they are five years old.

Romping with their mothers occasionally includes pouncing on her back as she sits. Maybe this leads to clinging there, for at least one Alaskan bear has been seen with a cub riding on her back. The she-bear must protect her cub from tigers, wolves, men, and male bears. The cubs are disciplined to stay where they are, to remain close to her, or to come as she commands them vocally. Sometimes they are cuffed or spanked. In spite of her caution and her teaching, between 10 and 40 percent are lost in the first eighteen months. Their deaths are frequently due to encountering adult males while away from their mother's immediate vicinity.

For the better part of three summers, not mating, the she-bear protects, teaches, feeds, and plays with her offspring. Where brown bears temporarily congregate, such as at salmon-spawning streams, the little bears may change mothers or simply accumulate with one mother. During the first days of this shuffling, the mother bears appear anxious and may even try to prevent the cubs from doing so, but as the days pass they seem to adjust to and accept it. Usually in their third summer the juveniles are chased away or abandoned by their mothers. These half-grown bears seem to do well enough if food is abundant, but may have lean years if it isn't. They continue to be bullied by bigger bears until they are themselves large and powerful, reaching full growth at about ten years. Even then they may face dangerous confrontations—though these are not usually fatal—since bears are socially hierarchic. The big, old males dominate, followed (and sometimes retreating from) females with new cubs, other adult males and females, and, at the bottom, subadult bears of both sexes not long separated from their mothers. She-bears with cubs seem to be more tolerant of single females and their own independent offspring than they are of strange bears, especially young males.

All brown bears are very sensitive to the approach of danger. In forests and rough terrain they slip away. In Yellowstone National Park the grizzlies monitor the movements of a human intruder, but get alarmed and leave if there are so many that the task gets too complex. In open country, the bear runs if danger is perceived at a distance, but if come upon suddenly—especially if the bear is a mother with cubs—it may attack. Such an attack may be a bluff, a threatening approach to get a better look, or an outright assault. In fighting (or killing large animals), bears do not "bear hug" but bite and strike with their front paws—the same versatile front limbs with which they scoop salmon, heave boulders, bury a cache, climb, drag, carry, and even swim breaststroke through deep snow. Brown bears sometimes rear up in fighting, but they do not attack in a bipedal position. Except for combat among males during mating season, unrestrained fighting is not a common resolution to social tension. The linear dominance/avoidance system inclines the subordinate bear in a typical encounter to retreat, although the withdrawal is broken by brief stands to threaten or defend. Submission postures and teeth-baring, such as occur in the social canines and primates, are not resorted to. Like most power structures in which the individuals vary in health, grow older, or get bigger and more confident, the arrangement is constantly tested and occasionally readjusted. Bluff, psychological factors, physical condition, prior experience, and other things play a part at least as important as combat. Sensitivity to the roaring of big males has been tested by playing recorded calls in the presence of subordinate bears implanted with radio transmitters relaying cardiac information. Their heart rates double when they hear such roars, and they appear to be "intensely frightened." Among grizzlies, the old males who are displaced from the top disappear rather mysteriously, perhaps to die in their dens.

Among Asian brown bears, at least twenty-three different social behaviors have been observed, such as head-high and head-low threats, stiff-legged walk, backing up, facing away, ears-back position, bluff charge, sidling, and staring. Most of these occur in situations of high density, where abundant carrion, salmon, or garbage attract dozens or scores of bears to an area where they form loose feeding aggregations, as along the falls of the McNeil River, at the base of the Alaska Peninsula. A "touchy truce" prevails, enforced by body language, facial expression, and vocalization. With a limited number of fishing places and much inter-bear tension, the smaller bears hang out at the periphery, scavenging leftovers and cadging scraps from the dominant animals. Intolerance on the part of the fisher bears increases in times of scanty salmon. The subadults do not join the fishing circle until they are more than six years old. In fishing, the bears use two variations of a basic technique, either plunging in and grabbing the fish in the jaws, then carrying it to shore, holding it down and biting it, or else standing in the stream and smashing down on it with a forepaw before taking it in the mouth. Bears have not been seen to smack fish out of the water.

Bears adjust their daily regimen to circumstances; they may be active at any time of the day. In Europe, brown bears are active mostly during the late afternoon and evening. The American grizzlies, the most nearly open-country bears, no longer move as freely in daylight as they once did. Like the other species, brown bears sometimes mark trees by scratching on or rubbing against them. There is evidence that they may roll in their urine first, as though they were dogs who had not yet thought of urinating directly on the tree. Pine-needle oil or turpentine also triggers this wallowing behavior. Some also roll on ants, for reasons unknown.

In general, bears are shy animals that avoid trouble. Even today the brown bear lives in peaceful coexistence with man and his domestic animals in the Caucasus and the Carpathians. The grizzly, so feared by the European settlers in North America, Lewis and Clark's *Ursus horribilis,* was known to American Indians as a fellow-being whose warnings, if he was grouchy, were clear enough. The reports of naturalists, photographers, and early travelers who behaved "bearishly," avoiding confrontations, reveal the grizzly not to be the monster portrayed in sensational stories.* Brown bears are widely known as circus performers and streetside acrobats, and solitary, itinerant musicians with their dancing bears still travel the roads of much of Asia. The false image of raging ferocity is in part the residue of spectacles in the plazas and "bear-gardens" of Europe and America, where bears were goaded into fights with bulls or dogs; it also derives from the fierceness with which bears defend their lives and space when surrounded by frontiersmen, hunted by ranchers with dogs, or crowded by tourists and hikers.

Over the world, hundreds of brown bears have lived out their lives as captives without ever being in a cage. The heraldic figure of the city of Bern, Switzerland, the emblem of the state of California, and the symbol of Mother Russia, this species is the world's best-known and most revered bear. Yosemite, perhaps America's most spectacular national park, derives its name from the Miwok Indian word for grizzly bear, *uzmati.* But this powerful animal can never be taken for granted. He is far more dangerous to his trainers in the circus than are lions or tigers, says Carl Hagenbeck, the foremost authority on the history of the circus. "Grizzly" Adams, an American showman of the nineteenth century, lived in hotel rooms for half a century with a bear named Martha Washington and other trained grizzlies, but was finally killed by one of his own bears.

---

*For example, Andy Russell, painter on the American frontier, observed grizzlies hundreds of times but was never attacked. W. J. Schoonmacher, who spent twenty years photographing wild animals, had no trouble with bears. Doug Peacock, who spends many weeks among grizzlies every year, says that he has often been threatened but never runs and has never been harmed.

The American Black Bear

Ursus americanus is native only to North America, from southern Canada to Mexico, and formerly in all of the continental United States. Typically, this is a forest bear of temperate climates; it is most abundant in the forested regions of western, northeastern, and southeastern states, and is scarcest in the Great Plains. Not generally as large as his close relative, the brown bear, the black is seldom taller than one meter or longer than two. Although big males occasionally reach 350 kilograms in weight, 250 kilograms is a more usual adult size. The difference between the sizes of males and females is in this bear (and the brown) as much as 100 percent—one of the traits that led early paleontologists to misinterpret bones and fossil remains as belonging to more than one species. Although pelt color, size, and skull shape set off the American black from his grizzly relative, the surest differences from a zoological standpoint are in the teeth and feet, specifically in the shape and size of the rear upper molar teeth, the profile of the claws, the amount of hair between the toe and footpad (more in the black), and the amount of skin webbing at the toe-pad base (more in the black).

In the eastern part of its range the bear is often truly black but sometimes cinnamon-colored. Its color variations are greater westward, where it may also be brown or blond. A white race, the Kermode bear, is found in British Columbia, and a blue-gray phase, the glacier bear, lives in central Alaska and the Yukon.

Although a forest animal, the black bear's habitat is highly varied. It does well in almost any temperate or boreal climate as long as there is vegetative cover in which to travel, escape, and den. Subarid thorn forest, evergreen chaparral, mesquite-greasewood thickets, beech-maple or oak-hickory hardwoods, juniper savannas, pine parklands, heavy conifer woods, rural countryside or village environs, swamp edges and wetland forests, subalpine areas and coastal thickets are all home to the black bear, who has, in some of these areas in the West, replaced the grizzly.

The home range of black bears varies in different parts of the continent, depending on how far the individual must search for food. The average is about 66 square kilometers for males and 21 for females, but can be as much as 173 square kilometers for a big Pennsylvania male and as little as 10 for an Arizona female.

An opportunist that will eat anything, from canned goods to crippled cows, this bear nonetheless has both preferences and seasonal needs. Sweets and meat are high on the list of choices. Like other northern bears, it follows a seasonal round, favoring tender greens such as clover, squawroot, peas, vetch, and aspen catkins in early summer, followed by grubs, rodents, flowers, carrion, dandelions, strawberries, juneberries, blackberries, hazelnuts, haw apples, wild plums, and ashberries as the season advances. When blight destroyed the chestnut (as a mature tree) in the eastern U.S. early in the twentieth century, a major food was lost and bears came more directly into competition with deer, grouse, turkeys, squirrels, raccoons, and hogs for acorns—which they also consume in large quantities in the evergreen oak brush of the far West. The dexterity with which it separates acorn shells and meats in its mouth, and catches some of the meats that drop on the back of a paw, reveals how fastidious and delicate an eater the bear is, contrary to its image as a crude blusterer. Breaking down the trees to get at apples is, after all, not bumbling carelessness but simply the only way to reach fruit on high, slender limbs. Nor does it hesitate to climb oaks to harvest the mast, clearly showing that adult bears *do* climb, folklore notwithstanding. Bears also like bird eggs and the underbark or cambium of some trees, as well as frogs, crayfish, and snails. They have tried everything found in cabins, barns, tents, smokehouses, cellars, and henhouses—providing the basis for innumerable bear anecdotes and tall tales about molasses-smeared specters in the moonlight, or monsters dusted ghostly white with flour or grimy with lard and soot. Black bears spend hours overturning rocks and smashing and turning logs. As much as one-third of their droppings contain the remains of bees, wasps, hornets, ants, and—especially—beetles, all of which are high-protein foods. One naturalist saw bears catching grasshoppers by flushing them into a stream and then scooping them up. No ordinary beehive is safe, and a single bear may open half a dozen in a foray. In Alberta and British Columbia, the black bear fishes like the brown bear in streams. In sum, 80 percent of the black bear's food comes from fifty-eight different plants, the animal portion from invertebrates, frogs, reptiles, fish, and some eight different mammals.

In mountainous areas the black bear, like the brown, follows the "greenup," starting in the bottoms and ending the season in the upper meadows and forests. In Oregon the pattern is to feed first in wet meadows, moving into streamside pastures on the slopes and on to the upper meadows, then traveling rather widely during late summer through mixed conifer forests, snacking on the fauna in dead logs, circling into manzanita brush and oak, and finally returning to mixed conifer woods for denning. One study showed the black bear keyed to a daily routine of working away from its preferred sleeping area early in the day, foraging in an exploratory way on the outward trip, then turning back and stopping only at the good spots as it made its way to its sleeping place.

The winter denning of the black bear, like its food habits, varies geographically with climate, and varies in any given area from year to year with summer food supply and fall weather. Arizona blacks dig under a big boulder in dense chaparral, going in to hibernate about November 15, but sunning at the den's entrance on warm February days and making daily sorties out of the den by mid-March. In Idaho, bears dig dens in October and enter in early November—earlier if the food supply has been good—at a time of low temperature and high precipitation. There and elsewhere in the north, the winter sleep may last six months. In North Carolina the bear may only scrape a depression under a smilax or fetterbush thicket, or it may look for a suitable tree cavity without too much draft from below, and sleep from mid-December to late March. In the Great Smoky Mountains National Park of the southern Appalachians, bears prefer a large tree as a kind of shield and nestle in at its base or scrape out a cavity between its roots. In Louisiana and other states in the Deep South, bears usually remain active all winter, except for pregnant females.

In all cases it seems that females den first and longest, followed by big males in good condition. Subadult bears, especially males, den least and last, probably because they usually get the short end of things and are not in as good physical condition as the dominant animals. Denning bears tend to lose about one-quarter of their weight, although the rate of loss is only half that during normal summer resting periods. They continue to lose weight for a week or more after leaving the den in the spring, depending on the quality of food available. In addition to hollow trees, the spaces between roots or under fallen timber, and holes that they dig, black bears have been known to hibernate in culverts, caves, and building subspaces.

Like other northern bears, blacks are born in the winter den, but litter size and frequency tend to be greater: where they are heavily hunted and well fed, females may reproduce every two years and begin reproducing in their third year; as many as five young have been seen in one family, although the average is closer to two. Reproduction in a single population of bears, such as Pennsylvania's, may vary by a factor of three from year to year. This is believed to be due to the bears' response to population density, the food situation, and a tendency among bears to have a synchronized, alternative-year reproductive emphasis that more or less matches the same rhythm in the acorn crop.

Mating takes place in May or June. Copulation is dog-fashion, yet catlike in that the male sometimes bites and holds the back of the female's neck. It lasts twenty or thirty minutes. In the uterus the fertilized ovum divides a few times, after which the little ball of cells (the blastocyst) floats free for six months. It attaches to the uterine wall after this time of arrested development, and an eight-week gestation begins. The cubs are born into a soft bed of plants in February, and weigh about one kilogram. They suck noisily and frequently, the diet of bear milk being high in proteins, fats, and solids. Forty days elapse before their eyes open. Mother and young leave the den about eight weeks after birth, when the newborn have grown to about nine kilograms. Many cubs have a white chest patch that will disappear in time. They are highly vocal and expressive, singing a "musical rainbow" up and down the scale when they nurse, muttering and grumbling a sleepy song afterward. They utter long, tremulous notes of pleasure, diminutive growls, and whimpers and cries of loneliness and fear. They like to hide in dark places, play in water, engage in games of tag, tumble while holding their own feet, and play-fight. Little bears mouth each other in play and greeting. They are shy of strangers and very timid around adult bears—who are indeed a mortal danger to them.

Attractive as they appear, little bears are, by human standards, very demanding and loutish, although their mothers are forceful disciplinarians. All bears, especially little ones, are vulnerable to pumas, dogs, wolves, bigger bears, poisonous snakes, alligators, men, fires, and accidents. In captivity, especially if separation from its mother was frightening, the cub's demands for comfort and contact are excruciating. It becomes a clinging, clawing, climbing, screaming brat, terrified by any sign of rejection, routinely turning over its food bowl (which is, after all, like turning over rocks in the food search), then wallowing in the mess and ferociously defending it; spilling, opening, tearing, it is a bundle of seventy claws and teeth—all in all, says Irving Petite, author of *Mister B.,* a "ludicrous tyrant." Of pet bears, Barbara Burn and Emil Dolensek, in their book on keeping pets, say in effect: Bears are impossible; forget it.

By fall the cubs weigh about 30 kilograms, and most den over with their mother the first winter after their birth. By midsummer of their second year, at eighteen months, the cubs weigh about 110 kilograms. The mother bear sends them up a tree and leaves them. She will no longer tolerate their presence, nor will she mate again until the next summer.

The yearlings have a hard and dangerous time. As cubs, about one-quarter lose their lives; during the second and into the third years another third will die. Besides finding their own food and avoiding danger, they must find home ranges of their own or, if the population is high, tread warily while in the proximity of others. Although they are masters of communication, black bears seem to injure each other more than do brown bears.

Despite the hazards of life, black bears are provocative and inquisitive. They have been seen playing with coyotes, and their escapades as recounted in American folklore are due to their probing, manipulative personality—a taciturn, churlish, hirsute little kid weighing 200 pounds. As cubs they dig, mouth, and paw everything from their first outing onward. It is clear that not all "campground bears" are only after food. Students of bear behavior describe an almost ritual sequence of the approach to novel objects: smell, handle, chew. Sniffing is a major sensory activity. Seeking subtle odors at a distance, the bear raises its head at an angle. When sniffing an object or smelling out food close at hand, the head is held or carried low, the ears partly back. During foraging, the bear's upper lip is extended and may touch or move the leaf litter of the forest floor. The animal moves along haltingly, stopping to tip over a rock or grasp an acorn with its lip. With a paw it deftly digs, rakes, lifts, pulls, and turns logs, rocks, earth, and debris. Small objects can be picked up singlehanded by holding them between a claw and foot-pad. When it catches a small mammal, the bear first slaps it once or twice, pins it down, then drags or pulls the prey toward its mouth and finally bites it. When eating grass it bites off the stems with its incisors (in contrast to brown bears, who often bite off vegetation with their back teeth). In captivity, bears amuse themselves with blocks, chains, dowels, and hoses even more than do primates or carnivores. Lying on their backs, they may pass a chain from hand to hand. Because of their persistence and great strength, bears, whether pets or wild intruders, tend to break things around human dwell-ings—but not through clumsiness. (Their destructiveness after breaking in suggests yet another explanation for the Goldilocks story, implying that the setting in the bear's house is perhaps only an externalization of our childlike, or bearish, tendency to destroy what is fragile.) Captive bears love to ride in backpacks as cubs and in trucks as adults.

In a bear's daily round, activity is usually heaviest in the morning and evening, sleep or rest occurring during midday and after mid-night. In their leisurely rambling and casual, observant resting, bears give an impression of speculative contemplation. They enjoy bathing and mud-wallowing, and are inordinately fond of back-scratching. In Minnesota, male bears have a regular series of familiar rubbing trees on which they wear away their hair so that some have a bare spot on their rumps. Standing on their hind legs, they reach up and tear or scratch-mark the trunks of cedar, fir, and hemlock trees with their claws.

Except for the odd dead horse or a garbage dump, food does not come in massive windfalls as often for blacks as it does for browns and polars, so that they are not as often observed in large aggre-gations. Yet their ranges are not as large and they may be slightly more social. More damage to one another is done among them by fighting, while at the same time adults appear more tolerant of those nearby, especially in the case of a mother and her grown daughter. Adults of unknown relationship have been seen traveling together. At garbage dumps and berry patches they feed in close proximity without trouble, and there is much home-range overlap and flexi-bility related to the patchy and changeable food supply. Bear-trainers describe the black bear as more of a here-and-now personality who grumps immediately if dissatisfied and is less complicated than his prickly cousin, who keeps a longer account of benefits and insults received. As a captive the black is sometimes short-tempered and boorish, an amusing if sometimes difficult personality not to be unduly feared or fully trusted by anyone not familiar with the system of bear signals consisting of expressions, postures, odors, and sounds by which moods are communicated.

Threat signals alone are numerous. There is much huffing and puffing, hoarse bellowing, grunting with the mouth closed, pop-snapping of jaws, teeth-clicking, panting, lip-licking, sniffing, and staring to the accompaniment of a stiff-legged walk. A yearling defending against a threat huffs in and out. A bear on the verge of initiating a serious charge huffs with his mouth open and upper lip lifted. An angry bear slaps the ground or a tree or limbs with its forepaws. A typical sequence is sniff, stare, stand up, charge, and stop; slap the ground, huff, jaw-pop, pant, and retreat. Some of these threats are also given without serious intent by cubs, once they have scrambled up a tree or behind their mothers. An experienced woodsman who knows when to huff and stomp can intimidate a threatening bear.

Compared to the brown bear, the black breeds fast and dies young. It can live as long as twenty-seven years, but that is unusual. The mortality rate is such that only half reach age three. They may breed at age three and a half, but do so more often at four. Since they do not require the degree of wilderness seclusion of brown bears and do well in places like Pennsylvania, Michigan, Wisconsin, and most humanized countryside if there are patches of forest cover, their human encounters are much more numerous and diverse. Because the bear's food supply is often linked to human land use, property damage is frequently related to its search for food, but does not often include the killing of livestock. Habitual "nuisance" bears in the national parks are live-trapped and relocated by rangers, or killed. Bears blundering into towns and villages usually meet a quick end at the hands of panicky policemen. Of the 20,000 or so that are killed every year, about half are done in by hunters—who kill them mostly in chance encounters while hunting other game. Deliberate bear hunting is usually done with a special breed of dogs initially developed in Tennessee.

The Polar Bear

Ursus maritimus, the "sea bear," is the great white or cream-colored survivalist of arctic snow and ice. Like its close relative, the brown bear, but living north of it, the polar bear is circumpolar in distribution, found as far north as 88 degrees latitude, and southward to the limits of pack ice and the regular flow of icebergs. Wherever there is open sea, it prowls the shores in northern Norway, Denmark, Russia, Alaska, and Canada. It travels on icebergs to Iceland and a great many other arctic islands, sometimes south to Japan or to Churchill on Hudson Bay. In Greenland it migrates to the coast in winter and back to the interior mountains for summer. In Norway it travels southwest in the fall, offshore to Spitzbergen, and back to the Barents Sea. At Hudson Bay the polar bear spends the whole summer on dry land, snoozing in summer beds of peat moss, while a thousand miles to the north it drifts for hundreds of miles on ice in the Arctic Ocean.

The white bear is a huge animal, up to nearly three meters long and 400 kilograms in weight. The longer guard hairs of its pelage are white, the underhairs orange or yellow. For its size it has a small head, with large canine teeth and small molars. The nose is arched or "Roman," the ears short, and the eyes small and dark. Polar bears are relatively narrow through the shoulders and long in the neck and tail, and have large, furry feet and partly webbed toes. Such a powerful animal has little to fear, but avoids killer whales, armed men, and adult bull walruses. Wolves are a danger to the cubs.

Considering where it lives, the polar bear has a surprisingly varied diet. It eats cod, krill, shellfish, waterfowl, lemmings, salmon, beached whales, narwhals, seals and their pups, walruses, sea birds and their eggs, hares, foxes, and young or disabled reindeer and musk-ox, as well as crowberries, blueberries, and other plant foods. Access to snow-free tundra in summer has much to do with the availability of plant food, so some bears may go for long periods eating only meat. Sometimes they obtain plants indirectly or secondhand when they eat the stomachs of hoofed animals.

The polar bear does not follow the general bear rule that the higher the latitude, the longer the hibernation. Most do not lay on heavy fat or den over winter like their relatives to the south, although they may lie up for a few days. Pregnant or cub-accompanied females do follow the fattening regimen and carefully select a den site as the arctic night comes on. In the northernmost regions they prefer deep, drifted snow, which in turn influences whether they dig in onshore or on fast ice, which they prefer to drift ice. They are secretive and timid about the den location and can be frightened to the less desirable drift ice by human activity. Dens are excavated quickly, some in less than an hour. It is essential that the snow does not thaw and melt at any time during the six months of hibernation. The den's shape and location and the thickness of its walls affect the bear's body-heat production and energy use. Once inside, the bear adjusts temperatures by making or closing vents or scratching snow from the walls and ceiling to change their thickness.

The anomaly in the distribution of this bear is a population far to the south, quite near the treeline on the Manitoba shore of Hudson Bay. Here the bears have access to a green summer world. The Hudson Bay population, and others in the Norwegian Svalbard archipelago and on Wrangel Island (north of the east end of Siberia) enjoy unusually good denning conditions—that is, places where holes can be dug through the snow into the earth. Here the near-shore areas constitute "traditional" locations, so ideal that dens are sometimes only a few meters apart. The sleeping chambers are at the end of a two or three-meter corridor, usually with only one or two rooms, but sometimes with as many as five, especially if the occupants are a mother and older cubs.

Hibernation begins in September, shortly after which, if the bear is newly mated, implantation occurs and development of the embryo begins. The cubs are born in December, after ten weeks of gestation. The furry newborn—as many as four but normally one or two (the mean is 1.72)—weigh about one kilogram. Mothers with new cubs are restless and, even in the den, dangerous. Some tolerate human approach, while others smash out through the den wall and threaten or attack. Even when undisturbed, mother bears come out occasionally to clean their fur of dirt or grease.

The bears emerge with the warming air of April. The cubs will nurse for about eighteen months, sucking for fifteen minutes six or seven times a day. The family remains near the den for several days, reentering it to sleep. All excrement, even though the bears are about to leave, is deposited more than ten meters away from the den. The cubs are taken for walks of a kilometer or two; then the mother and her cubs, in synchrony with other, nearby families, head for the edge of the sea. The journey may be only a few kilometers or as many as seventy-five. The trip is slow if the cubs are new, with stops to dig shallow hollows into the peat, which are lined with moss and lichen and used for naps. Sometimes the little bears ride on their mother's back. The cubs are fearful of big, strange animals, so terrified of dogs that they will even scamper toward humans for protection. Once having reached the shore, with its open leads in the ice, the family concentrates on catching seals—new cubs merely watching. Even after weaning, the cubs will remain with their mother for another eighteen months, so that in all she has their care for three and a half years. The females, therefore, like their brown relatives, breed every third or fourth year.

While with their mother, the young learn to glissade and tobog-gan, traveling rough glaciers or tumbled pack ice with great agility. They play together, biting, pawing, running, growling, shifting with mood intensity to solitary play. Play sessions are often less than a minute long.

Although spending most of its time on ice or on shore, the white bear enters the sea readily to cross open water or go back and forth between bergs to search for seals or carrion, or to escape from men. Kept warm and made buoyant by a 6-centimeter layer of fat, the polar bear is a powerful swimmer, paddling with the front feet and guiding with the rear, moving at a steady eight knots. It can leap and cavort in the water, somewhat like the porpoise, and seems to enjoy rocking small bergs. When it dives its ears are flattened and closed, and its nostrils are also shut. Underwater the eyelids remain open, while a third lid, the transparent nictitating membrane, closes to protect the eye and may function as a lens. The blood vessels to those parts of the body other than the brain, lungs, and front limbs are constricted, enabling the animal to conserve oxygen when it dives, and remain underwater for more than two minutes. This vascular adjustment to diving has some similarities to the partial shutdown that occurs during hibernation.

The arctic fox is a familiar companion of the polar bear, scavenging from its leavings like the jackal shadowing the lion, but the bear is a dangerous ally and occasionally kills a fox who gets too close.

Except when accompanied by cubs, the bear is less shy toward people than are its southern relatives, and like them is intensely curious about what man is up to, his garbage and his structures.

The Himalayan Bear

Selenarctos thibetanus is also called the Asiatic or Tibetan black bear—or moon bear, because of a white or orange-yellow crescent that appears on its chest. It is a bear of eastern Asia, filling in the habitat that lies between that of the brown bear to the north and the sloth bear and sun bear to the south. Individually this bear does not wander great distances, but as a species it lives in a variety of habitats and terrain: at 4,000 meters elevation in the montane forests of China and Tibet, in the broadleaf forest valleys of southern Russia, Afghanistan, and Baluchistan, in the arid high country of West Pakistan, and in the birch groves and pinelands of Indochina, Formosa, Manchuria, and the three southern islands of Japan.

Besides the white horseshoe on its chest, the Himalayan bear's distinguishing features are a soft, shaggy pelt with a manelike mantle of hair around the neck and shoulders. The length of hair is in inverse proportion to fat accumulation in the fall. If the acorn and cedar-nut crops have been good, the bear is fat for hibernation and the pelt is light. Usually it is glossy black but may be dark brown. Among older individuals the upper lip, muzzle, and chin become white. The head is short and wide, its heavy jaw-teeth giving it a roundheaded appearance, and its short, rounded ears are set far apart. The moon bear differs in proportions from its relatives, having slender legs, a narrow hind foot that tapers toward the heel, and relatively short front claws. As bears go, it is medium-sized, about 190 centimeters long and weighing up to 115 kilograms.

In winter it seeks broadleaf forests, preferring to den in hollow trees, particularly linden, in which it digs out a rotten center as much as sixty feet above the ground. Other dens are dug beneath tree roots, and sometimes natural caves are used. As with other ursine hibernators, an anal plug seals the alimentary tract—a clot of nut hulls, wood, and hair. In the den the skin of its paws is slowly sloughed off and replaced by new skin. The two or three young remain in the den with the mother for the first two or three months, and after their emergence for another three years. The species is unusual in having three instead of the usual two pairs of teats. If some reports are true, it is also unlike other bears in that it sometimes forms family groups composed of a pair of adults and two successive litters of young.

In summer the bear goes up the mountains into pine forests or close to the treeline, and the roaring of fighting males can be heard during the mating season. Its diet consists mostly of insects, fruit, and plant materials; it does not fish, nor does it pursue hoofed animals. In July it typically climbs trees to eat bird-cherries. Sitting in a fork, it bends branches down and holds them under a haunch while stripping the fruit with its forepaws. As branches accumulate under the bear, a kind of nest is formed. In Japan the moon bear strips bark up from the base of cedar, cypress, and other conifers, and such broadleaf trees as chestnut, cucumber, oak, linden, and wingnut, and then eats the sapwood. As with its close relative, the American black bear, which also damages trees by tearing off the bark, in some regions of bear country they do little or no damage, while in others the damage can be economically significant. In Japan it is worst where the forests have been transformed into single-species tree plantations, probably because some of the bear's food requirements are absent.

The Himalayan bear's principal enemies are wolves, men, dogs, and tigers—the Manchurian tiger is said to imitate the bear's mating call in order to lure it. Conversely, Jim Corbett, the famous hunter of man-eating tigers, claimed to have seen a bear drive a tiger from its dinner.

The Sloth Bear

Inhabiting diverse habitats, *Melursus ursinus*, the "lip bear," is found from northern India south to Sri Lanka. It shows typical bear flexibility in adjusting to jungle, savanna, and either broadleaf or evergreen forests, seasonally dry environments, so long as there are dense thickets or rocky outcrops where it can hide and lie in the shade. At 100 kilograms in weight and 170 centimeters in length, it is not large for a bear, but its shaggy black hair and the long ruff on its neck and shoulders make it seem bigger. Its belly and underlegs, on the other hand, are nearly bare—probably to facilitate heat-dumping or bellying down on the cool earth on a hot day, a widespread habit within the order Carnivora. The face and soles of the feet also have little hair. This bear has large, ivory-colored claws and a white Y or V mark on the chest.

Living in the subtropics, the sloth bear does not need to den up for weeks or months like its northern relatives, though it does retreat to caves during the rainy season. The one or two cubs are born during November or December and begin to travel sooner than other little bears. Adult males have been seen with the family, and the little bears are known to ride their mothers' backs.

Although it is sometimes active in the day in cool weather, this monsoon-climate bear is typically nocturnal. Its population in the Royal Chitwan National Park in Nepal suggests a distribution of about one bear in ten square kilometers. It keeps bear custom through marking trees by slashing the bark with its foreclaws, and in dry country it has been seen to dig for water. Because of the more even dispersal of its food, the sloth bear has no occasion to congregate at food sources and does not meet in feeding groups like the *Ursus* bears.

In one aspect this is a highly specialized bear: it is an expert in the hunting of termites, which are a major part of the invertebrate fauna in the world's tropics. To get them the bear smashes a rotten log or tears open a termite mound with its long claws. At the same time it alternately blows away the dirt and wood chips and sucks up termites so noisily that it can be heard 100 meters away. It is called the "lip bear" because its long lips form the end of a tube for this staccato in-huffing and out-puffing. The tubular system is made possible by the absence of upper front teeth, the reduction of cheek or molar teeth, and a long, grooved, bony palate. Valves close the nostrils. All in all, these modifications result in a rather different face among bears.

The sloth bear also feeds frequently in the treetops and is so excellent a climber that it can climb a smooth pole. It may sit in a tree to eat ants or honeycomb or shake fruit down. It likes mustard-tree and palm fruits, yams, guavas, mangos, berries, potatoes, paw-

paws, various flowers, and such tropical exotic specialties as fig, ber, uria, kon, mee, daruba, and ebony fruits. It does not kill or scavenge much meat, but does eat other insects than termites.

Paw-sucking occurs in this species, as it does in others, but whether for spilled fruit juices, for secretions from the footpads, or for psychological reasons is unknown. Perhaps it is only to soften or remove calluses, as the paws are extremely sensitive, giving the bear such delicate finger control that it can pick locks to escape from cages.

Among themselves, the bears communicate by sound and facial expression. It is so noisy an animal that people living within its home range tell of its many calls: screams, yelps, barks, grunt-wickerings, and a long, drawn-out, melodious, two-part call when mating. Huffs and chuffs signal threats, and it snarls and roars when fighting.

Occasionally the sloth bear is a victim of wild dogs or tigers, but more often of men, who kill it for the *os bacculum* or penis bone— valued for its magic potency—and for its fat, which is used as a hair restorer. Although usually timid and preoccupied with its diligent termite digging, it is widely feared in jungle areas because it may attack savagely when surprised, or sometimes at night when a pedestrian or bicyclist is unaware that the bear is nearby.

The Sun Bear

Helarctos malayanus, also sometimes called the Malay or honey bear, lives strictly in dense tropical forests in northeast India, southern China, Burma, and Malaysia, extending as far east as Borneo, Sarawak, and Sumatra. Sleek and small-eared, it is the smallest of the bears, weighing about 45 kilograms, and is 130 centimeters in length. It also is the most arboreal, a bandy-legged, long-tongued, loose-jointed feeder and nester in the treetops. Like other tropical climbers, it has long claws and bare soles.

The sun bear is basically black, but, like other tropical bears, has a yellowish or whitish mark on the chest. It differs from them in its very short hair and tan muzzle. The fur is patterned in unusual whorls and cowlicks on the forehead and behind the ears; the head is short, wide, and flat.

The bear is almost completely vegetarian, usually feeding in the trees on mushrooms, fruit, and honey, its "meat" consisting of insects and frogs. To give birth, the sun bear uses the hollow in a log or living tree, but sometimes makes a leafy tree platform in which to sleep. Reproduction can take place at any season, but in captivity tends to peak in spring and fall. Females first breed in their third year. The one or two cubs are born after about three months of gestation, uninterrupted by embryonic delay. More naked than other little bears, the tiny sun bear cubs weigh only 255 grams and are about 18 centimeters long. They cannot see or hear for two weeks or more, and their skin is nearly transparent. For two months they do not walk and are not weaned until they are four months old. During the first two months of life, the cubs' alimentary systems require external stimulation in order for urination and defecation to occur. This is provided by the mother bear's licking. Babies in captivity without mothers must be sponged several times a day to stimulate elimination or they do not live. Adults in captivity are restless and destructive—with their powerful front limbs, adapted to ripping open logs, they can easily tear down a wooden or plaster wall—and tend to do a lot of whining and foot-sucking. The sun bear's chief enemy in the wild is probably the wild dog.

The Spectacled Bear

The South American bear, *Tremarctos ornatus,* is perhaps a little better known than the sun bear of southeast Asia. Sometimes called the Andean bear, it is the only bear now living in the southern hemisphere and the only member of its family in the New World tropics. It occurs from Venezuela and Colombia southward, most abundantly on the eastern slopes of the Andes, but also on the coastal foothills of Equador, Peru, and Chile, and southeast to the near parts of Bolivia. Most of its year is spent in deep, wet forests, from which it moves with the seasons to alpine forest and *páramo,* or even into the high elfin forest, steppe, or thorn forest and desert. It is black and shaggy, named for the yellowish lines on its face which often form rings around the eyes. Like the bears of tropical Asia, it has a white patch on the chest and, like them, is typically small, weighing from 80 to 125 kilograms and standing 70 centimeters at the shoulder. Larger individuals are known, however, up to 175 kilograms and 266 centimeters.

In South America this bear is not simply called the spectacled bear but has different names indicating individual color or activity: *achupalla* (underbark eater), *yura mateo* (white-fronted), *yana puma* (black "puma"), *olo guanadero* or *ocunari* (cow-eating), or *pucca mate* (red-fronted).

Because of the heavy jaw muscles it uses for crushing palm nuts, its skull shape is unusual, rather resembling that of the giant panda, which has massive molars for grinding bamboo shoots.

To rest and hide, the spectacled bear makes a nest on masses of bromeliad plants high in the trees, but to give birth it prepares a nest between large buttress roots or under the edge of a boulder. One or two cubs are born in December or January—during the midsummer season of high rainfall and abundant fruit. The cubs are said to ride on the mother, and sometimes a family has been seen accompanied by an adult male. Like other bears, the cubs make a humming sound when nursing. When very young they are so un-developed that they require the mother's help to nurse for their first eight weeks, and this is the only bear reported to carry food to its cubs.

Although diurnal in the heavy forest—foraging in early morning and evening—the spectacled bear is mostly active at night in more open country. Everywhere it makes heavy use of steep ravines and precipitous, rocky slopes. In climbing, the bear does not depend only on large trunks that can be grasped in usual bear fashion, but is able to climb vines and small trees less than a paw-width in diameter. The tree beds are often used as feeding platforms. Food preferences include berries, fruits and hearts of bromeliads, orchid bulbs, lilies, the underbark of certain trees, palm nuts and frond petioles, figs, cactus pulp, sugarcane, and corn. Bromeliads (epiphytes growing on but not into the branches of trees) are used not only as food and bedding but as a source of drinking water because their leaves form a series of catchments for rain. In more mountainous areas the bear follows the fruiting season up the slopes. Less than 5 percent of its food is meat from larger animals—mostly carrion and some rodents.

In general, the spectacled bear is shy and cautious. It would be little known were it not for its raids on cornfields, where it is shot by field guards as a pest. Before entering a field the bear climbs a nearby tree to scout it, and even when it enters the field it seldom gets more than a few feet from cover or a ravine, coming out to snatch an ear or two and carrying it back to eat or take to its cubs. But it is blamed for eating half the crop in as many as 20 percent of the cornfields. When disturbed or stalked by men, the bear circles to get downwind, sniffing to identify its pursuers. Sometimes it is hunted with dogs, and older bears become extremely careful, staying in cover and traveling only in deep gullies when possible.

In many instances the bear is blamed for the death of cattle, even where the evidence indicates that the victim was killed by a puma. When it does attack cows, it chases them along a steep, rocky slope until the prey falls, whereupon the bear grabs it by the head and kills it.

The Giant Panda

The giant panda, or *beishung,* is found in north-central and southern Sichuan, southern Shanxi, and southern Gansu provinces of west-central China, along the eastern edge of the Tibetan highland. It was formerly more widely distributed in China and south into Burma. It inhabits a region of cold temperate climate, in mixed coniferous and broadleaf forests, between 2,600 and 4,000 meters in elevation in very steep and rugged terrain, going down to 800 meters in winter.

A typical adult weighs in excess of 100 kilograms and may reach two meters in length, counting a tail of twelve centimeters. The panda is soft and woolly, basically white with black on limbs, shoulders, and tail, with patches on its ears and eyes. The panda has been a world celebrity, particularly in the West, since it was first made known to Europeans in 1869. In China its pelt was used by farmer-hunters to pay taxes and has been considered a royal gift for centuries, although the living panda is now regarded as a "priceless heritage" and is protected in a series of eight nature preserves.

WHY THE GIANT PANDA
HAS BEAR'S BLOOD

The immunological evidence that the giant panda is a bear is based on the theory that the degree of chemical reaction (often resulting in an allergic symptom) by an organism to molecules of protein other than its own is determined by the degree of genetic unlikeness. (In organ transplants, for instance, it is desirable to use a donor as closely related to the recipient as possible in order to reduce the degree of protein difference and the intensity of the immunological response.) When certain proteins (transferrins) from the black bear, *Ursus americanus,* are mixed with the blood of other animals, a measurable reaction occurs. The degree of reactivity can be quantified and is interpreted as the degree of relatedness between animals descended from a common ancestor. The comparative results look like this:

Combination of black bear transferrin and blood of:	produces a reaction indicating this degree of genetic difference:
black bear, *Ursus americanus*	0
brown bear, *Ursus arctos*	6
sun bear, *Helarctos*	8
spectacled bear, *Tremarctos*	8
giant panda, *Ailuropoda*	18
red panda, *Ailurus*	52
raccoon, *Procyon*	55*

The giant panda, *Ailuropoda melanoleuca,* is also renowned among biologists for the details of its anatomy, which caused a schism regarding its classification for many years. To some it seemed to be a member of the raccoon family, to others it belonged to the bears, while a third group assigned it to a separate family of its own. Although unanimity has not yet been reached, the argument for its bear connection has gained strength with serological studies of its

While 18 units of difference between the giant panda and the black bear constitute a greater difference than that between any other bear and the black bear, it is still much smaller than the difference between the giant panda and the lesser panda or the raccoon. One conclusion is that the giant panda is more of a bear than a raccoon; another would be that the giant panda deserves the taxonomic status of a family (as well as genus and species) all to itself.

Many zoologists find the above evidence, along with the giant panda's overall bearishness, to be convincing enough to place it in the *Ursidae*. The skeptics are more impressed by the giant panda's unbearlike footpads, specialized stomach and gut, massive teeth and skull, unusual S-shaped penis, naked skin of the ano-genital area, and its bleating rather than roaring voice. For a more detailed account of the debate, the reader should see Ramona and Desmond Morris's *Men and Pandas.*

*This information is based on V. M. Sarich, "Transferrin," *Transactions of the Zoological Society of London* 33 (1976): 165–171.

blood proteins, even though its chromosome number is identical to that of the raccoons (42) as opposed to bears (52 or 74). Its shape and gait seem bearish to the casual observer, although its stride is longer than that of a bear and more rolling or waddling. The panda's most distinctive anatomical and behavioral features are linked to its food and habitat. Because of its predominantly bamboo diet, it has a wide and massive skull with forty-two large, grinding teeth (the same in number as other bears). Unlike either bears or raccoons, it has no heel pad on the rear feet (and therefore does not make a manlike footprint). Its front feet are even more unusual because of an extra bony pad on the heel of the thumb (or radial sesamoid), which it uses as an opposing digit for holding the bamboo it eats. This is typically done as the panda sits bolt upright. The esophagus has a horny lining and the stomach is very muscular. Surprisingly, the small intestine is rather short, reducing the efficiency of digestion, so that a huge amount of vegetal matter is continually passing through it, making the trail of a wild panda a staccato passage of droppings. In this sense, this bear is virtually a slave to its gut, consuming up to 15 kilograms per day. In their book, *Men and Pandas,* Ramona and Desmond Morris write, "The panda waved good-bye to the nimble-minded world of helter-skelter chases, bloated blood feasts, and sprawling catnaps. Instead it has become (literally) a manual laborer, toiling endlessly at its repetitive bamboo-picking tasks." Fortunately for it, vast amounts of the two species of bamboo it prefers grow in its mountain habitat, providing both cover and nourishment. Altogether it eats more than twenty species of bamboo, favoring different parts of the plant at different seasons.

Not that the giant panda eats only bamboo. It consumes other plants, small mammals, birds, fish, and eggs when available, as well as carrion. Occasionally pandas raid corn or wheat fields, and they will eat cultivated plants in captivity. Still, its dependence on bamboo is such that the occasional die-off of the bamboos result in catastrophe for the pandas. In the late 1970s and again in 1984, for example, Chinese scientists reported that as much as one-fourth of the population starved to death.

Males and females are identical in markings and size. Even in captivity the sex of an individual is difficult (for humans) to ascertain, as the external genitalia look much alike. The very small (4-centimeter) penis of the male is not normally visible. During mating, the female assumes a head-down position while the male mounts. Copulation takes from thirty seconds to five minutes. In captivity the female is in estrus twice a year, but in the wild she breeds in April. Evidence in captive animals also suggests that the animals may first mate at about three and a half years of age, at which time both sexes also begin scent-marking by rubbing a scent gland in the anal area against a tree or stone, or by cocking the leg like a dog.

More often, sexual maturity is reached at six years. In zoos, pandas live as long as fourteen years.

Gestation in captivity takes about five months, but probably includes a period of suspended development, as with other bears. Like the young of other bears, too, the newborn are tiny and nearly helpless, covered sparsely with white hair, and weigh about 100 grams. Only one or two are born at a time, the mother holding them while they nurse. Blind and toothless at first, the cubs do not see for eight weeks or crawl for three and a half months. A single cub can be carried by the mother, holding it against her breast while she walks on three legs. Birth takes place in a hollow tree or cliffy den or cave. Instead of hibernating, the pandas descend to lower elevations for the winter.

In captivity (and probably in the wild) little pandas like to play at somersaulting, doing headstands, rolling, and head- and body-shaking. All may be active day or night, but are especially lively in the evening and at dawn. They like to bathe and can climb, but do so slowly as they get big. In the wild they are retiring and elusive. By some accounts they are slow and do not run, but by others they are very swift; by some they are clumsy and stupid, by others nimble and sensitive. To escape, the panda swims without hesitation. The home range of adults is thought to be no more than two kilometers square, although it may travel more widely during mating and with seasonal weather changes.

Within the range of the giant panda also occur the Himalayan black bear and a pale race of the brown bear, but virtually nothing is known to science about the interactions of these three bears. The voice of the panda is described as more of a bark or a bleat than a roar, although at mating time a low, deep call is given. Gastroenteritis and roundworm infections are the panda's most common diseases. Besides man, its most dangerous enemies are the dhole (a wild dog) and the leopard.

·3·

CELEBRATIONS OF THE SLAIN BEAR

Bear myths tackle fundamental questions of human existence; they are a paragraph in the idea that nature is a language. Although there are other sacred animals in the traditions of the northern hemisphere—myths and ceremonies of the raven, coyote, tiger, elk, eagle, kite, whale, and so on—the bear has a role in human imagination for which it is endowed beyond all the rest.

The natural world frames the myth of the bear. Although that world is now removed from our daily life, we can imagine the bear in landscapes of the ancient north. As winter approached, all green things perished and the soil froze; except for the needles of the conifers, the leaves withered and fell. The sounds of frogs and insects ceased as the days grew cold and short. Many of the birds and small mammals vanished. With the snow, the pale face of death came over the world. The caribou and elk would dig for moss or dried grass, pursued in turn by the wolf and other predators. Men, too, hunted and savored the frozen berries and nuts they put by. The animals were themselves both food and teachers of food-getting, scavenging, storing, and pursuing. But which among them spoke to the season's inescapable analogy to the life of a man? Gradually, perhaps over many centuries, the human question went beyond "How do we survive the cold winter?" to "How do we survive the cold death?"

The bear, more than any other teacher, gave an answer to the ultimate question—an astonishing, astounding, improbable answer, enacted rather than revealed. Its passage into the earth, winter's death, and burial under the snow was like a punctuation in the round of life that would begin again with its emergence in the spring. "Spring" was three things: a season of renewal, the underground stream that came forth even in winter, and a "leap" from the earth. The miracle was double, for the bear burst out with young—birth and rebirth. Somehow the bear knew when to re-enter the world again, emerging just ahead of the snowmelt, as though its very heat set the new year in motion, timed to graze lightly on the tendrils of the first skunk cabbage and new sedges. The rebirth was synchronized for access to the cold storage of the frozen carcasses of reindeer, moose, bighorn, and deer beneath the shrinking snow mantle. Clearly the bear was master of renewal and the wheel of the seasons, of the knowledge of when to die and when to be reborn. Of all the animals who vanish from the north when the cold winds begin to blow, this phenomenal retreat and rejuvenation acts as a clue to the greater pulse of coming and going. The bear's ascetic freedom in the den from eating and excreting, its timing in concert with the solar cycle, and the she-bear's meticulous motherhood are peculiarly visible and thought-provoking. The bear seems to die, or to mimic death, and in that mimicry is the suggestion of a performance, a behavior intended to communicate.

The tutorship of mankind did not stop there. The bear was a midwinter feast for man, taken from a crypt in the snow. Its entrails would heal a dozen winter complaints; its fat was like liquid gold. Men had a feast of meat to warm their insides and a hide to bundle in. This slaying of the bear was never an everyday event, rare enough not to become a harvest of ordinary food, yet frequent enough to be experienced by everyone. It was as though men were summoned by such a hunt, invited to intrude in the middle of the bear's cycle of deathlike sleep, to receive a gift of nourishing food and astonishing spiritual awareness by participating in its reincarnation. From feast to festival, from stomach to sacrament, the idea congealed across the millennia as a rite. Like all rites it referred to an explanatory, exemplary, wonderful tale.

The powers of the bear and its relation to man have been preserved in a story with two main parts, the first of which may be the most persistent and widely told tale ever devised to entertain and educate.

Its details vary somewhat in different parts of the world, but the Haida version from British Columbia is typical:

> Long ago, a group of girls of the tribe were out gathering huckleberries. One among them was a bit of a chatterbox, who should have been singing to tell the bears of her presence instead of laughing and talking. The bears, who could hear her even though some distance away, wondered if she was mocking them in her babbling. By the time the berry-pickers started home, the bears were watching.
>
> As she followed at the end of the group, the girl's foot slipped in some bear dung and her forehead strap, which held the pack filled with berries to her back, broke. She let out an angry laugh. The others went on. Again she should have sung, but she only complained. The bears noted this and said, "Does she speak of us?" It was growing dark. Near her appeared two young men who looked like brothers. One said, "Come with us and we will help you with your berries." As the aristocratic young lady followed them, she saw that they wore bear robes.
>
> It was dark when they arrived at a large house near a rockslide high on the mountain slope. All of the people inside, sitting around a small fire, were wearing bearskins also. Grandmother Mouse ran up to the girl and squeaked to her that she had been taken into the bear den and was to become one of them. The hair on her robe was already longer and more like a bear's. She was frightened. One of the young bears, the son of a chief, came up to her and said, "You will live if you become my wife. Otherwise you will die."
>
> She lived on as the wife of the bear, tending the fire in the dark house. She noticed that whenever the Bear People went outside they put on their bear coats and became like the animal. In the winter she was pregnant, and her husband took her to a cliff cave near the old home, where she gave birth to twins, which were half human and half bear.
>
> One day her brothers came searching for her, and the Bear Wife knew she must reveal her presence. She rolled a snowball down the mountainside to draw their attention, and they climbed up the rockslide. The Bear Husband knew that he must die, but before he was killed by the woman's brothers, he taught her and the Bear Sons the songs that the hunters must use over his dead body to ensure their good luck. He willed his skin to her father, who was a tribal chief. The young men then killed the bear, smoking him

out of the cave and spearing him. They spared the two children, taking them with the Bear Wife back to her people.

The Bear Sons removed their bear coats and became great hunters. They guided their kinsmen to bear dens in the mountains and showed them how to set snares, and they instructed the people in singing the ritual songs. Many years later, when their mother died, they put on their coats again and went back to live with the Bear People, but the tribe continued to have good fortune with their hunting.

In the Bear Mother story, men acknowledge kinship with an ancestral bear, yet keep the distinction between bears and human beings. The bear abductors, obviously alarmed about the moral state of humans when they hear blasphemy, assume human form. The woman is mated with a divinity, becoming herself a sacred procreator, and thus is involved with a form of immaculate conception. The Bear God dies for the welfare of people, exacting atonement and propitiation from the hunters. He becomes the archetype of all bears who will judge the spiritual state of human hunters. As food, the slain bear becomes a sacramental entity. The Bear Sons, themselves divine, can change from bears to men, share in both natural and supernatural attributes, and thus, as hunters, become intermediaries. They know that hunting is a holy activity, and understand the religious procedures of reconciliation between the hunters and the hunted. The tale shows why both bears and people are part animal, part human. Men are descended from the Bear Mother, who is therefore the founder of the clan and who resides spiritually underground with the Bear People. She is to the clan as the root is to the tree. When bear spirits come into the everyday world they wear bearskins. Men's luck and prowess in hunting are the result of their exacting ritual acknowledgment of that gift in the way they bring home the bear itself.

The second part of the myth, the Bear Son legend, which follows the adventures of the youths, develops later on, and we will follow it in connection with stories of the miraculous return of heroes thought to be lost. The Bear Mother tale itself reveals that bears are kinsmen: true forebears. It tells that men descended from the Bear Mother, a woman who married (and became) a bear and founded a special race of immortal beings—ourselves—and that men are part human and part divinity, since the Bear Prince she married was a shape-shifting, all-hearing immortal who knew and controlled the cosmic power of conducting the sacred hunt. Such ancestors should be referred to in honorific terms only. The Bear Mother may also be the first great mythopoetic mother of all life (the first external incarnation among animals of our personal mothers), prior in history and deeper in the psyche than her humanlike expressions, the goddesses and madonnas of civilization.

The story of the ritual death of the sacred bear is the cornerstone of a cosmogenic scheme, a tale of the secret of perennial success, and therefore renewal. We may guess that this came about among hunting/gathering peoples with the first intuitions of metaphoric thought. Much later, classical philosophers would concur that the idea of *thereutes* or *venator* embraces all searching, all quests for love and understanding, bound up in the drama of the hunt. The tale is given a spatial setting. In time the cosmology of the bear would develop a dual form in space, a horizontal partition of the world along the axis of the river of life and the people: its headwaters the home of immortal souls; its middle that of the living; its lower reaches the netherworld of the dead. But it also assumes a vertical structure: the sky as the home of eternal beings; the earth's surface that of the mortal creatures; the underworld as the place of the dead kinsmen. Just as the river unites the three realms in one dimension, the figure of the tree unites them in the other.

Earlier we proposed that the many dictionary meanings of "bear" could be collected under three headings: navigation, transportation, and transformation. The settings of bear mythology likewise take place in three realms: the sky, the earth's surface, and the underworld. In an elementary sense the two groups correlate. The location and movement of the stars is the basic guide to place and travel, the middle earth of daily life is where we encounter the bear messenger from the gods, and the underworld is the essential place of renewal in the endless round of life and growth. At the same time, however, each of the three realms is complete in itself and all three definitions of "bear" are represented as events in the legends that describe spirit bears and men in the heavens, the ground, and the nether region.

In the Sky

Reference to the "celestial" domain may seem strange, for the great, lumbering bear seems poorly cast as an aerial sprite. Yet the bear shines brightly in the heavens. As the two conspicuous constellations of the northern hemisphere, Ursa Major and Ursa Minor, the bear occupies a significant position in the heavens. The brightest star in Ursa Minor, Alpha Ursae Minoris, is better known as the Pole Star, or Polaris. This celestial pole is the northern spot to which the earth's axis points. Ursa Major and Minor are closely connected: both are composed of seven stars, and the first two stars in Ursa Major, Alpha and Beta, are the "pointers" directing the viewer to the Pole Star. The Hindus called Ursa Major the Seven Bears or the Seven Rishis (Wisemen), and the constellation was named in Sanskrit *rakh,* which means "bright." Some historians conjecture that the Greeks confused *rakhtos* with their own word *arktos,* and hence arose the bear constellation and the bear stories to explain the animal's appearance in the heavens. In mythology, these two signal constellations are lumped together and both commonly referred to as the Great Bear.

Traditional symbols for the turning Great Bear include the cross and the swastika (the four revolving seasons, the four directions), and what might be the most basic of all symbols, the spiral. In his heavenly role, the Great Bear, for some ancient peoples, directly influences childbirth. The Hindus, for example, placed red spirals on the outsides of houses where childbirth was about to occur, dancing outside the house—always circling it to the right*—to ensure that the newborn child would make the passage safely into life by turning in the proper direction out of the womb. Etymological connections between *bear* and child*bear*ing and maintaining one's correct direction by keeping one's *bear*ings are all deeply rooted in the bear's power of renewing the world.

According to De Gubernatis's *Zoological Mythology,* the Hindus

---

*The pattern of movement of the Great Bear around the North Star is counterclockwise, hence the spiral would seem to be to the left. But the point is that the turning of the heavens carries with it the daily renewal of the sun. If you face south toward the sun in the southern sky, its motion appears to be from left to right.

believed that as the source and wellspring, the primeval whorl of all the energy in the universe, the Great Bear caused the "seasons to follow one another in regular succession, rains to fall, and crops to grow and ripen . . . it assured . . . a supply of food, but if it gave . . . health and strength, it also, as the controller of water and wind, caused droughts in season, and sent blights and diseases on evil winds." Keeping in mind the Seven Bears and the Seven Rishis of the Hindus, consider the following description from the *Rig-Veda:* "Those which are the Seven Rays, in them is my nave expanded." The Great Bear is the ever-turning mandala in the sky. Thus the Pole Star, called *druhva* in Hindi, provides more than mere navigational guidance—serving as the still center of the wheel, offering spiritual bearings for the religious wanderer.

Although the ancients knew seven planets and there are seven stars in Ursa Major, how the seven bears rose in the sky for the Aryan Indians remains a mystery. In the classical West, the story is less clouded. The bear owes his position in the heavens to the fate of Callisto, one of Artemis' virgin votaries, who becomes transformed permanently into a bear as punishment (or protection from punishment) for transgressions that are perhaps seen in the mythology as regressive, wild, or unchaste. At any rate, her behavior was unbecoming an attendant of Artemis, who, besides being surrounded by young virgins, was also the defender of chastity, young things in general, and childbirth. In one version of the myth, Artemis discovers that Callisto is pregnant. For copulating with men, Artemis transforms Callisto into her most familiar bestial incarnation, the side of her that is most unchaste, most unvirginlike—a she-bear. In another version, Zeus impregnates Callisto. Hera, Zeus' jealous wife, punishes Callisto by turning her into a bear; again, the bear is seen as the fallen, bestial side of Callisto. In both versions, Arcas, the son of Callisto, hunts his bear mother and pursues her to Mount Lycaeus, Zeus' sacred ground. To save her from matricide or as punishment for that trespass, Zeus fixes them both in the heavens as the constellations Great Bear and Little Bear, circling on the axis of the heavens.

The Finns, Ostyaks, and Voguls tell a story of the earthly bear's origin on a cloud near the Great Bear constellation. The bear came to establish the Barenfest ceremony, then returned to the sky. Like other bears since then, which are killed, its spirit was sent home by the ceremony that it taught men.

The Ostyaks, a tribe of western Siberia, explain the bear's descent from heaven in a different way. For them, bears began in heaven, born of a union between Moon, Sun, and Big Bear, a primal force or being. Bears lived solely in heaven, the story goes, until one day when Father Bear went out on a hunt, Little Bear broke the lock on their hut and entered the courtyard of heaven. An ungainly cub, his paw sank deep through the floor of heaven; and through the hole Little Bear glimpsed the people below. He was so pleased by what he saw that he pleaded with his father, Numi-torum, to allow him to visit the world below, and finally convinced him.

Numi-torum placed Little Bear in a golden cradle and lowered him on silver chains onto a honey blossom that grew on the noisy surface of the black earth. Numi-torum instructed Little Bear to leave the good people alone and to oppress the bad. He also told Little Bear to explain to the people the great bear ceremony, its acts and meanings. At the conclusion of the first bear ceremony, described later in this book, as performed by the Ket, a tribe of the Ostyaks, Little Bear fills his knapsack with silver as a present for his father, who raises him back up to heaven.

For the Ostyaks, the bear serves as a delegate from the world of the supernatural, the world beyond, to man. The feast of the bear is intended to make clear the connection between the holy places where the ceremony was performed and heaven itself. By enacting the feast, the Ostyaks ensure that their souls will wander to that holy spot where the fate of humans is finally decided. In a sense, then, their lives rest in the hands of the bear.

As for the "sky bear," we may summarize by noting that there are short-term and long-term powers of the sky over events on earth. Daily weather and the climatic changes of the seasons are widely seen as having their origins in sky conditions—in clouds, wind, the sun's heat, precipitation, and the association of these phenomena with the sun and stars' position, all signified by the corresponding behavior of birds and other animals. These sources in the sky of periodic events on the earth's surface connect and bind the universe together. Although bears do not fly like birds, their aerial reality is manifest in Ursa Major, a continuing sign of the bear's presence as a weather magistrate and prophet, particularly in connection with palingenesis, the power of renewal and the regeneration of the seasons. That same power is basic to the passage of the bear's own soul and its function as a spiritual envoy between the tumult of life in the ebb and flow of physical being on earth and its eternal pattern, exemplified by the wheeling of the Great Bear in the night sky.

The Eskimos tell an elaborate story to explain the origin of the Great Bear constellation. When the Eskimos hunt bear, they pretend they are hunting some other animal, for they are aware, as are the Finns, that the bears know what they're thinking. In the story, an Eskimo woman stumbles upon a house full of bears in human form. They leave their bearskins outside the house, but when they hunt they don their skins and become bears. The woman lives with them a long time until, yearning for her husband, she leaves them. The Bear Men make her promise not to tell anyone of their whereabouts, but her husband, curious, goes to find the strange house. The Bear Men know instinctively of her betrayal and angrily seek her out. One of them breaks into her house and bites her to death. When the bear leaves, the husband's dogs attack the bear. Suddenly, both bear and dogs burn wonderfully bright, and rise to the sky as stars. Bear and light merge for the Eskimo as a heavenly constellation.

These two constellations, fraught with mystery as they turn at the center of the northern heavens, provide the essential and vital power for the orderly functioning of the universe. In this context the Great Bear functions as the Prime Mover, who must be placated in order to ensure his continual turning. Donald A. Mackenzie, in *The Migration of Symbols, and Their Relation to Beliefs and Customs,* argues that the pagan ceremonies of circular, ecstatic dances were "originally . . . performed by magic-workers to stimulate the Great Bear Constellation." Otherwise, he says, the ancients believed that the Great Bear might jam, or else spin in the wrong direction. C. G. Jung indicates that in Mithraic cultures, Mithras himself is sometimes the *Sol invictus;* he holds in his right hand the constellation of the Great Bear, "which moves and turns the heavens round."

The Winnebago Indians of Wisconsin conceive the transcendent bear in four colors: white, red, gray, and black, each bound to a point of the compass. According to anthropologist Walter Funmaker, the youth on his vision quest must "visit" all four. The black bear signifies introspection and "that forward looking associated with one's own mortality." It is part of the renewed consciousness of adolescence, the sensitivity that in all mankind marks the psychological readiness in the individual for contemplation of life and death, his philosophical entry into adult status and concerns.

When the first whites came to North America, they found that the Algonkian tribes already identified the same stars as the Great Bear that they themselves did. In time they found that this was true from Nova Scotia westward to Point Barrow and down the Pacific coast, and even among the Pueblos—though not every tribe knew the bear in the sky. Some, apparently, had forgotten. To the Iroquois and Micmac Indians, the Great Bear was composed of four stars pursued by seven "hunters," the second of which was accompanied by a tiny star, his pot for cooking the bear. To them, also, a group of stars above the bear constituted its den. The hunters were the robin, chickadee, moosebird (Canada jay), pigeon, blue jay, owl (probably the horned owl), and saw-whet (a small owl). The pursuit begins in late spring. By fall the four at the end of the line have lost the trail. The robin, chickadee, and moosebird overtake the bear in mid-autumn and kill it, the red fall foliage indicating the slain bear's blood. Perhaps the four that drop out are the same species that migrate away in winter, while the successful hunters of the clan are those that either stay for the winter or remain through the fall. (Only the robin's presence in this theory is anomalous.) The Cherokee Indians, like the Greeks, live below 40 degrees north latitude, and from their perspective the four stars were "lost" below the horizon at midwinter. The Cherokee saw them as part of the hunters, like the Iroquois, while to the Chinese and classical Greeks those were the only hunters, the first three stars being the bear's tail. (That this bear has such a long tail has led to speculation that its model was the cave bear, *Ursus spelaeus,* which had a longer tail than any of the living bears, and became extinct 10,000 years ago.)

As already noted, the connection of birds to bears seems at first strange, but is in part due to their similar roles as weather prophets and their spiritual dominion over the seasons. The association is ancient and widespread. In the Balkans, Yugoslavia, and Greece, the birds in antiquity were major calendric spirits. Water-bearing pots and vases in the shape of bear paws also date from the sixth millennium B.C. Danilo culture of Yugoslavia. These are marked with rain and storm symbols, indicating the bear's role as one of the oldest weather forecasters, a living almanac, a major celestial power in the

Mediterranean region, where the rains occur only in one season. In northern Eurasia this emphasis is on waterbirds, focusing, says the distinguished archaeologist Marija Gimbutas, on the return of birds in spring. Among the Cree Indians, until recently and long before the time of megalithic seasonal clocks like Stonehenge and numerical charts of the year, bear hibernation and waterfowl migration were principal markers in the division of the year, "the basis," observes Gimbutas, "for models of a seasonal symbiotic parallel between the social life of men and animals." In the north country the disappearance of small mammals and invertebrates, like the fall of leaves and the ripening of fruit, is a sign of the end of summer, but the crucial onset of snow and the end of winter in the imminence of the spring thaw are most dramatically foreshadowed by the precise departure and arrival of geese and bears. In light of this shared oracular power, their intertwined presence in the stars is not surprising.

Much more fundamental and widespread is the belief that birds are the souls of the dead. The Evenk Siberians traditionally believe that one of the souls of a dead clansman, the *beyen* or body-soul, is accompanied by the shaman to the land of the dead—at the root of the clan tree or the mouth of the clan river. Meanwhile, the *omi* or shadow-soul flies off upstream, to the headwaters, where live the immortals. Mangi, the bear who is the chief ancestral spirit that controls entry into the lower world, discovers that the dead person lacks his reflection or shadow-soul and sends the goldeneye duck after it. But the duck fails and the bear itself goes to retrieve the *omi*. On its return the *omi* becomes a bird and flies back to the middle world of the living. The bird-souls are seen there by people, hopping around in the trees before reentering a woman's (or animal's) womb and vivifying a new being. While in the womb the feathers drop from its wings and they become arms.

A different version of the cosmic hunt in the night sky which is probably older than the hunt of the bear, as told in native America, is the Asian description of the hunt of the spirit elk, Kheglen, by Mangi, the bear and chief ancestor spirit. Linked to the base of the clan tree or *turu*—the larch—Mangi is also feminine, the mother-beast. The sky is the taiga of the upper world, where Kheglen and her calf (the stars of Ursa Minor) hide during the day among the thickets. At night they come out to graze and are pursued and killed

THE COSMIC HUNT

To realize what a great part of the northern sky was dominated by the great hunt, one needs to watch all night. Ursa Minor, Ursa Major, and Boötes, who make up the prey and pursuer, pivot around the North Star in the course of the night. The sky is swept by this great arm of lights, the drama of the chase from horizon to zenith, circling from right to left, dominating the visual field, awesome in its energy. In the Paleolithic era it was not Polaris but another "north star" that was hub of the revolving universe. The "pursuit" was like a great gear on an invisible axis, driving the whole stellar panorama through the night, bringing the rising sun, whose brightness was therefore also the bear's doing: the ultimate food chain. Hunters have always known that the chase liberates the energy that turns the world.

Although they agree on the nature of the spectacle, different peoples identify the players somewhat differently. Three examples follow:

1. In the archaic myth the "big bear" and "little bear" are the cosmic elk, Kheglen, pursued by Mangi, the bear spirit (Boötes).

2. In Europe the bear is not the hunter but the hunted. Along with the little bear, she is chased by the human hunter in the constellation Boötes.

3. To Algonkian Indians, the stars near the pole are the bear's den, the four stars of the bowl of the Big Dipper are the bear, and the seven hunters trail out behind.

Thus we have worked back from the Greeks, Finns, and Hindus toward an older, Paleolithic substrate, framed in notions of the hunt that nightly crosses the sky. The hunt is not a frenzied pursuit but the stately procession of final things, energy gained and spent, transferred, assimilated, and dissipated, only to be renewed again by the holy sun. Who knew better than those Paleolithic peoples (and bears) that food chains or some cosmic equivalent turn with their energy the great wheel of the universe? The bear dominating the northern sky as predator in one view, prey in the other, reminds us of its high place in the food chains on earth, hunted by men and yet an avatar of the forces that rule all life.

by Mangi, whose ski tracks are the Milky Way. The cosmic elk is overtaken annually, at the end of winter, and with her death the middle earth where men live bursts into new life, the ice breaks up, the snows end, the waterfowl appear, and calving takes place in the fresh green pastures. The new life springs from the various parts of the body of the elk butchered by the hunter-bear. The Siberians' early-spring ceremonies of the sun's return pantomime the great hunt. The dissection of earthly elk by men is ritualized so as to echo the myth of new life springing from its death. To some groups the whole constellation is the elk, Ursa Minor its calf, and the constellation Boötes, the hunter-bear. In that upper world the succession of day and night is produced by the chase. The path of these figures around the Pole Star is so much a part of northern life that the Soviet ethnologist G. M. Vasilevich says that the young people of today read it like a watch, and can tell the time of night to the minute by the position of these constellations.

In the Underworld

The aristocratic maiden who was destined in the transarctic myth to become the Bear Mother of men was taken to the underworld, the entrance to which was located on a high mountain slope. There the Bear People took off the skins they wore when they went out into middle earth. Oddly enough, the girl, waiting at the edge of the flickering fire to learn her fate, notices that the hair on her own cloak has become more bearlike. True to the rule that reality is reversed in the Other World, she "puts on" her bear robe upon entering the underworld just as the bear spirits put theirs on when entering the middle world.

This underground life (and deathlike state) of bears must have been one of the most surprising discoveries in the history of human thought. The brown bear prefers to dig a den among the roots of a great tree, and spends as much as half its life underground, neither eating nor drinking the entire time. The cave bears—and sometimes the brown bear—known to Neanderthal people used natural caves whose passages extended to who knew where. Black bears sometimes hibernate inside hollow trees, but usually go underground. If the sky reigned over the calendar of events on earth, it was nonetheless in the subterranean world that generation began. In the world of analogies essential to mythical consciousness, life begins and renews in *interiors*. Unlike foxes, mice, and beetles, which are also born in holes, the bear reenters the hole in a mimicry (or ritual pantomime) of death. Deep among the roots of the tree, whose trunk is marked by the bears in middle earth and whose branches connect the lower realms with the sky, the bear demonstrates that death is a journey toward the mother, just as birth is a departure from her.

Like the branches that frame the clan's tree of life, a profusion of stories sprang from this concept of the bear as the consummate master of regeneration. The bear became not only the exemplar of the nether journey that precedes new life, but the keeper and chief of that realm. Thus the bear is seen by many peoples as a bringer and giver of life, for the bear's body is itself an "interior." The Evenks of Russia tell this story of the bear:

A girl, Kheladan, was walking and came to a bear. The bear said, "Kill me and cut me up. Place my heart to sleep beside you, put my kidneys behind the hearth, my duodenum and rectum opposite you; spread my fur in a dry ditch, hang my small intestine on a dry, bent-over tree, and put my head near the hearth." Kheladan did as the bear ordered. In the morning she awoke and looked. Behind the hearth were two children (the kidneys) playing; an old man (the head) slept near them, and opposite were an old man and an old woman (the intestines). She glanced outside; there were some reindeer (the fur) walking about, and the little valley was full of reindeer.

The spirits of the lower world are the object of the shaman's magic. His access to them is indicated in his costume among the Selkup Siberians and others of the north by bear-fur adornment on its lower parts. In healing ceremonies he makes contact with Mangi, the bear and chief ancestor spirit of the underworld. Thus *renewal,* like *interior,* has multiple meanings in which the bear remains a central figure. Our own interiors are also caves, inaccessible to the rational ego with its need for conscious light. The vestiges of an older style remain even in the conscious psyche. In dreams, the animals are as they were when they linked the dreamer to another world. We may explain their lively meanings as autonomous expressions of our emotional lives. Nightmares of bears, for example, are said to represent childhood and infantile fears latent in the adult. *Bar* and *gebaren*—"bear" and "to give birth"—are the German roots for the English *bear* with both meanings. Thus, says a psychiatrist, bear dreams come from the mnemonic trace of our birth. In dreams associating the bear with a mountain (like the mythical ancestor in Siberian stories), the terrain is the *mons veneris* and we are the helpless cub. The dream of climbing a tree to escape a bear is interpreted as a return to the tree of life or the womb; to be "bare" is to be helpless; hugging bears indicates homosexuality.

Folktales may be regarded as the containers of similar psychodrama. Thus "Goldilocks and the Three Bears" has been variously described as an "internalized" expression of ancient ritual, a drama of oedipal conflicts, a tutorial of logical thought, and a formulation of anal problems. But what has become of the real, grumpy, shaggy, dangerous bear? Is the bear simply a large hulk upon which the infantile mind projects the human figure, and are we to accept the myth of the Bear Mother as the simple confusion of personal ontogeny with human history? No, says Carl Jung. Each night in sleep we hibernate a little: our breathing and temperature are modified; ingestion and elimination are forgotten. The bear, he says, is at the center of this excursion toward death's second self. Of this experience, James Hillman has said of animals, "To look at them from an underworld perspective means to regard them as carriers of soul, perhaps totem carriers of soul, perhaps totem carriers of our own free-soul or death-soul, there to help us see in the dark. To find out who they are and what they are doing there in the dream, we must first of all watch the image and pay less attention to our own reactions to it. As from a duck blind or when downwind stalking a deer, our focus is on the image, acute to its appearance, ourselves abashed, eclipsed in that intensity in order to follow the precise movements of its spontaneity. Then we might be able to understand what it means with us in the dream. But no animal ever means one thing only, and no animal simply means death."

The subterranean sleeper comes into our own time in a somewhat different context—in the modern expression of the "underground." Gary Snyder, in a poem entitled "The Way West, Underground," has called to our attention a different version of history in a countercultural sense. White America traces its roots to the East and the coming of Europeans; but there is a prior history. America was first peopled by men from Asia, who brought with them the myth and ceremonies of the bear. They themselves perhaps owe something to even more distant ancestors represented by the great underground sanctuaries even farther east in the Paleolithic cave art of Europe. Thus the oldest American traditions did not arrive by westward Atlantic crossings, but by way of Siberia and Alaska—the route by which bears themselves arrived in a series of evolutionary surges. Of this view, the anonymous author of the Bear Claw Press calendar for 1977 says, "The earliest cultures followed the paths of animals: hunters from the Siberian taiga tracked bears and caribou into North America. . . . In retracing the bear's ramblings from the West Coast back around Asia to Europe, Snyder's poem describes a cultural continuity as well, returning us to our own deepest origins. . . . It utterly reverses the European view, not only by reconnecting human destiny with its habitat and fellow-creatures, but by recovering the natural history of Northern peoples and animals, moving together across the land masses." From this we see that in tracing the circumpolar traditions of the bear ceremonies, we transcend the usual opposition of European and Native American origins, and that of Asian versus European, because the metaphysical bear legends are a shared heritage, perhaps part of the oldest traditions of mankind. This modification of our history reflects also our new sense of the bear as more than an external being—as part of the deep reality of the human self.

On the Earth

From the time their ancestors first wandered into the forests and grasslands north of the equator, men have been watching, following, listening to, sometimes avoiding, and finally mimicking and studying animals. Myths tell of animals as the teachers of men.

The Inuit Eskimos, for example, think of the bear as both ancestor and tutelary guide to the food quest. They claim that their hunting strategy imitates the stalking of seal and walrus by the polar bear, who moves against the wind, crouching below the horizon, moving only when the prey looks away, pushing ahead a concealing chunk of ice, using rock or ice as projectiles, even covering its conspicuous black nose with a white paw. Elsewhere, men are led by bears to the medicinal herbs, the location of honey, or the wild fruit in season.

It has been suggested here that hundreds of millennia of attention to their fellow creatures helped to hone human intelligence. As the seasons and the hunt became storied phenomena, men saw animals acting in the drama of their own lives, key characters in the slowly rising conscious/unconscious structure of human culture. To this awareness of reality as recollection and intent, the marvelous array of animal life ceased to be simply *others,* and the species took their places as skilled and talented practitioners. Each in some way seemed to know a secret and to be wise in the metasocial fabric of the world, to be keyed by mysterious means to the needs of the hour, to the lunar pulse, and the season's passage. Being specialists—over against man, who needed something different from each in his own un-specialized way—few among the animals reflected directly the human situation, and fewer still seemed wise beyond its singular genius. For most, even as they came to be regarded as the tangible aspects of invisible presences, the animal gods were limited in their particular powers. The bear was the outstanding exception.

Why should the bear be so prodigious a model? From a natur-alistic and perceptual point of view, there is nothing else like a bear in human experience: its humanlike foot and dexterity of forepaws, its tendency to stand erect, its binocular vision in spite of the big nose, its amazingly manlike anatomy when skinned. But its major qualification for viziership is a consequence of its omnivorousness, its versatility. It may be difficult to overestimate the importance of this one fact, that the personality of the bear is largely the conse-quence of a big omni-eater, the finder of whatever is ripe and the killer when necessary. It is the bear's broad, searching, persistent openness that makes contact with us, that flash of recognition in which men instantly perceive a fellow being whose questing prov-ocation, whose garrulous, taciturn, lazy ways, even whose obliga-tions and commitments to hunt, to hole up, and to dominate the space he lives in are familiar. The bear is a special model of human flexibility, a generalist set against a world of specialists. To para-phrase an old saw about the fox and hedgehog, the bear knows many things while the elk knows only one.

But the bear's similarity to man is not all that has so captivated human imagination. It is what he does and how man encounters him in the middle world of life that brings to mind his uniqueness, that suggests even that he is observed and eaten by men for a purpose. We may wonder if the bear did not seem to early men to be the creature who knew everything. Man's association of the bear with the river and the tree was probably close to the earliest act of human scrutiny, for it was the tree and the river that connected the three levels of the universe.

The bear has many watery connections. A Siberian story is recorded about the relationship of the bear to the creation of tools that is reminiscent of Australian aboriginal stories telling how the land took its contours from the activities of a giant. As recounted by G. M. Vasilevich: "The bear started to cross a river, getting deeper into the water—up to the heel, the ankle, the knee, the thigh, the hips, the belly, the navel, the armpits, the shoulders, the throat, the chin, the mouth, the nose, the eyes, the crown of the head, until he disappeared altogether. Then he said: 'My heels shall be whetstones; my knees grinders; my shoulder blades stones for trying out colors; my blood the color red; my excrement black.' Since that time one could find in the taiga colors, grinders, whetstones, and other things."

The bear plunges into water to soak when ill or injured, to cool itself at the height of summer, and to escape from pesky horseflies and midges. It is to water that the polar bear flees for safety and to which the she-bear leads her young cubs for their first seal hunts. Swamp thickets in the South are common hiding, day-bedding, and denning places, for the trees there grow especially big and their trunks rot hollow. Like his little cousin the raccoon (or "wassenbear"), the bear prowls wetlands and seashores, seeking windfall meals. Clear to the centers of the continents, the rivers of the ancient world teemed with anadromous fish, especially the salmon, whose annual runs were as tightly time-factored as the migration of birds or the mass emergence of certain caterpillars (such as the "woolly bear"). The salmonoid fishes ascend from the mouth of the river— that distant source in the sea or a great lake. Headed for the upper tributaries, which are also remote, they die, and their bodies wash back down toward the place of origin. Or, intercepted, they pass into the gut of the bear, and the elemental remains are turned back downstream. Like the waterfowl that follow the streams in their flight, they seem bent on a transcendental voyage, a passage in which the familiar middle world is but a segment.

The Greek bear goddess, Callisto, was said by Hesiod to have been a river nymph. Her other name was Themisto, her river-god father Inachus. Callisto's tomb was near a spring at Krounoi in central Arcadia, connecting her not only with a watery environment but to a source from the underworld. The bearish places of pre-classical Greece were all near springs, as to the north where the bear-cult pottery of the ancient Danubians was decorated with chevrons symbolizing flowing water.

But it was probably long before anyone thought of pottery that the river was first perceived as a metaphor of destiny, the "clan river" of eternity connecting the three worlds. The bear signaled—perhaps seemed even to oversee—the arrival of the salmon. The salmon were human food too, which made the first link in the man-bear-river-salmon system a tangible reality. We can only guess how the river's eternal flow, the upstream movement of the miraculous fish from the depths of a watery matrix toward the almost ethereal springs at the headwaters, or their fate in the stomach of the bear might have stimulated the concept of reincarnation. In time, the spiritual forces represented by the physical realities would be grappled with by a shaman, who would travel the river to the ancestral downstream and the immortal upstream in a trance instead of a boat.

The other branching image penetrating the three levels of exist-ence—the tree—also had natural bearish connections. In the south, from China to the state of Georgia in the United States, bears are born in hollow trees and crawl back into them to sleep, to hibernate, or to elude pursuers. Little bears scamper up trees for safety. All species except the polar bear can and do climb trees. Willow and alder buds, like fruits and nuts, are sought as food. The underbark or cambium of fir and spruce is widely eaten. The forest is the bear's cover; out of it or deprived of it, its habits are altered: he travels by barrancas and gullies or between moraines, becomes more strictly nocturnal, or gets gruff and aggressive toward intruding people rather than stealthily evasive.

Again, in all of this, the bear seems to be a guide for men. We will never know whether men simply discovered that they and it lived parallel lives or, taking note of the bear's example, sought out the same forest resources. But in oral tradition it is said to be the latter. Even man's use of wood as fuel for his fire came to be linked to the bear's celestial role, as its pursuit of the cosmic elk around Polaris keeps the wheel of the universe turning and brings the daily return of the sun's heavenly fire.

A Prometheus-like story of the Ainu tells how the bear obtained fire. In mountainous, volcanic countries like Japan, the forest home of the Animal Chief and the Bear People is in the mountains. The bear's association with the underworld makes him knowledgeable of the fire inside the earth, and his solar connections are implicit in the sun's control of the season and denning. Among several Siberian tribes, the bear ceremony includes a procession in which the bones are carried around the fire in a solar pattern.

Perhaps the most telling connection between bears and trees, from the standpoint of human imagination, is the ursine habit of "signing." Pandas spray their urine directly on trees, like some cats; Balkan brown bears have been seen to roll in their urine and rub their backs on trees. Even without the urine, bears' rubbing-trees are familiar to naturalists, and certain trees are used regularly. The bears appear to be scratching—but is that all? Even if such itch-posts are not being deliberately marked, there can be little doubt that other bears, all animals with keen noses, will take note of the scent, when passing, perhaps for days or weeks.

Bears also reach up, while standing on their back legs, and scratch hemlock, spruce, fir, and pine trees. Individual trees are scratched again and again over a period of years. What the bear is doing, within his own sphere, is unknown, but it is clear to the human observer that few other animals in the northern hemisphere other than themselves could make so striking a five-fingered print. Other than the bear, perhaps only the big cats give the impression of making a meaningful mark on a tree.

While the bear is certainly not always part of the worldwide mythology of the tree of life, of knowledge, or of good and evil, in the northern hemisphere it is widely and intimately a part of that imagery and story. The tree is a nearly universal symbol of renewal and the yin/yang relationship of life and death. In the bear the tree has a metaphysical symbiotic partner, a companion in the art of immortality. The bear, like the tree, seems to die but, in the spring, is discovered not to have died. And so it is said that, even when killed, it does not truly die. Like the tree, with its roots, trunk, and limbs in different layers of the cosmos, the bear is seen in the stars in the night sky, underground as the sleeper, and on earth as an animal. Yet there is a sense in which there is but one bear, even on earth. William Gronbech, a Danish historian of religion, early in this century, said, "When the animal steps out of our view we fancy that it trails a line of existence somewhere hidden among the thousand things of the earth until it reappears across our path. . . . The universe is crossed by millions and millions of threads, each one spun by an isolated individual. According to primitive experience, the facts arrange themselves into a different pattern. All bears are the same soul, and every new appearance of a bear—whether it be no other than that we saw yesterday or the most distant of all among the kin, as we reckon—is a new creation from the soul. A bear is a new birth every time it appears anew, for the deep connection in the existence of the soul is a steady power of regeneration."

Gronbech's observation clarifies a remark made by a Mistassini Cree Indian in a film made by the Canadian Film Board in 1973: "If we do not show respect for the bear when we kill him, he will not return." Thus the bear's capacity for renewal is based on a soul that outlasts death. Among the Siberians, who developed this concept to an elegant degree, the bear has four or five souls (in female and male respectively) that have different destinies and associations with the body. One of the crucial elements in the soul's return is the recognition by those who attend its death that they play a part in its renewal as well. Such was the nature of the instructions given to his children by the Bear Chief husband of the Bear Mother in the traditional story. Other animals have also tutored men in this matter, according to other stories, and all of them have in common the physical capacity to survive disintegration: the butterfly, who is totally transformed from the caterpillar; the snake, whose phallic shape and vaginal rippling movement combine with skin-shedding; the frog, changing from tadpole in the water to adult on land; the beetle, turning a ball of dung into new life. In all cases two things are true: translated into human life, such symbolic passage must be ritually framed—that is, elements of the story that associates them with men must be enacted or artistically revivified; and the passage from life to death has something fundamental in common with all transformations—birth, puberty, marriage, new social status or rank, and death.

The Festival of the Slain Bear

The rituals that the dying bear in the myth of the Bear Mother instructed men to keep vary in detail among circumpolar peoples, even within Siberia, though they retain a common infrastructure. The festival of the slain bear was observed in 1958 among the Ket, a tribe of Siberian Ostyaks, by E. A. Alekseenko, a Soviet ethnologist. The Ket believe that the bear is chief among animals, that beneath its skin is a being in human shape, divine in wisdom. When a hunter has located the den of a bear, he returns to camp. From his tent he pounds his snowshoes with a stick and waves to others in the dispersed settlement to indicate his discovery, and the signal is relayed from tent to tent across the snow. When the other hunters have assembled, he describes the trail and the den or "tent" of the "old man." The generic term *bear* and the words *hunt* and *kill* are never used. These euphemisms signify respect for the bear's kinship to man, and the ambiguity and mystery of the bear as both spirit and animal put a restraint on his expression, for the bear is listening.

Early the next morning the group assembles near the den and builds a fire. By its light they prepare their weapons. The men approach the den at dawn and cry out, "Come out, Grandfather!" The bear is goaded out with spears and killed by an ax-blow on the head. Care is taken that no blood is shed on the ground. The hunters continue to speak to the bear after it is dead, for its soul is alive and present. They implore it not to be angry and invite it to become their guest. The right forepaw is cut off and flipped several times— palm up or down meaning "yes" or "no"—to determine whether the soul of a dead relative is present and, if so, to what clan and family he belonged and exactly who he is. Tossing the paw also tells how many days the guest will remain. The paw will be kept as a talisman. The bear is skinned, following the cutting of an incision from the throat down. The head is severed from the body, but remains attached to the skin; the carcass is flayed and dissected in a precise way; the stomach, lungs, and bowels are buried on the spot. The butchering of ribs, back, and shoulders is done so that no bones are cut. One of the hunters gives a bit of the heart to any boy who is present, which he eats while sitting astride the still warm animal. The heart, liver, and fat are cooked in a copper kettle on a nearby fire and each hunter eats some of them all. The butchered body of the bear, along with skin and head, is then dragged home on sleds.

The festival that follows, lasting for several days, involves everyone in the camp—usually from three to five families. The men cook the bear's flesh in a large copper kettle at a fire in the host's tent. Everyone takes at least a bite of every part, except for the head, which is eaten only by the hunters, each of whom is obliged to taste all edible parts of it. The lard is smoked and later taken by the host to his relatives, even though they may live many miles away. The participants take meat home in big wooden dishes—nothing is left or wasted. The next day there is another feast, this one for the bear himself. First the host's tent is cleaned, the floor is covered with fresh fir twigs, all bear flesh is removed, and the tables are cleaned. The host draws the bear's picture, which embodies the bear's soul, on an oval piece of birchbark. Sometimes bits of copper are attached to it as bracelets and collars, and it is then covered with another piece of bark and the two are pegged together. Among some of the Ket, the bear's skull is used instead of a drawn image. The bark drawing is placed near the tent entrance, in a newly painted chest, head forward. With it are placed skin from the bear's face and snout, the gallbladder, and sometimes the eyes and penis. A cedar twig, bent into a ring and tied, has a bundle of twigs—the bear's "ribs"—attached to it. Bits of fish glue, the bear's tongue, and pieces of copper are hung from the ring. Copper is called "the bear's gold," and connects its bones while the glue binds other parts of its body. Thus the cedar ring with its adornments is said to hold the bear's body together. The symbolic bear is put into the chest, which is made of cedar, a sacred wood of which drums and drumsticks are also made. At the end of the festival, the bark drawing will be hung on the branch of a cedar tree.

With all assembled, the host sits beside the chest and tells the story of the hunt of the bear, beginning with his own rising on the day he discovered "the old man's tent." At a crucial point the narrator breaks a miniature lance, jumps up shouting *"Uzdj!"* and swallows the bear's eyes from a bark goblet. This container, called the *ittyn,* and the broken spear are thrown into the fire. If the host chokes a bit, he is felt by others to be somewhat humiliated; if he is asphyxiated he is being punished. The narrator proceeds to describe the movements and mimic the growls of the bear. He imitates it, holding up the snout as a mask. Occasionally warming the snout over the fire, he passes it to each hunter in turn. They repeat the performance, asking the bear for successful hunting. Each hunter mimics or dances the bear in his own way, bringing vividly before everyone the encounter with the "animal king" and appealing directly to its soul for good hunting in the year to come.

When the hunters' stories have ended, the objects are returned to the chest, and tables are set, including one before the chest. When the food is served, all wait while the bear "eats." The host then sets seven glasses of tea on the bear's table, sips each of them, and passes six on to the elders, leaving one. After the feast, the bear paw is tossed to select a member of the host's family to eat the last of the bear. In doing so, he earns protection from bears for the year.

The next day a final feast is held to see the bear off. Before the assembled community, the bear is asked not to be offended and to send other bears. The cedar bear-surrogate is carried around the fire in the direction of the sun's movement, then the chest with its sacred remains is also walked seven times around the fire. The bark drawing is taken into the forest and suspended from a notch cut into a young cedar tree, or the bear's skull is placed on the end of a broken branch in a tree or on the end of a pole stuck in the ground. The bear's bones are carefully collected, bound together with bark, and buried by the host in a hollow tree or in the ground. When the picture hung on the tree dries and falls to the ground, the bear begins a new life.

The festival of the slain bear is, with embellishment, an enactment of the myth of the Bear Mother, centering on the death of the bear. Like all ritual mimesis, it is not seen by the participants as a portrayal but as a recurrence in which the brothers of the hunt participate, giving all due honor once again in the ceremony that ensures their release from beardom into humanity yet sustains their respect for their dead kinsman.

Variations of the Festival

Rites for the dead bear, similar enough to be linked by numerous details and all based on the myth of the Bear Mother, occurred until recently in Lapland, Finland, western and eastern Siberia, Kamchatka, Japan, Alaska, British Columbia, and Quebec. Although the bear was deeply respected and his body treated with reverence across both America and Eurasia, ceremonies of the slain bear were practiced least in the continental interiors, such as the plains and grasslands. There is some evidence of a wide and ancient distribution in virtually every country of Western and Eastern Europe, in Asia south to Iran, and among many of the Indian groups of the United States, even into Central and South America. The diversity of details of this vast body of cultural relicts reveals a human creativity and adaptive flourish without loss of reference to real bears or the underlying theme. Each phase of the hunt and festival, like the details of the Bear Mother story, was modified in specific ways by the tribes of the northern hemisphere. Preparations for the hunt, which normally took place in late winter, sometimes included abstinence from sexual intercourse, sweat baths, saunas, fasting, incantations, or visionary and dream experience. At times the hunters departed through unhinged doors wearing their clothes inside out (tokens of the reversal of things in the underworld of the dead). The fire near the bear den was said to require as many as nine kinds of sacred wood, and jumping through the fire and engaging in wrestling matches near it were not uncommon. Some groups formed a file or chain of men from the fire to the den. Sometimes a gap was left in the ring of men around the den for the passage of a forest spirit to the bear. Arrows and spears were used, as well as the ax, to kill the bear. Among old Germanic groups the participants shook the dead bear's paw and the bear was butchered at the den rather than in the village.

The Lapp procession to the den was led by a "ringer" who carried a staff with a brass ring at the end (signifying the sun?), followed in turn by a sorcerer, the spearman, woodcarriers, and others. The Lapp word for "alder" is the same as that for "bear's blood" and "menstrual blood." Alder-bark ceremonies centered on the "alderman," a term derived from *Laeib-olmai,* the name of a hunting god. As recently as 1868, when the Lapp hunters returned to their village with a slain bear, the women spat alder-bark juice at them through a brass ring. They also sprinkled the bear with the same "protective" substance, as well as the hunters, the dogs, the reindeer pulling the sledge with the body of the bear, the tent in which the bear was to be flayed, and the children who carried the women's portion of the meat to them. At these feasts everyone was smeared with bear blood, and a birchbark cone filled with chewed alder bark was placed before the bear's nose. Later, blindfolded women shot alder arrows at the bear hide to determine who would marry next or whose husband would be the next great bear hunter. The "blood" of tree, woman, and bear signify the multiple layers of fertility, regeneration, and the maternal principle at the heart of the ceremony, with its transposition of the hunt and marriage.

The Lapps spoke of "consulting" the drum before the bear hunt, and for centuries songs to the bear were also accompanied on the drum. Its universality is an archaeological fact; though its true antiquity is difficult to trace, since skin and wood do not usually endure, its widespread use in the last few centuries implies very old beginnings. The unifying and signaling value of the drum is obvious, so that the drumbeat became an early victim of missionary fervor. When the Lapps were forced into Christianity early in the eighteenth century, the drum was still part of the bear ceremony, and all but a few score of the sacred drums were publicly burned. Magically decorated, someimes made of bearskin, the Lapp drum was thought to come alive in the hands of the adept. It was designed as an evocation of the sun, connected in turn with the bear because the latter is the master of the seasonal round manifested in the shifts in the sun's arc and in the bear's underground sleep-death and awakening-birth. Some drums were the animal itself, its laces and bases designated as anatomical parts.

When the Koyukon of Alaska kill the bear in the den, it is always pulled out by hand, never with a rope or chain. Like the Siberians, they keep dogs away, for they are felt to be highly polluting to the bear spirit. The Koyukon slit the bear's eyes so that it cannot see while it is butchered on the spot. The ceremonial feast is held in the woods rather than in the village, although leftover meat may be brought home. An old man is quoted by anthropologist Richard Nelson as saying, "What we eat here is the main part of the bear's life." As among other subarctic peoples, the different parts of the bear are rigidly proscribed for eating by the different sexes, age groups, and participants in the hunt. The above remarks refer to the black bear. The Koyukon women eat none of the brown bear, whose power is even greater (but who is less tasty), and its hide is not even brought into the village.

Among the Ugarians along the Ob River in western Siberia, returning bear hunters and the carcass of the bear are sprinkled by women with water or snow. In some groups the men are pelted with snowballs, a box of snow is put alongside the dead bear in the host's house, or the hunters are thrown into the river. Songs accompanying this "welcome" refer to the "snow game" or the "water game." The logic is one of cleansing in a playful and joyful mood, although the pantomime of a snowfall suggests the early-winter signal to the bear for "going down" into his winter den and deathlike sleep. The creative aspect of water for all life is joined in the natural history of the bear to its affinity for aquatic habitats, its love for swimming and fishing, as well as the metaphysics of the clan river.

The singing and chanting associated with the snow and water games are only a small part of the music associated with bear ceremonialism. Song and dance are more frequent than the example of the Ket might indicate. Group singing at the edge of the village welcomes the bear and is part of the sending-home ceremony. Among the Koryak of Kamchatka, one of the women goes out to meet the returning hunters. Carrying a torch, she puts on the fresh bearskin and dances. A choral dialogue follows in which she plays the bear in a rhythmic reenactment of the chase. Such pantomimes are considered by anthropologists to be among the more ancient and widespread parts of bear ceremonies and hunting rituals of all kinds. (In the psychological development of the child, enactment precedes speech.) Among the Evenks of west central Siberia, the words for "to leap" and "to overtake" and "to dance" have a common origin— which adds to the evidence of the origin of dancing as symbolic dramatization, part of a narrative. The psychologist Erik Erikson has observed that leaping is the first step in linking unlike realms. Similarly, the anthropologist James Fernandez describes metaphor as having prelinguistic forms in ritual leaps that connect otherwise totally different domains. Mimic performance may be as old as, or older than, speech itself, and the dance of the hunt may have served to communicate about it before storytelling emerged.

As the bear's body is brought into the village, the Mistassini Cree women, unlike the dancing women of Siberia, cover their faces.

The Finns sang a welcome:

> The illustrious is coming,
> Pride and beauty of the forest,
> 'Tis the master come among us,
> Covered with his friendly fur-robe,
> Welcome, loved one from the glenwood.

Among many of the American Algonkian tribes, the middle toe and claw of the bear's right forefoot were cut off and given as a talisman to the wife of the man who carried the bear from the woods. Sometimes the animal was butchered on a special table or taken into a "temple" in the village. When the host's dwelling was used, the bear might be brought in through a special door or through the smokehole, as among the Gilyaks, whose houses were built into the ground.

Typically, the slain bear is carried into the house and placed before the hearth where "the old goddess of fire, guarding the fire in the center of the house, is said to have welcomed the guest." The association of the bear spirit and the hearth may be in part connected with the heat of the depths of the earth where he retires for renewal. But it is more. The bear's sun connections probably stem from his celestial power and the paradigm of renewal. "Brightness" is part of his etymological origins. The Kaska, an Athapascan tribe of British Columbia, believed that fire was first the possession of a bear who could obtain sparks from a firestone. The stone was stolen from him by the other animals and broken by the fox so that a piece could be given to each tribe of men.

At this time the bear is adorned. The Labrador Indians decorated the head and paws with beads, quills, and vermillion; the Ojibway festooned the head with silver and wampum. Father DeSmet observed that the Assiniboine also decorated the head. Among the Northwest Coast Indians there was a dressing-the-slain-bear ceremony, after which the Kwakiutl hunter addressed the bear, saying, "Thank you, friend, for meeting me. I did not do any harm to you. You came to meet me, sent by our Creator that I should shoot you, that I may eat together with my wife and friend."

Throughout the festival, especially during butchering, cooking, and eating, vernacular gender rules. That is, the roles are different for men and women—who skins and butchers, who cooks and eats what parts, where the celebrants sit at the feasts, and so on. From the Bear Mother story, to which the celebration looks for its basic outline, throughout the ceremony, the tale and its rites extol a sacred marriage, murder, and funeral. It is not unlikely that some of the most archaic parts of this legend of love and death have been lost. Such a loss may be indicated by the remnant of an extraordinary ritual marriage which was still part of the festival among the Finns in the nineteenth century. Setting out for the bear's den, the hunters were said to go "to wed the forest virgin." During the feast, marriage symbols and songs embellished a festive procession with a bride, groom, and bride's father at the front. One account also tells of a man in these processions who married a female bear.

In all cases the bear is looked upon as a guest in the house, its spirit believed to be still alive and watching. Finnish guests arriving for the feast all greet the bear politely. A forest spirit, the "little mother of honey" is invited to this wedding. The duality of the sexes was in the past expressed in the formation of two Finnish clans, the Bear and the Elk, forming a bimodal tribal structure, anthropologically called a *moiety*. A similar totemic division was also true of the Ostyaks, Kergulians, and other Siberian peoples. A function of moieties is to define potential mates in marriage.

The Finnish myth that describes the bear's origin in heaven, a story apart from the Bear Mother tale, is also unique to them and neighboring peoples, telling of the bear's descent from a cloud near the Great Bear constellation after getting permission from its father, the Numi-torum, to take to the humans instructions for the Barenfest. The Finns are also unique in drinking from the skull of a bear during the feast, humming a bearlike *brummte* as they do so (reminiscent, perhaps, of the humming of little bears as they nurse). Among the Lapps, the feast songs were sung by three separate choral groups—men, women, and bear—and were made up of forty-eight verses, each with its own melody.

Other variations in the festival include the use of herbs and tobacco, painting of the bodies of the participants, making a surrogate image of the bear, playing of rattles, drums, and other instruments, recitation of personal visions or spirit guides, forms of dance, and the use of an altar—though no one festival has all these elements. Sex, age, marital status, prestige, and kinship are often a basis of human roles in the celebration.

A typical feature of the rites among American Indians that was not common in Asia or Europe was the use of tobacco. For example, the Neskapi of Labrador smoked after the hunt, "sharing" tobacco with the bear. The Northern Algonkians placed tobacco in the bear's teeth and smoked over it and, at a later point in the feast, smoked in a circle around the head and skin of the bear. The Blackfoot, who have been described as bearers of some of the oldest Asian traditions, say that the medicine-pipe bundle was first given to a girl who married a bear, and so they held the pipe with two hands in imitation of the bear, from whom its power comes. Tinder smoke and beaver musk were used for this across Eurasia, the body of the bear being surrounded by censers. The American Northwest Coast Indians, especially the Tsimsyan, carved scenes from the Bear Mother myth into their totem poles, and also depicted there the bear as it related to other totem ancestors.

In eating the bear, some Siberians disperse the meat beyond the camp to distant kinsmen. In America, among the Montagnai, the Cree, and others, a bowl of hot bear grease was passed around and the hunters dipped their hands in it and smeared it on their hair, after which the roasted head was given, each man taking one bite. In no case was any part of the meat given to the dogs or thrown away. As few bones as possible were broken or cut, for all were collected at the end of the sacramental feasting. In most cases the skull was hung in a specific tree, usually a fir, or sometimes put on a pole, but it was not seen as a hunting trophy—the bear's soul is more closely associated with the skull than with any other part. The tree kept it from desecration by scavengers, and since the tree is itself a sacred image of renewal, the skull's attachment to it was perhaps the ultimate ritual of palingenesis, the cycle of the soul into new life. The German historian of religion Ivar Paulson has observed that the most persistent part of the slain-bear festival in those places where only traces of it remain is the preservation of the skull.

The other bones were usually buried, but not always; sometimes all were placed in tree platforms, or the smaller bones interred in the ground while the long bones were wrapped and tied to a tree trunk. Bone rites everywhere, says the historian of religion Ake

Hultkrantz in *The Religions of the American Indians,* especially emphasize the head and are associated with hunting success, renewal, the guardianship of passages, and the turn of the seasons. Keeping the bones whole, collecting them together, rearticulating some of them, and representing them in art are all directed to the metaphysical continuity bridging the tension between unity and division, in which the body of the bear represented social and earthly forces in counterpoint.

The spirit of the bear was addressed by the people at various times during the hunt and the funerary rites. It was usually hailed as a respected kinsman—"grandfather" or "grandmother." The bear was petitioned to allow itself to be killed or to die of its own choice, and later not to be angry with the hunters, who deny responsibility for its death.

The Asiatic Eskimos not only used synonyms for the animal itself; they would "get hold of" or "reach" the bear instead of "killing" it. "According to their ideas," says the Soviet ethnographer G. A. Menovščikov, "the game was not killed, it came spontaneously to the man as a guest. This guest, however, had to be brought down with the help of a harpoon or spear. The killed game was highly praised and persuaded not to be offended but to return again to the hunters."

It is clear that the death was more like a change in key than the end of the life of the animal, so that to kill properly did not carry the same onus for Eskimo hunters as it would in the civilized world, with its history of wars and exterminations. This rodomontade of conciliation and pretense of innocence may sound to us like guilty self-deception, but the Eskimos and others did not think they were fooling the spirit of the bear, nor was there among them the guilt associated with the killing of animals by modern people. Their rhetorical language was part of a delicate, ongoing negotiation with the soul of the bear and with the powerful divinity who gives the bear to men. They were reminding the bear that it was sent, that its death was not due to their own will and pride. Invocations and prayers addressed to the soul of the bear during the ceremony also sought appeasement and reconciliation in which the people urged the bear to take account of the honor and respect paid him.

This reverent attitude was held not only during the festival but at all times. The bear's shadow-soul could hear and understand all speech of animals and men, no matter where they were. Because of its unique place in their world, generic terms of speech were not appropriate. Hence it was impolite and dangerous to refer to the bear simply as "bear" or to criticize it. To do so might summon it in anger, an experience known to all peoples who live near the taciturn and unpredictable real bear. Circumlocution, rhetoric, and formality characterized all speech to and about bears.

The indirect reference to bears, both in direct address ("Cousin," "Grandfather," "Old Man") and in the third person ("Old Honey Paws," "Crooked Tail"), influenced the way in which hunters told each other about discovering the bear's den. In this they were everywhere, by tradition, circumspect. Among the Gwich'in Athapascan Indians, this discretion was carried to an extreme. The announcement that a den had been found was always phrased as a riddle. A man might quietly ask, "What's the brown stuff on your cheeks?" referring to the brown hair on the nose of the black bear. Or he might say of a meal, "Where is the fat and grease that goes with it?" Another way was to imitate the bear by rubbing his back on a post or walking pigeon-toed.

Although the bear was said to hear everything that humans say, and was likely to take offense at the mention of its true name, it was, strangely enough, unable to grasp the riddles or to recognize itself in the synonyms. Another possible reason for the euphemisms among the Athapascans lies in the legend of the male ancestor who married a bear, a reverse form—but with many similar implications—of the myth of the Bear Mother. Any of one's hunter friends might secretly be married to a woman who could transform herself into a bear and who, if she knew of the forthcoming hunt, might warn the bear, which, in turn, could attack the hunters. Thus the riddle was usually asked, and always answered, out of earshot of women. In a tale about a hunter who revealed the location of his bear-wife's den, the man was killed by the bear.

When they encountered it on the trail, men were likely to address the bear euphemistically. Women expressed their kinship to bears differently. Among the Cree Indians the woman averted her eyes from the bear. Among the Athapascans, if caught out in the woods alone, some Tagish women who meet a grizzly will address it directly as "brother" in hopes that it will be reminded of the incest taboo and run away embarrassed. In a similar situation, Koyukon women of Alaska show their genitals and say, "My husband, it's me." So,

SOME SYNONYMS FOR THE BEAR

HOMAGE OF ADDRESS

cousin	elder brother
grandfather	old man
grandmother	great-grandfather
uncle	stepmother

EUPHEMISMS

the animal (Michikaman)	forest apple (Finn)
big-feet (many groups)	four-legged human (Cree)
big great food (Montagnais)	fur man (Ostyak)
big hairy one (Blackfoot)	golden feet (many groups)
black beast (many groups)	golden friend (Finn)
black food (Cree)	golden king (many groups)
blue-tooth (Lapp)	gold friend of fen and forest
bobtail (many groups)	(Ural Altaic)
broadfoot (Estonian)	good-tempered beast
chief's son (Cree)	grandfather on the hill (Ural
the dog of God (Ostyak, Lapp)	Altaic)
dweller in the wilds (Ostyak)	great-food (Tungus)
dweller in the woods (Ostyak)	holy animal (Lapp)
food of the fire (Montagnais)	honey paw (Tungus)

too, among the ancient Greeks, says psychiatrist-historian Erich Neumann, where in "ritual exhibitionism . . . these goddesses [Artemis, etc.] display their genitals" as shown in "numerous representations."

When a Ket man or woman met a bear on the trail, he or she was likely to say, "Go away, Old Man, I'm not guilty," meaning that one had done nothing to offend the forest spirit who is master of the animals, with whom the bear is an intermediary.

To speak of the bear as such is to risk evoking a response by him. Just as the old Hebrews never spoke the name of Yahweh, subarctic men used synonyms for that which was most sacred. The Tungus of the Altai Mountains of Siberia, like the old Caucasian, Amerin-

illustrious pride (Finn)
light-foot (Finn)
little mother of honey
  (Finn)
lord (Ural Altaic)
lord of the taiga (Nanai,
  Tungus)
master of the forest (Lapp)
my father's brother-in-law
  (Tlingit)
old man of the mountains
  (Lapp)
old man with the fur garment
  (Lapp)
one going around the woods
  (Tlingit)
one who owns the chin
  (Montagnais)
one who prowls at night
  (many groups)
owner of the earth (many
  groups)

sacred man (Lapp)
sacred virgin (Lapp)
short-tail (Montagnais,
  Tungus)
step-widener (Lapp)
sticky-mouth (many groups)
the strong one (Tagish)
takes large leftovers home
that which went away
  (Koyukon)
thick fur (Lapp)
the thing (Koyukon)
uncle of the woods (Votyak)
unmentionable one
  (Blackfoot)
venerable one (Vogul)
wide-way (Lapp)
winter-sleeper (Lapp)
wise man (Lapp)
woodmaster (Samoyed)
woolly one (Lapp)
worthy old man (Ural Altaic)

dian, and other Asiatic peoples, are not unusual in having more than fifty euphemisms for the bear's name, such as "Lord of the Taiga," "Honey Paws," "Short-Tail," or "Black Food." The courtesy of address and oblique reference are among the most universal, and probably the most ancient, aspects of the veneration of bears.

Until the nineteenth century, and in some cases even more recently, the festival of the slain bear was celebrated by peoples in many parts of the two continents of the northern hemisphere. Like other aspects of human culture, the feast probably had a center of origin and was altered in detail by widely different societies, yet remained profoundly constant in its central themes. Its parts were essentially as follows:

1. locating the bear's den
2. performing rituals of purification and preparation
3. reciting tabooed words and euphemisms
4. calling out the bear and apologetic speeches
5. killing the bear in a prescribed way
6. welcoming the bear to the village
7. skinning and flaying, leaving the bones intact, separating of head and paws from the body
8. decorating of the head and fur
9. socially structured, sacramental cooking and feasting
10. telling the story of the hunt and other myths of the bear as kinsman
11. setting aside of certain parts for healing or talismans
12. representing the bear in art
13. singing, dancing, divining
14. sending-home ceremonies, special funerary disposition of the skull and other bones

The soul of the bear was said to return home to a distant place in an underworld in the mountains or forest, where it would convey the events of the bear's death and celebration to a chief or animal master. The body of the bear was regarded as a gift to humans, its soul an intermediary between them and the powerful deity or guardian of the earth. Perhaps above all, this ceremony addresses a question central to the human conscience: the necessity of killing other beings in order to live. It implicitly denies that such killing is heroic or that the prey is insignificant in any spiritual sense. By focusing on the most manlike of animals (who is, like all living things, a kinsman) it raises the issue to its most intense expression. In attending to the animal that is not regularly hunted and is not pursued in the kill, it emphasizes the gift-quality of all things in life provided for man by the natural world, and therefore the gift of life itself. Throughout the festival, the religious quality of all the details of mundane life is brought to the fore, so that all of human activity can be seen in its participatory resonance with the cosmos.

What G. A. Menovščikov wrote of Asian peoples is also true of American Indians. Cheyenne author Hyemeyohsts Storm, in *Seven Arrows,* says that the only animals killed are those who allow themselves to be caught because ceremonies sending their spirits home have been properly done on previous occasions. Thus the bear is not booty or the trophy of a vainglorious enterprise, but provides a collective occasion for courteous transaction between the people and a powerful divinity as well as with the bear itself.

The attitude of hunting/gathering peoples the world over is similar to that described by Charles Hill-Tout, a nineteenth-century ethnologist, of the Lillooet Indians: "Not a single plant, animal or fish, or other object upon which he feeds is looked upon as something he has secured for himself by his own wit and skill . . . or as mere food and nothing more. . . . He regards it as something which has been voluntarily and compassionately placed in his hands by the good will and consent of the spirit."

Apart from its conciliation of the spirit of the forest and its obvious socially integrating effects, the festival of the bear carried multiple metaphors of human life and death. The fate of men is more or less like that of bears; death was acknowledged with similar funeral rites and the soul was said to depart to a sacred realm.

The Bear Festival and the Politics of Centralization

In parts of Asia, and to a lesser degree in America, the bear to be killed was first held captive. Sometimes the Kets, whose festival is described above, killed a bear that had a cub. The cub was taken to the village and given to a childless family to rear. Called *yskit,* which means "son" or "daughter," it lived in its host's or "parent's" tent, slept in its own bed, and was treated much like a human child. The cub was also honored as a guest. It wore copper earrings, bracelets, and collar. Sometimes, as it got older, it accompanied men on bear hunts. When the cub was three years old it was taken into the forest and released.

Other tribes of the far north and east—the Ainu, Gilyak, Orochi, and Olcha—kept such cubs and, instead of freeing them, reared them to kill in a ceremony clearly derived from the archaic festival of the hunted bear. Such holidays most fully studied by Western anthropologists are those of the Ainu and Olcha, which are admired for their richness and complexity, and sometimes cited as models of rapport between man and nature. But the sacrifice of a captive rather

than a free-living bear shifts the psychology of the relationship between man and bear—and the natural world—in profound ways.
The Olcha ceremony lasted as long as sixteen days and was planned
as a January commemoration for a dead kinsman. (When a bear was
not available, a dog was used in its place and was said to be a *panjau*
or *presku*—an embodiment of the dead soul.) A pre-festival was held
involving the live animal. The bear was fed before guests in the
house, while tied in the center of the "father's" house, pulled flat
with ropes at each of its legs; it was doused with water, collared,
led about the village, beaten, and teased.

From the second to the sixth day, friends gathered from a distance.
There were dogsled races and much visiting. The bear was "regaled"
in various houses as a "guest," transported from one residence to
another on a sled drawn by many dogs. On the seventh day there
was a feast of fish and berries, and the sacrificial area was decorated
with fir and willow branches. The next morning a pile of willow
shavings was made and the bear was dragged out to see them and
tied while boys showed their courage by jumping on its back. An
all-night feast followed in the host's house.

On the ninth day the bear was dragged out for a tour of the
village, and fed fish. The killing and carving instruments were brought
from a special hut where the skins, paws, and heads of other bears
were stored. The bound bear was turned in circles and beaten by
an old man with a stick, who told the bear he was "cleansing" it. A
drum shaped on one end like a bear's head was played by women
dressed in their finery, and everyone went to the sacrifice area at the
edge of the village, where the people formed a circle around the
bear. The host chose a man to kill the bear and gave him a bow.
Arrows were shot over nearby trees; then the bear was shot in the
heart. Others shot arrows into it. The bear was unchained, laid on
a willow mat, and eviscerated. It was then taken "home" on a sledge,
and little boys met it in the doorway and grabbed for its fur. Only
then did clansmen enter, build a dais for the head and skin of the
bear, and have a meal. That night everyone came for a feast of raw
fish, soup, and brandy.

From the tenth to the fourteenth day there was more visiting and
the departure of all but the clan groups. Everyone ate boiled bear
meat and drank brandy. On the fifteenth day the head was cut from

the skin and the *ngarta* ritual, an eating competition, followed. Two sides, the men of two moieties—the "men of the forest" and the "men of the water"—were seated opposite each other. Three times the men got up and went outside, where the women pelted them with snow. They returned to eat a bilberry dessert, then all china dishes were removed, the floor was covered with fir branches, and different parts of the cooked bear were served—upper paw, mandible, head, intestines, and grease—to individuals of specific rank. Following this formal meal, everyone ate boiled bear: the oldest men ate the biceps and genitals; the women and children were denied tongue. A dog was tied to the doorpost and the host pushed its nose against the post, the hearth, and the bed. The bear bones were carefully collected and taken to the sacrificial area and put in a receptacle. The guests then departed, and along with gifts of bear meat, the host gave away his dogs in a kind of potlatch-like gesture.

On the final day the villagers ate the last of the bear and cleaned up. The bear's skull was smoked in a fire and a song was sung to it. It was then put in a birch tree and a sending-home prayer was said. The festival ended with a meal of fish and brandy.

The Olcha call the festival "play with the bear"—*bojum hupu*. The bear is "played" for meat, for communion with relatives, for luck in hunting and fishing, and for the memory of a dead relative. The bear is not a god but a "dog of the forest men," the *duanteni*, who dress as bears. The killed bear is said to return to the forest men, taking with him provisions—all that was eaten at the festival. The Olcha explain this by appending to the story of the Bear Mother an episode in which she takes her cub-children with her to the forest to get provisions. Her brothers follow and kill her without ceremony, taking the cubs. One of the cubs, however, dies and redeems the men by performing the rites. The story interprets the sacrificial killing of the bear thereafter as an act of reincarnation, sending the bear back to the forest men.

It is apparent that the Olcha have expanded the festival to achieve a variety of social and interpersonal ends, and have reduced its religious tenor. The Ainu of Japan also "sent home" the soul of a hand-reared, sacrificed bear. If the cub was very small when captured, it was nursed by Ainu women, then reared as an honored guest until it was two or three years old. Like many other celebrants of the bear fest, the Ainu believed that the manlike gods were garbed as animals only in the land of man, that meat and fur were gifts to men from them, and that the slain bear returned to its divine form. The Ainu retained many of the details of the more "basic" festival— the honorific references, the bringing of the carcass in through a special window, the ornamentation and arrangement of the skin and head by the hearth, the non-spilling of blood, and, above all, its religious address and sense of reciprocity with a powerful divinity. However, as is the case in the Olcha festival, the bear was a captive whose death was scheduled for January; there were also other foods, such as fish, millet, and sake; and the trussed bear was teased and goaded before it was strangled. A shaman played a central role. Among the Ainu and Gilyak, a woman who was foster mother to the cub danced the sorrow of the slain bear's mother. Several elements seem to come into the picture of the bear festival with the transformation represented by the Ainu and the Olcha:

1. the presence of domestic organisms, i.e., dogs and millet
2. the ingestion of alcoholic beverages
3. the presence of a shaman
4. the slaughter or sacrifice of the animal

In spite of the divergence of the secular/religious directions in the Olcha and Ainu bear festivals, there is a modernity which they share. The planned, public execution of a man-reared animal can hardly be perceived like the hunt, with its uncertainty and its moment-to-moment poignancy. Generally, sacrifice of something *owned* is a bargain with the gods. Does not the bear, reared in captivity, lose some of its power to represent the unsought gift of life? The sacred feast, according to Jane Ellen Harrison, the distinguished classicist, is the prototype of all religious sacraments. To be joined with the god was experienced first—and continues to be most deeply felt— in the eating of the sacred body. But when preceded by a sacrifice it becomes a late, specialized form of sacrament. "It presupposes," Harrison says, "the existence of a well-defined personality with whom one can 'carry on business' . . . as if he were a man." Long before the Olympians ousted animals from the Pantheon, and Hebrews and Christians conceived of a single, anthropomorphic god, the sacramental meal of the divine bear had begun to be altered by the sacrificial idea.

Claude Lévi-Strauss, writing of "The Bear and the Barber," observes that animals are not only edible but thinkable. As the totemic bear gives way to the captive bear, the latter can be seen, like a domestic animal, to signify a human product rather than the ancestor of a religious clan. It tends to become an object instead of a kinsman who keeps before men his connection to nature and separateness from it.

The occupation to which the bear becomes an appendage is shamanism. The oldest explanation of the Great Bear constellation is that Mangi is the spirit Bear Mother. This hunter-bear in the sky is later represented as male, then regarded as human. According to Soviet ethnographer A. F. Anisimov, this shift is marked by the rising power of the shaman among Mesolithic peoples. It has been suggested that the shaman's role was at first a gift or a calling rather than a position sought, inherited, or trained for. Among the Siberian Evenks, for example, the ancestor spirits that lived "at the root of the clan tree" were "the mother-beast" and had positive significance among the earliest shamans, who may have been women healers. With the concentration of political power associated with the agricultural occupations, men sought and bequeathed the office. Rites increasingly became performances rather than egalitarian group activity. The pantheon of spirits, once accessible to all, became the shaman's spirit helpers. Evidence for this change can be seen in the word *niamat* (the rite of giving the killed bear to another), which was enlarged to *nimnganivka* (the shaman's work). This work was the building of a wall of friendly, lower-world spirits around the village to protect it from evil, a magic fence, the *marylya,* signifying a defended territory.

By the time the Russians subjugated the Siberian tribes in the seventeenth century, a diversity of social organizations could be found across Asia, representing several stages of this process leading to shamanic control. The most "advanced" had a shaman with enough concentrated power to negotiate with the Russian outsiders, having inherited rank, wealth, and political power as well as spiritual leadership. It is hardly surprising that the tidiness of the Ainu bear ceremony should appeal today to the modern imagination more than does the rather scruffy Ket or Algonkian group surrounding the bear's den, whose chants and dances were without a choirmaster. Although feminine generative and renewal power was central to bear ceremonialism, its religious expression—or secular redirection—was increasingly organized by males.

Of the shift of view which eased the shaman into a priestly role with the coming of agriculture, Joseph Campbell has said, "The highest concern of all the mythologies, ceremonials, ethical systems, and social organizations of the agriculturally based societies has been that of suppressing the manifestations of individualism."

The emergence of the shaman within the bear ceremonies is characterized by Joseph L. Henderson in *Thresholds of Initiation* as a "defeat and mastery over the feminine." In Longfellow's version of the Algonquin legend of Hiawatha, for example, the killing and robbing of the bear amounts to the suppression of the feminine principle in corn-growing by "culture-ambitious" men. The captivity of the bear, the overshadowing of sacrament by sacrifice, territorial concepts, patriarchal power, shamanism, and religious spectatorship all seem to mark a shift in the older participatory theriophany toward a more man- and male-centered cosmos.

Shamanism in turn would be eclipsed by priestly orders. In a sense it contained its own seed of destruction by an extension of its centralizing force. Shamanism tended to diminish individual self-reliance, the significance of the primary concepts of the personal fast, vision, and guardian animal, and the honoring of unique realizations of divinity. Yet it retained, says Campbell, a ritual whose meaning was clear to all and "a lighter, more whimsical character" involving familiar deities rather than "profoundly developed gods." Ake Hultkrantz notes that shamans and secret societies are associated in agrarian life with the products of agriculture, group work calendars, and labor-saving specializations, and therefore with such intermediaries as curators, fraternities, and masters of ceremonies. In Campbell's words, the planters would bind "everything into the compass of their own hieratically organized world society, offering the power of the group as a principle finally and absolutely superior." It is not surprising that such socially controlled ideologies should pay increasing attention to domestic animals, who are also submissive, or to the carnivores like the wolf and lion who may be seen as both dangerous and symbolic of their own warrior brotherhoods. The bear, a loner, seems by contrast obsolete or even subversive. Finally, priests, arriving from outside the tribe, whose secret knowledge and training and power represented what social critic Ivan Illich calls a "new scarcity," merely had to replace the shaman with their own man.

·4·

OTHER CEREMONIES
OF THE BEAR

Judging from their distribution, the customs associated with the
bear are ancient, intercontinental, and boreal, and have a common
origin in the prehistoric Old World. Their oldest elements are part
of the traditions of the hunt and the ceremonial feast that marks its
success. The myth of the Bear Mother may also be part of the old
core culture that spread west and south in Europe, and across Asia
into North America.

As this tradition dispersed with human migration and through
tribal contact, its details were altered. On the whole, a veneration
of the bear became part of the lives of scores of peoples across this
vast geographic extent; over many thousands of years the exact forms
of this system gradually changed, modified locally in diverse ways.
Like language itself, as the practices diffused they became supplemented, abbreviated, sometimes radically altered. Even so, certain
common threads continued to reveal their mutual origin—the conciliatory spirit, the euphemisms and terms of honorific reference to
the bear, the prayerful address or propitiation directly to the spirit
of the bear, the careful disposal of the bones, and the myths of
kinship with man.

One of the variations on the theme reflects directly the bear's
ferocity and danger to man. Among the Kutenai, for example, the
grizzly had a malevolent aspect against which men were helpless
without the power of magic. The destructive energy of the grizzly
could be invoked against an enemy by shamans using effigies. Competition sometimes occurred between shamans in a struggle to con-

trol the bear magic. Sometimes the Assiniboine, Cree, and Taos Pueblo people sought this power in their war preparations against other tribes. Among the former, the warrior-cult had distinctive ritual equipment—shirt, hairdress, shield, face paint, knife, and lodge, for example. Among some of the Pueblo Indians it was customary to treat a dead bear as though it were a slain enemy—with the same rites of decoration and war dance performed at the killing of a man. One of these dances was intended to convert the dead enemy into a friend.

Closely related to this concept of the bear as a warrior spirit is the protection not only *from* but *by* the bear. The bear was dangerous whether or not prompted by witchcraft. An annual spring ceremony among the Kutenai to obtain immunity from bear attack followed a dream, notifying a member of the tribe to lead the rite. The participants assembled in the dreamer's lodge, reaffirmed their friendship with the bear, wished it good luck, and petitioned for good health before an altar holding a bear's skull and paws. The songs, accompanied by a deer-hoof rattle, sometimes took place in a specially constructed, skin-covered tepee whose floor was covered with fresh soil; a willow branch was bent and staked near the door. A pipe was passed and songs were sung, led by individuals singing to their own spirit guardians. Imitations of the bear were danced. After several nights the rites ended in a berry feast, after which the participants went home to their own lodges and the bear spirit to the bear's den. Indeed, the whole ceremony amounted to a "visit" by the people to the sleeping bear in its den, the songs acting as the equivalent of the hunt, the offerings, recitations, petitions, mimetic dances, and supplications being combined as a conciliatory renewal of the spiritual relation of man and bear.

Similarly, the Blackfoot, who did not hunt the hibernating bear, killed it only in a kind of war mentality. That is, they treated it as a sometimes sacred enemy, one whose name they did not speak, and whose powers they called upon in other than sacramental ceremonies.

One of the most widespread ceremonies reflects the bear's power as healer, the oldest forms deriving, perhaps, from observations of the bear as his own herbalist, who picks and chooses among a wide variety of plants for those needs of his physiology related to hibernation, as well as medicinal uses. The many associations of bear and plant names are indicative of the bear's herbal sagacity. For example:

bearbane, *Aconitum*
bearberry, or whortleberry, a tonic and astringent, *Arctostaphylos uvaursi* or *Oxycoccus macrocarpus* or *Ilex decidua*
bearbine, a *Convolvulus*
bear brush, or inkberry, *Garrya fremonti*
bear clover, or mountain misery, *Chamaebatia foliolosa*
bear corn, or American hellebore, *Veratrum viride*
bearfoot, *Helleborus viridis*
bear grape, or bear plum, bearberry, bilberry, *Aconitum*
bear grass, a grass or *Yucca* in the American Southwest, a lily in the Northwest, *Camassia,* a *Polypogon* or *Andropogon*
bear huckleberry, *Gaylussacia baccata* or *Vaccinium hirsutum*
bear moss, or haircap moss, *Polytrichum,* or a *Yucca*
bear oak, *Quercus pumila*
bear's breech, *Acanthus*
bear's ear, *Arctotis,* or primrose or *Auricula*
bear's foot, or stinking hellebore, *Helleborus viridis*
bear's garlic, or ramson, *Allium ursinum*
bear's head, a fungus, *Hydnum caputmedusae*
bear's paw, *Arctopus echinatus*
bear's tail, an Asian perennial herb, *Celsia arcturus*
bear's weed, yerba santa, *Eriodictyon*
bear's wort, spicknel, *Meum athamanticum*
bear tongue, *Clintonia*
bearwood, the cascara buckthorn, *Rhamnus purshiana*

These are only a few of the scores of plants, worldwide, named in part because the bear uses many of them for his own health, and in doing so "teaches" men about them. Many American Indian tribes saw the bear as a master healer.

Of all plants, tobacco is the most frequently associated with the bear, at least in North America. The Kutenai, for example, saw the bear as the plant's protector. Each year the spirit grizzly appeared to one of the men in a dream, making him the "tobacco chief." The man drew the image of the bear on an altar in his lodge, and the place and time to sow the tobacco seed that year were revealed to him.

Among the other tribes who regarded the bear as a physician were the Cheyenne, Eastern Cree, Penobscot, and especially certain Southwest tribes: the Pomo, famous for their "bear doctors," the Zuñi, who used the paw in healing ceremonies, and the Tewa, for whom the word *kieh,* or "doctor," is synonymous with "bear." Typically, certain parts of the bear have their special uses in medicine. Thus the bear is not only a guide to and protector of the plants that heal, but he himself is a pharmacopoeia in Asia as well as America.

Eastern as well as western Indians called on the bear as healer. Southern Asian Indians believed that bears collected ripe apples, removed the rinds, and heaped together the pulp. Adding honey and sweet-smelling flowers, the bears threshed the concoction with their feet, and then ate the mixture. Hunters would rob them of it, and sell it as something called Karadi Panchamritham, or "bear delicacy made of five ingredients." Panchamritham could also be made without the bear's intervention, from plantains, fruit, sugar, coconut shavings, ghee, honey, and cardamom seeds. Indians drank it as a general health elixir. These same Indians collected the hair of the bear, which they encased in a cylinder and tied to the groins of young boys and the necks of young girls to prevent fever and bed-wetting.

Perhaps more than the Asians, the American Indians exploited the bear's alleged powers of healing. The Blackfoot, for instance, derived the power of their medicine pipes from various bear concoctions; to intensify the power of the pipe, men dressed themselves in grizzly skins during the pipe ceremony. A hill near the mouth of the Cheyenne River in South Dakota is called Matoti, or Bear's House. There, Cheyenne women prayed to a boulder to grant them feminine strength and power; if a brave touched the same boulder, his arm immediately withered. Some Indians believed that the grizzly breathed various colored dusts from his nostrils—red, yellow, blue—and spit out colored earths while performing his healing arts. The ancient Chinese believed that the bear's paw contained powerful medicinal properties, and so they cooked it in stews. (Bear paw, tender and gelatinous, was a delicacy of some North American Indian tribes, perhaps related to the belief that by sucking on his paw the bear was able to survive a winter's sleep without food.) "Bear paw" is still available in some Chinese restaurants, but the dish is now prepared from bean curd.

Claude Lévi-Strauss, in his seminal work *The Savage Mind,* lists the many parts of the bear that the Siberians utilized in their cures: "The flesh of bears has seven distinct therapeutic uses, the blood five, the fat nine, the brains twelve, the bile seventeen, the fur two." The Kalac, in Russia, collected the frozen excrement of the bear as a cure for constipation. Pliny the Elder, in his *Natural History,* recommends bear grease as a preventative for falling hair; those afflicted with thinning hair in first century A.D. Rome were instructed to use bear grease mixed with laudanum and adiantum. Medieval man believed in the curative power of bear flesh, taking his direction from the *Regime du Corps,* a French medical book, which recommended the cooked flesh of bears for its general medicinal properties, based on the testimony of the ancients. With authority from the *Regime,* medieval English and Scottish folklore has it that general bodily vigor may be gained from drinking the blood of the bear. Saint Augustine is more specific. He recommends eating the testicles of bears as a cure for epilepsy, proclaiming them as "famous against the falling sickness. . . ." According to Augustine, epilepsy was punishment for conceiving a child on a forbidden occasion. Anne Clark, in *Beasts and Bawdy,* sharpens the connection: "The moral, presumably, was that men and women should abstain from sex on Saturdays, or on the eve of certain other religious festivals, as any children begotten on such occasions would inevitably be born with major defects."

The bear is thus also identified with spiritual well-being and with physical health and healing. Not only is it the animal of beginnings, but also of re-beginnings—of recovery from spiritual malaise and physical illness and, metaphorically, revival from death. Above all other animals, the bear is considered to be the supreme physician of the woods.

Unlike most physicians, however, people throughout time have believed that the bear can heal himself. For many illnesses, the medieval bestiaries say he strokes himself with an herb named florius— sometimes called mullein. If the bear suffers from stomach trouble, he supposedly cures himself by eating ants.

Jung, in describing dream symbolism in relation to alchemy, assigns to the bear a many-hued healing ability: "The dreamer is falling into the abyss. At the bottom there is a bear whose eyes gleam alternately in four colors: red, yellow, green, and blue. Actually, it

has four eyes that change into four lights." The abyss here symbolizes, perhaps, the passage between life and death, between wake-
fulness and sleep (as in the phrase "I'm falling asleep"); the bear, in
his healing and redemptive power, proclaims that everything will
be all right—the dreamer, in his sleepy hibernation, will make it
back safely to the world of the healthy and the living. As the winter
passes and the ground once more begins to warm, the bear stirs.
Something fundamental is taking place. The bear's mysterious stirring enters arcane lore, for his miraculous transformation back to
life is assumed to have begun. That underground awakening becomes a natural part of the symbology of alchemy, the medieval
science of the transformation and elevation of the soul. Spiritual
healing requires agitation and movement underground, in the soul's
dark caves. Thus the bear represents in alchemy the *nigredo* of prime
matter, the blackness and darkness of the *prima materia* that must
be transmuted on the path toward enlightenment. Without heavi-
ness and darkness the conversion to health is impossible; that is,
without darkness there can be no movement to light.

Even naturalists of a more recent time looked upon the bear as
an extraordinary physician. Legend has it that when wounded the
grizzly gathers leaves of the greasewood plant *(Sarcobatus)* and forces
them tightly into his wounds. An old hunter, Benjamin Wilson,
describes pursuing a wounded bear only to find it immersed in mud
up to its nose. He comments: "I have heard tell by others that bears
have the sagacity to seek the healing of their wounds with application
of mud." In either case, the bear seems to use plants or earth as a
primitive poultice. One nature writer remarked that the black bear
in particular possesses a remarkable ability to recover from broken
bones or mutilated limbs. In fact, most eighteenth- and nineteenth-
century hunting accounts testify to the difficulty of penetrating the
bear's thick fur and skin with a bullet. Hunters would wound a bear
one season, track him again the next, wound him again, and so on,
until they would finally kill him. When examined, old wounds were
found to have healed, leaving little visible trace. Hunters formulated
a theory about the bear's unusual healing ability: they believed that
the bear's thick skin prevented bleeding, while his coarse, matted
fur helped to keep the wound closed. The bear was said to heal most
of his wounds by licking them. Ernest Thompson Seton, the naturalist, said, "The licking removed the dirt, and by massage reduced

inflammation, and it plastered the hair down as a sort of dressing over the wound to keep out the air, dirt, and microbes." Another naturalist asserted that bears are susceptible only to rare diseases, arguing that the bear is one of the few wild animals that die of old age. The grizzly in particular stores fat beneath the skin and between its internal organs, perhaps offering greater than normal protection.

Other ceremonies associated with the bear retain his connection with the "control" of the seasons, as seen in the concept of the constellation Ursa Major, with his hands on the axis of the universe. The bear is the major figure in the turning of the sky around the axis that runs through the poles of the earth, connecting them with the Pole Star. Thus the bear rules the hours of the night, the coming of the sun each day, and the seasonal cycle. This is often associated with the coming of rain and the success of planted crops. The Bear Song Dance of the Crow Indians, for example, was a seasonal dance in which the resurgence of the animal element in specific individuals was expiated. The Utes and Paiutes danced the bear in a late-winter ceremony that mimicked the awakening of the animal in its den. The lodge became the den itself, and men and women moved in two facing lines. Together with tobacco offerings, this ritual was essentially a behavioral metaphor of the year's renewal as determined by the bear's emergence. For the Shoshoni also, the bear's stirring, as signified by the first thunder of early spring, announced the cosmic awakening, the time to break up the winter camp, and to stage a festive social and courtship celebration.

Still another body of evidence connects the bear with a different emergence—the transformation of the youth into an adult. The Dakota tribe performed a "making of a bear" dance in which the initiate imitated the bear and was ritually hunted by other youths as part of the death that must precede the new birth into adult status. "Among the Ammasilik Eskimos," writes the anthropologist Mircea Eliade, "the apprentice spends long hours in his snow hut, meditating; at a certain moment, he 'falls dead,' and remains lifeless for three days and nights; during this period an enormous polar bear devours all his flesh and reduces him to a skeleton. . . . Life is reduced to the essence concentrated in the skeleton, from which [he] will be born again." For the Pomo Indians the ceremony centered in an all-night dance. Among the dancers a "bear" ran back and forth; boys were shoved in front of it and got knocked down. Later, inside the lodge, the bear circled the center pole, accompanied by the sound of birds from "two little bears" on each side of him. He climbed the pole, fell to the floor, danced to the drum at the rear of the lodge, took off his bearskin, sat down as a man, and smoked a pipe.

Of bears and initiation, J. L. Henderson writes: "The bear ritual points to integration of the new personality following a period of dissociation." The fundamental task of such integration, he says, is the unification of "the seed and the sprout," that is, the feminine wisdom of being and the masculine wisdom of knowing. Only initiation, he believes, achieves the simultaneous capacity for experience and being conscious of that experience. The transformation into an animal recovers his "power to be," to "achieve ego strength in the face of the onslaught of the collective unconscious, the infantile primary powers." The bear is both mother and father, a whole and an association of parts, a spiritual and physical being who "dies" and is renewed; hence it is the ideal model for the new birth into tribal participation.

Finally, formalities that derive from, but do not require, the killing of a bear are based on the belief that bears overhear all that is said by men, and that a spirit bear or its master judges the veracity and sincerity of human respect. The Ute Indians told a version of the Bear Son story in which a foundling child, in the care of a mother grizzly, sees how the bear judges the prayers directed to it by humans, and how the integrity of the petitioners is revealed by their gift tokens. Scoffers are subject to punishment, while the truly reverent are favored. The child later returns to his people and exhorts their genuine honesty and sincerity. The Samoyed, Ostyak, and Vogul peoples of Siberia formerly swore oaths by the bear before testifying at a trial. They were handed a nose or paw, which they bit, saying, "If I am wrong, so bite me as I now bite thee." If the swearer perjured himself, a bear would eat him. In settling disputes, the Ket give the suspect a bear ear to kiss and chew; if he can do so without pleading guilty, it weighs in his favor. Their word for "honest truth" is *kojubat*—from *koi* for "bear" and *bat* for "truth." "The fundamental notion," says Irving Hallowell, the preeminent student of the bear festival, "is that the activities of the bear are closely associated with the ministration of a kind of supernatural justice." Sinful men are killed by bears, and those bears who have offended the Numi-torum, the master of the forest, will be killed by men. "Men and bears, in relation to each other, thus become instruments of supernatural justice."

In the foregoing, we have briefly summarized seven types of bear ceremony besides that of the slain bear:

1. protection from bears
2. protection by the bear spirit
3. evocation of warlike themes
4. healing ceremonies
5. seasonal or fertility rites
6. initiation ceremonies
7. formalities of a judicial nature

We have also noted that veneration of the bear is not necessarily accompanied by bear ceremonies. Some peoples have several of the above rites in addition to that of the slain bear; others may have only one.

Is there a unifying theme or underlying concept? We think there is. Each one of the rites addresses a transformation, a process of change. In a world view in which man plays a cosmic participatory role, nothing is taken for granted. The rising of the sun, the turning of the seasons, the passages of a human life all require human action. But the basic process is always that of a wheel of existence whose movement is epitomized as a genetrix—the work of a metaphysical mother. A feminine principle of birth, growth, death, decay, and rebirth lies at the heart of the veneration of the bear, for the bear is the supreme model—and therefore the guiding spirit—of the theme of renewal.

It appears that all formalities and myths connected with the bear are rooted in the Bear Mother story and the rite of the killed bear. These are the most widespread and probably the oldest elements of bear veneration. If so, the other rites and legends—and reverence for the bear without formal rites—may be derivative. Many of the latter ceremonies tend to occur in isolation in regions that are also at the fringes of the geographic distribution of hibernating bears—in the American South and Southwest, in the Near East and Mongolia and China, and around the Pole north of the range of *Ursus arctos*.

As Irving Hallowell observed in his classic essay on bear ceremonialism, the most elaborate ceremonies do not necessarily correspond to the deepest respect for the bear. Perhaps those more complex rites—such as were practiced until recently in eastern Asia by Gilyaks and Ainu—can be likened to a baroque phase of art, in which increasing attention is given to form and display at the expense of central idea. Such a view is consistent with our suggestion that the most elaborate expressions of the bear ceremony seemed to mark a historical shift in focus away from the independent power of the bear and toward human control and mastery.

·5·

THE GETIC AND GREEK CONNECTION

Only fragments of the ancient hunting cultures of Paleolithic Europe and Eurasia have found their way into the modern world. The traditions of prehistory were reordered by agriculture, which spread north and east from the eastern Mediterranean as a series of waves. The practical side of daily life was profoundly changed, and so was the cosmology of which life was felt to be a realization. Between the earliest domestications of animals, some 12,000 years ago, and the peak of Sumerian civilization, about 5,500 years ago, the representation of divinities as animals was slowly altered by combination with human features. The emphasis and details of the myths of which they were expressions were altered, so that by the time of preclassical Greece, such sacred presences as the bear loomed only in the shadows, certain of its qualities being brought forward into the light of the shrines and stories of the time.

Perhaps the most profound change affecting the figure of the bear was the eclipse of the Bear Mother legend by accounts of the adventures of her sons. Among recent "Paleolithic" cultures the accounts of the two half-human, half-bear children of the Bear Mother were minor, diminished by the radiant story of the woman who married the bear and thereby related men for all time to it as kinsmen. Her sons were simply the first of the hunters to understand the purpose of the rituals of the bear hunt, to show all men that it is indeed a grandfather who is slain each time a bear is killed.

An early elaboration of the Bear Son story may be represented by a myth among the Mistassini Cree of Quebec, involving a father's search for a "boy who was kept by a bear." The bear, knowing of the father's approach, teaches the boy the secrets of hunting. After a song-fight, the bear is killed at the den, and the boy's father takes the bear's sacred forearm, with which it "throws out" all game to be taken by human hunters, back to his village with the boy. The youth grows into a great hunter, but when a jealous woman unwraps the forearm, the young man vanishes underground, leaving his human clothing behind.

More typically, the Bear Son story follows this pattern:

A wedded but childless woman meets a bear in the forest, is taken to his underground cave, and remains there to bring forth a son to him. The child, Bear Son, is born hairy, with bear's ears, and is held captive in the bear's cave. Thanks to Bear Son's prodigious strength, mother and son are able to escape back to the surface of the earth and to their people. The woman's husband adopts the child, who grows up to be strong, but is generally thought to be a no-account.

Bear Son then embarks on a series of adventures, accompanied by friends of great physical prowess and carrying a weapon that he uses with great skill. In the main adventure, Bear Son and his friends spot a house in the woods and enter it. The house is unoccupied, but filled with food and furniture; Bear Son and his companions eat their fill and fall asleep. The owner, usually a dwarf, returns and maltreats each of the occupants. When it is at last Bear Son's turn, he seizes the dwarf and either suspends him from a tree by his beard, or cuts off his head or arms. In either case, the dwarf escapes to the underworld, Bear Son in hot pursuit.

The entrance to the underworld is down a deep well into which Bear Son must lower himself by means of a rope. The underground journey is fraught with hazards—fire and cold, wind and water, pitch darkness. Bear Son finally emerges into a world abundant with meadows, trees, and flowers. He finishes off his enemy, and rescues several young and beautiful princesses who have long been held captive by the dwarf. As Bear Son tries to reenter the world, however, his comrades tarry and almost prevent his escape. Eventually he prevails and returns to his home, to everyone's surprise— they all thought him dead—bringing with him both the princesses and great wealth.

The adventurous, heroic content of the Bear Son story signified a change in the values and consciousness of Old World cultures. In a sense there has been no more crucial shift in the turbulent history of the past ten millennia than this new emphasis and allegory. A central theme of Frazer's *The Golden Bough,* for example, is the annual renewal of the vegetation as personified in the dying and reviving god, the son and lover of a goddess. "The Year-God cycle," says Marija Gimbutas, "starts with the birth of the Divine Child," which was, in turn, "at the heart of the whole complex of images of an agararian religion. . . . Naturally the goddess who was responsible for the transformation from death to life became the central figure in the pantheon of gods. . . . Almost all Neolithic goddesses are composite images with an accumulation of traits from the pre-agricultural eras." The Divine Child itself, she says, "represents the awakening of a new-born spirit of vegetation." Typical among such divinities is the Cretan Zeus, the holy babe born in the Cave of Dikte, who was not reared by his mother, Ge (Gaea), the earth goddess, but by Artemis or others. Thus do the traces of the bear as the perfect and wild mother, rearing her sons, furnish the Old European early agriculture with its ideal of the renewing and protecting Bear Mother. Nine thousand years ago she was represented as a woman wearing a bear mask. But in time, Old Europe was swamped and overlaid by the Indo-European cultures with their celebration not of the mother but of the son. As the warrior patriarchs shaped the world of male power and masculine ideals, the nurturing feminine image became subordinate to that of the wonderful son who renewed himself underground.

The new worship of manlike gods incorporated the Bear Son legend in humanized form. The geography of this connection to Greek classical thought centers in the region of Thrace, west of the Black Sea. According to the Greek historian Herodotus, the inhabitants of that land, the Getai, annually sacrificed a man to a god of immortality, Salmoxis. The dead man's soul was considered to be a messenger or emissary to the god. A story about Salmoxis was conveyed by Greeks down the Black Sea coast and the Bosporus to Greece itself. It told of a man of Thrace who was captured and taken away as a slave, and who returned to his home many years later, a wealthy and mysterious stranger. He invited everyone of importance to his home for a feast at which he propounded a concept of ever-

A baked-clay bear figure of 23,000 years ago, from Czechoslovakia, corresponding in age to the cave art of France and Spain. *Moravian Museum, Brno*

A Czechoslovakian rhyton or drinking pot of 5,000 years ago. In her book *Prehistoric Art in Europe*, Nancy Sandars contrasts this pot to the 23,000-year-old bear figure from the same region: "The wild animal still receives more respectful treatment than the domestic 'slave.'" As a pot the bear has become a worker; its bloated body and reduced head show typical effects of the "domestic" animal. The Paleolithic bear carried a god's grace or vengeance, while the Neolithic bear carries only the materials its human owners put into it. *Moravian Museum, Brno*

Although bears have been absent from the British Isles for at least a thousand years, this stone carving from the sacred site at Armagh, Ireland, suggests the bear's presence (or the memory of its presence) and importance. *Ulster Museum*

Known in myths and legends as the carrier of good will from the gods or the giver of special food, the bear came to be represented as a vase in Neolithic pottery. This pot, from a sixth millennium B.C. Yugoslavian site, is decorated with zigzag and triangular markings, thought to signify the bear's water- and rainy-season connections. *Archeological Museum, Zadar*

"The maternal devotion of the female bear," writes archaeologist Marija Gimbutas, "made such an impression upon Old European peasants that she was adopted as a symbol of motherhood." Many small clay figurines of Madonna and child, both "wearing bear masks," were made by people of the Vinča culture in the fifth millennium, B.C. — this one from Yugoslavia. It is likely, however, that the idea of the bear as a model of motherhood is much older than peasant society and that the little statuettes indicate a transitional expression of the idea. *National Museum, Belgrade*

The legend of the transformation of Callisto, the companion or form of Artemis, into a bear, was depicted on an Apulian vase in ancient Greece. A fragment of that chous shows Callisto, her ears already grown long, hair appearing on her body, and her hand turning into a paw. To save her from being hunted down, Zeus transferred her into the sky as Ursa Major. *The J. Paul Getty Museum, Malibu, California*

To combat the ancient divinity of animals, Christian artists often depicted them as vain imitators of man. The mocking of the bear in this fifteenth-century Flemish drawing reveals the clown on the bear, a vain imitator of the mounted knight and a parable of man's foolish striving to transcend his human status. *Bodleian Library, Oxford*

It is widely held in folklore that the bear's young is born a shapeless lump and has to be licked into shape by the mother. For medieval Christians this became the ideal parable for the Mother Church shaping the human soul. *Bodleian Library, Oxford*, Ash. 1511 f.31

The bear, the hibernator, was a major and early manifestation for man of the cycle of renewal and reincarnation. So deep is the bearish energy of this theme that the resurrection of Christ, in this illustration from a medieval manuscript, shows bears supporting the sarcophagus. *Bodleian Library, Oxford*

BELOW: Albrecht Dürer's Northern Celestial Hemisphere of 1515 was one of the first published maps of the sky. Both Ursa Major and Ursa Minor are shown as long-tailed bears, despite the fact that all bears are short-tailed. For peoples of the northern hemisphere, these constellations, together with Boötes, sweep the sky in a sacred hunt each night. *The Metropolitan Museum of Art, Harris Brisbane Dick Fund, 1951. (51.537.1)*

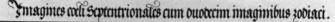

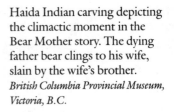

Haida Indian carving depicting the climactic moment in the Bear Mother story. The dying father bear clings to his wife, slain by the wife's brother. *British Columbia Provincial Museum, Victoria, B.C.*

BELOW: This nineteenth-century American painting, "Bear in Tree," shows a black bear as frontiersmen might often have seen it, treed by dogs. *National Gallery of Art, Washington, D.C.*

This 1873 drawing of "Native Cali-
fornians Lassoing a Bear" shows the
means by which a bear was captured
for a bear-and-bull fight, held in the
plazas of coastal California towns.

In this engraving, "The Enraged
Bear," by eighteenth-century artist
Johan Elias Ridinger, the bear was
transformed into something resembling a werewolf. We do not see what
has startled the animal, which glares
back directly at the viewer, and thus
the picture describes a confrontation
between civilized observer and wild,
monstrous nature. *Henry E. Huntington
Library, Santa Monica, California*

Bear carving on the door of the house
of Chief Shakey, Tlingit Indian, at
Wrangell, Alaska. To enter, one enters
the bear. *Peter Nabokov*

A Tlingit totem pole from Alaska showing "Kats and His Bear Wife." The sculpted sequence represents the reverse of the Bear Mother story, as it tells the tale of a man who married a female bear. Returning to live in the village with his bear wife and cubs, he was warned by her not to look again at his human wife. When he saw her by accident, he was killed by his cubs and the dirge sung by his bear wife became a traditional song of Tlingit Indians. The carvings show the bear wife perched on Kats's head, and his cub children below. *Otto Schallerer*

The "Teddy bear" got its name from an incident in which President Theodore "Teddy" Roosevelt, while hunting, refused to shoot a small bear. This 1902 cartoon was by C. K. Berryman.

Despite its burly appearance, the bear is capable of precise balancing and dexterity. Trained to perform, bears with itinerant keepers and in circuses have entertained audiences for 2,000 years. In a Polish bear school of the seventeenth century, a bear was "taught" to dance on heated metal plates. In modern circuses, like that of Barnum & Bailey, the bear reached an apogee of complex performance and appeal. *Barnum & Bailey*

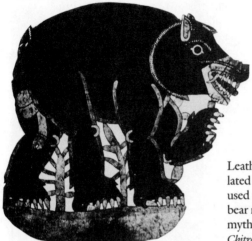

Leather marionette of a bear with articulated joints. In India such figures are often used in folk plays. The unlikely penis on this bear may emphasize his masculinity or his mythical sexual appetite. *Chitra Kala Parished/ Chitrakar Studio*

In his painting "The Princess on the Bear," Theodore Kittelson has illustrated a Norwegian folktale, "White Bear King, Valemon," in which a princess marries a bear in order to get a golden wreath — both a matrimonial ring and, like the golden bough, a symbol of renewal. The bear, bewitched by a troll-hag, was a bear by day and a man by night.
Theodore Kittelson

lasting life. Then he built a secret underground chamber and shut himself in it for four years.* There he fasted. His sudden reappearance—like his return from exile—seemed to confirm his claim of immortality. His name, Salmoxis, was derived from the Thracian word *Zalmo,* for "skin," because he was said to have worn a bearskin.†

Later Greek comment on this story, while the Salmoxis sacrifice was still being made in the Danube area, added that the god was a master of meteorological prediction, of the "signs of the seasons," a daimon weather-prophet. Part of the ritual included shooting arrows at thunder and lightning.

But the story continues. Salmoxis became in turn a co-regent with the king, then the priest of the god of immortality, and finally was addressed as the god himself. From a sacred cave he made oracular prophecy, but was always approached on behalf of pilgrims by intermediaries. From this tale Euripides created the Muse in *Rhesos,* the mother of a slain Thracian king, who refers to the king's immortal soul as an oracular daimon in a cave on the sacred mountain Pangaion, and, though dead, it "shall lie in secret in a cavern of the silver land, half human, half divine." Near the cave, Socrates later met people who healed in the name of Salmoxis, and the Greeks of Socrates' time regarded the Thracians as cave-connected people who could foretell the future. On Mount Laphystion an oracle, Trophonios, reigned in a sacred enclave. Those who sought his help sometimes disappeared into his cave for days and were given up for dead—then reemerged, renewed and radiant. The ceremonies of the Trophonios cult were an evocation of the descent to the underworld of the dead and return, included both feast and fast, and clearly

---

*In Balkan folklore the bear enters his cave for forty days after the winter solstice, suggesting an antecedent for other famous forties in religious history and myth. Its transposition into four years also suggests various calendric fours, as well as the points of the compass.

†In reading Mircea Eliade's book *Zalmoxis,* we were puzzled to find that he considers the subject centered on wolves instead of bears, until we realized that for Eliade "primitive" meant cultures of the Neolithic and the environs of preclassical cultures, that his emphasis was on warrior fraternities and the cults and sagas of barbarian adventuring. In our view this is a late, not a primal, stage of pre-Europe, when the ideal of the individualistic and independent bear had given way to a new imagery—the fighting clan, the blood and bloody brotherhood of power and vengeance, symbolized by the hierarchy of the wolfpack and the cults of the lion.

collapsed the cycle of life, death, and renewed life into a single ceremonial episode of initiation.

The Salmoxis legend was brought into Greece, if the classicist Rhys Carpenter is correct, by migrating Thracians. From it came the impiety, murderousness, and underworld adventures of the Aeolids—Salmoneus, Athamas, and Sisyphus. The essence of the story is descent and return, in which the traveler visits the place of renewal and transformation which harbors implicitly within it the forecast of the future. The ritual of Trophonios integrated the theme of death and resurrection with the "new birth" of the initiate. The candidate, probably an adolescent boy, descended into a thirty-foot-deep "circular chasm," in the floor of which was a hole through which he entered or was drawn, feet first. Later he resurfaced, also feet first, frightened and having had a vision that instructed him on the future (the same daimons preside over prognostication as over initiation). Part of the ritual preparation is often bathing: it corresponds to the psychological immersion in Anamnesis (forgetting) and links the loss of childhood with its primal parallel, death. The initiate new birth, which follows, is like that of the newborn infant, an awakening of memory at fresh, mythic levels. In the Trophonian gorge, the oracle's home near Labadea, the candidates were probably immersed or drank from the spring of forgetting and the spring of remembering.

From the Getai and Dacians of the Balkans, the Thracians brought the cult of renewed life into Greece, where it sired the ceremonies of the Eleusinian mysteries. The Getai, in turn, had been influenced by the northeastern European forest people, where the bear is a true hibernator. Thus Epimenides, a Cretan sage, slept fifty-seven years in a cave, had prophetic knowledge, and ate little—a sacred bear antecedent of Rip Van Winkle.

As the mythology of the bear entered Neolithic Europe, its multiple qualities were divided and the single image broken. Its connections with the moon went one way, its solar powers another. The forerunner of Artemis was, in her genesis, fragmented into Demeter, Isis, Iphigenia, Hecate, and so on. Artemis' twin, Apollo, born with her under the mountain in Delos, deprived her of sun mastery. Finally, to the Romans she is the stern virgin Diana, stripped of her older, fecund connections with the underworld which were transformed into Gorgons, she herself marginalized and isolated as a free but backward spirit. The bear's power was broken by heroes like Heracles and Perseus and shrunk to chaste femininity in Artemis, its masculinity given to various Greek gods.

The Greek metaphor/ambiguity of the bear/person, the shift from animal figure to that of human—from bear to the goddess Callisto—marks the anthropomorphic tendency of emerging Greek thought. Callisto, in her earliest form, when she mated with Zeus, says the classicist Joseph Fontenrose, was probably a bear. In the oldest version of the story she was not raped at all; she was a willing mistress. She appears in paintings at Delphi "wearing her bearskin" and as a bear on fifth century B.C. coins minted in southern Greece. In the form of Artemis she is Arklos, the bear-woman. With the anthropomorphizing of the gods and the polarity of Orion and Artemis, the theme of sexual misconduct becomes more prevalent, as in Ovid and Euripides. This is probably a "late" confusion of the archaic Bear Mother myth with the widespread cynegetic taboo against sexual intercourse before the hunt as the bear-Salmoxis-Callisto theme was gradually disengaged from its original base in a hunter-gatherer culture and subordinated to the abstracting and humanizing Olympian world. So, for a while, Hades was represented in sarcophagus carvings as wearing a bear headdress, and thereafter the bear image was lost altogether. But beneath the human visage there remained a core of organic connections, an underground meaning that would survive its eclipse at the hands of hubris and mono-theism, to be awakened by the survival of real bears as civilization crept north.

Elsewhere in Greece, the "Arkades" of Arcadia (that is, "bear folk") traced their descent from Arcas, son of Callisto, the she-bear divinity. On Mount Lykaion (misnamed after the Greek for "wolf" because of the very old confusion between the words for wolf and bear*) as late as classical times, there was a sacrifice to Zeus Lykaios (who was born in a cave), in a sanctuary to which a legendary hunter drove the game but could not himself enter, but waited for it to

---

*The confusion attests to the acumen of the ancient hunters, who perceived the biological kinship of dog and bear, and by whom, in Europe, the bear was sometimes called "bee-wolf" and who sometimes regarded the bear as the "dog" of the gods. Elderkin sees the confusion arising in the term for "slash" or "hook," which referred first to the bear as in "Zeus the Slasher," Zeus Lykaios, but was mistaken for the other slasher, the wolf. Sir George Lox called this a "confusion of homonyms . . . converting Lykaon into a wolf."

emerge, without its shadow, from the realm of death. The animal so driven was Callisto, the bearess. The hunter was Arcas, her son, who failed to recognize her. It was Arcas who had somehow survived being served as a meal for Zeus by Lycaon, his own grandfather.* To prevent the young hunter from killing his mother, Zeus transported them to the sky, Callisto becoming the Great Bear constellation, Arcas Arcturus. The birth of Arcas was the result of Callisto's mating with Zeus. In another version, Callisto was executed with an arrow by her hunting companion, Artemis, because of her pregnancy, then set in the sky, and Arcas was given to Maia in Arcadia to rear. In yet another form of the story, it was Hera, Zeus' jealous wife, who punished Callisto by turning her into a bear—the bear seen here as the fallen, bestial side of Callisto. Arcas, the son of Callisto, hunts his mother and pursues her to Mount Lycaeus, Zeus' sacred ground. For that trespass, Zeus fixes them both in the heavens as the constellations Great Bear and Little Bear.

A curious twist to the version in which Zeus saves Callisto from death at her son's hands is that Hera asks Ocean and Tethys not to permit Callisto (as a constellation) to dip beneath their waters, that is, to set below the horizon. This seems a strange punishment, as a perpetual circling in the sky would accord her a kind of immortality. The answer, according to Jane Ellen Harrison's description of the changing view of immortality in Greece, is that in the older traditions, to be truly immortal was to participate in the great round of seasons, of life, death, and new life. In that context, to be fixed in the sky would indeed be punishment. But the Olympians would later "slake off the year daimon" to claim a "deathless immortality" free of the endless cycle. In the mythic world of the Thracian bear, that would be "really a denial of life, for life is change. . . . Such is the very nature of life that only though the ceaseless movement and rhythm of palingenesia [regeneration] is immortality possible." What later was to become the positive, deathless eternity of the Olympian gods was earlier, to an older religion, a negation.

The priests at the cave sanctuary on Mount Lykaion were "weather magicians," among whose incantations was the bringing of rain by dipping an oak branch into a spring. In the maze of kindred connections in Greek myth, Callisto also has river-god connections, as

---

*We are reminded that adult bears readily kill and eat cubs, even their own kin.

the granddaughter of Inachus.* In Attica, the Thracian root traditions place a bear cult around Artemis, centered at her temple at Brauron. For her, little Athenian girls who came to be initiated danced in yellow-brown robes, calling themselves bears. Carpenter suggests that the story of Iphigenia, who was saved from sacrificial death by Artemis, may be associated with the ritual sacrifice of one of these bear-children.

Iphigenia, the daughter of Agamemnon whom he attempted to sacrifice to Artemis to placate her for having killed one of her sacred deer, may have been a bear prior to becoming human. As the classical scholar Lewis Farnell says, she was "the anthropic animal of sacrifice . . . a bear slain in the ritual of a bear goddess." At Brauron, on the coast of Attica, offerings were made to Iphigenia (perhaps representing Artemis) of the clothing of women who had died in childbirth. This back-and-forth movement between the bear as goddess and the bear as sacrifice to the goddess, and between the sacrifice of the bear as animal and as a person probably represents fragments of an ancient but changing story. Farnell speaks of the complex of legends of Artemis, Brauron, and Aules which "enables us to discern the prehistoric figure of a bear goddess and a ritual in which the bear was sacred and yet slain"—a prescient remark in the light of the circumpolar ceremony of the slain bear. The connection of Artemis with childbirth (or the "slaying" of women by her in childbirth) may also seem puzzling in the light of her virginal character. Yet, among those committed to the more ancient cult of the bear, sexual abstinence often preceded the hunt, and woman's sexuality and menstruation carried heavy taboos in relation to hunting— prohibitions that may have changed, taking the state of virginity as a final, baroque expression when the woman herself became the hunter.

The Greeks are said to have burnt bears in a ceremony honoring Artemis at Patrae. If so, the bear was very early sacrificed for the goddess who was herself bear-Artemis. Like the sacrifice of bears reared for the purpose by the Ainu and other Asian peoples, the

---

*In natural history, the association of the bear and water may be in part that of underground water and of caves, in which bears sometimes hibernate, but more exactly of the bathing and feeding by bears in rivers and lakes. The oak in the Mediterranean region is evergreen, and therefore a sign of the continuity of life. Everywhere, however, the bear is a major feeder on mast.

DEMETER AND ARTEMIS: THE BEAR GODDESSES

In the Bronze Age twilight of Neolithic religions, as many of the old animal divinities faded in popularity, the rich figure of the legendary bear spread itself across the conclave of Mediterranean gods. Among these the Greek goddess Demeter was the most important. Literally, Demeter means "the grain of the bear mother"—that is, "barley mother." Older than Artemis, she was sometimes spoken of as Artemis' mother. Demeter was called "the broad-faced one" and, by Euripides, "the mountain-ranging mother of the gods." As a form of Rhea, she turned the spindle of the celestial universe, its energy focused nightly in the master figure of the Great Bear. Demeter was also a form of Gaia, "a great goddess of the lower world," a supreme chthonian power of the Greek cosmos.

Demeter's underworld associations are multifold. She was the nurse of Trophonios, the cave-dwelling oracle and master of initiation rites. A temple in her honor stood in the Grove of Trophonios at Lebadea. Demeter's ceremonies at Phigaleia and elsewhere took place in a cavern, sometimes referred to as an "underground sleeping room" or sanctuary. The myth of her descent into and return from the underworld precedes the tales of later Olympian heroes who embodied dramatic elaborations of the metaphors of rebirth. Among the most famous Greek ceremonies, the Eleusinian mysteries, performed at Eleusis, which means a "place of birth," were Demeter's rites. They were celebrated with a barley water–mint drink, *kykem,* and a torchlight parade reflecting on earth the seasonal march of stars across the heavens. As the mistress of renewal, Demeter came in time to oversee fruition in agriculture, but in her origins there were no farms, only, says Lewis Farnell, "the shadowy form of an aboriginal earth spirit."

Artemis, whose name means "bear," is the goddess who absorbs some of the sacred bear's ultimate qualities as the animal image itself disappears, Cheshire-cat-like, in the anthropomorphism of the Classical gods. It is she who is most other and wild. Artemis is a vital spirit in both the mythical tale and the human spirit. Observed as an aspect of her own psyche by Christine Downing in her book *The Goddess,* the Artemis-bear lives not only in the polar realms of sky and underworld but in both the landscape and the heartscape. For Christine Downing, Artemis represents three things: "she who slays, she who is other, she who comes from afar." Least of all the divinities in the Greek pantheon is she at home on Olympus. "Artemis embodies," says Downing, "a profound denial of the world of patriarchy, the world where some persons have power over others, the world of dominance and submission, where one can be hunter *or* hunted."

The Classical Greeks stripped the goddess still further of her traits. In Ovid's *Metamorphoses,* Callisto, a "companion" or form of Artemis, was in myth punished for pregnancy, demoted from her human form back into that of the bear, and turned into stars, leaving to Artemis the pure, final aloofness of virginal wildness, not a sentimental shepherdess but a solitary *anima* who will never be tamed, removed from the civilized world.

In her votary power as protectress of mothers in childbirth, Artemis is closer to her fecund spiritual mother, Demeter. She is, continues Downing, the one who "knows each tree by its bark or leaf or fruit, each beast by its footprint or spoor, each bird by its plumage or call or nest . . . each tree, laurel or myrrh, oak or ash . . . each brook or stream," a maternal source beyond motherhood. For all her wildness, Artemis is not transcended in consciousness. She is the "recreation (or recovery) of a world within which we live as a realm of souls, of living, meaningful-in-themselves beings." She is not the past, but, as Hippolytus says, "Artemis seems to beckon from the future, to call me toward who I am now to become."

ceremony gave a new twist to the older slain-bear ritual, transposed into the more anthropomorphic imagery. So, too, the quinquennial dance of the ten-year-old maidens "for Artemis," as a premarriage requirement, trails remnants of the woman-bear marriage myth.

Before noticing other Greek connections, we can see that the figures and stories mentioned so far express the primal set of two tales, one involving the seduction and marriage of a woman by a bear, and the other the adventures of the extraordinary son of that marriage. These two bodies of connected narrative, the Bear Mother and the Bear Son, were shaped by Greek thought in ways that were meaningful in that culture, just as the details differed for the same reason among scores of other peoples. At the time they reached Greece, such stories were already a rich and mature body of legend, probably tens of thousands of years old. The Bear Mother seems to be the more widely disseminated and therefore the oldest. Indeed, the concept of the hero in human form, to which the Bear Son lends itself, is much more prevalent among adventuring warrior people, subsequent to the development of agriculture, seafaring, military might, cities, and trade.

To continue with the evidence, other Greek stories derived from the Getic connection include the legends of the house of the Aeolids, which fostered a son who was a weather prophet, the return of a son to a forbidden banquet hall and his death, and a son, Melicertes ("honey-eater") whose tomb or sleeping place on the Corinthian isthmus became a chthonic shrine under the guardianship of an uncle, Sisyphus, the father of Odysseus. In the *Odyssey,* it was Sisyphus who defeated death. When he died a second time, a great rock was placed over him to keep him down, and he was forever destined to heave it upward.* Once again, what is punishment and what is The Way shifts in Greece with time. Jane Ellen Harrison remarks that Sisyphus is Titan, the Sun, and that his "labor" is no penalty but simply *dike,* or intrinsic reality, and that only later the Olympians saw his eternal round as fruitless work. For them, she says, "those of the old order of palingenesia", like Orpheus, had become criminals being punished in Hades.

---

*Heaving up large boulders is, of course, an almost incessant activity of the brown bear in search of rodents and insects.

As for the *Odyssey*, Rhys Carpenter believes it to be a form of the Bear Son story. Odysseus' son, Telemachus, speaks of his ancestry, and refers to a grandfather as Arkeisios, from an adjective for "bearish" or "ursine." The same adjective was used in reference to the cave on Mount Ida, where the infant Zeus was nourished in the *arkeison antron* or "bear cave." Used as a patronymic, the adjective means "bear son." The ancestor referred to was Cephalus, one of the Aeolid family, who mated with a she-bear to produce Arkeisios, the "bear son." In this story Carpenter sees an expression of the ancient and widespread myth of the bear-human marriage that founds a line: "From Finland and Lapland across the whole of Siberia to the Japanese Islands, through Kamchatka and across Bering Strait, across Red-Indian North America to Labrador and Newfoundland, in a vast belt of many thousand miles, there has been traced a bear ceremonial of eventually identical form and content."

Of the *Odyssey* he says:

> The bear names cluster so close about Odysseus that it would be mere blindness or obstinacy to overlook their clue. . . . The central theme of the sacred legend of Salmoxis . . . with its distant homecomer with his treasure, who feasts the chief citizens in a great hall, who disappears unexpectedly and is given up for dead, who sleeps in an underground chamber, who suddenly returns to the amazement of all—does not this supply the thematic material also for the Odyssey?

The Greek mythology of Dike is strangely parallel to the more archaic concept of the great bear spirit. Dike is the underlying order of the world, with which human customs must be harmonized. Above all, Dike is manifested in star passages, the seasons, and in palingenesis, the eternal cycles. As Eurydice, Dike is connected with Orpheus and becomes an example of the punishment of those who do not respect natural order. Orpheus, an adventurer in the underworld and a native of Thrace, was a "sun worshipper." This idea echoes fragments from the bear's connection with season and sun, the mastery of renewal, his manifestation in the constellation, the bad luck of those who fail to show regard for the animal gods, and the Pythagorean slavery of Salmoxis.

But Orpheus was discredited by the Olympians at Athens, and the classical Greeks repudiated those connections. The gods around Zeus demanded sacrifice like a pirate demanding ransom, and the Greeks became increasingly separated from the year-daimons and the cycle of periodic reincarnation. The bear was so totally eclipsed in this shift that the ursine beginnings have almost vanished.

·6·

THE LITERARY BEAR

Just as the ancient tales of the bear found their way—disguised as human figures—into classical mythology, and from there into the printed word, the oral traditions of old northern Europe also provided the source of early literature. Such stories are not literature in the sense of the modern work of a single, creative author but, like the Bible and the work of Homer, are part of a prehistoric stream of ideas put on paper in historic times. Among these, none links more clearly the myths of Finland to its oldest piece of literature, the *Kalevala,* than the bear spirit.

In the moving, sometimes lyric epic, the hero of the poem, Vainamoinen, pauses for a moment in the narrative to recount the creation of Otso, the bear:

> Otso was not born in straw-bed,
> Nor was born on chaff in malt-house;
> There was Otso brought to being,
> There was born the honey-pawed one,
> Near the moon, in gleams of sunshine,
> And upon the Great Bear's shoulders,
> There beside the Air's fair maiden,
> Near the daughter of Creation.

The fair maiden then casts a piece of wool from the heavens into the waters below, which the winds gently flow to the forest's edge. There, Mielikki, the forest's mistress, places the soft wool into a maple basket and hangs it on a golden chain from a branch of a fir tree:

> Then she rocked the charming object,
> And she rocked the lovely creature
> Underneath a spreading fir-tree,
> Underneath a blooming pine-tree.
> Thus it was the bear was nurtured,
> And the furry beast was fostered,
> There beside a bush of honey,
> In a forest dripping honey.

And the Finnish bear "grew up most handsome, / And attained his perfect stature." Then the bear swore an oath to Mielikki that if she would grant him sharp claws and strong teeth he would never use them for mischief or evil. And in the sagas that follow the *Kalevala,* the bear keeps his word and protects the people of the North. In return he is treated by them with awe and respect.

Yet the shift in tone represented by the *Kalevala* and other Scandinavian hero stories from prehistoric bear rituals, places an emphasis on heroic valor. In the course of this shift, one sense of the bear gave way to another, and as man gradually assumed the power of the animal, he also gained the courage to repudiate the sacredness of the animals themselves. For example, William Gronbech writes, in his *History of the Teutons:* "In the neighborhood of Eric the Red's homestead in Greenland, there appeared one winter a great white bear which ravaged around, and when Thorgils, then a guest of Brattahlid, slew the beast to save his little son's life, he gained the praise of all men. Only Eric was silent, and though he made no objection to the customary disposal of the body for useful ends, it was understood that he was incensed at Thorgil's deed. Some said that Eric had cherished 'ancient faith' in the beast." One suspects that it was not the killing or the use of the bear, but the *way* it was done, without ceremony, that bothered Eric.

The rise of the importance of the Bear Son legend in early historic times coincides with the rise of the wandering adventurer, of which Odysseus is among the earliest in literature. Norse and Teutonic legends are heavily invested with the conflicts of honor and courage among swashbuckling heroes, and their monumental pillage.

Shape-changing stories in which men transform themselves into animals characterize the Old Norse sagas. In the saga of *Hrolf kraki,* the hero turns out not to be King Hrolf of Denmark, but one of his followers, a shape-shifter named Bodvar Biarki, or Bodvar Little Bear. Bodvar's father Biorn (Bear) had been changed into a bear by a wicked stepmother, but he was able to assume human form at night, and took as a paramour Bera (She-Bear). Before he was killed, he warned Bera never to eat bear flesh; but the stepmother forced her to do so. After Biorn's death, she bore three sons: the first was half man, half elk; the second had dog's feet; and the third was Biarki, who possessed human form. When Hrolf fought his final and most vicious battle against enemies who were controlled by supernatural forces, Biarki was absent. Hrolf's troops saw, however, that a great bear remained close to the king and protected him, slaying the enemy in great numbers by swiping at them with his forepaws.

Biarki's men began to look for him, and finally found him resting in his own tent; they berated him for deserting the king; he reluctantly went to the battlefield, announcing that he would be far less good there than in his own tent. As he entered the field, the bear left, and Hrolf was defeated. Clearly, Biarki had been fighting as a bear, engaged in what is called in the Icelandic sagas *hamfarir*, "shape journey," in which a warrior sends out his spirit in the form of an animal, typically a bear, to wage fierce battle. The Old Norse belief in animal transformations continues today, if we are to believe the introduction to *A Collection of Popular Tales from the Norse and North German:* "Even now in Norway, it is matter of popular belief that Finns and Lapps . . . can at will assume the shape of bears; and it is a common thing to say of one of those beasts, when he gets unusually savage and daring, 'that can be no Christian bear.' "

A thirteenth-century account of the settlement of Iceland at the end of the ninth century, *Landnamabok*, tells of two settlers, Dufthak, a freed slave who purchased some land, and Storolf, a landowner. They were both *hamrammr* "shape strong," and able to assume other forms. One night they fell to quarreling over grazing rights. "One evening at sunset a man with the gift of second sight," the story tells us, saw a great bear leave Storolf's house and a great bull depart from Dufthak's; they met and fought furiously. The bear won. The story concludes: "In the morning a hollow could be seen in the place where they had met, as though the earth had been turned over, and this is now called Oldugrof."

But if a Norseman was not *hamrammr*, he could still partake of the power of the bear by impersonating him—he might wear a magic pelt, a bearskin.* This magical investiture produced Scandinavian warriors who fought with all the ferocious strength and power of a bear and who were called *berserkers*. *Ber* derives from the root word for "bear"; *sark* means "shirt." Although no descriptions exist of Norse warriors wearing bearskins into battle, there are decorations on helmet plates and scabbards of human forms with bear heads and feet that date from the pre-Viking period in Sweden. And we do find, for instance, in *Grettir the Strong*, a thirteenth-century Icelandic saga, men fighting with the "berserkers' rage." The comrades of Odin in the *Ynglinga Saga* also fight with the "fury of the berserkers."

Bearskins are also associated with the ordeals of initiation. In some Icelandic initiation ceremonies, the youth wears a bearskin until he returns from a hunt with a bear's snout to prove his victory; in some other versions of the initiation, the youth has to toss the skin at his testers, and retrieve it and cut off the paw to prove his manhood. In initiatory combat, the bearskin heats a candidate to a sacred frenzy of ferocity to make him act, according to the historian of religion Mircea Eliade, "like a beast of prey or a shaman." Eliade sees such *berserk* behavior as moving the young warrior to a higher plane of existence. This thesis is echoed in his study of *Zalmoxis*, the Thracian man-divinity who, in Eliade's view, is aligned with the wolf as a model for the warrior class. In both Scandinavia and Thrace, these myths express the ideology of medieval buccaneering and valorous deeds—an ego-centered shift from the old, egalitarian band existence, with its mood of accommodation to a natural world, toward the centralized magic of the shaman, with a concomitant rise in his political power. As Claude Lévi-Strauss points out, when the metaphors of totemic metaphysics begin to break down, the poetic parallels between human and animal decay into a convergence

---

*Bearskins possess power outside the Norse world. American Indian shamans wore bearskins for various rituals. The naturalist Tracy L. Storer, in *California Grizzly*, tells of an Indian shaman who neglected to remove his bearskin while having intercourse with his wife; she reportedly gave birth to a bear cub. In the Grimm fairy tales, the devil will accept a bearskin as payment of a debt. In the fairy tale "Bearskin," the devil is in fact placated when the victim remains wrapped for seven years in a bearskin. In another story, a pregnant woman becomes frightened by a bearskin; her baby is born with a patch of bear fur on its leg.

of literal similarities. Men begin to act like animals. Such is the *berserker*.

The Norse put bearskins to other ritual uses. For instance, they might be used as biers to carry the dead; or, as the historian H. R. Ellis Davidson suggests, to wrap the dead in their graves, "as is shown by the traces of claws surviving in graves in Norway and Sweden in the period before the Viking Ages." One of the descendants of Storolf, the shape-shifter who fought in the *Landnamabok,* was a Lapp named Orvar-Odd, who used a bearskin to drive back his enemy. Marooned with his crew off the Baltic coast, the story tells us, Orvar-Odd was attacked by hostile mainlanders. He set up a wooden cross and draped the skin of a bear across the poles, placing the head on top of the pole. When a female giant was sent to attack, Orvar-Odd set burning embers in the bear's mouth and drove back the giant with magic arrows. Bearskins displayed in this manner also form a part of the Lapp bear-slaying ritual.

For the Norse, the bear performed as a *fylgia,* a guiding spirit protecting the virtuous. In *Nial's Saga,* the hero Gunnar's *fylgia* is a massive bear. Some wise men may be able to see these spirits. A simple Old Norse folktale tells the story of a boy, Thorstein, who was abandoned as a baby and raised by peasants. One day he visits the hall where his true parents live. His wise father, Geitir, sees the boy enter in a rush, and trip, and then fall. Geitir laughs. Confused, the boy asks why the old man laughs at him. Geitir answers: "I could see what you could not—a white bear cub came in behind you and ran under your feet. When he saw me, he stopped, and you ran over him." He explains that the bear is the young boy's guardian spirit, and that the presence of a bear augurs great things for the young boy's future.

The Celts venerated Dea Artio, a bear goddess whose cult is depicted in a bronze statue at Bern: a seated goddess offers fruit in a patera to her bears. Another Celtic bear goddess may have been Andarta (Strong Bear), and still another, Artaios, may have served the Celtic people as a bear god. Although the cult of the bear in Celtic Ireland can only be inferred from fragmentary evidence, the bear's importance is suggested by such common surnames as Mathghamna, Son of a Bear.

Themes of shape-shifting, transformation, and union with bears

SIOUX METAMORPHOSIS

1.

He comes from the north
he comes to fight
he comes from the north
see him there

I throw dust on me
it changes me
I am a bear
when I go to meet him

2.

Send word, bear father
send word, bear father
I'm having a hard time
send word, bear father
I'm having a bad time

3.

My paw is holy
herbs are everywhere
my paw
herbs are everywhere

My paw is holy
everything is holy
my paw
everything is holy

and offspring also came to Ireland. They are perhaps best summarized in an elaborate Irish Celtic legend called "The Brown Bear of Norway."

A king of Ireland once had three daughters, and he asked each whom she would like to marry. The first two answered predictably, but the third surprisingly announced, "I'll have no husband but the Brown Bear of Norway." Everyone laughed and sent the princess off, but that night she woke from her sleep to find herself in a rich hall, where a beautiful prince asked her to marry him. She consented, and the prince explained that he was enchanted: "A sorceress who had a beautiful daughter wished me for her son-in-law; and because I didn't agree, she made me take the form of a bear by day, and I was to continue until a lady would marry me of her own free will, and endure five years of great trials after." He ended by telling her that if she ever mistrusted him or grew tired of him, they would be parted forever and he would be forced to marry the witch's daughter.

They spent a year together and a lovely boy was born to them, but he was soon taken away by an eagle. She grieved, and twelve months later gave birth to a beautiful little girl. But a greyhound came into the room and snatched the little girl away and ran into the woods. When the third child was born, a woman appeared before the princess and wrapped the child in a blanket and disappeared down through the ground. The princess grew tired of the hardship and asked her bear husband if she could return to her parents for a time. He allowed the visit, and told her if she wanted to come back, she must only mention her desire and it would come true.

She returned to her parents and explained to them what had happened and asked them to help her retrieve her children. Her parents consulted an old woman who sold them eggs, for she was very wise. She advised that the only plan was to secure the bear's skin that the prince was obliged to put on every morning, and burn it, for then he couldn't help being a man night and day. Thus, the enchantment would be at an end. After eight days the princess felt a longing to see her husband again, and so she made the wish and found herself at his side in bed.

The next night she got up after midnight and found the prince's bearskin hanging in an alcove. She threw it into the parlor fire and never took her eyes off it until she saw it a pile of ashes. Her husband was waiting for her in the bedroom. "You have separated us forever!" he screamed. "Now I must take a three days' journey and live with the witch's daughter. The skin was my protection, and the woman who gave you the advice was the witch." He then bade her farewell forever.

The rest of the story details her elaborate efforts to reach the prince's bedroom in the witch's castle. After many unsuccessful attempts, she finally enters his bedroom, sits on the edge of his bed, and sings him this song: "Four long years I was married to thee; / Three sweet babes I bore to thee; / Brown Bear of Norway, won't you turn to me?" He finally remembers that she is his wife, which breaks the spell, and not unlike the fall of the House of Usher, the witch's entire castle crumbles to the ground.

When the English retell the legends of the North, they make the stories tamer by draining them of most of their magic; the English seem more interested in the details of adventure. The Bear's Son story, for example, is one of the principal sources for *Beowulf,* the first great work of English literature, which was written sometime in the middle of the eighth century. The name of the poem's hero, Beowulf, translates literally as "bee-wolf" or, more commonly, "bear"; he possesses the strength of thirty men—or one bear?—in his hand (his special weapon).* Like his animal namesake, Beowulf runs swiftly, swims strongly, and fights fiercely. But the Bear's Son story hovers only as a dim outline behind that poem. What provides shape instead is the bear's miraculous ability to return from an underground death, a power dramatically transferred to Beowulf. In three marvelous adventures—with Grendel the monster, with Grendel's vicious mother, and with an unnamed dragon—Beowulf rids the world of evil. In the second of these episodes, Beowulf, accompanied by a band of warriors, journeys to a distant lake, where his deep dive into the murky waters to reach the monster's home, a muddy cavern at the lake's bottom, takes most of the day. After nine hours, many of Beowulf's companions sadly leave the edge of the lake, weary of waiting and grieving for their lord, who, they assume, must certainly

---

*The left hand is the source of magical power. For this reason, the Kamchadal and the Eskimo both believe the bear to be left-handed. While we do not know whether Beowulf is right- or left-handed, we do know he carries the strength of thirty men in one hand. And at least one critic, Donald Fry, has argued that Beowulf, with his left hand, ripped off Grendel's arm.

have perished. Indeed, a pool of blood has slowly formed on the surface of the water. Those who faithfully continue their vigil, however, are rewarded with a miracle: Beowulf emerges from the fen, having vanquished the "witch of the sea floor." In this, the most animistic of English poems, the Anglo-Saxons projected onto Beowulf their own basic animal yearnings and, in so doing, revealed their historic connections with the bear.

Deriving its power perhaps from Beowulf, the bear as a symbol attaches itself to King Arthur, to whom every English nobleman in the Middle Ages and the Renaissance delighted in tracing his lineage. Arthur, sixth-century leader of the Knights of the Round Table, and the first great nobleman in the history of the English people, stands as the model in the Middle Ages of the good and righteous ruler. His Latin name, Arcturus or Arturus, translates as *bear,* and his ensign is the bear, a device adopted by other medieval knights of lesser light in their attempts to stand in Arthur's historic/legendary glow. Guy of Warwick, for instance, the hero of one of the most popular romances in the Middle Ages, carries the bear and the shaggy staff on his ensign.*

Medieval literature, particularly the ballads and the romances, has its own share of shape-shifters that assume the forms of many wild animals—including the bear. The most notable example appears in "Tam Lin," a ballad filled with ancient folklore. Tam Lin has been abducted by the queen of the fairies and, on one dramatic evening, falls in love with Janet, the king's daughter, and they conceive a child. In order to disenchant her lover, Janet must unseat Tam Lin from his horse while he rides amid the fairy troop and hold him fast as he changes into a series of repulsive shapes. As Tam himself explains: "They'll turn me to a bea [bear] sae grim, / And then a lion bold, /But hold me fast, and fear me not, / As ye shall love your child." This is not unlike the test that the young bride undergoes in the Grimm fairy tales, when, in her marriage bed, she comes face to face with a huge bear. In "Tam Lin" the transforming action

---

*It was common practice for aristocratic families in the tenth and eleventh centuries to trace their lineage to bears. H. M. and N. K. Chadwick, two famous literary historians, point out notable examples: "The genealogies of Earl Siward of Northumberland, who died in 1055, and of Svend Estridsen, king of Denmark 1047–76. Siward's father is described as *Beorn cognomento Beresune, hoc est Filius Ursi;* and it is added that he had the ears of a bear."

takes place on Halloween, a scary, enchanted night associated still with shape-shifting.

It is in the bestiaries, however, those moralized descriptions of animals which flourished in the twelfth century in England, where the theory is laid for the medieval perception of animals. The bear is seen both as motherly and affectionate, while the Latin name *orsus* firmly connects it with "beginning." Furthermore, according to the bestiaries, bears are extremely sleepy animals, becoming "so deeply drowsy that they cannot be woken up, even by wounds, and they lie hid after bearing for three months." In addition, bears are perceived as particularly sexual, for "they do not make love like other quadrupeds, but, being joined in mutual embraces, they copulate in the human way. The winter season provokes their inclination to lust." The bestiaries see the bears as human counterparts in other ways and even assign to them a sense of modesty: "The males respect the pregnant females with the decency of a private room, and, though in the same lairs for their lying-in, these are divided by earth-works into separate beds."

The bear occupies a contradictory position in the bestiaries. Living beyond civilized life, sexually and boldly aggressive, the bear gives vent to a massive and uncontrolled appetite, upsetting rule and restriction. But in its display of maternal care and concern, the bear is the very essence of civility and order. Standing for both male and female characteristics, the bear would appear to have no gender. But the Church will take advantage of the bear's ambiguous position. Aggressively antagonistic, yet possessed of a soul capable of infinite love, the bear becomes emblematic of the Christian in his unformed state. Thus the bestiaries ready the way for the Church's conversion of the bear from unredeemed, feral creature to faithful servant.

This movement is dramatized in a popular French romance, *The Masquerade of Orson and Valentine,* printed in Lyons in 1489; it was printed in England in 1550 under the title *The Historye of the Two Valyannte Brethren: Valentyne and Orson.* The story involves twin brothers who, when infants, are abandoned in the woods. One reaches the den of a bear and is raised as a wild creature; he wanders the woods and is known only as Nameless. The other twin makes his way to the court of King Pippin, where he is christened Valentine. When the brothers finally meet, Valentine assumes responsibility for domesticating his feral twin, who becomes a court servitor and a faithful companion to his brother. His Christian name, Orson, reminds the rest of the court of his animal past. In their principal adventure together, the two brothers rescue their mother, Belisant, from the clutches of an angry giant.

Man has two sides, this medieval story suggests: a loving and civil one, plus a wild and unruly one. The former must reform the latter, a transformation enunciated in the names of the two brothers. Valentine is the name of two early Italian saints, both of whom were commemorated in the Middle Ages on February 14, a day when birds, not humans, reached joy and harmony by selecting their love mates. Saint Valentine's Day also celebrated religious love: medieval worshipers often took God as their "valentine." Later in the period, February 14 became a traditional day for honoring secular love. The name Orson means, of course, "bear." *The Masquerade* shows us that only through the power of love can man conquer his animal side, become whole, and thus acquire his true identity and live harmoniously. Then he will finally be reunited with the source of maternal, protective love: Belisant the Beautiful.

Christianity

In his book *Carnaval,* René Gaignabet points out that Saint Blaise represents the Christian culmination of a dominant pagan myth, of which the most popular example is Orpheus. According to Gaignabet, Orpheus' descent into the underworld and his eventual successful return represents a model borrowed and adapted from prehistoric bear ceremonies, and Orpheus frequently appears iconographically in the shape of a bear. At the Louvre is a picture of Orpheus as a bear dating from the fifth century, the period when the cult of Saint Blaise was most active; another appears in a palace of Onmeyade, where Orpheus is painted as a bear sitting on a mountain peak, bewitching attentive animals.

In Christianity, Gaignabet maintains, Christ's descent into hell mimics Orpheus and thus the bear. One of the symbols of Christ, the sun, also echoes the sun/light connections with the bear. Those connections with light are further recalled in the Anglo-Saxon root *bher-,* which means both *bright* and *bear.*

Described as a bear of a man, Saint Blaise functioned as the keeper of the winds, and more importantly, he marked the rebirth of the year—the advent of spring—by breaking wind, as the bear's "fart of dehibernation" announced springtime. Saint Blaise, as revealed in the numerous stories that surround him, blesses people by conferring continuous years of light on them—thus, a candle mass—and is the patron saint of Candlemas.

Up to this point the bear has stood mainly for power and magic, fierceness and courage in fighting. He possesses certain magic, in part because he stands beyond civilized life, and perhaps because he has been outside organized religion. The Church had to struggle to have a powerful and unruly bear in his wild state symbolize anything positive, but it certainly could not ignore such a pervasive pagan symbol—it needed to convert him. In his unfettered state, he stood in the Bible for viciousness and vengefulness, overwhelming and uncontrolled power; he was ultimately destructive. Tamed and refined, he presented a picture, however, of wonderful caring and concern. Every bear possessed this devilish character; but the Church could redeem him.

The Bible provides the key to the bear's new role in religion. The most famous episode in the Old Testament involving the bear occurs when the prophet Elisha is mocked for his baldness by some children; "old bald head" curses them, whereupon a she-bear rushes out of the woods and kills forty-two of them.

This puzzling scene may in part be understood in the light of biblical reference elsewhere to the fury of the she-bear deprived of her cubs, and to the familiar six-week period of traditional Syrian bear hibernation applied to such other regeneration cycles as the Flood, Christ's forty days in the wilderness, and Moses' forty years of wandering. It would appear that the destructive power of the terrible mother operates now under the aegis of a patriarchal summons, even to destroy children. Bad-mannered cubs do get a whacking from their mothers, but the mixing of such chastisement with the savagery of the feminine devourer requires one backward and two sideways leaps of the imagination.

Biblical interpreters usually see the bear here as a symbol of God's vengeance—perhaps an echo of the pagan berserker's rage—as it is unleashed on the faithless. Jeremiah, in Lamentations, sees God in His anger as a bear lying in wait, for Jeremiah sees God's vengeance as uncontrollably wild. That connection between divine anger and the bear is finally made clear in the Book of Hosea: "I am the Lord your God . . . they forgot me. So I will be to them like a lion, I will fall upon them like a bear robbed of her cubs. I will tear open their breast, and there I will devour them like a lion, as a wild beast would rend them." The Book of Proverbs tells us later, however, that it is better to meet a sow robbed of her cubs than a fool possessed of his folly.

But when the bear is not identified with God's wildest anger, he is simply raw power. So, for example, he symbolizes the Persian Empire, and he is the second of the four beasts in Daniel's vision of the Apocalypse: a bear was raised up on one side; it had three ribs in its mouth between its teeth; and it was told, "Arise, devour much flesh." But while David goes on to equate the bear with the unrepentant, uncircumcised Philistines, who have defied the "armies of the living God," the hope still lies in Isaiah that "the cow and the bear shall feed; their young shall lie down together."

That hope can be met only in the tamed, transformed bear. Before that could occur, however, it was necessary for the Church to present the bear as evil and vicious—witness the biblical descriptions. Saints became the instrument by which the bear could be overcome. Saint Ursula, for instance, is the central figure of an important medieval cycle of tales in the Catholic Church. She received her bear name from defending her 11,000 virgins against the bear's onslaught. The true test of any saint's power, however, was not merely in overcoming the bear, but in taming it.

Saint Sergius of Radonezh possessed miraculous powers over animals. He lived in a forest and shared his bread with a bear cub that eventually became tame, a story similar to Saint Gall's exchanging bread with a wild bear for wood to build his house. Saint Columba is usually shown with a palm branch and a bear on a chain. Saint Korbinian is also shown with a tame bear. He was riding to Rome with a packhorse that was attacked and killed by a bear; Korbinian forced the bear to carry his load to Rome.

Other medieval literature continued to represent the bear as an evil force that must be overcome or at least kept at bay, but it was given more definition than it received in the Bible, and began to symbolize one or more of the Seven Deadly Sins. This was especially true in a book like the *Ancrene Riwle,* a rulebook for cloistered

RESURRECTION, THE MADONNA,
AND THE DIVINE CHILD

Writing in the *Journal of American Folklore* in 1945, Marius Barbeau summarized the Eurasian and American mythology of the bear as having the following motifs: a mystic union between a human and a divinity, producing offspring who became intermediaries between men and a powerful god; the self-sacrifice and immolation of the supernatural Bear Father in order to benefit humans; a tradition of a sacramental feast on the flesh of the divine animal; and atonement, rituals, offerings, and prayers to the spirit of the sacred animal. He notes that the Laplanders called the male bear the "sacred man" and the female the "sacred virgin."

The classical scholar Lewis Farnell, writing of the Thracian/Greek oracles Zalmoxis and Trophonios, says, "A vegetation god was likely to have his annual appearances and disappearances, and one who lives in the dark beneath the earth might come at times to be regarded as dead or sleeping, at other times as awakened or revived.... The death of the god, followed no doubt by his resurrection, was an idea expressed in genuine Thracian ritual." Such a vegetation god was the sun king, accompanied by a mother-consort, the central theme of Frazer's *The Golden Bough*.

One may see in this widespread and diverse mythology a history of ideas and consciousness leading from the bear toward the divinities of the Mediterranean world, including the sacred mother and the son-king of the Near and Middle East, the genetrix whose son's inevitable death was a resonance of the two-season Mediterranean year. Just as in Bohemia, where the shrovetide bear is, says Frazer, a "corn spirit" in animal shape, a vegetation god, as suggested by Farnell, reflects the work of a deeper, seasonal power, a weather prophet associated with the sky, where the bear's great might was exercised. Perhaps the transition to a plant spirit is easily made from the bear because it is a plant-eater that is closely and seasonally linked to the calendar of plant growth and fruiting. Does the bear furnish the agricultural peoples with their earliest intuitions of the Great

Mother Earth, first worshiped in caves, whose sons must die like the withering grasses and whose daughters must be lost to the underworld with Persephone, like grain planted but not yet germinated? Perhaps the half-human, half-bear figurines venerated in Yugoslavia seven thousand years ago are tracks of the shift from animal to human images in human thought (allowing that the same process may have been in different stages at the same time in different parts of the world). Greek gods of non-Greek origin—Hecate, Cybele, Ishtar, and, notably, Artemis—each kept some bearish quality or power of the shadowy ancestor. Apollo the healer and "shining one," Demeter the "barley mother," Hermes the fertility and underworld guide, Themis the oracle of the sacred seasons, and many others absorbed and inherited different powers of the ancestral bear.

A long interval of complex and often obscure history separates the primordial bear, even the Bear Son, from later concepts of the god's resurrection. Even so, the Christian Madonna still occupies her cave in the sculpted grottoes of a thousand churchyards. A Byzantine illustration shows the ascent of Christ, his sarcophagus supported by bears. We cannot know whether these are the same bears with glowing eyes that Jung said were the renewing force of the deepest self, or those the Algonquins associated with the four points of the compass, or the four corners of Ursa Major. Perhaps the idea of eternally renewed life, alternating with death and descent into the lower world, is not *derived* from the example of the bear, but, because it is expressed in so many different cultures and languages, the example of the bear releases the concept from its culture bonds. The bear's example precedes all specific manmade ceremonies and stories of the perennial but transformed being who unites the poles of life and death. As Jung's associate C. Kerenyi says, "In the domain of myth is to be found not ordinary truth but a higher truth, which permits approaches to itself from the domain of *bios.*"

women written in the thirteenth century. The Seven Deadly Sins are represented as animals—the bear, seen as Sloth, perhaps recalls his somnolent character from the bestiaries. In a fifteenth-century illustration of Geoffrey Chaucer's *The Canterbury Tales,* Gluttony rides fat on a bear in "The Parson's Tale." Again, his character may be lifted from the bestiaries, where we are told that bears are constantly ravenous for honey: "Bears look out for the hives of bees and long for honeycombs very much. Nor do they grab anything else more greedily than honey." In another manuscript illumination, Luxuria (lasciviousness), another of the Seven Deadly Sins, rides astride a bear. At the same time, the bear is more directly associated with male sexuality—and Saint Peter Damian tells us that Pope Benedict was transformed into a bear in the afterlife in part for his carnal life on earth. The Church obviously believed in the myth, popularized by the bestiaries, that the bear copulates face to face, but more than that, the Church could not easily brush aside or forget the memory of the Old Norse legends of the bear as a human sexual partner.

Entering the world anew at the beginning of February, the bear became closely allied with the Christian holiday of light celebrated on February 2, Candlemas. Candlemas is the Christian occasion for celebrating new life, a time when the sun/son is welcomed back from its winter absence. According to Gaignabet, the bear signals that return:

> Candlemas itself falls just six weeks after the sun's deepest retreat into winter darkness, and six weeks is the length of the bear's sleep (both in Aristotle and, more important, in popular superstition). The bear has just emerged from his sleep of death. He is the prophet of the seasons, and his reappearance foretells the return of spring.

In southern France during the Middle Ages, at Arles-sur-Tech, a bear festival was performed on the Sunday immediately following Candlemas Day. A cave was constructed in the middle of the town square; a man dressed in a bearskin ran wildly through the streets, and a "victim," appointed by the townspeople, was seized by the bear and dragged into the cave. Inside the cave, a table was prepared with cakes and wines, and the bear and victim were ritually married there in the presence of all the townspeople. Perhaps not only was new life being celebrated here, but also a strengthening and reuniting of a belief in the connection between man and bear.

In Silesia, Hungary, and Carinthia, the feast of Candlemas is still called Bear's Day, and on that day the bear emerges from his den, the belief goes, to discover whether or not he has cast a shadow. If he casts a shadow, he must remove himself to his den for six more weeks of slumber.

In the tradition of the Arcadian bear cult of Mount Lykaion, the bear lost its shadow upon entering the cave, for the shadow symbolized the soul, and any being who dared enter the underworld of death must leave his soul there. Thus, if the bear has indeed entered the underworld, he must have left his shadow behind. If he emerges with any trace of shadow, he has obviously not slept the sleep of death and must return for another, longer try. Only when he has no trace of a shadow can he effectively announce the advent of spring—the continual rebirth of the land from the dead of winter.

Somehow the ritual observation was transferred to the badger, also a hibernant. The German immigrants to Pennsylvania used the groundhog, whose now obsolete scientific name, *Arctonys monax,* affirms its bearlike properties. Americans still anticipate February 2, Groundhog Day, to determine whether spring is just ahead or still six weeks off. In fact, what we yearn after is the sacred rite of spring— the miraculous possibility of the return of new life from the land of the dead.

The Catholic Church reaffirmed the archaic concept of the bear's maternal concern and care, its ability to promote its own transformations. All bears were now, in the eyes of the Church, females, emblematic of the *pietas materna*. The Church did not have to fetch its theory from afar. The bear's motherliness is even suggested grammatically in both Greek and Latin, where the word *bear* is feminine in gender. And, if Aristotle is to be believed, there would be no mature bears without the sow's primal, maternal intervention: "Having produced them [cubs], by licking them with her tongue she completes their warming and concocts them, matures them." Vergil is said to have compared his first drafts to bear cubs that needed revising and reshaping. Later observers of the bear embellished on Aristotle; they were convinced that bear cubs were born blind, hairy, and shapeless, a mere fat ball of fur. They concluded that the sow had to lick her cub forcefully into shape, or else the small cub would never develop into a mature bear.* Thus, Shakespeare gives us the following images: "So watchful Bruin forms, with plastic care, each growing lump, and brings it to a bear"; and "like to a chaos or an unlicked bear whelp." The French still use the phrase *ours mal leche,* a badly licked bear, to describe an incorrigible, ill-behaved child. The assumption behind the phrase seems to be that the mother had not performed her task well, hence the child needed to be shaped up, to be given a "licking," or "tongue lashing," to become bearable.†

J. L. Henderson points out that the ability of the sow to shape her cub out of *prima materia* finds a parallel in Pythagoras, who referred to she bears as "the hands of the Goddess Rhea—an allusion to the formative skill of Mother Nature who, like the mother bear, leads to beauty and perfection what was imperfect before." Christianity capitalized on both the bear's primal ability to express concern and care and to provide shape. The bear is the first animal in Christian tradition to be called "brother," because he cares for those in trouble. In his *Life of St. Francis,* Saint Bonaventure describes a monk, Florentius, who, in dire need of a guardian for his flock, prays for divine aid:

A bear appeared, and bowing his head to the ground and showing nothing hostile in his behavior, clearly gave it to be understood that he had come to serve the man of God. Florentius acquired great affection for the obliging beast and of his simplicity often called him "brother." The story of this pet, as of so many, has a sad ending, for jealous monks belonging to another monastery slaughtered the kindly creature.

---

*Evidence to refute the notion of a shapeless cub was first documented by Pietro Andrea Mattiali in his commentary on Dioscorides, in 1544, when he described a pregnant bear that had been cut open by huntsmen, and noted that cubs with distinctly formed limbs were found inside.
†The first instance indicated by *The Oxford English Dictionary* for the word *licking* in the sense of *whipping* is dated 1756. T. H. White, in his translation of the *Bestiary,* notes: "Until that period, the parents or schoolmasters who proposed to lick the young idea into shape were offering no threat: they were, on the contrary, referring to the gentle and maternal solicitude which Pope mentions playfully in his couplet, and to which Shakespeare refers. . . ."

Clemens Alexandrinus, one of the Church Fathers, who was born around A.D. 150, expanded the ursine symbol of care. For Alexandrinus, the bear's loving care makes him the perfect emblem of the Christian teacher; one of the most important lessons the bear teaches is piety. Gregory the Great tells how King Tortila found Cerbonius, Bishop of Populonia, giving shelter to some imperial soldiers; for that transgression he was sentenced to be eaten by a huge bear:

> Crowds such as attended the Roman circus gathered and the bishop was led forth. The bear was released and advanced toward the prelate, but suddenly abandoned his ferocity, bowed his neck, lowered his head in humble submission, and began to lick the bishop's feet. The crowd which had expected to witness the man's death loudly expressed their admiration and veneration.

The Middle Ages further refined the religious emblem of the bear; he came ironically to stand for Christianity itself. After all, the Church provided the means for spiritual shaping; it offered guidance and presented a model for the novitiate. The Church was, moreover, responsible for rescuing its members from moral and spiritual death, for reforming and regenerating heathens. The idea has some historical antecedents: in the Icelandic *Eyrbyggia Saga,* one character is called *eigi einhamr,* "not of one shape," until he is converted to Christianity. The bear is thus identified with well-being in general, with recovery from spiritual malaise and physical illness, and, in dire cases, with rebirth from a spiritual death.

His healing, magical power periodically resurfaced, in medieval poems such as *William of Palerne,* divested of its Christian cover. This poem, first written in the twelfth century in France, was translated into English soon after 1350, and was rewritten back into French as a prose romance in the sixteenth century. Its long and peripatetic history attests to the popularity of its story: Prince William is stolen as a child by a werewolf to save him from a murder plot. After diligently raising the young prince, the werewolf helps William to elope with his love, Melior. In order to escape safely, the couple must wear bearskins as protection against evildoers.

The Fables

Fables became popular during the High Middle Ages, and their appeal continued strongly through the Renaissance. Drawing on Aesop as a source, the fabulists dramatized the characteristics of the bear as they found them in twelfth-century bestiaries. The bear is still shown as sometimes mean, sometimes friendly, but he is never simply a wild animal, admired for his "bearness." Rather, he exists for us to learn our daily moral lesson.

Whether Aesop actually lived is a subject for scholarly debate. Most historians describe him as a Greek slave who was freed in the sixth century B.C., and who used his fables to point out the injustices of contemporary society. The earliest collection of Aesop comes to us from the Latin poet Phaedrus, a slave who was freed by Augustus. Babrius, the second-century poet, provides the first Greek translation, which already seems to exhibit influence from its travels to India, possibly from the fables of Pilpay, animal stories derived from the *Panchatantra*. One of those Indian fables, "The Gardener and the Bear," underscores the bear's benevolent but dumb nature.

> A gardener loved nature so much that he left the company of men for plants and flowers. He had no wife, no children, but his garden became a terrestrial paradise. He grew lonely, however, and decided to search for a companion. The next day he traveled to the foot of a great mountain, and there spotted a bear, who looked warm and friendly. They quickly became fast friends, living together, the bear protecting his gardener friend. When the gardener fell asleep one warm afternoon, the bear remained awake, shooing flies from the gardener's face. One persistent fly would not leave, so the bear swatted it with a large rock, breaking two of the gardener's front teeth. This fable, told to Damna the fox by his wife, Kalila, carries this moral: Better to have prudent enemies than ignorant friends.

Aesop's fables were printed in England by William Caxton in 1484. By that time, however, the bear had already appeared throughout medieval Europe in a wide range of animal stories. He is Bruno the bear in *Ysengrim*, a 6,000-line poem written in Flanders by Navardus of Ghent about 1150, which details the adventures of several animals: Ysengrim the wolf, Reinardus the fox, Grimus the boar, and the gullible Bruno. One of Aesop's fables, "The Bear and the Fox," gave rise to the *Roman de Renart,* a French poem of some 30,000 lines printed in installments between 1170 and 1250, in which the bear plays a leading role. These stories about two animals, the wily fox and his naive bear friend, provided the model for many other Reynard adventures during the thirteenth and fourteenth centuries in France and Germany which continued in popularity through the Renaissance and finally worked their way into the present-day Uncle Remus tales.

In "The Bear and the Fox," the bear comes off once again as an innocent, silly, but well-meaning creature: Bear boasts to Fox of his excessive love of man, saying he never worried him or mauled him— when he was dead. Fox observes with a smile: "I should have thought more of your profession, if you never ate him alive." Aesop appends this pithy moral: Better to save a man from dying than salve him when dead.

But for Aesop, the bear is not merely a dumb creature; he also exhibits greed. In "The Lion and the Bear and the Fox," the lion and the bear discover a carcass of a fawn, and fall to fighting over its disposal. After a long and bloody fight, the lion and the bear, half dead and half blind, find they are too tired to touch their prize. A fox comes by, sees how tired and helpless both creatures are, and carries off the booty. Bear speaks the moral: "Poor creatures as we are, exhausting our strength and tiring each other to give a rogue a dinner." So while the bear is greedy, he at least has the good sense to realize both of their mistakes. The reader must give the bear at least some credit.

The bear's stock characteristics in Aesop were picked up by the writers of Renaissance emblem books, descriptions of the plant and animal kingdom, each with its own emblematic service. One such book, the *Minerva Britana,* compiled by Henry Peacham in 1612, combines both the bear's ferocity and his friendliness in a fable derived from Aesop titled "The Two Fellows and the Bear":

> Two friends there were that did their journey take,
> And by the way, they made a vow to either,
> What'er befell, they never would forsake,
> But as sworn brethren, live and die together:

Thus wandering through deserts, here and there,
By chance they met a great and ugly *Bear*.
At whom, amazed with a deadly fear,
One leaves his friend, and climbeth up a tree:
The other falls down flat before the *Bear,*
And keeps his breath, that seeming dead to be,
The *Bear* forsook him (for his nature's such,
A breathless body never once to touch.)
The beast departing, and the danger past,
The dead arose, and leapt along his way:
His fellow leaping from the tree at last,
Asked what the *Bear,* in's ear did whispering say,
Quoth he, he bade me, evermore take heed,
Of such as thou, that failest in time of need.

The friend who feigns death here reenacts perhaps the bear's miraculous return from his own cave-death each year. The bear's advice, "a friend in need is a friend indeed," recalls the perception of the bear as an animal of practical wisdom. But the bear is not always viewed as a wise or benign animal—especially in the Reynard cycle, a series of animal stories that arose in the twelfth century around the border of France and Flanders, and which were retold in many collections in the Renaissance. Most of the tales pit Reynard the Fox against Isengrim the Wolf. In some of these tales, however, the wily fox beguiles the innocent, gullible Bruin the Bear.

The folklorist Stith Thompson lists five basic bear tales in the Reynard cycle, and in each of them the bear is duped. In the first, a fox sees a man hauling a load of fish, and plays dead in the road. The man loads the fox onto the back of a wagon, enabling the fox to eat the fish. Fox tells bear, who tries the same trick and is killed by the wagon. In the second, fox persuades bear to fish through the ice. Bear attempts it, freezes fast to the ice, and loses his tail. This version, Thompson points out, is sometimes used in folklore to explain why the bear's tail is so short. The third is a continuation of the second: Fox enters a woman's house and tells her about bear on the ice. While she goes out to catch bear, fox devours her milk and butter. She returns, and drives out fox by beating him with a dish. Covered with butter, fox convinces bear that his brains have been knocked out. In the fourth, fox feigns illness. Out of sympathy, bear carries fox on his back. In the fifth version, bear chases fox, who escapes under the roots of a tree. Bear catches fox, and just as he is about to bite his leg, fox yells, "It's only a root." Bear lets loose, and they go their separate ways.

There are two variations. Fox established a bet as to who can name three different trees. Bear naïvely names three varieties of the same tree. In the second variation, bear sees magpie and envies its colors. Fox offers to paint bear. Bear lies down on a haystack, which fox promptly sets on fire. This version is sometimes used to explain why the bear's fur seems to have a slightly gray, singed appearance.

There are three other types of bear tales, derived from the Reynard tales, which are better known in parts of the world other than central Europe. The following story, for example, is found in most parts of Asia, throughout Africa, in Negro, Spanish, Portuguese, and French traditions in America, and among the North American Indians:

Fox pretends to be excited about being the godfather of a child, and insists he must keep leaving bear's company to see the newborn infant. Actually, he leaves to steal honey that he and bear have stored in common. Eact time fox returns to the cave, after having stolen some of their mutually owned honey, bear asks fox for the name of the child. Fox replies obliquely. He first says, "Well Begun"; after his second round of stealing he answers that the name of the child is "Half Done"; and then "Almost Gone"; and so on. Bear finally realizes that he's been tricked, and starts to fight with fox. At the end of the fight, the badly beaten fox smears bear's nose with honey in a vain attempt at victory.

In the second bear tale, fox disguises himself and violates a she-bear who has gotten herself hopelessly caught in the crotch of a tree. To add insult to injury, fox then covers himself with soot and impersonates a pastor and offers condolences to the distraught she-bear. He even offers graciously to find a nursemaid for the bear's distraught cubs. Fox, of course, takes the job himself and, in the final insult, eats the cubs. Later, bear builds a house of wood, and fox one of ice. They live comfortably through the winter, but in the summer, when the fox's house begins to melt, he tries to drive the bear out of his house. Finally there is a third, rather pale story in which fox persuades bear to bite the tail of what appears to be a dead horse. To humor fox, and because he is good-natured, bear agrees. The horse awakens from his sleep and drags away the bear.

The *Roman de Renart*, a beast epic, is carefully calculated to satirize feudal institutions. The big and burly bear must be portrayed as a naïve and dumb creature, even though he in fact possesses uncanny ability to avoid man's traps and snares in the wild. The small, defenseless fox needs to hoodwink the powerful bear. In the poem's political context, the wily but weaker fox is cast as a poor peasant, courageous enough to outsmart the fat and dumb aristocracy. There is further irony here if we recall that the bear is fundamentally connected with the first royal house in the Arthurian romances, later with Guy of Warwick, sometimes called the Kingmaker, and also with the aristocratic families of the Earl of Kent and the Earl of Leicester. Besides being satiric, these tales deliver an arsenal of morals: size doesn't ultimately matter; don't be too gullible or good-natured; and on and on. It is the fox who drives these lessons home through his schemes and elaborate plots. He appears to be the hero.

But on close reading the bear turns out to be more humane than the other animals in the *Roman de Renart*. While the fox is a type, an embodiment of wile and deceit, the bear on occasion feels sympathy and compassion; he forgives. Ultimately the bear wins our sympathy. The fox exhibits the same behavior in each of the Reynard fables, making it easier in the long run to dismiss him as one-dimensional; the bear is more ambiguous, easier to take to our hearts. A. A. Milne's popular *Winnie-the-Pooh,* which appeared some seven centuries later, capitalizes on the same endearing, naïve, but compassionate soul. Milne credits the Reynard stories with providing inspiration for Winnie and his friends. Another modern favorite, Paddington, demonstrates a similar compassionate, caring bear-soul. The bear's capacity for human emotions sets him apart.

Bears do not generally appear in the popular literature of France and England from the seventeenth to the nineteenth centuries, because they are not a part of the classical Greek or Latin traditions from which these literatures draw. But they clearly star in the fables. Jean de La Fontaine, the seventeenth-century poet, wrote moralized fables that also rely on Aesop for their source. First published in 1668, his *Fables* may provide the origin of our phrase "a bear market" to refer to investors who sell high now, in the hopes of buying the same thing later at a lower price. In Fable 20, "The Bear and the Two Schemers," La Fontaine points out the dangers of such a practice:

> Two schemers whose purse had grown thin
> Sold to a nearby furrier
> A live bear's serviceable skin;
> As experts, they'd bring him down; at least they said they
> were,
> And swore he'd be the best one ever subdued by guns,
> A furrier's bonanza—immense wealth all at once—
> Furred till impervious to frost however keen;
> And fur for more than just one coat should be a boon.
> Dindenaut prized his sheep less than these men their bear:
> Theirs in their eyes, but not in bruin's sight.
> They'd be back in two days and have had time to spare,
> Then after the hunt, set a price that would be right.
> The quarry was found, shuffled toward them at a trot;
> The men stood as if halted by a cannonball.
> The contract hung fire, and neither could recall
> Why they'd come out or that the bear was to be shot.
> One climbed a tree to the top (the one by whom the skin
> had been sold).
> The other, like marble—even more cold—
> Played dead, face to the ground, lying prone,
> Since he'd heard that a bear against which to guard,
> Is inclined to let alone
> A body that has no life, does not move or breathe hard.
> Master Bear, like a fool, was taken in by the ruse,
> Saw the rigid form devoid of mobility
> And, fearing some kind of trickery,
> Rolled it over, back again, brought his nose close
> To the nostrils to see if breath went in.
> "It is a corpse," he said. "I'll make off, to escape the stench."
> Whereupon the bear sauntered toward the woods again.
> One of our two fur dealers came down from his branch,
> Ran to his friend and said, "Narrow escape you've had,
> But you weren't mauled, and suffered mere fright after all.
> Well and good"; then, "What about the skin of the animal?
> When he whispered, what was it he said?
> His nose very nearly touched your ear
> As he rolled you here and there."

—"What he said was, 'It might cost you dear
To sell a bear's skin before killing the bear.' "

La Fontaine's little story brings to a close the interest in fables; for him, the bear stands as an innocent, stupid bystander, animating the greed of the merchants. Seemingly more intelligent than his human consorts—though perhaps more gullible—the bear utters the moral. But he is clearly on his way out—a cash commodity. We only smile at his wisdom, for it is a message of the marketplace, not the woods. He has nothing to tell us about our souls, only about our pocketbooks.

Not until nineteenth-century romanticism, with the influence of Lamarck and Darwin, coupled with a growing interest in national preserves and the protection of wild animals, does the bear reemerge into literature. In the literature of the Romantics, large, wild animals begin to express God's powerful aspects. William Blake's "Tyger" is probably the most familiar example. Where the bear still roamed wild and people had close contact with him, for instance in America, he appeared, with more frequency, to symbolize grand ideas, like the majesty of the land, freedom, and even God himself.

Fairy Tales

Fairy tales are closer to us in time than Reynard and Aesop, and so perhaps are more familiar. Many have bears as central characters, and the two most popular tales might help us to understand the bear in all fairy tales. "Goldilocks and the Three Bears," the more popular of the two, will serve as one illustration; "East of the Sun and West of the Moon" the other. Though one earlier version exists, Robert Southey is usually credited with publishing "Goldilocks" in 1837. The tale is interesting for several reasons. First, the bears are upstanding and honest: when they leave their house for a walk in the woods, they do not lock the front door "because the Bears were good Bears, who did nobody any harm, and never suspected that anybody would harm them." And "they were good Bears—a little rough or so, as the manner of Bears is, but for all that very good-natured and hospitable."

Second, in Southey's version of the story the human character is an old woman, who intrudes on the bears—they are minding their

A CHILD'S SONG

Grizzly Bear

If you ever, ever meet a grizzly bear,
You must never, never, never ask him *where*
He is going,
or *what* he is doing;
For if you ever, ever, dare
To stop a grizzly bear,
You will never meet *another* grizzly bear.

own business—and *she* is lost and dishonest. The bears form a strong familial unit. In *Mother Goose's Fairy Tales of 1878,* Great Huge Bear, Middle Bear, and Little, Small, Wee Bear become Father, Mother, and Baby Bear. They live in an appropriate house, with food and furniture, and are generally pictured wearing clothes. (In a Norwegian version of the tale, the bears are in actuality three Russian princes who live in a cave and at night cast off their bearskins.) Father Bear asserts his authority—even speaking in boldface type in Southey's story—while the child grows more and more upset.

Southey gives his version of "Goldilocks" a moral ending. We are told that the old woman jumped out the bedchamber window, "and whether she broke her neck in the fall; or ran into the wood and was lost there; or found her way out of the wood, and was taken up by the constable and sent to the House of Correction for a vagrant as she was, I cannot tell. But the Three Bears never say anything more of her." The bears' relationship is perhaps strengthened by going through the ordeal presented by the old lady intruder.

"Goldilocks" begs for psychological interpretation; Bruno Bettelheim responds in *The Uses of Enchantment: The Meaning and Importance of Fairy Tales:*

With this spelled-out designation of the beasts as forming a family, the story unconsciously came to relate much more closely to the

Oedipal situation. . . . The intruder is seen to interfere with the integration of the basic family constellation, and thus is threatening to the family's emotional security.

Fairy tales that describe families surviving visits from an alien, disrupting force may enable a child to lay to rest fears about its own family falling apart. Indeed, Momma and Poppa Bear are admirable models of parental authority: they are strong; they take action; they settle things. Baby Bear remains safe. In a sense, they resemble modern, fantastical super-heroes—in an average family. Perhaps it is this combination that appeals to the speaker in the first stanza of Greg Kuzma's contemporary poem "In Love with the Bears," a nostalgic celebration of that famous Momma, Poppa, and Baby:

> To see them coming headstrong
> battering the air
> home to Goldilocks and three chairs
> three bowls of porridge
> three beds
> taking the steps three at a time
> barging into the rooms
> this is what I grew up on
> three bears with nothing to do
> no terror of woods each with
> a small anger toward the usurpers
> that easy knowledge of something
> taken and not returned
> something broken and not fixed
> something pressed
> in which the hump still lay
>
> Now years later I love them for what
> they are
> the common stutter of their fears
> the worse stutter of their deeds
> capable of being neighbors
> capable of running for a short ways
> essentially speechless
> their fur hooked by thorns
> wearing shabby coats
> and passing in the street

> sometimes glad to greet me
> sometimes afraid to meet me with
>   their eyes

In the second stanza, the speaker has grown up, and the bears, too, have grown older. While their coats may look shabby, "their fur hooked by thorns," they still hold meaning for the speaker. For the bears did what they needed to do at the moment: they ejected the intruder from their idyllic world. Now, like the speaker, the mature bears struggle into reality, "capable of being neighbors"— capable, that is, of moving into the world of everyday details. In their tentativeness and fear, their imperfection, they fall short of their earlier image. But perhaps that makes them all the more heroic. Thus the heart of the poem: if the speaker can only maintain his feeling—"I love them for what they are"—then he may more easily accept himself. So if the bears are sometimes frightened to look the speaker directly in the eyes, it is only because the speaker, too, is sometimes frightened to look at them.

For Bettelheim, fear of another kind underlies "East of the Sun and West of the Moon," the other important fairy tale in which the bear stars. This tale belongs to a genre known as the animal as groom, stories in which young, beautiful girls marry only to find that on their wedding night, in bed, their husbands have become ugly monsters—in many versions, a grotesque bear. W. R. S. Ralston published an article in the nineteenth century entitled "Beauty and the Beast" to document the pervasiveness of this genre. He outlined a number of tales, popular in such disparate places as Norway, Germany, Sicily, India, Russia, Crete, and Mongolia, in which young girls marry a variety of animals, including wolves, monkeys, goats, and bears.

Bettelheim has argued that these animal/groom tales are crucial for a child's emotional health, for they provide necessary psychological conditioning by objectifying normal sexual anxieties. The desired result is happiness through satisfaction:

> [They] offer the child the strength to realize that his fears are the creation of his anxious sexual fantasies; and that while sex may at first seem beastlike, in reality love between man and woman is the most satisfying of all emotions, and the only one which makes for permanent happiness.

Fairy tales promote feelings of satisfaction when the young bride successfully passes certain tests. If she agrees, for instance, to be nice, to kiss her animal mate, or to lick his nose or snout—that is, to overcome her feelings of fear or disgust and revulsion—then her groom can be transformed miraculously back into a handsome prince.

The Grimm's fairy tale "Snow White and Rose Red" allows the child to glimpse that transformation. One winter, the story goes, a bear visits the home of Snow White and Rose Red. Their mother, a poor widow, invites the bear inside to warm himself by the fire and urges her daughters not to fear the huge animal. The bear stays the winter, sleeping in the house each night, in a kind of domestic hibernation, and leaving each day in search of food.

Meanwhile, the young daughters undergo three adventures with a wicked dwarf, helping him out of trouble on three separate occasions. After the first two rescues, the dwarf swears and curses at the two girls. After the last, the dwarf becomes more enraged at their good nature and threatens to kill the two kind sisters, but at the final second the bear intervenes, strikes the dwarf with his mighty paw, and kills him. At that same instant, the bear changes into a prince, and explains to the astonished Snow White and Rose Red that the dwarf had placed him under a magic spell that prevented him from ever again becoming a prince until his spellbinder had died. Unwittingly, the two sisters have saved the prince. Despite the dwarf's unkindly treatment of them, the two girls willingly helped him out of trouble: they clearly personify absolute, unconditional love, the force of which ultimately makes possible the transformation of the bear/prince. At the story's tidy conclusion, Snow White marries the prince and Rose Red marries the prince's brother— putting into practice the poor widow's advice to her two daughters: "What one has she must share with the other."

In the stories from the North, as in the well-known Norwegian fairy tale "East of the Sun and West of the Moon," the lover assumes the form of a bear only by day.* The story, collected by Andrew Lang in the late nineteenth century, tells of a white bear who one autumn morning raps on the window of a poor farmer's house,

---

*In a Norwegian variant of "Goldilocks," a princess stumbles upon a cave inhabited by three bears. Entering, she finds a meal waiting on the table, which she devours, and then she falls asleep under one of the beds. The bears arrive home and turn out to be Russian princes who during the day wear bearskins.

promising to make the old man rich if he will only consent to give him his youngest, and prettiest, daughter. Torn between her fear of the bear and her wish to provide her family with wealth, the daughter finally agrees to leave with White Bear, who takes her to live with him in a beautiful castle built inside a huge mountain.

When she lies down each night and snuffs the candle, a man arrives in her bed, and he always departs before dawn breaks. She never actually sees him, for he comes in the dark and leaves in the dark, but we are told "it was the White Bear, who cast off the form of a beast during the night." After a time, the young girl grows homesick; the bear agrees to carry her home for a visit if she will promise never to talk to her mother in private about her new life.

Back with her parents, who now live in regal splendor, she breaks her promise and tells her mother how happy she would be if only she could glimpse the White Bear when he is a man. "Oh," cries the mother in horror, "he is very likely a troll. You shall have a bit of one of my candles. Look at him when he is asleep, but take care not to allow any tallow to drop on him."

The next night, back in bed in her bear castle, she holds the candle over her lover only to discover the handsomest young prince she has ever seen. She leans over to kiss him, and by accident three drops of wax fall on his chest. He awakens in horror and admonishes her for inspecting him, for, as he explains, his stepmother has placed him under a spell to live as a bear by day and as a man by night— for one full year. Had the young girl only waited, he tells her, they would have been able to marry. Now he must wed an ugly troll princess with a nose three ells long, who lives in a castle east of the sun and west of the moon.

The young girl, full of remorse and shame, promises to follow the prince. After many complicated adventures, in the last of which she rides on the back of the North Wind to the distant castle, she is reunited with her prince, who presents her with a final task: she must wash the tallow from his shirt—a deed that trolls find impossible to accomplish, but that Christians perform with ease. She removes the tallow with great finesse, and the stepmother and the ugly princess with the nose three ells long both explode instantly. The happy prince promises to marry the girl, assuring her that he will remain a man both day and night.

Bettelheim points out that the young girl is willing to break her promise—to remain silent about her life with the bear—because of a powerful desire to know about her lover's animal nature. Bettelheim's psychological interpretations presuppose that the bear always frightens us and that we must overcome deep feelings of repulsion and disgust to know its beauty. His conclusions indicate the great distance we have come from ancient bear ceremonies in which performers merge with bears. But Bettelheim may fall short of the complete truth. The bear in "Snow White and Rose Red" is indeed described as frightening, but he is also friendly and protective; the young girl in "East of the Sun and West of the Moon" is certainly terrified by White Bear, but he is also described as gorgeous. It may just be that these bears would not be so attractive if they were not so frightening.

In addition to allaying fears about human aggression, then, these fairy tales may also reveal a primitive desire for that animal spirit, as the contemporary poet Denise Levertov recognizes in her embellishment of "Snow White and Rose Red," aptly entitled "An Embroidery." Levertov strips away every event, detail, and character from the fairy tale—even the presence of the protecting and instructing mother—that does not illuminate Snow White and Rose Red's longing for bears and bear husbands.

She also reverses significant details. In the fairy tale, Snow White is a stay-at-home, content to remain with her mother and attend to domestic duties; Rose Red runs in the woods all day with the little animals; Snow White, "quiet and good," is rewarded by marrying the bear/prince. Levertov, on the other hand, stresses Rose Red's uninhibited nature, and—unlike what happens in the fairy tale, where gentility and domesticity are rewarded with marriages that endure happily ever after—Rose Red's ardent heart and burning cheeks find immediate fulfillment. Not only is the bear simply attractive, then, but his powerful strength and sexuality—his primal being—make him an object of desire.

The Roses have matured past any anxiety that may be reflected in the fairy tales, and so the bear does not have to be invited into the house. He opens the door and lies down by the fire. Rose Red gives in to her fantasy: at the poem's end, she dissolves into the Bear Mother, dreaming herself back into "a cave that smells of honey," where she combs "the fur of her cubs/with a golden comb." Rose White lies awake, thinking about the husband who might step out of the bear's hide. For Levertov, the two sisters are perhaps best seen as twin aspects of love—one drawn from the most primal and powerful myth, the other born in reality. Both are necessary for an accurate embroidery:

> Rose Red's hair is brown as fur
> and shines in firelight as she prepares
> supper of honey and apples, curds and whey,
> for the bear, and leaves it ready
> on the hearth-stone
>
> Rose White's grey eyes
> look into the dark forest.
>
> Rose Red's cheeks are burning,
> sign of her ardent, joyful
> compassionate heart.
> Rose White is pale,
> turning away when she hears
> the bear's paw on the latch.
>
> When he enters, there is
> frost on his fur,
> he draws near to the fire
> giving off sparks.
>
> Rose White catches the scent of the forest,
> of mushrooms, of rosin.
>
> Together Rose Red and Rose White
> sing to the bear;
> it is a cradle song, a loom song,
> a song about marriage, about
> a pilgrimage, to the mountains
> long ago.
>   Raised on an elbow,
> the bear stretched on the hearth
> nods and hums; soon he sighs
> and puts down his head.
>
> He sleeps; the Roses
> bank the fire.
> Sunk in the clouds of their feather bed
> they prepare to dream.

Rose Red in a cave that smells of honey
dreams she is combing the fur of her cubs
with a golden comb.
Rose White is lying awake.

Rose White shall marry the bear's brother.
Shall he too
when the time is ripe,
step from the bear's hide?
Is that other, her bridegroom,
here in the room?

Fairy tales are both serious and fun, tough-minded and at the same time humorous. Perhaps they became so popular because they seemed to fit so perfectly the tastes of the later nineteenth century. Like Charles Dickens's novels, they consist of dramatic stories alive with quirky, eccentric characters, but they are far from chaotic. Their neat endings leave the reader with a subtle but satisfying taste of morality. In Grimm's "The Willow-Wren and the Bear" (sometimes retold as "The Bear and the Kingbird"), for example, two tiny wrens launch a battle royal against all the four-footed animals when the bear calls the wrens' children "disreputable." King and Queen Wren lead all the winged creatures, while Commander Bear and General Fox direct the animals. In a humorous battle that follows, in which only three gnat stings are delivered—all three to the fox's behind—King and Queen Wren cause such a commotion that the rest of the forest folk retreat in fear. Humiliated, Commander Bear is forced to humble himself in front of the little wrens and apologize for his former, dumb-bear behavior. The mighty bear has been toppled, and justice triumphs. Peace reigns once more.

Eccentric behavior appealed to Victorian and Edwardian England because it illuminated so well its mannered, stylized life. People eat like pigs, laugh like hyenas, yammer like crows, insult each other like dumb bears and highfalutin foxes. The bully and the bear both act like beasts. Rudyard Kipling's *Jungle Book*, published in 1894, capitalizes on the literary possibilities of exposing a pretentious, highly mannered society by weaving a string of animal tales, interlaced with humor and morality. A strict code of law permeates even the jungle, and it is administered by Baloo, the schoolmasterly bear.

But while the Victorians like Kipling could find a spot in their hearts for Baloo, the wise and benevolent master, they also knew that sentimentality must be guarded against. One could respond too strongly and fully to the seductive call of the wild. We can turn once more to Kipling for that warning, in a poem titled "The Truce of the Bear," a statement against the Tsar's overtures of peace and friendship.* The poem advises against an open-hearted trust of the wild, or even more, against surrender to a self-aggrandizing sense of pity:

· ·
Horrible, hairy, human, with paws like hands in prayer,
Making his supplication rose Adam-Zad the Bear!
I looked at the swaying shoulders, at the paunch's swag and swing,
And my heart was touched with pity for the monstrous, pleading
    thing.
Touched with pity and wonder, I did not fire then.
· ·
I have looked no more on women—I have walked no more with
    men,
Nearer he tottered and nearer, with paws like hands that pray,
From brow to jaw that still-shod paw, it ripped my face away.
· ·

Folk Tales and Customs in America

In America, the "law of the jungle" was enacted on its frontiers. In the West this was staged as a fight to the death between a bull and a bear, a sport made popular in the Middle Ages.

This entertainment, which can ultimately be traced back to ancient Rome—Theodora, wife of Justinian, was in fact the daughter of

*The bear as symbol of the Russian state seems not to have been chosen by the Russians themselves but to have been invented by French writers of the nineteenth century, particularly the Marquis Adolph de Custin. He introduced the Russians to French readers as a wild, powerful, backward people who, in their huge bear-fur coats, made the streets of Moscow resemble a "zoo." In addition, the tall, strong, bearlike figures often greeted each other with a hearty embrace, or bear hug.

the bear-keeper at the Constantinople Hippodrome—delighted the medievals, who loved to watch spectacle fraught with Christian significance. Medieval audiences thrived on graphic presentations, and thus were eager to see acted out the taming of the wild bear. In one of medieval England's favorite sports, bear-baiting, they got their chance. There, they could see evil, the devil, or one of the Seven Deadly Sins overcome by man's determination and perseverance. Several bear-baiting rings survived into Chaucer's London, and in Southwark, in St. Saviour's Parish, there were also two bear gardens. The first house for bear-baiting was built in England sometime in the middle of the sixteenth century; and it is perhaps an irony of history that, like the bear, it, too, was transformed—from a place of ugliness and pain to the first English theater house. To advertise a bear-baiting, the medievalist Beryl Rowland points out, "a bear-ward would parade the streets with his bear and in order to excite interest would demonstrate the ferocity of his charge. Illustrations of the bear and his leader which appear on misericords and in manuscripts testify to the friction between the warden and the bear, and the warden often holds a cudgel or whip." In a typical fight, a bear would be chained to a sturdy tree in the center of a ring. He would then be blinded, and baited with dogs. Five or six men would then encircle the bear, whipping him, while he was forced to defend himself, or in the process he might have to dance to music. The bear received his dance training by being forced to walk on hot plates.

In California, the grizzly became the object of a spectacle that flourished there from 1816 to the early 1880s. In arenas up and down the coast, in a modified version of medieval bear-baiting, bears were pitted against wild bulls on sunny Sunday afternoons, on holidays, and on religious festival days. On a typical afternoon, posters and advertisements could be seen announcing fights at San Juan Capistrano, San Gabriel, San Bernardino, Oakland, San Francisco, Nevada City, Carmel, San Jose, and countless other towns and cities. The event was so popular that in most of these places a special arena was constructed, enclosed by a strong wooden fence with a raised platform for the audience; sometimes the *plaza mayor* was utilized, or sometimes the town's mission. The bulls used were Spanish bulls, which one observer called "the noblest game in America, with possibly the single exception of the . . . California Grizzly. He knows no fear, and shrinks from no enemy, having been accustomed all his life to fighting his rivals and other formidable animals. . . . He will come a mile for his enemy, and will as lief charge a hundred men at once." The bear and its most formidable match, the Spanish bull, fought, then, in much the same way that two rival heavyweight boxers would be matched in a modern-day "fight of the century."

The bear and the bull were introduced into the arena, the hind foot of the bear tied by a leather cord to a forefoot of the bull, both to keep the animals at fighting range and to discourage the bear from bounding over the fence. Then assistants withdrew from the arena and, as a contemporary account observes, the action began:

> The bull roared, pawed the earth, flung his head in the air, and at every moment seemed inclined to escape, but a lasso checked his course, and brought both of them with a sudden jerk to the ground. Bruin, careless of the scene around him, looked with indifference upon his enemy . . . but the jerk of the lasso aroused him as if to a sense of danger, and [he] rose up on his hind legs, in the posture of defense.

If the grizzly refused to fight, which sometimes happened, an assistant leaped into the arena and goaded him with a stick that had nails protruding from its end. But usually, according to contemporary accounts, the bull would paw around the arena a couple of times, gaze hard at the bear, then charge, head lowered, full speed. The bear typically held its ground: "The usual way by which the bear countered the bull was to crouch and, as the horns smashed against his own ribs, sink his teeth into the opponent's sensitive nose, swing his arm over and behind the head, and squeeze mightily." The grizzly might be bowled over by the impact, but there were times when the grizzly would turn the bull's head with such force that he would immediately snap its spine. While the record of wins and losses is hazy, one study that totted up the results of all the recorded fights found that more often than not the winner was the bear.

An unusual bear-and-bull fight occurred in Mexico between a bear named Samson, which belonged to Grizzly Adams, and a Spanish bull. Albert Evans, an eyewitness to the fight, provides this description:

In January, 1870, I saw that . . . bear . . . dig a hole large enough
to hold an elephant, take a bull which had been sent to fight him
in his paws as if he were an infant, carry him to the pit, hurl him
into it head foremost, slap him in the side with his tremendous
paws until his breath was half knocked out of his body, and then
hold him down with one paw while he deliberately buried him
alive by raking the earth down upon him with the other.

To stage these fights, grizzlies were captured by an Easterner
named Capen Adams—better known as Grizzly Adams. Born in
Massachusetts in 1812, Adams headed out at an early age for the
mountains of Montana, Utah, and California. While it is difficult
to separate fact from his own fanciful accounts and the legends that
surrounded him—witness the description above of Samson's fight
with the bull in Mexico—Adams was adept at capturing bears, wild-
cats, foxes, and birds—all alive. His specialty, however, was killing
mother bears and carrying off their cubs, training them to carry
loads and to walk on a leash. He periodically staged wrestling matches
in various coastal cities, in which he would do battle with a huge
grizzly until he had pinned it to the ground for the count of three.
Later he arrived in towns with a menagerie of animals and showed
them in a tent for a small admission price. But his most startling
act consisted simply of leaving his San Francisco apartment and
walking down the streets accompanied by his two closest friends,
Ben Franklin and Lady Washington, a pair of grizzlies.

Adams's feats of taming the bear in the nineteenth century embodied our fast-growing mastery over the country's wilderness. While
stories and hearsay about hunting this king of beasts abounded in
the popular journals, the bear hunt reached serious literature when
Washington Irving wrote a dramatic account of two buckskin-clad
hunters confronting a huge grizzly in the Rockies, "Adventures of
William Cannon and John Day with Grizzly Bears," collected in his
book *Astoria* (1836), a history of the post, which was founded by
Lewis and Clark as Fort Clatstop on their 1805 expedition. But the
spirit of Grizzly Adams, the man who could work miracles with
bears and who took as his own name the appellation "Grizzly," was
kept alive, in literature at least, by the famous California poet Bret
Harte. Besides a poem titled "Grizzly," Harte wrote an intriguing
short sketch about Sylvester, a grizzly cub that was kept as a pet in

a California mining camp, which he published in *Tales of the Argonauts* in 1875.

To move from a serious to a humorous strain in the literature, we must leave California for New England and the Southwest, and in so doing we pass through an important piece of Southwestern literature—more properly called a legend, though it was published in numerous places—the story of Juan Oso, or John Bear. A modern retelling of the Bear Mother and Bear Son stories, interspersed with bits and pieces of Norse legends, it may provide the link between the serious Western stories and the literature of the Southwest humorists.

The story of Juan Oso follows these general lines. A young woman named Consuela lived with her mother and father in a remote part of the rugged Sierras. One day, as she was filling her *olla* at a stream, she felt a large arm around her waist; she turned to discover a bear. He carried her off to his cave in the wildest part of the mountains. The bear fed the woman berries and venison and, in time, allowed Consuela to accompany him to gather food. They seem to have achieved a believable domestic arrangement. Frank Dobie, the nature writer, matter-of-factly observes:

> The bear is more like a man than any other animal. He can walk upright; he has hands to use; he eats the same food that *cristianos* eat, his brain is quick to understand. No, it is not impossible that a bear and a *cristiano* could live together.

After a year, Consuela gave birth; from the waist up, the child was a boy, from the waist down, a bear. When the boy was six— now faster, smarter, stronger, and bigger than other six-year-olds— he inquired about his mother's home before the cave. She explained about humans and houses and hearths. The boy pleaded to visit the world of people, and Consuela finally relented. She dressed him in skins to disguise his hirsute identity, and one day they both escaped from the bear. She told her people about her stay with the bear, and they, though initially skeptical, believed her when they saw the naked boy. He was taken to a *cura* and christened Juan Oso.

The rest of the story of Juan Oso recounts his adventures in the mountains, usually with his cane of pure iron that weighed two tons. In most versions, Juan Oso meets and defeats a black devil who lives in the bottom of a deep cavern, and rescues from the devil four beautiful sisters. The prettiest of them, a prince's daughter, is given as reward to Juan Oso. The couple, bear-groom and wife, live happily ever after in the land of the humans.

In the Juan Oso legend, the bear is referred to as the Enchanted or Mysterious One. He is a fantastic, supernatural creature capable of affecting profound transformations. The spirit of that enchanted bear was kept strongly alive by a group of nineteenth-century writers in New England before it flowered with the Southwest Humorists. Both of these groups of writers adopted the style of the tall tale and their imagination was fueled by isolated bits of wild-bear information like the following that were used perhaps to gull the greenhorn.

John Lawson, surveyor-general for the colony of North Carolina, wrote in 1709 that "if a dog is apt to fasten and run into a bear, he is not good, for the best dog in Europe is nothing in their paws; but if they ever get him in their clutches, they blow his skin from his flesh, like a bladder, and often kill him." And in 1748, the Swedish botanist Peter Kalm who was visiting John Bartram, an American naturalist in Philadelphia, wrote in his diary: "Mr. Bartram told me that when a bear catches a cow he kills her in the following manner: he bites a hole into the hide and blows with all his power into it till the animal swells excessively and dies, for the air expands greatly between the flesh and the hide."

In his humorous autobiography, *A Narrative of the Life of David Crockett, of the State of Tennessee,* published in 1834, Crockett climaxes a life given over to wild stories about hunting. In the *Narrative*, Crockett piles anecdote on anecdote about his hunting exploits with bears: killing 105 bears in a single year; fighting for four days without rest with a single bear; wrestling bears in creeks and up trees; confronting bears that take ten men to lift; and so on.

Crockett's wild fantasies about bears were given shape by a group of New England writers who produced hundreds of tales about bears. One, "A Bear Hunt in Vermont," published in 1833, is typical. The narrator brags that he has just been reading "Sketches of the Eccentricities of David Crockett" and thinks that nothing compares to a Vermont hunter "who will tear up a live oak tree with one hand, and wring off a bear's neck with the other, who will carry home panthers in his vest pocket, and eat wild cats with a spoon."

Crockett, he continues, used to take more than four hours to subdue one bear, "but a Vermounter don't want over fifteen minutes if the bear is anything less than nine feet long. . . ."

He decides to tell the story of Zeb Short—only six feet two inches tall—who on a bear hunt finds an unusually large bear. His hunting companion wants to shoot the bear, but Zeb intrudes: "Don't waste your powder, man, I want to shoot him just under the off ear, that's the spot. . . ." Zeb himself pulls the trigger, but the gun misfires, and Zeb and the bear wrestle it out on the ground. Zeb puts his hand in the bear's mouth and, his arm being mauled in the process, rips out the bear's tongue. The bear runs away and Zeb chases it for over a hundred yards, and once again wrestles the brute to the ground. The friend once more asks what he can do, and Zeb flatly responds, "be striking a fire, man . . . I want to eat some of this fellow." Zeb waits for the bear to turn its back, then picks it up, throws it into a mud hole, and holds its head under the mud, "as he would a child." He then casually leaves the bear tail-up in the mud, walks out of the hole, wraps a hankie around his mauled arm, and is once more ready to continue the day's hunt. What would Davy Crockett have done in such a predicament? the narrator asks, and then quickly provides the answer: "Why, Zeb could tie a bear in a double bow knot round him and heave both [Crockett and the bear] where they would never see daylight again."

While not as well cast as the stories of the Southwest Humorists, "A Bear Hunt in Vermont" contains the basic details of the tall tale: a huge bear that requires supreme strength and endurance to subdue; a rifle that won't work, so that man and bear must go at it with their own wits; a slight enchantment surrounding the bear—here it must only be shot in a special spot, which is typical of folklore animals; and, perhaps most important, a narrator who must appear tall—in this case to approach the bear's own size. But the gem of the tall-tale genre is "The Big Bar of Arkansaw," by Southwest Humorist Thomas Bangs Thorpe, published in 1841 in the journal called *Spirit of the Times*. The *Spirit* was the most popular humor journal of the period, and provided countless hunting stories of all kinds, but especially about the bear, with titles such as "Mike Hooter's Fight With the Bar," "Mike Hooter's Bear Story," "Jumping Over a Bear," "Ruff Sam's Bear Fight," and so on. The journal was edited by William T. Porter, who also edited two volumes of tall tales that featured Thorpe. Thorpe's "Big Bar" story is one of the most frequently anthologized tall tales, and its humor and sophistication make it well worth reading.

As the story opens, the narrator is taking a steamboat ride down the Mississippi when he hears a yelp from the social hall: "Hurra for the Big Bar from Arkansaw." He enters the room to find a man, known as the Big Bar from Arkansaw, holding forth about bears. The man brags that he hunts bears year round, the only difference being that in the winter the bears are fatter and slower; but to run a bear in a fat condition "improves the critter for eating . . . it sort of mixes the ile up with the meat, until you can't tell t'other from which." He remembers a morning in particular, chasing one such fat bear:

> . . . to see his tongue sticking out his mouth a foot, and his sides sinking and opening, like a bellows, and his cheeks so fat he couldn't look cross. In this fix I blazed at him, and pitch me naked into a briar patch if the steam didn't come out of the bullet-hole ten feet in a straight line. The fellow, I reckon, was made in the high pressure system, and the lead sort of burnt his biler.

The narrator, intrigued by this fellow, asks for a hunting story. Big Bar agrees to tell about the time "the greatest bar was killed that ever lived, none excepted." He knew the "bar" was large because of the scratching it left on the sassafras tree, eight inches higher than any other bear.

The first day he chases the bear eighteen miles with his hunting companion and his dog pack, led by Bowie-Knife, the best dog. The dogs pursue the bear until the animal decides to climb a tree and sit in its crotch, eyeing the dogs "as quiet as a pond in low water." His hunting friend, a greenhorn, fires a shot into the bear's forehead, which he shakes off, but climbs down enraged. Big Bar tries to shoot, but his gun misfires. The bear runs off and swims to an island, where he is chased by the dogs into the water, and finally killed. But when Big Bar fishes the carcass out of the water, he discovers that the dogs have killed the wrong bear. Somehow the bears changed places.

Frustrated, Big Bar tells his neighbors that he will catch "THAT BAR" on Monday. On Sunday morning, he goes into the woods with his gun and dog to defecate. Crouching there, his breeches down, he sees "THAT BAR" over his fence. He stands up and shoots. The bear "gave a yell, and walked through the fence like a falling tree would through a cobweb." He was dead. So enormous was the bear that " 'twould astonish you to know how big he was: I made a bed-spread of his skin and the way it used to cover my bar mattress, and leave several feet on each side to tuck up, would have delighted you. It was in fact a creation bar, and if it had lived in Samson's time, and had met him, in a fair fight, it would have licked him in the twinkling of a dice box."

But the story is not over. Big Bar announces that he actually *missed* the bear. Perhaps, he explains, the bear learned of the preparations to kill him and he came by early to save his breath. But more likely, he concludes, "the bear was an unhuntable bear, and died when his time came." Everyone falls silent. Big Bar remains silent, the narrator tells us, because of some mystery connected with the animal's death, some superstition, "a feeling common with all 'children of the wood' when they meet with anything out of their everyday experience." Bar then takes the edge off his surprise ending by inviting everyone into the bar for a drink.

In the middle of the narration, a bystander interrupts by saying that the story has begun to smell "rather tall." The line is a key to the importance of the tale. It is the first instance recorded by the *Oxford English Dictionary* of *tall* used to mean exaggerated. Previously the word was used to mean a lofty, grandiloquent style. The bystander's comment means to suggest that Big Bar is lying: but he chooses to use the word *tall*. The bear is, he believes, bigger than he ought to be. But therein lies the key: for if the bear is tall, so is the narrator; they have the same names. Besides, Big Bar the narrator "stood up" to shoot his victim. He's tall in stature—not only in hieght, but also in bearing.

The bear functions in this story to transform the narrator through its supernatural qualities: it can't be hunted, dies of its own accord, switches places with another bear, seeks out its hunter, and so on. Bear and narrator have been joined, not perhaps in the physical manner described in Juan Oso or in Bear Mother, but joined in deed. Beowulf's name is synonymous with bear, and he fights like one; Big Bar assumes the patronymic and, in the process of telling the story, becomes elevated.

Thorpe's "creation bar" is indeed dead. The unhuntable, larger-than-life bear can no longer star in serious narrative literature; comedy has become his habitat. The fable has reached full flower. Not that we cannot see him as a serious character; but writers seem unwilling to see the bear as a living animal. Majestic Otso has been emptied of heroic meaning. Witness Henry Wadsworth Longfellow's "Hiawatha," whose meter and spirit have been borrowed from the heroic northern past, from the *Kalevala*.

Hiawatha's father, Mudjekeewis, overpowers the "great bear of the mountains" by stealth, and steals from him the magic belt of wampum. Mudjekeewis does not welcome the bear, and utters no prayer for his soul. Instead, the bear is simply killed. Neither hunt nor ritual nor sacrifice takes place. And hence this description of the death of the great bear:

> With the heavy blow bewildered
> Rose the great bear of the mountains;
> But his knees beneath him trembled,
> And he whimpered like a woman.

Longfellow intends to imply, through the line "whimpered like a woman," that the bear refuses to die "like a man." He stereotypes both sexes through the poem, and thus degrades each. By killing the bear, Mudjekeewis establishes himself as master. He then begets the hero of the poem, Hiawatha. As J. L. Henderson observes: "Here we see an enormous change in man's relation to the animal—a transition from a primordial archetypal animal image to an image of culture-conscious, culture-ambitious man." Unlike the *Kalevala,* where the bear appears and reappears throughout the long poem, he lurks at best as a shadow in "Hiawatha." The bear was ready to be retrieved by twentieth-century authors.

At the turn of the century, the naturalist Ernest Thompson Seton began to publish a series of nature books that became popular with children as well as with adults. These books coincided with a growing interest in preservation, camping, and the out-of-doors in general. His most popular book, *Wild Animals I Have Known* (1900), provides a counterpoint to the moralized animal fables that preceded it—for example, Br'er Bar and Br'er Fox, which Joel Chandler Harris had resurrected from the medieval *Roman de Renart* and published in 1881 under the title *Tales of Uncle Remus*.

As in Reynard, Br'er Bar is hoodwinked by the wily Br'er Fox in a series of loosely connected incidents. Harris sets the scene in the deep South, and the social satire stands out in bold relief: maltreatment of uneducated blacks by the fast-talking, slick white establishment. Instead of talking for the bear, as Harris had done, Seton lets the bears come into view naturally, by describing their environment and their behavior. Supplemented by his own drawings and sketches, his books *Monarch, the Big Bear of Tallac, Biography of a Grizzly,* and *Wild Animals* came magnificently alive for generations of children.

The beginning of the twentieth century marks a dramatic change in people's attitude toward the bear—symbolized in one famous incident: Teddy Roosevelt's refusal to shoot a cub—or a sow, the accounts of the hunt vary—while on a bear hunt in 1902. Cartoons immediately appeared in national newspapers showing Roosevelt proudly taking his moral—or political?—stand. Almost one hundred years before, in 1805, Lewis and Clark had collected their first specimen, and described the savage *Ursus horribilis* in their journal. By refusing to kill a little bear, Teddy Roosevelt created the stuffed "teddy bear."

Modern Literature

The teddy bear's popularity was immediate; by 1907, people were even speaking Grammbear, a language that puns on "teddy" and "bear": "I am bearable," "celebriteddy," "bearadise lost." The juxtapositions in the Roosevelt event are enlightening: the huge bear mother and the toy; the gun and the stuffed doll; the Rough Rider and the soft teddy. It is as if the medieval Church had authorized a modern emblem of the transformed, benign, and tamed wild bear. From pagan sexual bear to female Christian bear to neuter stuffed bear—the animal had traveled the entire gender circuit.

The teddy bear exerted an enormous influence on children's literature. Fairy tales about bears, so popular in the nineteenth century—"Rose Red," "Goldilocks," "Beauty and the Beast"—grew into children's books about bears. But the bear was no longer a real bear living in the woods; he became a toy, a teddy, who may live in the woods as Winnie, or in a toy store, as in *The Shoe Shop Bears,* or in a house, as Paddington.

These books work their magic in part because of their illustrations. In books of the twenties and thirties, such as the Rupert Bear stories by Mary Tourtel and Alfred Bestall, the drawings suggest a real bear—long snout, round head, big furry ears—but stitch lines are visible around the head. He is still a toy. Rupert, a lovable bear who lives in a small cottage in the woods, wanders out periodically, gets lost, and has adventures—stories are titled "Rupert Gets Captured," "Rupert and the Robber Wolf," and "The Willful Princess." He returns home at the end of each episode to a triumphant reunion with his bear parents.

Two series of children's bear books have dominated the twentieth-century: the stories of Winnie-the-Pooh, and the Paddington books. Over the years, illustrations for Winnie-the-Pooh show him getting fatter, his arms and legs becoming shorter, his head flopping farther forward, as if in haphazard thought. His appearance parallels the changes in teddy bear design; he is, after all, a talking toy. Winnie can turn witty, urbane, or shy and naïve when you least expect it—and at times even brilliant. Though Pooh's problems revolve around honey—how to get it, and how to get more of it—his language is at times philosophical, even mystical. But Pooh's creator, A. A. Milne, makes it all seem natural, for each animal has a strong personality and never wavers from it. The world of Pooh is a solid, interesting, reassuring one that seems most times more attractive than the adult one. Christopher Robin, a young boy with a bird's name, pops in when he's needed and provides the necessary human complement. The real world does exist, out beyond Pooh Corner somewhere, but it touches the animal one only occasionally. Winnie-the-Pooh occupies the seat of honor: Pooh is the first famous fictional bear, to whom every other bear owes his existence.

The other famous teddy is Paddington, found one day by the Brown family as he sat on top of a piece of luggage in Paddington Station, hence his name. Michael Bond's Paddington stories offer us the opposite picture from Pooh's: Paddington is surrounded by humans and is visited by an occasional animal. Unlike Pooh, with his seemingly passive, out-of-control manner, Paddington takes charge. More slapstick than Pooh, Paddington exhibits enough human qualities, including his many costumes, to have made him prosper for almost thirty years. The outcome in both Pooh and Paddington is the same—we are enabled to see the human world in sharper focus—and both books reveal the enormous distance between us and our spiritual ties to the cave bear.

By 1935, the teddy bear had established itself so firmly that a serious novelist, Graham Greene, could write an experimental piece of fiction, *The Bear Fell Free,* with a teddy bear as a major character. In this little story, printed in a limited edition in London, Greene plays off the symbol of the teddy as an object of innocent and youthful love against the other characters in the story, who all drink too much and die too young, and who occasionally win grand sums of money in the Irish Sweeps. One sweepstakes winner, a character named Tony Farrell, who is desperately trying to recapture his youth, buys a plane and decides to fly solo across the Atlantic. At a farewell party hosted by his phony, drunken friends, Farrell's old flame, Jane, tosses a teddy bear into the cockpit—for luck, or for a whim, or perhaps even as a malicious reminder of their love.

In any case, the teddy becomes a constant presence. When Farrell noses his plane into the clouds, the teddy bear presses its plush paws against his back; when he dives, the bear beats his shoulder blades. As they glide along, the bear is Farrell's closest companion. Very quickly, however, Farrell encounters a severe storm. Terrified, he tries to head the plane back to land. Greene tells us that Farrell, blinded by the rain, is powering headlong into the sea. The scene inside the cockpit turns macabre, as Farrell's condition is revealed in the bear's: like the inanimate bear flopping from one side to the other, Farrell is helplessly trapped. Perhaps because of Paddington and Pooh and other clever bears, readers might hope that Greene's teddy will hatch a clever escape for his human friend. But this bear has no will, no imagination.

The plane crashes—Farrell's lark suddenly turned into grim reality—and the teddy bear falls free. For a second, with our attention on the little toy, we forget Farrell's plight—Greene has maneuvered us into a children's story. But that move only underscores one of the story's important points. For as with everything else in *The Bear Fell Free,* the teddy cannot avoid being sullied: "A slow green wave rose under the teddy bear, lifted it, and dropped it into the trough. Its black shoe-button eyes were glazed with water, its small arms spread wide, salt water soaked into the brown plush, loosening the black threads on its paws. Presently a strand of seaweed coiled round one ear."

But while teddys pursued their own literary careers, real bears appeared in more than one hundred modern poems—from Delmore Schwartz to James Wright, Robert Frost to William Carlos Williams, Marianne Moore, Galway Kinnell, and Theodore Roethke. The bear symbolizes the largest things, mankind itself, and the "modern condition"—sexuality, death, rebirth, feeble-minded strength, cunning, lost youth, and alienation. Speakers in these poems see similarities between their own life and the bear's. They find vision (in Richard Pflum's "The Silence of Bears"), joy (in Greg Kuzma's "The Dancing Bear"), and hope (in Kelly Cherry's "Resurrection Quatrain").

In very few of these modern poems, however, does the reader truly experience what Denise Levertov has called the "holy presence" of animals, the immediacy of power that one experiences in ritual. Instead, the bear acts more often than not as a cute old man in a furry coat, or some dark, vicious, primal symbol. In either case he is removed from the speaker, placed at some greater distance. In fact, the bear probably best known to students of modern poetry shambles across the lines of Delmore Schwartz's "The Heavy Bear Who Goes With Me" (1938), a poem in which the bear stands for the awkward, clumsy persona of the speaker:

> The heavy bear who goes with me,
> A manifold honey to smear his face,
> Clumsy and lumbering here and there,
> The central ton of every place,
> The hungry beating brutish one
> In love with candy, anger, and sleep,
> Crazy factotum, dishevelling all,
> Climbs the building, kicks the football,
> Boxes his brother in the hate-ridden city.
>
> Breathing at my side, that heavy animal,
> That heavy bear who sleeps with me,
> Howls in his sleep for a world of sugar,
> A sweetness intimate as the water's clasp,
> Howls in his sleep because the tight-rope
> Trembles and shows the darkness beneath.
> The strutting show-off is terrified,

Dressed in his dress-suit, bulging his pants,
Trembles to think that his quivering meat
Must finally wince to nothing at all.

That inescapable animal walks with me,
Has followed me since the black womb held,
Moves where I move, distorting my gesture,
A caricature, a swollen shadow,
A stupid clown of the spirit's motive,
Perplexes and affronts with his own darkness,
The secret life of belly and bone,
Opaque, too near, my private, yet unknown,
Stretches to embrace the very dear
With whom I would walk without him near,
Touches her grossly, although a word
Would bare my heart and make me clear,
Stumbles, flounders, and strives to be fed
Dragging me with him in his mouthing care,
Amid the hundred million of his kind,
The scrimmage of appetite everywhere.

The bear is a heavy klutz, and the speaker acknowledges that he would be better off without him. The speaker has not embraced the bear, he is instead stuck to him and with him. In Schwartz's poem, the bear becomes a measure of the man's distance from his own physicality; all that is natural and uncontrollable in him is here presented as brutish and rough.

Writing around the same time, Robert Frost also used the bear as symbol. Unlike Schwartz, however, Frost's bear is not a symbol of man's concern with his physicality, but of his "arrogant quest for scientific knowledge." In a letter to his friend Louis Untermeyer, Frost explains that the poem was inspired by bear activity in Franconia, New Hampshire, one summer day in 1925: "We are enjoying a descent of bears upon this region . . . six of the Fobes sheep have been eaten. A mother and two cubs went up the road by our house the other evening tearing down the small cherry trees along the wall. You could see where one of the cubs had wiped his bottom on a large stone and left traces of a diet of choke cherries and blueberries. I almost got one cornered in our pasture last night, but he lifted the wire and went under the fence."

It takes someone keenly observing a bear to retrieve that animal spirit and write it boldly back into literature; a person would have to notice its diet, see the scat, recognize one berry from the next, be able to identify a sow from a boar, and so on. Frost possessed that ability, and in his poem "The Bear," first published in *The Nation* in 1928, he makes real contact with the animal. The poem represents an important transitional piece in the history of the bear in modern literature, for Frost sees the bear both as living animal and as symbol. The first ten lines provide us that keen observation:

> The bear puts both arms around the tree above her
> And draws it down as if it were a lover
> And its chokecherries lips to kiss good-by,
> Then lets it snap back upright in the sky.
> Her next step rocks a boulder on the wall
> (She's making her cross-country in the fall).
> Her great weight creaks the barbed-wire in its staples
> And she flings over and off down through the maples,
> Leaving on one wire tooth a lock of hair.
> Such is the uncaged progress of the bear.

The rest of the poem, which satirizes man's inquisitiveness, sounds oddly like Schwartz's heavy alter-ego:

> The world has room to make a bear feel free;
> The universe seems cramped to you and me.
> Man acts more like the poor bear in a cage
> That all day fights a nervous inward rage,
> His mood rejecting all his mind suggests.
> He paces back and forth and never rests
> The toenail click and shuffle of his feet,
> The telescope at one end of his beat,
> And at the other end the microscope,
> Two instruments of nearly equal hope,
> And in conjunction giving quite a spread.
> Or if he rests from scientific tread,
> 'Tis only to sit back and sway his head
> Through ninety-odd degrees of arc, it seems,
> Between two metaphysical extremes.
> He sits back on his fundamental butt
> With lifted snout and eyes (if any) shut

(He almost looks religious but he's not),
And back and forth he sways from cheek to cheek,
At one extreme agreeing with one Greek,
At the other agreeing with another Greek,
Which may be thought, but only so to speak.
A baggy figure, equally pathetic
When sedentary and when peripatetic.

Four years later, in 1942, William Faulkner published one of the great modern literary works, "The Bear." With Faulkner our discussion will begin to close circle: we began with Beowulf the Bear, where man and animal were united, at least linguistically, and we near the end with Faulkner's ambiguous story in which man both reveres and respects the bear but is driven to hunt and kill him. It presents the bear as sacred, but alive at the wrong time.

The story describes young Ike McCaslin's preparation in the woods for the yearly bear hunt by his leader, Sam Fathers, and the eventual killing of the bear, Old Ben, by Boon Hogganbeck. Faulkner's story presents us with a powerful wilderness that was quietly passing away. Deeper and deeper incursions were being made by the logging trains at the end of the nineteenth century, and the haunted old bear is Faulkner's symbol for that untamed but fading wilderness. It is not the train that kills Old Ben, but the new spirit that the train carries into the woods—the power, greed, and competitive mentality of the logging companies and the society of which they are part. The same shrill steam whistle that drove Thoreau from Walden Pond also trees a solitary, frightened bear at the railroad's edge in the last pages of "The Bear."

For Faulkner, the impetus for America's change at the end of the nineteenth century sprang from an uncomfortable drive for money. That change is reflected in "The Bear." Toward the end of the story, when Ike returns to the woods, he learns that Major de Spain, a wealthy landowner, has sold his timber rights to a Memphis lumbering company; further, the old hunting group has incorporated itself into a new club, and now leases its hunting privileges. Ike's recognition of how the woods have changed presents itself in an appropriate animal metaphor: they changed the leopard's spots, he points out, when they could not alter the leopard. The death of Old

ONE-SMOKE STORIES

One-smoke stories must be told in the length of time it takes to smoke a traditional corn-husk and native tabac cigarette. Blowing smoke to the four or six world corners—depending on the tribe—the teller inspirits his story with breath. Smoke, story, and breath spiral upward, merging with the world's own breathing, repeating ancient patterns. In this story, "The Spirit of the Bear Walking," retold by Mary Austin, who keenly observed Southwest American Indians and wrote with passion about them, the bear's spirit appears when the spirit fire is lighted, offering comfort for an otherwise sad and disabling situation—the loss of one's child.

Hear now a Telling:
Whenever Hotándanai of the campody of Sagharawíte went hunting on the mountain, he took care to think as little as possible of Paháwitz-na'an, the Spirit of the Bear that Fathered Him. For it is well known that whoever can see Paháwitz-na'an without being seen by him will become the mightiest hunter of his generation, but he can never be seen by anybody who is thinking about him.

On the other hand, if a tribesman should himself be seen by the Spirit of the Bear Walking, there is no knowing what might happen. Hunters who have gone up on Toorape and never come back are supposed to have met with him. So between hope of seeing and fear of being seen, it is nearly impossible to hunt on the mountain without thinking of Paháwitz-na'an.

Hotándanai alone hoped to accomplish the impossible. He might have managed it at the time his thoughts were all taken up with wondering whether the daughter of Tinnemahá the

Ben signals, then, as with Beowulf, the coming of a new way of life. The desire for material wealth has replaced ritual, bravery, and things unspoiled.

The triad of the wilderness is established before the critical day of the last hunt: Old Ben, Sam Fathers, and the mongrel dog, Lion. Faulkner points out that only these three are "taintless and incor-

Medicine Man could be persuaded to marry him, but at that time he did not hunt at all. He spent his time waiting at the spring where the maidens came with their mothers to fill their water-bottles, making a little flute of four notes and playing on it. After he was married, however, he tried again to dispossess his mind of the thought of Paháwitz-na'an. "For," he said, "when my son is born he will have pride in me, and keep a soft place in the hut for the man who was the mightiest hunter of his generation." Thus it was that he never went out to hunt on Toorape without thinking both of his son and the Bear Walking.

In due time the son was born, and though Hotándanai had not yet become the mightiest hunter, he was very happy. Always when he went on the mountain of Toorape he remembered his wish, and so missed it.

In the course of years the tribe fell into war with the people of the north and the son of Hotándanai went out to his first battle. But, as it turned out, the battle went against Sagharawíte, and the son of Hotándanai was brought home shot full of arrows. Then the heart of Hotándanai broke when he buried him. He said, "Let me go, I will build a fire on the mountain to light the feet of my son's spirit, and then I will lament him."

Clad in all his war gear he went up on Toorape, and all the way he thought only of his son and how he should miss him. So, when he had lighted the spirit fire, he said, "Oh, my son, what profit shall I have of my life now you are departed!" And as he wept he saw something moving on the slope before him. He looked, for his eyes were by no means as keen as they had been, and behold, it was the Spirit of the Bear Walking.

ruptible." But it is not Sam who kills the bear, nor is it his disciple Ike. Boon Hogganbeck, the drunken Negro, the man who has difficulty firing a gun, kills Old Ben with his primitive tool, a hunting knife. And he kills trying to protect the only thing he has ever loved, the dog. The description of the bear's death is a vivid and telling one:

Then Boon was running. The boy saw the gleam of the blade in his hand and watched him leap among the hounds, hurdling them, kicking them aside as he ran, and fling himself astride the bear as he had hurled himself to the mule, his legs locked around the bear's belly, his left arm under the bear's throat where Lion clung, and the glint of the knife as it rose and fell.

It fell just once. For an instant they almost resembled a piece of statuary: the clinging dog, the bear, the man astride its back, working and probing the buried blade. Then they went down. . . . It didn't collapse, crumble. It fell all of a piece, as a tree falls, so that all three of them, man, dog, and bear, seemed to bounce once.

"As a tree falls" accurately describes the bear's death: a part of the natural world has fallen. Old nature is collapsing.

Shortly after the bear dies, there is a commotion in some other part of the woods. Sam Fathers lies motionless in the mud. He has not stumbled off his mule, he has not been shot. Sam has just quit living. Ben and Lion are both parts of nature, and so is Sam. When *they* die, so does he, for they are all related. Sam dies without kin, without children, so that everything he can pass on he has bequeathed to Ike McCaslin: "The old man, the wild man not even one generation from the woods, childless, kinless, peopleless. . . ." Beowulf, too, dies kinless. He can pass nothing on, except to the young man, Wiglaf, of the tribe of the Waegmundings, who helped Beowulf in his last and most crucial fight with the dragon. Sam, the chief, the father; Beowulf, the ring-giver, the leader: these are the people, each author seems to suggest, the likes of which we will see no more. Their family trees are rooted where they lie. The principal character in each of these two stories is a bear.

Beowulf shows that the Anglo-Saxon heroic ideal was giving way to something new—perhaps it was the Christianizing of England— and Faulkner recognized, in his own way, in his own time, that something was finished in America. Faulkner's choice of names reveals a curious irony. Old Ben certainly echoes Grizzly Adams's Ben Franklin, the wild bear on a leash. In his later years, Adams teamed up with several circuses, the most prominent of these started by a man whom many believe to be the father of the circus, Carl Hagenbeck, again certainly an echo of the man who kills the bear in the story, Boon Hogganbeck, and who ends up at the story's conclusion sitting under a tree, dazed, perhaps crazy, banging his rifle parts together.

Hagenbeck's nineteenth-century circuses were only a culmination of the persistent desire to tame and control the bear. Great public shows were held in Rome in which substantial numbers of bears were on display as early as 169 B.C. And perhaps the first record of bears performing in a kind of circus dates from Childaric I, who founded the Frankish Merovingian Kingdom; he had a circus built in Saissons around A.D. 460, and featured in his playbill trained bears. One branch of bear history has culminated in the teddy, the stuffed plaything. The real bear is just too much for many of us— he is too blatant a reminder of our primitive ancestry. Perhaps he threatens us by showing us what we might become.

But there is another branch to the bear's history, one that continues Old Ben's power—awesome, slightly bewildering, frightening, and fascinating power. This is how the more modern writers have perceived the bear, and they have attempted to return to the animal *as* animal. Symbols seem to recede, while the primitive, raw power of the animal is allowed to emerge—so much so, for C. S. Lewis, that Mr. Bultitude, a major character in *That Hideous Strength,* is a bear:

Mr. Bultitude's mind was as furry and as unhuman in shape as his body. He did not remember, as a man in his situation would have remembered, the provincial zoo from which he had escaped during a fire, not his first snarling and terrified arrival at the Manor, not the slow stages whereby he had learned to love and trust its inhabitants. He did not know that he loved and trusted them now. He did not know that they were people, nor that he was a bear. Indeed, he did not know that he existed at all: everything that is represented by the words *I* and *Me* and *Thou* was absent from his mind. When Mrs. Maggs gave him a tin of golden syrup, as she did every Sunday morning, he did not recognise either a giver or a recipient. Goodness occurred and he tasted it. And that was all. Hence his loves might, if you wished, be all described as cupboard loves: food and warmth, hands that caressed, voices that reassured, were their objects. But if by a cupboard love you meant something cold or calculating you would be quite misunderstanding the real quality of the beast's sensations. He was no more like a human egoist than he was like a human altruist. There was no prose in his life. The appetencies which a human mind might disdain as cupboard loves were for him quivering and ecstatic aspirations which absorbed his whole being, infinite yearnings, stabbed with the threat of tragedy and shot through with the colours of Paradise. One of our race, if plunged back for a moment in the warm, trembling, iridescent pool of that pre-Adamite consciousness, would have emerged believing that he had grapsed the absolute: for the states below reason and the states above it have, by their common contrast to the life we know, a certain superficial resemblance.

Three modern poets, William Carlos Williams, Adrienne Rich, and Gary Snyder, have continued to be fascinated by the bear's power. In his deceptively simple "The Polar Bear," Williams returns to the animal's quiet ferocity by focusing on our need to see the bear as a cute, seductive toy. But he forces us to remember that *his* bear is real, as we watch the innocence of *white* sliding into the whiteness of death:

> his coat resembles the snow
> deep snow
> the male snow
> which attacks and kills
>
> silently as it falls muffling
> the world
> to sleep that
> the interrupted quiet return
>
> to lie down with us
> its arms
> about our necks
> murderously a little while

Adrienne Rich, a marvelous and imaginative contemporary poet, yearns for the power of the bear. She tells her poem from the apparent viewpoint of a child, though the poem clearly describes an adult's desires in "Bears:"

> Wonderful bears that walked my room all night,
> Where have you gone, your sleek and fairy fur,
> Your eyes' veiled and imperious light?

Brown bears as rich as mocha or as musk,
White opalescent bears whose fur stood out
Electric in the deepening dusk,

And great black bears that seemed more blue than black,
More violet than blue against the dark—
Where are you now? Upon what track

Mutter your muffled paws that used to tread
So softly, surely, up the creakless stair
While I lay listening in bed?

When did I lose you? Whose have you become?
Why do I wait and wait and never hear
Your thick nocturnal pacing in my room?
My bears, who keeps you now, in pride and fear?

But it takes a contemporary poet of the land like Gary Snyder to move us into the "holy presence" of the bear. In a 1960 poem entitled "this poem is for bear," he welcomes the magic of bear—the bear in its entirety. It is one of the few poems that refuses to elevate the speaker's "I" over the bear—in fact, the last part of the poem achieves precisely the opposite effect:

"As for me I am a child of the god of the mountains"

A bear down under the cliff.
She is eating huckleberries.
They are ripe now
Soon it will snow, and she
Or maybe he, will crawl into a hole
And sleep. You can see
Huckleberries in bearshit if you
Look, this time of year
If I sneak up on the bear
It will grunt and run

The others had all gone down
From the blackberry brambles, but one girl
Spilled her basket, and was picking up her
Berries in the dark.
A tall man stood in the shadow, took her arm,
Led her to his home. He was a bear.

In a house under the mountain
She gave birth to slick dark children
With sharp teeth, and lived in the hollow
Mountain many years.

    snare a bear: call him out:
honey eater
forest apple
light-foot
Old man in the fur coat, Bear! come out!
Die of your own choice!
Grandfather black-food!
    this girl married a bear
Who rules in the mountains, Bear!
      you have eaten many berries
      you have caught many fish
      you have frightened many people

Twelve species north of Mexico
Sucking their paws in the long winter
Tearing the high-strung caches down
Whining, crying, jacking off
(Odysseus was a bear)

Bear-cubs gnawing the soft tits
Teeth gritted, eyes screwed tight
    but she let them.
Till her brothers found the place
Chased her husband up the gorge
Cornered him in the rocks.
Song of the snared bear:
    "Give me my belt.
    "I am near death
    "I came from the mountain caves
    "At the headwaters,
    "The small streams there
    "Are all dried up.

—I think I'll go hunt bears.
    "hunt bears?
Why shit Snyder,
You couldn't hit a bear in the ass
    with a handful of rice!"

KWAKIUTL PRAYER
ON HUNTING AND SLAYING
THE BLACK BEAR

*When the black bear is dead, when it has been shot by the
hunter, the man sits down on the ground at the right-hand side
of the bear. Then the man says, praying to it,*

Thank you, friend, that you did not make me walk about in vain.
Now you have come to take mercy on me so that I obtain game,
      that I may inherit your power of getting easily with your
      hands the salmon that you catch.
Now I will press my right hand against your left hand

*—says the man as he takes hold of the left paw of the bear. He
says,*

O friend, now we press together our working hands, that you
      may give over to me your power of getting everything easily
      with your hands, friend

*—says he. Now it is done after this, for now he only skins the
bear after this.*

Snyder recounts the entire history of man's treatment of the bear
in this poem—from the Bear Mother legend through our various
perceptions of it and appellations bestowed on it, to its eventual
destruction. Yet he insists, in his own perception of the animal
kingdom, on referring to the pursuers of the bear as his own brothers. The bear remains, even in our adverse treatment of him, a distant
cousin. As Snyder insists in *Earth House Hold,* when the poet attends
to animals, he goes beyond society. The last five lines of Snyder's
poem, in fact, seem to create a more tightly knit society precisely
by focusing on the animal.

Since about 1970, bears have begun to appear in surprising numbers in contemporary fiction. Robertson Davies ends his novel *The*

Manticore in an old cave-bear cave. The main character, in Jungian analysis throughout the book, finally is forced on Christmas Eve into an abandoned cave in an attempt to help him rediscover untapped strength and power. In *The Clan of the Cave Bear*, Jean Auel creates an entire prehistoric family who trace their lineage from the cave bear and who perform elaborate bear ceremonies periodically throughout the novel. Here is an early instance:

> They all knew what came next, the ceremony never changed; it was the same night after night, but still they anticipated. They were waiting for Mog-ur to call upon the Spirit of Ursus, the Great Cave Bear, his own personal totem and most revered of all the spirits.
>
> Ursus was more than Mog-ur's totem; he was everyone's totem, and more than totem. It was Ursus that made them Clan. He was the supreme spirit, supreme protector. Reverence for the Cave Bear was the common factor that united them, the force that welded all the separate autonomous clans into one people, the Clan of the Cave Bear.
>
> When the one-eyed magician judged the time was right, he signaled. . . . Mog-ur reached into a small pouch and withdrew a pinch of dried club-moss spores. Holding his hand over the small torch, he leaned forward and blew, at the same time he let them drop over the flame. The spores caught fire and cascaded dramatically around the [bear] skull in a magnesium brilliance of light, in stark contrast to the dark night.

John Gardner used the bear in his novel *Mickelsson's Ghosts* to suggest the supernatural, the occult. Madeleine L'Engle, in her novel *The Bear*, describes, in more vivid detail than the Bear Mother legend could ever have imagined, a marriage between a woman and a bear. Richard Adams's *Shardik* tells a story about a people who "worship the memory of a gigantic bear, which they believe to have been divine." The story may rely for its ending, in which a bear wreaks havoc on an army, on the Icelandic saga of Hrolf kraki, in which Biarki battles for the king in the form of a bear. Bears appear in each of John Irving's novels. The bear in *The Hotel New Hampshire*, lifted from *The World According to Garp* and given fuller treatment, represents a way of life, attractive but removed; he also represents power, stark and sometimes uncontrolled, something beneficial to retrieve. The bear is *literally* retrieved in Irving's *Setting Free the Bears*. Two young men, perhaps crazy, hatch a plan to free the bears from an Austrian zoo, in a political act of liberation. The center of John Ehle's recent *Winter People* is a powerful bear hunt.

In each of these novels, the bear is neither cute nor wildly distorted in size or strength—contemporary authors are willing to look at the bear directly. Retrieving him from fairy tales and fables began in earnest with Faulkner, who removed the hokum from the "Big Bar of Arkansaw" for "The Bear." But he saved the elements of enchantment: a huge bear who is impossible to hunt, who seems to die only when *he* is ready; a gun that strangely misfires; an animal that falls more like a tree; and so on. Faulkner took the tall tale and made it broad—as broad as the land.

Our image of the bear draws its power once more from ritual and myth. Even Allen Ginsberg, a poet we usually associate with the subjects and concerns of the city, expresses that primal longing for the bear. In an early poem, "A Desolation" (1961), the speaker laments that he must build a home in the wilderness, fearing otherwise that he will "perish"; that he "must tame the hart/ and wear the bear." The speaker's pain comes from seeing a discrete choice: bear *sark* or business suit; the wilderness or "an image of his wandering." He resignedly settles for the home "by the roadside." Hence *a desolation*—to feel unhoused and deserted in the midst of cozy society.

Poetry may be the proper literary home for the bear; its compressed and incantatory language best invokes the magic, as in Galway Kinnell's "The Bear," in which Kinnell moves beyond the longing expressed by Ginsberg, and permits his speaker to dream himself back into a bear. Waking, he yearns for his short-lived power. "The Bear" is at once a spell and a charm, spinning its own myth and magic, as old as the oldest legends of the bear.

The speaker in the poem kills the bear, suggesting that the bear may only be fully recovered in its killing. That is, some hunters may know the bear more intimately than do many well-meaning preservationists. A wonderfully moving example of this occurs in the earliest example of bear literature covered in this section, the *Kalevala*. Vainamoinen must kill a bear who has been sent specifically to ravage his land. Before he leaves on the hunt with his dog, he recites a prayer to the bear:

> O my Otso, O my darling,
> Fair one with the paws of honey,
> Do thou rest in hilly country,
> And among the rocks so lovely,
> Where the pines above are waving,
> And the firs below are rustling.
> Turn thyself around, O Otso,
> Turn thee round, O honey-pawed one,
> As upon her nest the woodgrouse,
> Or as turns the goose when brooding.

And after the kill, Vainamoinen asks the bear "not to be filled with causeless anger," then, with another song, sends it majestically on its way to a new home:

> Golden cuckoo of the forest,
> Shaggy-haired and lovely creature,
> Do thou quit thy chilly dwelling,
> Do thou quit thy native desert,
>
> . . . .
> Go to wander in the open,
> O thou beauty of the forest,
> On thy light shoes wandering onward,
> Marching in thy blue-hued stockings,
> Leaving now this little dwelling,
> Leave it for the mighty heroes,
> To the race of men resign it.
> There are none will treat thee badly,
> And no wretched life awaits thee.
> For thy food they'll give you honey,
> And for drink, of mead the freshest,
> When thou goest to a distance
> Whither with the staff they guide
>   thee.

There is compassion in the song, and a keenness of detail that comes only from close observation, none of which is possible without a profound connection between the hunter and the hunted. Even in the tall tale of "Big Bar," the bear comes to the hunter; there is a partnership. Vainamoinen says to the dead bear, "I myself have not o'erthrown thee, / Thou thyself hast left the forest."

When ritual evaporates or is forgotten, what remains appears to be brutish and savage. This is perhaps best seen in an activity like hunting. Without a profound respect for the sacredness of the animal's life, hunting devolves into mere butchery. That seems to be Norman Mailer's point in *Why Are We in Vietnam?*, a novel narrated by an eighteen-year-old psychotic Texan named D. J., who, the day before his army induction, describes a bear hunt he had been on sometime in the past. Every character in the novel sees the bear as a trophy, rifles as armament, and ritual as crude paganism. Power and sexuality rule their lives, and they value both, for each leads to conquest. That vision of life, where love and affection have been replaced by unbridled passion and possessiveness, has led us, according to Mailer, to Vietnam. Technology has overthrown skill and finesse. These hunters use helicopters and .375 Magnums; if they could use cannons and jet fighters, they would. The bear doesn't stand a chance. Here is one brief hunting description from the novel:

> "Break the shoulder bone and they can't run. Sure. That's where I want my power. Right there. Right then. Maybe a professional hunter takes pride in dropping an animal by picking him off in a vital spot—but I like the feeling that if I miss a vital area I still can count on the big impact knocking them down, killing them by the total impact, shock! It's like aerial bombardment in the last Big War. . . ."

Since every ending contains the thread of a new beginning, it is appropriate to end this section with Galway Kinnell's "The Bear," for it is a modern bear song, a twentieth-century *Kalevala*:

1

In late winter
I sometimes glimpse bits of steam
coming up from
some fault in the old snow
and bend close and see it is lung-colored
and put down my nose
and know
the chilly, enduring odor of bear.

2

I take a wolf's rib and whittle
it sharp at both ends
and coil it up
and freeze it in blubber and place it out
on the fairway of the bears.

And when it has vanished
I move out on the bear tracks,
roaming in circles
until I come to the first, tentative, dark
splash on the earth.

And I set out
running, following the splashes
of blood wandering over the world.
At the cut, gashed resting places
I stop and rest,
at the crawl-marks
where he lay out on his belly
to overpass some stretch of bauchy ice
I lie out
dragging myself forward with bear-knives in my fists.

3

On the third day I begin to starve,
at nightfall I bend down as I knew I would
at a turd sopped in blood,
and hesitate, and pick it up,
and thrust it in my mouth, and gnash it down,
and rise
and go on running.

4

On the seventh day,
living by now on bear blood alone,
I can see his upturned carcass far out ahead, a scraggled,
steamy hulk,
the heavy fur riffling in the wind.
I come up to him
and stare at the narrow-spaced, petty eyes,

the dismayed
face laid back on the shoulder, the nostrils
flared, catching
perhaps the first taint of me as he
died.

I hack
a ravine in his thigh, and eat and drink,
and tear him down his whole length
and open him and climb in
and close him up after me, against the wind,
and sleep.

5

And dream
of lumbering flatfooted
over the tundra,
stabbed twice from within,
splattering a trail behind me,
splattering it out no matter which way I lurch,
no matter which parabola of bear-transcendence,
which dance of solitude I attempt,
which gravity-clutched leap,
which trudge, which groan.

6

Until one day I totter and fall—
fall on this
stomach that has tried so hard to keep up,
to digest the blood as it leaked in,
to break up
and digest the bone itself: and now the breeze
blows over me, blows off
the hideous belches of ill-digested bear blood
and rotted stomach
and the ordinary, wretched odor of bear,

blows across
my sore, lolled tongue a song
or screech, until I think I must rise up
and dance. And I lie still.

7

I awaken I think. Marshlights
reappear, geese
come trailing again up the flyway.
In her ravine under old snow the dam-bear
lies, licking
lumps of smeared fur
and drizzly eyes into shapes
with her tongue. And one
hairy-soled trudge stuck out before me,
the next groaned out,
the next,
the next,
the rest of my days I spend
wandering: wondering
what, anyway,
was that sticky infusion, that rank flavor of blood, that poetry,
by which I lived?

·7·
THE BEGINNINGS

Where and when did the lore of the bear enter human thought? Of course we cannot say, but there is evidence that men have been "thinking" bears for hundreds of centuries. According to archaeologist François Bordes, the oldest object marked by the human hand was engraved on a bison rib about 300,000 years ago and was dug up at a site called Pech de l'Aze in southern France. It might have been carved by a member of our ancestral species, *Homo erectus*. Like many other such "batons," "pendants," or "churingas" examined by Alexander Marshack at Harvard University, the figure is accompanied by scratches or marks that appear to be a kind of notation. Marshack thinks such marks link the animal with temporal awareness, timekeeping, or "time-factored thought." Such objects, Marshack comments, relate the hand that made them to broader, possibly mimetic gestures and to speech, so that the movement of the hand becomes a "nouning" or "verbing" when the carved image is brandished to signify, or, perhaps, "to bear."

Thousands of such objects have been found, indicating that the concept of time and the annual round of the seasons are among the earliest records we have of the evolution of human intelligence. By 50,000 years ago, men and bears (both cave bears and brown bears) lived together in Europe. In a cave near Erd, Hungary, are the bones of more than 500 cave bears killed by Neanderthal men, dated by carbon-14 testing at more than 49,000 years old. Evidence there and elsewhere indicates widespread bear hunting. The most astonishing of five such caves is the Drachenloch Cave in Switzerland, excavated by Emil Bachler between 1917 and 1923. Here, at 2,400 meters in the eastern Alps, he found rectangular stone tombs containing carefully arranged bear skulls and bones. The animals had been killed by blows from stone axes and then decapitated.* In other chambers of the Drachenloch he found fireplaces and arrangements of skulls in wall niches. The thigh bone of a bear had been placed through the eye socket of a skull. All belonged to *Ursus spelaeus,* the cave bear, which became extinct about 10,000 years ago. The human occupants of the Swiss caves, Neanderthalers, themselves ceased to exist as a race in the archaeological record 40,000 years ago. Bachler declared that the cave "supplies the first evidence in man of an already awakened higher spiritual life which belongs in the realm of spiritual culture." The cave bear was a huge animal with a domed forehead, in appearance "the most bearish of bears." Bjorn Kurten, an archaeologist and author of a book on cave bears, doubts that the stone bins in the Drachenloch were made by men, and speculates that they were washed together by running water. But he does accept a Neanderthal–brown bear association at Regourdon Cave near Lascaux, found by Eugene Bonifay, a French prehistorian. Among the accoutrements in the Neanderthaler's grave is a bear arm bone. In the Petershohle, near Nürnberg, wall niches contained skulls and leg bones of bears when the cave was discovered in the nineteenth century. At the Hellmichhohle, in Germany, E. F. Zotz found both cave-bear and brown-bear bones buried near the entrance with two neck vertebrae connected and the large molar teeth filed down, as the heads are cut and the teeth of the dead bears are still filed by some Siberian peoples. At Monte Circeo, southeast of Rome, the bodies in a multiple Neanderthal burial had their heads removed in the same way and were surrounded by an arrangement of stones

---

*The separation of the bear's head from its body and the special disposition of the skull are details in which the circumpolar rituals of the slain bear, studied by ethnographers in the nineteenth century, showed similarity to the evidence from the Paleolithic caves. In our own time, Promsias Mac Canna, the noted authority on Celtic culture, remarks on the similarity of stone heads in Irish cathedrals to the heads set in niches in the Gaulish monuments in southern France. This Celtic "motif of *têtes coupées* or severed heads," far from being trophy mounts or the final insult of warrior traditions, is a widespread custom among hunters. In a manuscript called *The Taymouth Hours,* in the British Museum, there are more than thirty hunting scenes in which, says scholar Yates Thompson, "the hunting rituals are here meticulously depicted, the *curée* or removal of the beast's entrails, the *présent* in which its head is set on a pole, and the *mort,* announcing the kill." While such similar rites for the dead prey all cannot possibly be shown to have had a single historical beginning or connection (although that is not impossible), it is noteworthy that among the oldest records of the *présent* are the skulls of bears and that hunters on two continents and a score of tribes observed it until recently; certainly this places the bear close to the heart of the meaning of the act, if not its origin.

suggestive of the bear-skull crypts and wall-niche arrangements. Thus the veneration and special "funerary" disposal of the skull and other main bones of the bodies of men and bears have features in common. The implication of some concept of similar reincarnation related to burial rites is indicated.

There is further evidence of Neanderthal reflections on immortality through rebirth from their graves in Near Eastern caves, where pollen in the burials shows flowers to have been interned with the corpse. At Regourdon Cave, in France, a human grave offering included the arm bone of a bear.

Thus, prior to 30,000 years ago, human attention was drawn to the theme of cosmic renewal. Parallels in the disposal of bear and human bones suggest an analogy, perhaps the concept of immortality in which the bear was both metaphor in its hibernation cycle and ritual instrument in the earliest human funerary practices.

Between 30,000 and 10,000 years ago, there appeared a somewhat different body of archaeological material—pictograph and petroglyph cave and rock-shelter art. In his monumental study of the rock art of European caves, André Leroi-Gourhan plotted the exact location of some 2,188 figures in sixty-six caves. He distinguished between the entry, central chamber, peripheral passages, and rearmost parts of the cave. Certain kinds of animals appeared characteristically in these different sections of the cave sanctuary, and were typically shown in association with specific "mated" species. Leroi-Gourhan hypothesized that most animals and abstract symbols in these Paleolithic galleries were regarded as either male or female and that their pairing indicated the essential polar theme of the religious concepts underlying the cave art. The rhinoceri, lions, and bears were unusual in that they were seldom paired and nearly always occurred in the deepest part of the cave. Only about 30 bears (in contrast to 610 horses) are seen, but, like the lion, may be of supreme significance. The non-paired representation and remote location of the bear seem to suggest an androgynous principle of creativity even more fundamental than that of the polarity of masculine and feminine. Somehow the bear, and a few other large predators and man, appear to transcend, or perhaps incorporate, what is divided and external among the other forms of life. The meaning of this separateness can only be guessed at, but it is consistent with the dual aspect of the bear in folk cultures—it is referred to as "grandfather" and "stepmother," and the separate roles of men and women in the ceremony of the slain bear.

At La Vache Cave there was found a long bone shaving, and etched into it was possibly a group scene: six human figures in "reverential posture," a horse, a wounded aurochs (wild cow), and a bear shown face-on. It is, says Marshack, a ceremonial object, "a body of crucial seasonal images . . . a time-factored ceremony and myth involving man with a pantheon of creatures and symbols." The face-on position of animals in this art is extremely rare.

In a cave near Montespan, France, is a clay sculpture of a headless bear. Nearby, between its forepaws, lay a real bear's skull. Beneath it was a hole that probably was the base for a wooden stake on which the head was hung. The life-sized form was suitable for covering with a real bearskin.

At the Wildenmannistock Cave in Switzerland, at about the same time (perhaps 13,000 years ago), men were still placing bear bones and skulls in niches in the cave walls as their ancestors had done for thousands of years. And the bears were still hunted—at the Dragon Cave near Mixnitz, the remains of more than 30,000 bears were concentrated, and some forty-two skulls placed in a line. At the Brillenhöhle Cave in southern Germany, the bears alternated seasonally with men. Human reindeer hunters from the plains to the north migrated south to the mountains in summer, following the herds, and camped in the cave that bears used in winter.

Across Eurasia and America, men were busy etching the symbols of their metaphysics into stone. Among these petroglyphs are scores of bear figures. At Pechialet, in the Dordogne Valley of France, an engraved stone shows two men who may be dancing with a bear. Another, from Mas d'Azil, shows a masked dancer before the paw of a bear, possibly, says Marshack, "aspects of a bear rite, ceremony, or myth, with associated symbols and signs, including the horse, related to the bear story," with the marks of a "time-factored notation." If the story of the Bear Mother and her "rescue" by men who slew the Bear Father was already being told, a famous "bleeding" bear, engraved at Trois Frères Cave in France, may represent not only a typical bear hunt but (perhaps at the same time) the primordial event, the killing of Grandfather Bear.

How did bears come to be drawn on cave walls in the first place? Johannes Meringer, a pioneer archaeologist and religious prehistorian, has called attention to the "idea" of making communicative scratches on the walls as similar to a cave-bear habit. Their cousins, modern brown and black bears, are notorious among foresters for the damage they do to coniferous trees by standing on their hind legs and reaching up to make deep gashes in the trunk, somewhat in the manner of cats "sharpening" their claws on furniture. Meringer describes the petroglyphs as a way of "signing" the walls as men knew the bears to do.

Both the bear's signing marks and human handprints in caves are widely recorded. Thus, says Marshack, "we may say that the Master Bear was the first teacher of this animal art and where he touched was a proper place for animal magic." Human "hand imprints were perhaps placed on the walls in imitation of the imprints of the bear."

Such marks by the bear, both in caves and on trees, were typically seasonal—related to fall occupancy of the cave and spring emergence. Marshack reminds us that human calendars, a lunar notation, have long been kept by hunting peoples. Such archaic calendars, he observes, were used to mark periodic ceremonies, "including aspects of an ancient bear ceremony." Of some fifteen different patterns etched in amber and stone, "in one way or another, each pattern was an act of participation in the story of the bear."

Another unusual aspect of the bear effigies is that several are shown wounded and dying. Pockmarks in the stone image show where actual arrows or spears may have been thrust in a mock hunt. The other species shown, such as the horse, bison, deer, mammoth, and aurochs, were more typically the "everyday" food species, while the bear, being less abundant, was killed and eaten less often. Evidently something other than simple hunting magic was going on. Among tribes celebrating the festival of the slain bear in more recent times, similar circumstances prevail and the explanation could be that the bear, above all others, symbolized the religious aspect not only of the hunt but of a more general exchange of spiritual respect for the gift of food and life. If the same was true of the peoples of the Paleolithic caves, then perhaps the fauna represented in the drawings signified many aspects of a theology of which a part was represented by the sacred hunt and the spirit of the bear.

As for the cave environment itself, certain psychological effects may have been intrinsic to the meaning of cave art. Speaking of Basua Cave in Savona, where footprints left by Neanderthalers 450 meters underground are associated with a "zoomorphic stalagmite," there was apparently a ceremony "long before the birth of art," according to archaeologist Alberto C. Blanc. This was also a cave-bear den. In this "extremely uncanny environment," animal-like stones were the targets of clay pellets. Some of these targets, he notes, "consisted of the intentional modification" of the natural forms. Perhaps such modification was seen by the celebrants as a way of participating in the emergence of living forms from the vague shapes in stone, just as the mother bear is said to lick her cubs into form.

In any case, the analogy of the tunnel and the womb probably flashed into the human imagination long ago. Also, as Bertram Lewin has said, the cave interior reminds us of the interior of our own heads, where we "carry images." It is the place where dreams occur. If the head is regarded as male—as is true in the festival of the slain bear—and the chamber itself as the female womb, both elements of the generative power are present.

But the genetrix—the Bear Mother—is surely predominant, for, in mythology, she is the keeper of the underworld realm. Initially she is the Bear Mother; how she becomes simply the Great Mother of classical times is not known, but there are some clues in the final history of the Bear Mother art from Old Europe.

A third phase in the archaeology of the bear—if we count the Neanderthal constructions as the first and the rock-and-bone art of the caves and shelter as the second—the third represents a transition from the hunting/gathering cultures of the Paleolithic to the earliest farmers of Old Europe—that is, the region circumscribed by present-day Romania to the north, Greece to the south, Austria to the west, and the Black Sea to the east. In this area, between 9,000 and 5,000 years ago, Neolithic or early farming peoples flourished, leaving an enormous archaeological heritage in hundreds of mounds representing early villages and towns. From the lowest strata come bear-shaped "cult vases" decorated with the water symbols that associate the bear with springs and the underworld.

Somewhat later the bear takes a different form, half human and half bear. Hundreds of figurines begin to appear in this debris. Sometimes she appears as a "woman wearing a bear mask," sometimes this Bear Mother is seated, holding a cub, or carrying the cub in a bag on her back. She is often represented with human breasts, sometimes with one hand on a breast. She is referred to as the Lady of Vinca (Vinca being the name of the culture complex).

According to Marija Gimbutas, whose book *The Goddesses and Gods of Old Europe* describes these objects, "Hundreds of such schematized bear-nurse figurines imply the role of the goddess as a protectress of weaklings or of a divine child."

What a falling-off there has been. The great Bear Mother, the keeper of the secrets of generation, birth, and death, has been reduced to a nurse. At first the whole bear appears—as it had in art from the beginning—but she is transformed into a woman with a bear's head (to signify, perhaps that she still represents the nurturing power of the bear) or merely with the mask of a bear. She is dependent on a sky god who is in control, to whom she is subordinate. In her keeping is a "divine child," who is without doubt the Bear Son in his new role as hero.

Evidence for the emergence of the idea of an earth-mother goddess from the older, maternal bear can be seen in traditions at the sanctuary of Ge (or Gaea, the Earth Mother) at Athens. There was a chasm in the earth into which "every year cakes of barley and honey" were thrown in a ritual act, according to Lewis Richard Farnell. What could be a clearer offering to a bear than cakes of the "bear-grain" and honey? In time the great goddess came to be more closely associated with the soil and the cycle of crops and vegetation, but the bear was the first ruler of the underworld to forecast the seasons by his annual entry and emergence. Farnell continues, "We have countless examples from the Mediterranean and other religions of that association of ideas in which the deity of vegetation is naturally regarded as partly belonging to the world below the surface of our earth, hence as a buried and at times dead divinity, into whose realm the soul of the departed enters, to live there—it may be—in divine communion with the lord or the mistress of the souls. Such a divinity may easily come to add to his other functions the role of prophet, in accordance with the widespread belief that all the earth is the source of oracles and prophetic dreams. All these characteristics are found in the Hellenized Dionysus, and they all can be traced in the various parts of the Thracian religion." Farnell's identification of that earlier divinity with Dionysus and the Getai of Thrace leaps ahead in time another 4,000 years, to the era of Greek patriarchal

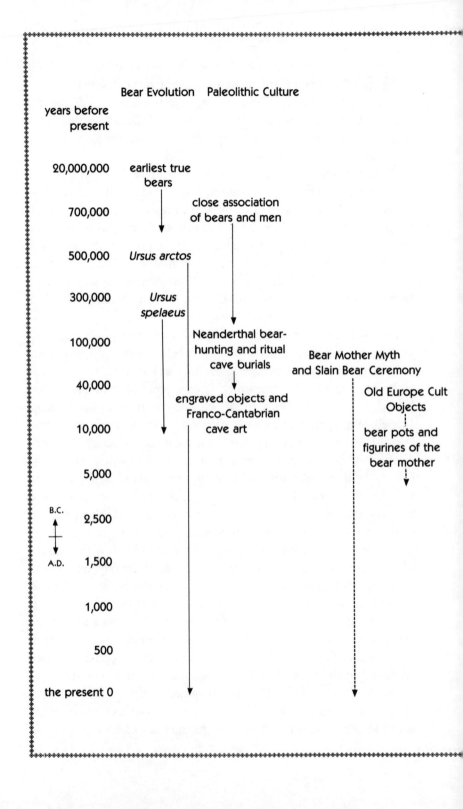

TIME SCALE IN BEAR/MAN INTERACTION

------------indirect evidence

_____"modern" documents

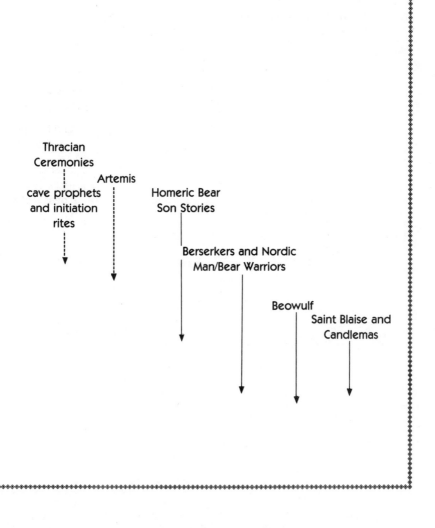

Thracian
Ceremonies

Artemis

cave prophets
and initiation
rites

Homeric Bear
Son Stories

Berserkers and Nordic
Man/Bear Warriors

Beowulf

Saint Blaise and
Candlemas

heroes, but before that it was the great goddess herself who ruled the underworld—and who was probably descended from the Bear Mother.

The figurines from Yugoslavia, Bulgaria, and adjacent countries may mark a local transition of the Bear Mother to the Great Mother. Among these early farmers the creative principle shifts from the animal image to the Great Earth Mother—to the soil itself—personified in the human figure. The emphasis is toward male control; the myth of the Bear Son is flourishing. The next step, at least for the culture of the Occident, is epitomized in the Getic connection, the replacement of the bear altogether by the human image—Artemis, Callisto—and the absorption of the Bear Son myth into the purely human adventurer-hero.

EPILOGUE
The Past and Future of Bears

From the beginning, bear myths and rituals centered on the theme of renewal, whether it was the reincarnation of the soul, the symbolic replenishment of human food, the passage of initiation, or the renewal of clan power in its heraldic image and brave deeds. But the emphasis and meaning of these forms of transformation have changed over the centuries. The question underlying all of them might be: Are the good things of life a provender given or are they an opportunity seized? The Bear Mother story and the archaic ceremony of the hunted and slain bear seem to emphasize the position that man is a beneficiary of a benign providence. It is not so much his power as his humility that brings success in the hunt. The bear, representing all the needs of life, is sent, and its killing is but the final act in a cycle in which men acknowledge the spiritual side of all reality and the centering of power outside themselves. From the earliest preservation of cave-bear bones to the funeral rites for human dead, the theme of the continuing life and the soul is linked to the holiness of the hunt. In his cycle of hibernation the bear may have given men the model for immortality. From the funeral of the dead bear, who has the wisdom of the soul's rebirth, arose the prayers and propitiations that could be directed as well to the renewal of the human spirit.

The emphasis began to change as the economic and social life of man changed. With the coming of the horse as a mount, the ship, combat between village chiefs, the traditions of personal honor and valor in war, territoriality and resource conflicts, the permutations of trade and buccaneering—in short, with the birth of the individual,

LEARNING ABOUT OURSELVES
FROM BEARS

Ever since ancient times, says anthropologist William S. Laughlin, men have argued "from animals to men and back again with sophistication and success." But what do animals tell us most about ourselves? Since man "rediscovered" that he was an animal with the publication of Darwin's *Origin of Species* in 1859, three kinds of animals have stood above all others in this regard. The first is the rat, especially in its white or laboratory form. In hundreds of ways the rat has predicted human reaction to stress, environmental poisons, nutritional deprivations, overcrowding, organ transplants, alcoholism, and so on. Thanks to rats, we understand much about cancer and conditioned reflexes. The second is the primate, especially monkeys and apes. Anyone familiar with Harry Harlow's experiments with mother-deprived monkeys, or Jane Goodall's and Richard Lee's observations of chimpanzee and wild baboon societies is aware of this. Finally, Farley Mowat, George Schaller, and others have shown that we owe much to the study of wolves, wild dogs, and lions in understanding sex roles, group hunting, and cooperation in evolution, human and otherwise.

But none of the above animals is a large omnivore. None tells us about the speculative range of mind over possibilities, the choosing of alternatives in a strongly seasonal climate. Stuck perpetually with pack life, monkeys, rats, and wolves hardly know

heroic ego at the center of consciousness—the bear's role in human thought shifted. At first the story of the Bear Mother was at the source, as was the concept of life as a gift of meat and fur from the Bear Father, and of man's ceremonial responsibility in the acknowledgment and honoring of these gifts. In this earlier tradition, the Bear Sons are but the inheritors, the hunter-teachers of the myth and the rite. In the new phase, attention shifts to the Bear Son as the center. His life is not simply bounded by respect toward the forest-spirit, but is enlarged by his own ursine strength. He becomes

true solitude or the needs and joys of independence. The individual counts little among them. What more do we cherish as humans than these things that the bear can perhaps illuminate—the freedom and capacity for personal decisions and individual idiosyncrasies that decide our fate?

In their social interactions bears seem more like humans whose life is always on the knife-edge between the soliloquy of the self and the chorus of the group. Evolving man moved toward individual uniqueness, liberation from group-think, away from the invisibility of the one in the many, or the final tyranny like that of the ant colony. Who better to demonstrate to us autonomy and its special style of attention and introspection than the social yet irascible, supreme recusant, *Arctos*?

In the third stanza of her poem "Many Winters," Nancy Wood speaks of this lesson from the bear:

> There is the young girl in me traveling west
> With the bear which taught me to look inside.
> The bear stood by himself and said,
> There is a time for being alone
> So that you do not take on
> The appearance of your friends.
> There is a time for being at home with yourself.

a traveler, a mighty fighter, or a vicious avenger and cunning survivor. As a true Bear Son, his adventures carry him into the underworld and he is believed by others to be lost. He overcomes many obstacles, but by dint of his imagination and strength he returns victorious, as though risen from the dead, bringing with him the spoils.

In both the Bear Mother story and the Bear Son continuation of it, there are great feasts, the penultimate celebration of the use of the fruits of the earth. The older ritual emphasizes the role of man as actor-receiver, the later ritual as actor-taker. Likewise, the feast has a different quality. Where the hunted bear was the sacramental object of the feast, the timing was only broadly fixed by the men themselves. Usually it took place at the season of the year's renewal, but the "discovery" of the den was part of the "luck" of the hunter. The festival was centered on the religious nesting of the divine animal. Offerings of tobacco and sharing of the hearth and table with the spirit of the bear itself were inherent in it. As time passed, the aforementioned shift in mentality came to prevail. The bear was reared in captivity; its life and the time of its death came under human regulation. Increasingly, domestic animals were also sacrificed as part of the festival. The idea of sacrifice, foreign to the hunt, emerged—a sharing of harvest by ambitious men seeking the favor of a god, or paying a debt for a successful venture. Sacrifice was the calculated dispersal of wealth or booty, a negotiation between like minds, typically part of the Bear Son story.

Bears and other animals gradually disappeared from the Bear Son legend, to be replaced in the classical West by men or monsters— or gods and goddesses who looked human. Just as the metaphysics came to resemble a power struggle among men, the priests (as shamans at first) themselves gathered power that formerly, in the ritual enactments of the Bear Mother myth, had been scattered among the participants where the individual role changed in different years, the choice of actors depending on the vicissitudes of the hunt or on the personal dreams and visions that came sometimes unbidden. The sacredness of nonhuman life did not vanish from the religion of the heirs of the Bear Son. But it was, over many centuries, dispersed among domestic animals, the slaves or pawns in the dramatic mimicry by which the analogy of the struggle for power among the immortals affects the fate of men.

In the modern view, the main cultural baggage of modern Europe and the West is essentially Mediterranean. History is mostly a series of pulses emanating from the religious and philosophical traditions of the Indo-European and Latin world. The arts proper, as well as the arts of statecraft and civil rights are rooted in the Romans, Greeks, and Hebrews—and more remotely in the peoples of Egypt or the Near and Middle East. In writing and reading about the bear, we have been awakened to the extent of our loss of the northern connection, of the great silence of its rich traditions in the modern world. Without denying the wealth of Mediterranean civilization, we have had our eyes opened to the spirit of ecological partnership between men and the biotic world so true of the North and so scanty by comparison in the South. History has obscured the sense of kinship with the natural world and the reverence of nonhuman life in all its forms as profoundly sung, danced, and storied by ancestors in Eurasia and America who did not write, and whose drums were silenced by force. Taught to see the northerners as barbaric plunderers—that is, to see the whole of that heritage in terms of its late prehistory—we have accepted the bookish view of human progress and spirituality. Symbolizing only the bear's strength the northern legends of piratic wayfaring—the plundering Norsemen, Goths, Vandals, and pillaging Vikings—are but distortions of traditions that earlier had a very different tenor, often expressed as a subtle and beautiful collaboration between creative men and the natural world around them. We have become aware through study of the bear that the older pagan thought was a culture in many ways as spiritual, elegant, and intelligent as that shaped by men anywhere. At the very least it cherished the earth and all its life. At its best it may have been a true source of civilization's most valued ideas.

Only in a few places are the bears themselves doing well. Because of their conspicuous size, competition with man for food, and shyness in the face of machines and roads, bears are rapidly declining in numbers and disappearing from much of their earlier range. The major exceptions are the American black bear, the brown bear in some parts of Asia and the American island refuges, and the polar bear. These still have populations that are self-sustaining, although their disappearance from many local areas still occurs. Bears have been killed for centuries for their gallbladders, penis bones, paws, and other "medicinal" parts. In recent years, however, an international trade has begun in which professional hunters illegally poach brown, black, and polar bears for these organs, often leaving the rest of the bear as waste. In northwestern America, particularly, such hunting threatens black-bear populations.

In the last 300 years the brown bear has almost vanished from Western Europe; in Britain it became extinct nearly 1,000 years ago, having already disappeared from Denmark; it ceased to exist in Holland three centuries ago, and in North Africa, Germany, and

Switzerland in the nineteenth century. In Eastern Europe it fares somewhat better, but is declining in many localities: a few hundred each live in Greece, Czechoslovakia, Hungary, Bulgaria, and Poland; in Yugoslavia there are around 2,000, in Romania 3,000. All told, perhaps about 18,000 brown bears now live in twenty to fifty widely scattered European populations. The great reserve of brown bears in the Old World is the USSR, with an estimated 100,000 bears, mostly in the Sikhote Alin, Altai, and Baikal regions, and the Sayan Mountains. A few probably persist in Iran, Syria, Afghanistan, Kashmir, and Iraq; Japan has 3,000.

In America the brown bear has had a disastrous century. Though more than 20,000 remain in Alaska and Canada, in the other states of the U.S. it now numbers in the low hundreds. The details of the eradication of the grizzly from the American West have been widely published, the final disappearance in most states occurring between 1870 and 1930. It remains today only in four of the contiguous states. Even in the U.S. national parks (Yellowstone and Glacier) the grizzly faces an uncertain future because the density of tourists increases the frequency of confrontations with men, and the bears are subject to heavy mortality when they travel beyond the park boundaries. The brown bear is a shy animal and retreats from road-building, logging, mining, and other construction, especially if machines are used. For this reason its potential habitat is reduced, even when the bears are not directly killed. As for hunting, only rarely has a population of any species of bear been threatened by deliberate hunting. Of the thirty-three grizzlies known to have been shot in 1980, for example, only six were killed by hunters. Many more bears are shot (or poisoned or trapped) by people who kill bears on the assumption that bears and people (or livestock, orchards, and beehives) are incompatible.

The American black bear is now found in all the Canadian provinces, twenty-three of the United States, and two or three states of Mexico. At present, its greatest populations are in southern Canada and the northern United States. No doubt its populations will continue to adjust to the pattern of land use. Since it is less shy than the brown and more adaptable to human impact on the land, this bear is not likely to suffer extinction in the foreseeable future.

The polar bear was at serious risk at mid-century, when aircraft began to be used in hunting it, but since then the five nations on whose northern frontiers the bear is found have moved to protect the polar bear from levels of killing or capturing that would be likely to destroy it as a species. Pipelines, drill rigs, military activities, roads, and other human activities in the Arctic tend to drive the bear from such areas, so that its circumpolar population of roughly 15,000 may be further reduced. One thousand live in zoos, where they have begun to be bred successfully in recent years.

Little information exists on the status of the Asiatic black bear (which is a bad sign in itself). As a reputed killer of livestock it is persecuted throughout most of its range, and it is also said to be reduced due to forest clearing throughout south central and southeast Asia and Japan.

The sun and sloth bears are suffering the same loss of forest cover. The sun bear is accused of damaging commercial coconut trees, and both are feared for their occasional aggressive attitude toward people. Together with the spectacled bear of South America, these tropical bears are in jeopardy. Legal protection is poorly enforced, poaching is common, and drastic forest clearing and modification of native habitats point to diminished space and safety for them.

Asian bears are killed as they have been for centuries, especially for their fat, used for healing purposes, and the *os bacculum* (penis bone), which is considered an aphrodisiac.

The giant panda, although strictly protected in the three or four provinces in which it occurs in western China, probably does not number much above 1,000. Such numbers for a wild species approach a level of genetic and ecological risk. Twenty or so exist in Chinese zoos, and probably another dozen in other zoos of the world.

The northern bears have the rather paradoxical advantage of being classed as "game" animals, which means (in all but a few places) that they are no longer "pests" or varmints on which bounties are paid. While this usually means that they can be legally hunted, restrictions on hunting are enforced by wardens, and in most places money from the hunting license increases research and management programs so that much more is known about the bears' populations. The sun, sloth, and spectacled bear remain poorly differentiated from pest status. In some American states (such as Maine) and European countries (such as Norway), farmers or ranchers suffering bear damage to their property are compensated from government funds.

Current research on hibernating bears includes study of the excretory physiology—the animal's capacity to carry on life processes without excretion and without poisoning itself with its own nitrogenous wastes. Since excretory failure is a widespread corollary of age and disease in man, there may be hormonal controls or other biochemical secrets yet to be discovered that could have medical uses. Also, the metabolic control in hibernation which produces a state of self-contained deep sleep might be useful in surgery or even in future space travel. So it is that each year dozens of sleeping bears are dragged from their dens to become outdoor laboratories—drugged, measured, and sampled in many ways—and put back again in the hope that their experience will be no more harmful for them than a bad dream.

Field research on bears, especially their space and habitat needs, is essential in order to provide for their survival in a world of competing land uses. The pioneering work by John and Frank Craighead in the remote tracking of the daily and weekly movements of grizzly bears by the use of radio telemetry has greatly advanced our understanding of that species. As the Craigheads have noted, the dark side of such research is that it tends to become scientifically fashionable and is imitated with bureaucratic monotony, with endless "reevaluating" of what is already known or "testing" of new electronic devices. Perhaps there is some point at which we should say "Enough!" and cease to drug, ear-clip, paint, tattoo, tooth-pull, vaginal-smear, implant, collar, and probe.

In general, bears need abundant space and solitude, and as omnivores they require diversity of food. Since they are not likely to have large areas of wilderness given over to their sole use, their greatest need is for men to participate with them in coexistence. In such a rapport, respect for the bear is essential, for it can be a dangerous animal. But more often the fear of bears is exaggerated. The news media sensationalize the occasional deaths and injuries of people by bears, even though the frequency of such incidents is comparatively low. Being highly intelligent, bears can learn to live with man, as well as man with bears, if given the opportunity and "education." Where there are abundant wild resources—or, as in some parts of Eastern Europe, where grains and fruits are planted for the bears—they learn not to harm crops and livestock. On the other hand, people can learn much that will help them to live peacefully with bears—to make their own presence known in the wilderness, to remove tempting food from them as much as possible, to remain at a distance, and to deal properly with an aggressive bear.

But the risks of living in a world with wild bears can never be totally removed. Only when we are ready to accept that risk as part of the price of having wild bears will we contain the irrational fears and thoughtless habitat destruction that result in the loss of bears from the world.

AFTERWORD
Fear of Bears

The image that most people have of Hokkaido (where I traveled the month of July 1972) is one of trees, bears, and the Ainu—the north, and virgin forests—miles of dense woods with dirt roads and few towns. A respectable area of forest for a smallish island, though not comparable to the great sweeps of trees in Siberia or British Columbia. And yet an eminent botanist whose life work has been the study of North Pacific island forest ecology, and in particular Hokkaido, told me, "Virgin forests! They call this place and that place a virgin forest. There's scarcely a true virgin forest on the whole island." Hokkaido, for all its untamed aspect, has been pretty well exploited, logged at least once and now entering the second or third time around. The great lowland woods and bogs have been drained and converted to pasture or agriculture. Now, on the southern coast, giant industrial combines are making plans for more instant cities. The decentralization of Japanese industry will mean that the quiet shores of Hokkaido will come to suffer the same pollution as afflicts the Pacific coast of Honshu. The demand for timber continually increases, and forestry scientists reluctantly revise their estimates of what "sustained yield" means to satisfy the greed of the economy. (The virgin forests of British Columbia, which are being clear-cut right now, are largely being sold to Japan.) Water pollution is such that I have been told the salmon enter only one river in all of Hokkaido now, the Tokachi. At the same time an aggressive commercial tourism pushes roads and inns deeper and deeper into the mountains or onto isolated coasts, disrupting the remaining natural ecosystems and degrading the intangible essence called wilderness, which evaporates when too many people come to look at it.

The thrust of industrial civilization is toward growth and continual expansion. The capitalist system measures all success by growth and profit and, as an economic system, has no chance of ever achieving a condition of balance, harmony, and stability. The socialist countries are committed to their own vision of growth and progress, which could conceivably achieve a state of balance, but certainly not as long as an abrasive competition between the socialist and capitalist nations forces both into ever more expansive planning. "Infinite growth is not possible on a planet with finite resources."

Although mankind has had an increasingly destructive impact on the earth over the centuries (loss of soils through deforestation and erosion; extinction of species), the accelerated growth of the past few decades—both in population and in counterecological technology, has brought the problem to crisis proportions.

Social consciousness in the Occident began with revulsion against slavery and serfdom. People came to see that an owning class grossly exploiting a working class was wrong. Then some came to comprehend the errors of racial prejudice, and to see that the exploitation of undeveloped peoples by developed nations was not a proper way for a society to sustain itself. Ecological consciousness expands this process one step more: we begin to grasp that nature has its own kind of "standing," and that "the people"—"the global community"—should mean all living beings. As the Plains Indians would say, "The trees are the standing people, birds the flying people, fish the swimming people. There are four-legged people; we are the two-legged peoples." A revolutionary ecological morality tells us we cannot forever exploit the world of nature, any more than a healthy society can maintain itself by the exploitation of other human beings. We can work with nature, trade with it, borrow from it, and repay it, but we must not misuse it. And this is not just a "moral" rule; it is a hard scientific rule; if we break it for too long, we shall surely be destroyed.

In late July 1972, deep in the Daisetsu range of Hokkaido, at about ten-thirty in the morning, on the little summit called Goshikidake, I found myself in conversation with some fellow hikers while taking a rest and looking at the view. We stood there in the

wind and sun, looking out over the vastest and wildest scene in all
Hokkaido. Our talk turned to bears. Three young men, meteorology
students at Hokkaido University, said they were worried about bears.
Now everyone knows that the Hokkaido brown bear or *higuma*—
Ursus arctos—is a formidable and cranky bear. Knows, that is, from
what they've heard and read. Everyone in Hokkaido seems ready to
tell you again about the two (or was it three?) students who were
killed by a bear in the Hidaka mountains several years ago. So hikers
walking the trails of the high ridges fear to venture off the path,
and prefer to camp in bunches. They hang little bells on their packs,
or carry dangling transistor radios playing music all the way. To
scare off bears. But—the actual danger? I ventured to ask. I'd been
watching closely from every vantage point for many days (based on
acquaintance over the years with the North American brown bear
in the Sierra Nevada and Cascade Mountains of the West) and hadn't
seen the least trace of a bear. I argued, "I doubt that there are bears
in this area right now, and if there were one or two, the statistical
chances of being attacked by a bear are much slighter than the
chances you'd have of getting hit by a car in Tokyo; and besides,
with a little knowledge one could probably avert the attack of a bear
through some skillful psychology. . . . " I argued thus because I was
getting tired of being warned about bears by everyone in the mountains. My own pleasure and habit is to camp alone and walk alone;
in fact, I had hoped to see a bear. They were adamant. "I am afraid
of bears up here," one sturdily insisted. I felt it wasn't bears, but
the idea of bears that he feared: the unseen, dark forces that lurk in
the forest of our mind. To be too concerned with bears while hiking
in the mountains means you cannot become one with nature; nature
appears to harbor evils. Perhaps we should shoot all bears? And the
next thought is, Perhaps we should cut down the forests. Clean it
up. Get that messy stuff out of the way. This line of fear and thought
brings us back to the environmental crisis. Clearly it won't do.

But still, what are we to do about bears? It is very well to say
that we must feel and practice brotherhood and solidarity with all
living beings, but what about bears? Thinking about the food chain
is not much consolation here; man, who usually eats other smaller
animals and various plants, could well be just another sort of bear-
food.

Village and tribal peoples in Africa and India live close to large predators in relative ease and learn to be comfortable with tigers in the jungle just beyond the garden, but modern civilized society simply shoots them all. The Buddha, in some of his previous lives, according to the *Jataka* tales, entered the food chain fearlessly, and there is a story of his feeding himself to a hungry mother tiger. This is too much to ask of most of us, except as a reminder that we have a part to play in the wheel of life too, and it would be well if we could play our role elegantly and graciously when the time comes. The Cheyenne Indians have a saying: "Let us all be meat, to nourish one another, that we all may grow." The anthropologist Weston LaBarre says, "The first religion is to kill God and eat him." Or her. And the second is to give yourself away.

Revolutionary thought, in the vanguard of society, purports to be compassionately and intelligently concerned with the ultimate welfare of man. Human welfare goes beyond mere survival. What most of us desire for ourselves and others is a vivid life, a life that is real, with work, sharing, occasional ecstasy, and occasional deep contemplation. The bear, as the Ainu say, is the God of the Mountain. His energy, vigor, and alertness are pure expressions of the power of the wild forest. To meet him is not just an occasion of fear, but of delight and awe. We learn to accept bears in the mountains as part of the risky beauty of life. A rancher losing a few head of horses or cattle to a raiding bear should be seen to be paying "taxes" to nature—and the whole society should help him bear the burden by paying the rancher back for his loss. Our world would be sadder and poorer if there were no bears. The creative energy that makes poems, revolutions, civilizations, needs the spontaneity that nature demonstrates. A truly accomplished society would be dynamic, stable, lean, and playful—with a power that came from within.

Yet we must be practical. "A century of development" has not been so bad for Hokkaido; for most people who live there, life has gotten easier and better. Only the Ainu are worse off than before. When Ainu culture is finally gone, those persons who are genetic survivors of the Ainu but Japanese in language and culture will probably emotionally side with the conqueror. But don't be too sure—five hundred years after the first white men set foot in North America, some American Indian groups still tenaciously fight for their heritage. The Hopi and other Pueblos, the Navajo, Mohawk,

Iroquois, Cheyenne, Pit River, and a dozen other tribes could be named.

Brazil, in the name of developing the hinterland of the Amazon, is engaged in a kind of genocide at this moment. Small, peaceable cultures of Amazon Indians who have lived for millennia in the jungle with amazing plant knowledge and highly specialized, efficient techniques are being displaced or downright murdered. American and European companies are standing in the wings. The ecological tragedy is the loss of a vast natural ecosystem before anyone has had a chance to really study how it worked. There is a high chance of irreversible soil damage following on attempts at opening the forest to mechanized agriculture. The human tragedy is twofold. As the Amazon Indians are destroyed, with them dies their subtle and ancient system of plant knowledge. And with them dies one of the few remaining living examples of how human beings can survive in quiet, nondisruptive, energy-conserving, and apparently spiritually satisfactory ways in what appears to be a very hostile environment. The developed world's attitude is that a few Indians cannot be allowed to stand in the way of progress, or social evolution. Most people confronted with such problems don't know what to say, they've been so indoctrinated with a simple consumer or materialist concept of progress. They would rationalize that the plight of the Indians is unfortunate; but the process of history is bound to overtake these backward peoples, and, in the long range, it's for the benefit of the majority.

The shocking paradox is this: the progress of civilization by which we justify the dislocation and destruction of small aboriginal societies is the same process that is bringing all mankind to the environmental crisis! Much of modern civilization is useful, beautiful, a superb testament to the human spirit. But one fact cannot be avoided: what we call modern civilization leads away from variety and diversity and toward monoculture (as in agriculture, or as in mass television culture); it leads away from rich genetic information storage and toward a poverty of life-information—that is, fewer sorts of living beings. Civilization is not in harmony with the process of biological evolution, but runs counter to it. "Man is literally undoing the work of organic evolution," writes Edward Abbey. It may prove to be that the Ainu, or the Indians of the Amazon, in their slower but surer way, are the true vectors of human history and human social progress.

A gloomy outlook for the near future:

- growing oil and coal shortages, leading to reckless gambles with nuclear power plants and the many dangers thereof
- increasing pollution, especially from petrochemical industries
- more population growth
- soil depletion and agricultural crises, leading to localized famines
- extinction of wild animal species, and reckless last-minute exploitation of all animal and plant resources
- more and worse wars

All of which brings us to the question: What is to be done? A great revolution or transformation is called for. But what revolution could aspire to bring down a vested interest as huge as the world technological-industrial cancer? And must we destroy it all? Some possibilities exist. We must shed an economic system that fosters wasteful growth and pointless expansion. With help from the scientific community we must restudy our technological options and move in the direction of energy-conserving, low-pollution, high-efficiency technology, which might produce adequately for basic human needs using less net energy and less exotic materials. We must seek technologies and economic systems that renounce short-term gain in favor of long-range stability.

We must move away from the centralist, statist conception of government and see that a "country" should be a natural biological region (a biome, or watershed region) and its people an actual ethnic entity, as far as possible. In our parliaments or soviets we must include the votes and voices of trees, rivers, and animals, as well as human beings. In part (and here we can learn from the Ainu) this is done with ritual, dance, and myth. She who becomes a bear in the bear-dance for a brief while can speak for the bear. Thus the world of nature penetrates the political meeting-chambers of mankind.

Some of the wealth of the overdeveloped regions will have to be invested wisely back into the sustainable economies of the undeveloped countries. The third world and the fourth—or aboriginal—world must not be forced into alien political models that deny their own cultural integrity; in fact, we may have more to learn from tribal models of society, in the matter of organization, than they have to learn from us.

And each of us, where we live and in association with our neighbors and comrades, must join in a struggle that is not only against oppressive social systems, but in defense of the land. In defense of the earth, air, water, where we live. In taking up this defense, we will become in our own place "aboriginals" of that place—and cease to fear bears.

Humans are marvelous animals, but now we must prove our real worth. At the Stockholm environmental conference in June of 1972, the Chinese delegation stated, "Man is the most precious of all things." This should be changed to say, "Man will be the most precious of all things when he comes to realize the previousness of all things."

—GARY SNYDER

Sources

Bear imagery, lore, anecdote, and natural history are not scarce resources and we have undoubtedly forgotten some who have helped or shared their ideas and experience with us. But we do wish to thank all who have said, "A book on bears! Have you seen . . . ?" as well as the experts whose remarks, however casual, may have been seminal in an encounter that itself has slipped from memory while the idea lingered, and we ask the indulgence of the friends, family, and colleagues overlooked in our list below.

For their help we are indebted to Don Brenneis, Albert B. Friedman, Harvey Botwin, Dolores LaChapelle, Virginia Renner, Joseph Meeker, Lance Olsen, Charles Jonkel, Barbara Duden, Ivan Illich, Robert Walker, Henning Dunker, Maurya and Robert Falk, Florence Krall, Grace Sanders, Tuula Stark, Dick Shepard, Susan Hertel, Paul Falstich, Kali Sanders, Margaret Mathies, Charles Schweighauser, Werner Warmbrunn, Stephen Glass, Dorothea Yale, Carl Hertel, John Rodman, Lucian Marquis, Winifred Ragsdale, William Pietz, Barre Toelken, David Rockwell, Peter Nabokov, Harry Senn, Ronald Macaulay, Gary Snyder, Richard Cooley, June Shepard, Kate Stafford, Beverly Scales, Teresa Hildago, June Berman, Bill Winn, Doug Peacock, and Judson Emerick. Staff members were cordial and helpful without exception at the Honnold Library, the Huntington Library, the Frick Art Reference Library, the J. P. Morgan Library, the Bodleian Library, Trinity College Library in Dublin, the British Museum, the Museum of Man, and the Library of Congress.

We do not feel that this book is the product of an exhaustive review of any aspect of the bear. Much depended on what was, in the chancy course of things, available to us. This is but a sample of the enormous literature in many languages relating to the impact of the bear on human consciousness. We much appreciated the patience of Barbara Burn, William Strachan, and others at Viking Penguin who waited for a manuscript delivered years beyond its due date (and even then we yielded it reluctantly, for we felt that the bear was only beginning to come out for us).

The sources we used are given below in three general categories: natural history, mythology, and literature.

NATURAL HISTORY

Bromley, G. *Bears of the South Far Eastern USSR*. New Delhi: Indian National Science Documentation Center, 1973.

Brothwell, Don, and Eric Higgs, eds. *Science in Archaeology*. London: Thames and Hudson, 1969.

Caras, Roger A. *Monarch of Deadman Bay: The Life and Death of a Kodiak Bear*. Boston: Little, Brown, 1969.

Chorn, John, and Robert S. Hoffman. "*Ailuropoda melanoleuca.*" *Mammalian Species* 110 (1978): 1–6.

Cockrum, E. Londell. *Introduction to Mammalogy*. New York: Ronald, 1962.

Collinder, Bjorn. *The Lapps*. Princeton: Princeton University Press, 1949.

Collins, Larry R., and James K. Page, Jr. *Ling-Ling and Hsing-Hsing*. Garden City, N.Y.: Anchor, 1973.

Couffer, Jack. *Song of Wild Laughter*. New York: Simon and Schuster, 1963.

Craighead, Frank C., Jr. *Track of the Grizzly*. San Francisco: Sierra Club, 1979.

Craighead, Frank C., Jr., and John J. Craighead. *Grizzly Bear Prehibernation and Denning Activities as Determined by Radiotracking*. Washington, D.C.: Wildlife Society, 1972.

Dolensek, Emil, and Barbara Burn. *A Practical Guide to Impractical Pets*. New York: Viking, 1976.

Dumezil, Georges. *Archaic Roman Religion*. Vol. 3. Chicago: University of Chicago Press, 1966.

East, Ben. *Bears*. New York: Crown, 1977.

Egbert, Allan L., and Michael H. Lugue. "Among Alaska's Brown Bears." *National Geographic,* September 1975.

Eisenberg, John F. *The Mammalian Radiations*. Chicago: University of Chicago Press, 1981.

Ewer, R. F. *The Carnivores*. Ithaca, N.Y.: Cornell University Press, 1973.

Flyger, Vagn, and Marjorie R. Townsend. "The Migration of Polar Bears." *Scientific American,* February 1968.

Gilbert, Bil. "The Great Grizzly Controversy." *Audubon Magazine,* January 1976.

Gordon, Lesley. *Green Magic, Flowers, Plants and Herbs in Lore and Legend.* New York: Viking, 1977.

Grinnell, Joseph Bird, *et al. Fur-Bearing Mammals of California.* Vol. 1. Berkeley: University of California Press, 1937.

Hagenbeck, Carl. *Beasts and Men.* New York: Longmans, 1909.

Haynes, Bessie Doak, and Edgar Haynes. *The Grizzly Bear.* Norman: University of Oklahoma Press, 1966.

Herrero, Stephen. "A Comparison of Some Features of the Evolution, Ecology, and Behavior of Black and Grizzly/Brown Bears." *Carnivore* 1 (1978): 7–17.

————. "Man and Grizzly Bear." *Bioscience* 20 (1970): 1148–53.

Hoagland, Edward. *Red Wolves and Black Bears.* New York: Random House, 1976.

Jorgenson, Jeffrey P. "Annotated Bibliography of the Spectacled Bear (*Tremarctos ornatus*) and Related Fossil Species." Ms., 1980.

Kittredge, William. "Grizzly Too Close." *Outside,* December–January, 1982.

Krott, Peter. *Bears in the Family.* New York: Dutton, 1964.

Kurtén, Björn. *The Age of Mammals.* New York: Columbia University Press, 1971.

————. *The Cave Bear Story.* New York: Columbia University Press, 1971.

Laurie, Andrew, and John Seidensticker. "Behavioral Ecology of Sloth Bears." *Journal of the Zoological Society of London* 5 (1977): 187–204.

Laycock, George. "Everybody's Favorite Bear." *Audubon Magazine,* May 1977.

Lentifer, Jack W. "Alaskan Polar Bear Movements from Mark and Recovery." *Arctic* 36:3 (September 1983).

Lindsey, F. G., and E. C. Meslow. "Home Range and Habitat Use by Black Bears in Southwest Washington." *Journal of Wildlife Management* 41:413 (1977).

McCracken, Harold. *The Beast That Walks Like a Man.* Garden City, N.Y.: Doubleday, 1955.

McNamee, Thomas. *The Grizzly Bear.* New York: Knopf, 1984.

Mallenson, Jeremy. *The Shadow of Extinction.* New York: Macmillan, 1978.

Martinka, C. J. *1968 Bear Management Activities, Glacier National Park.* National Park Service Progress Report. Washington, D.C., 1968.

Martinka, Clifford J., and Katherine L. McArthur, eds. *Bears—Their Biology and Management.* 4th International Conference on Bear Research and Management, Bear Biology Association. Washington, D.C.: U.S. Government Printing Office, 1980.

Matson, J. R. "Bears—Their Dormancy." *Journal of Mammalogy,* 27:3 (1946): 203–12.

Matthews, L. Harrison. *The Life of Mammals*. New York: Universe, 1971.

Morris, Desmond. *The Mammals*. New York: Harper & Row, 1965.

Morris, Ramona, and Desmond Morris. *Men and Pandas*. New York: McGraw-Hill, 1966.

Nicholas, C. W. "The Sloth Bear." *Loris* 13:4 (1974): 203–10.

Olsen, Lance. "The Cognitive Complexity of the Grizzly Bear." Ms., n.d.

Peyton, Bernard. "Ecology, Distribution and Food Habits of Spectacled Bears in Peru." *Journal of Mammalogy* 61:4 (1980): 639–52.

Sarich, V. M. "The Giant Panda Is a Bear." *Nature* 245 (1973): 218–20.

———. "Transferrins." *Transactions of the Zoological Society of London* 33 (1973): 165–71.

Schaller, George B. *The Deer and the Tiger*. Chicago: University of Chicago Press, 1967.

Schaller, George B., and Gorden R. Lowther. "The Relevance of Carnivore Behavior to the Study of Early Hominids." *Southwestern Journal of Anthropology* 25:4 (1969): 307–41.

Schmidt, John K., and Douglas Gilbert, eds. *Big Game of North America*. Harrisburg, Pa.: Stackpole, 1978.

Schneider, William. *Where the Grizzly Walks*. Missoula, Mont.: Mountain Press, 1977.

Schommaker, W. J. *The World of the Grizzly Bear*. Philadelphia: Lippincott, 1968.

Sheldon, William G. *The Wilderness Home of the Giant Panda*. Amherst: University of Massachusetts Press, 1975.

Sitwell, Nigel. "The Inscrutable Panda and Professor Hu." *International Wildlife Magazine,* May–June 1982.

Stanley, Steven M. *The New Evolutionary Timetable*. New York: Basic Books, 1981.

Sternhart, Peter. "Getting to Know Bruin Better." *National Wildlife* 16:5 (1978).

Storer, T. I., and L. P. Tevis. *California Grizzly*. Berkeley: University of California Press, 1955.

Storey, Harry. "Bears and Water Holes." *Loris* 14:6 (1978).

Stroganov, S. U. *Carnivorous Mammals of Siberia*. Washington, D.C.: National Science Foundation, 1969.

Wilber, Ernest P. *Mammals of the World*. Vol. 2. Baltimore: Johns Hopkins University Press, 1968.

MYTHOLOGY

Alesenko, E. A. "The Cult of the Bear Among the Ket (Yenisei Ostyaks)." In *Popular Beliefs and Folklore Tradition in Siberia,* edited by V. Dioszegi, 175–92. Bloomington: Indiana University Press, 1968.

Anisimov, A. F. "Cosmological Concepts of the Peoples of the North" and "The Shaman's Text of the Events and the Origin of Shamanistic Rite." In *Studies in Siberian Shamanism,* edited by Harry N. Michael, 157–229, 84–123. Toronto: Arctic Institute of North America, University of Toronto, 1963.

Asbjornsen, Peter Christian, and Jorgen Moe. *Norwegian Folk Tales.* New York: Pantheon, 1960.

Barbeau, Marius. "Bear Mother." *Journal of Folklore* 59:231 (1945): 1–12.

Barrett, Samuel Alfred. *Pomo Bear Doctors.* Berkeley: University of California Press, 1912.

Barrionuevo, Alfonsina. *Cuzco, Magic City.* Lima: Editorial Universo, S.A., n.d.

Birkey-Smith, Kai. *The Eskimos.* London: Methuen, 1936.

Blanc, Alberto C. *Social Life of Early Man.* Chicago: Aldine, 1967.

Brothwell, Dan, and Eric Higgs, eds. *Science in Archaeology.* London: Thames and Hudson, 1969.

Brumfield, Allaire Chandor. *The Attic Festivals of Demeter and Their Relation to the Agricultural Year.* New York: Arno, 1981.

Bullfinch, Thomas. "Callisto." In *Bullfinch's Mythology.* New York: Macmillan, 1973.

Campbell, Joseph. *Historical Atlas of World Mythology.* Vol. 1, *The Way of the Animal Powers.* New York: Harper & Row, 1983.

———. "The Master Bear." In *The Masks of God,* vol. 1: *Primitive Mythology.* New York: Viking, 1959.

Carpenter, Rhys. *Folk Tale, Fiction and Saga in the Homeric Epic.* Berkeley: University of California Press, 1956.

Chernetsov, V. N. "Concepts of the Soul Among the Ub Ugarians." In *Studies in Siberian Shamanism,* edited by Harry N. Michael, 3–45. Toronto: Arctic Institute of North America, University of Toronto, 1963.

Collinder, Bjorn. *The Lapps.* Princeton: Princeton University Press, 1949.

Cox, George W. *The Mythology of All Nations.* London: Kegan Paul, 1882.

Darnell, Regna. "Hallowell's 'Bear Ceremonialism' and the Emergence of Boazian Anthropology." *Ethos* 5:1 (1977): 13–30.

Diòszegi, V., ed. *Popular Beliefs and Folklore Tradition in Siberia.* Bloomington: Indiana University Press, 1968.

Downing, Christine. *The Goddess.* New York: Crossroad, 1981.

Dumezil, Georges. *Archaic Roman Religion.* Vol. 2. Chicago: University of Chicago Press, 1966.

Elderkin, George W. *Kantharos.* Princeton: Princeton University Press, 1924.

Eliade, Mircea. *Birth and Rebirth.* New York: Harper & Row, 1958.

———. "The Rites and Symbols of Initiation: The Mysteries of 'The Ainu Bear Sacrifice.' " In *Man and the Sacred.* New York: Harper & Row, 1967.

Elms, Alan C. "The Three Bears: Four Interpretations." *Journal of American Folklore* 90:357 (1977): 257–73.

Ewers, John C. "The Bear Cult Among the Assiniboin and Their Neighbors of the Northern Plains." *Southwestern Journal of Anthropology* 11 (1955): 1–14.

Fodor, Nandor. "Nightmares of Bears." *American Imago* 6 (1949): 341–52.

Fontenrose, Joseph. *Orion: The Myth of the Hunter and Huntress.* Chapter 10, "Kallisto and Zeus." Berkeley: University of California Press, 1949.

Frazer, James G. "Killing the Sacred Bear." In *The Golden Bough.* New York: Macmillan, 1951.

Funmaker, Walter W. "The Bear in Winnebago Culture: A Study in Cosmology and Society." Ms., 1974.

Garman, Douglas. *Greek Oracles.* London: Elek, 1965.

Gimbutas, Marija. *The Goddesses and Gods of Old Europe.* Berkeley: University of California Press, 1982.

Hagar, Stansbury. "The Celestial Bear." *Journal of American Folklore* 13 (1900): 92–103.

Hallowell, A. I. "Bear Ceremonialism in the Northern Hemisphere." *American Anthropologist* (n.s.) 28 (1926): 1–175.

Harrison, Jane Ellen. *Themis.* New Hyde Park, N.Y.: University Books, 1962.

Hollingshead, Mary Brooks Berg. "Legend, Cult and Architecture at Three Sanctuaries of Artemis." Ph.D. diss., Bryn Mawr, 1979.

Hultkrantz, Ake. *The Religions of the American Indians.* Berkeley: University of California Press, 1979.

Huxley, Francis. *The Way of the Sacred.* London: Aldus, 1974.

James, E. O. *Sacrifice and Sacrament.* New York: Barnes and Noble, 1972.

Jung, C. G., and C. Kerenyi. *Essay on a Science of Mythology: The Myth of the Divine Child, and the Mysteries of Eleusis.* Princeton: Princeton University Press, 1949.

Kerenyi, C. *Eleusis: Archetypal Image of Mother and Daughter.* London: Routledge and Kegan Paul, 1967.

———. *The Religion of the Greeks and Romans.* London: Thames and Hudson, 1962.

Lanwel, Andreas. *Prehistoric and Primitive Man.* New York: Abrams, 1967.

Larsen, Helen, and Froelich Rainey. "Ipintak and the Arctic Whale Hunting Cultures." *Anthropological Papers of the American Museum of Natural History* 42 (1948).

Leroi-Gourhan, André. *Treasures of Prehistoric Art.* New York: Abrams, n.d.

Leroi-Gourhan, Ariette. "The Flowers Found with Shanidar IV: A Neanderthal Burial in Iraq." *Science* 190 (1975): 562–64.

Lévi-Strauss, Claude. "The Bear and the Barber." In *Reader in Comparative*

Religion, edited by William A. Lessa and Evron Z. Vogt. New York: Harper & Row, 1965.

Levy, C. Rachel. *Religious Conceptions of the Stone Age.* New York: Harper & Row, 1963.

Lewin, Bertram. *The Image and the Past.* New York: International Universities Press, 1968.

Lincoln, Abraham. *The Collected Poetry of Abraham Lincoln.* Springfield, Ill.: Lincoln and Hernden Building and Press, 1971.

Lindow, John. *Swedish Legends and Folk Tales.* Berkeley: University of California Press, 1978.

Lowie, Robert H. "The Material Culture of the Crow Indians." *Anthropological Papers of the American Museum of Natural History* 21 (1924): 201–70.

MacCana, Proinsias. *Celtic Mythology.* Hamlyn, Middlesex, England: Newnes Books, 1983.

MacCulloch, John Arnott, ed. *The Mythology of All Races.* New York: Cooper Square Publications, 1964.

MacKenzie, Donald A. *The Migration of Symbols and Their Relations to Beliefs and Customs.* New York: Knopf, 1926.

———. *Myths of Crete and Prehellenic Europe.* London: Gresham, n.d.

Manker, E. "Seite Cult and Drum Magic in the Lapps." In *Popular Beliefs and Folklore Tradition in Siberia,* edited by V. Diòszegi, 27–40. Bloomington: Indiana University Press, 1968.

Marshack, Alexander. *The Roots of Civilization.* New York: McGraw-Hill, 1972.

Martin, Calvin. *Keepers of the Game.* Berkeley: University of California Press, 1978.

———. "Subarctic Indians and Wildlife." In *Old Trails and New Directions,* edited by Carol M. Judd and Arthur J. Ray. Toronto: University of Toronto Press, 1980.

Menovščikov, G. A. "Popular Conceptions, Religious Beliefs and Rites of the Asiatic Eskimos." In *Popular Beliefs and Folklore Tradition in Siberia,* edited by V. Diòszegi, 433–49. Bloomington: Indiana University Press, 1968.

Michael, Harry N., ed. *Studies in Siberian Shamanism.* Translations from Russian Sources. No. 4, *Anthropology of the North.* Toronto: Arctic Institute of North America, University of Toronto, 1963.

Mishler, Craig. "Telling About Bear." *Journal of American Folklore* 97:383 (1984): 61–68.

Myers, John Linton. *Who Were the Greeks?* Berkeley: University of California Press, 1930.

Nahodil, O. "Mother Cult in Siberia." In *Popular Beliefs and Folklore Tradition in Siberia,* edited by V. Diòszegi, 459–77. Bloomington: Indiana University Press, 1968.

Nelson, Richard K. *Make Prayers to the Raven.* Chicago: University of Chicago Press, 1983.

Neumann, Erich. *The Origin and History of Consciousness.* New York: Pantheon, 1954.

Okladnikov, A. P. *Yakutia Before Its Incorporation into the Russian State.* Montreal: McGill-Queens University Press, 1970.

Opler, Morris E. "A Colorado Ute Indian Bear Dance." *Southwestern Lore* 7 (1941), Colorado Archaeological Society.

Paulson, I. "The Preservation of Animal Bones in the Hunting Rites of Some North Eurasian Peoples." In *Popular Beliefs and Folklore Tradition in Siberia,* edited by V. Diòszegi. Bloomington: Indiana University Press, 1968.

Philippi, Donald L. *Songs of Gods, Songs of Humans.* Princeton: Princeton University Press, 1979.

Phillips, Ann Patricia. *The Prehistory of Europe.* Bloomington: Indiana University Press, 1980.

Potapov, L. P. "Shamans' Drums of Altaic Ethnic Groups." In *Popular Beliefs and Folklore Tradition in Siberia,* edited by V. Diòszegi, 205–34. Bloomington: Indiana University Press, 1968.

Reed, Vernon. "The Ute Bear Dance." *American Anthropologist* 9 (1896): 237–44.

Sandars, N. K. *Prehistoric Art of Europe.* London: Pelican, 1968.

Santer, Marc R. *Switzerland from Earliest Times to the Roman Conquest.* London: Thames and Hudson, 1976.

Schaeffer, Claude E. "The Bear Foster Parent Tale: A Kutenai Version." *Journal of American Folklore* 60 (1947): 286–88.

Scully, Vincent. *The Earth, the Temple and the Gods.* New Haven: Yale University Press, 1962.

Skinner, Alansen. "Bear Customs of the Cree and Other Algonkian Indians of Northern Ontario." *Papers and Records* 12 (1914), Ontario Historical Society, Toronto.

Solecki, Ralph S. *Shanidar: The Humanity of Neanderthal Man.* London: Allan Lane, 1972.

Speck, Frank G. *Naskapi: The Savage Hunters of the Labrador Peninsula.* Norman: University of Oklahoma Press, 1935.

———. *The Celestial Bear Comes Down to Earth.* Reading, Pa.: Public Museum and Art Gallery, 1945.

Steward, Julian H. "A Uintah Ute Bear Dance." *American Anthropologist* 34 (1932): 263–73.

Swanton, John R. *Social Conditions, Beliefs and Linguistic Relations of the Tlingit Indians.* Berkeley: University of California Press, 1970.

Tanner, Adrian. *Bringing Home Animals.* New York: St. Martin's, 1979.

Vasilevich, G. M. "Early Concepts About the Universe Among the Evinks." In *Studies in Siberian Shamanism,* edited by Harry N. Michael, 46–123.

Translations from Russian Sources. No. 4, *Anthropology of the North*. Toronto: Arctic Institute of North America, University of Toronto, 1963.

White, T. H. *The Bestiary: A Book of Beasts*. New York: Putnam, 1950.

Wissler, Clark, and D. C. Duvall. "Mythology of the Blackfoot Indians." *Anthropological Papers of the American Museum of Natural History* 2 (1908).

Zolotarev, Alexander M. "The Bear Festival of the Olchi." *American Anthropologist* (n.s.) 39 (1937): 113–30.

LITERATURE

Adams, Richard. *Shardik*. New York: Avon, 1974.

Aesop. *Caxton's Aesop*. Edited by R. T. Lenaghan. Cambridge, Mass.: Harvard University Press, 1967.

Aristotle. *Historia Animalum*. Translated by D'Arcy W. Thompson. Oxford, England: Oxford University Press, 1910.

Armstrong, Edward A. *Saint Francis: Nature Mystic*. Berkeley: University of California Press, 1976.

Asbjornsen, Peter Christian, and Jorgen Moe. *Norwegian Folk Tales*. New York: Pantheon, 1960.

Auel, Jean. *The Clan of the Cave Bear*. New York: Bantam, 1970.

Austin, Mary. *The Children Sing in the Far West*. Boston: Houghton Mifflin, 1928.

———. *One Smoke Stories*. Boston: Houghton Mifflin, 1934.

Barakat, R. A. "Bear's Son Tale in New Mexico." *Journal of American Folklore* 78 (1965): 330–36.

Barbeau, Marius. "Bear Mother." *Journal of American Folklore* 59 (1946): 1–12.

Barrett, Samuel Alfred. *Pomo Bear Doctors*. Berkeley: University of California Press, 1917.

Bettelheim, Bruno. *The Uses of Enchantment: The Meaning and Importance of Fairy Tales*. New York: Random House, 1977.

Bierhorst, John, ed. *Sacred Path: Spells, Prayers and Power Songs of the American Indians*. New York: Morrow, 1983.

Blair, Walter. "The Technique of the Big Bear of Arkansas." *Southwest Review* 28 (1943): 426–35.

Blount, Margaret Joan. *Animal Land: The Creatures of Children's Fiction*. New York: Morrow, 1975.

Bond, Michael. *A Bear Called Paddington*. Boston: Houghton Mifflin, 1957.

Botkin, B. A., ed. *A Treasury of American Folklore, Stories, Ballads and Traditions*. New York: Crown, 1944.

Bouissac, Paul. *Circuses and Culture*. Bloomington: Indiana University Press, 1976.

Bridger, Jim. "A Famous Bear Story." In J. Cecil Alter, *Jim Bridger*. Salt Lake City, Utah: Shepard Book Company, 1925.

Brown, Charles. *Bear Tales: Wisconsin Narratives of Bears, Wild Hogs, Honey, Lumberjacks and Settlers*. Madison: Wisconsin Folklore Society, 1944.

Brunvand, Jan Harold. *The Study of American Folklore: An Introduction*. New York: St. Martin's, 1968.

Burke, Peter. *Popular Culture in Early Modern Europe*. New York: Harper & Row, 1978.

Buttrick, Arthur George, ed. *The Interpreter's Dictionary of the Bible*. Nashville: Abingdon-Cokesbury, 1951–57.

Chadwick, H. M., and N. K. Chadwick. *The Growth of Literature*. 3 vols. Cambridge, England: Cambridge University Press, 1932–40.

Chekhov, Anton. *Plays*. Translated by Elisaveta Fen. Harmondsworth, Middlesex, England: Penguin, 1959.

Cirlot, J. E. *A Dictionary of Symbols*. New York: Philosophical Library, 1962.

Clark, Anne. *Beasts and Bawdy*. New York: Taplinger, 1975.

Clark, Joseph D. *Beastly Folklore*. Metuchen, N.J.: Scarecrow Press, 198.

Colgrave, Bertram. "Mexican Version of Bear's Son Tale." *Journal of American Folklore* 64 (1951): 409–13. Reply: C. Claudel. *Southern Folklore Quarterly* 16 (1952): 186–91. Second Reply: A. I. Hallowell. *Journal of American Folklore* 65 (1952): 418. Third Reply: F. Goodwin. *Journal of American Folklore* 66 (1953): 143–54.

Crane, Stephen. *Sullivan County Tales and Sketches*. Edited by R. W. Stallman. Ames: Iowa State University Press, 1968.

Crockett, Davey. *A Narrative of the Life of David Crockett, of the State of Tennessee*. Philadelphia: E. L. Carey, 1834.

Crossley-Holland, Kevin, trans. *Beowulf*. New York: Farrar, Straus & Giroux, 1968.

Cushing, G. F. "Bears in Ob-Ugrian Folklore." *Folklore* 88 (1977): 146–59.

Danielli, M. "Initiation Ceremonial from Norse Literature." *Folk-Lore* 56 (1945): 229–30.

Dasent, George Webbe. *A Collection of Popular Tales from the Norse and North German*. London: Norroena, 1905.

Davies, Robertson. *The Manticore*. New York: Penguin, 1972.

Dawson, G. E. "London's Bull-Baiting and Bear-Baiting Arena in 1562." *Shakespeare Quarterly* 15 (1964): 97–101.

Dembeck, Hermann. *Animals and Men*. London: Nelson, 1966.

Dobak, W. A. "Eighteenth-Century Bear Story." *Journal of American Folklore* 85 (1972): 274.

Dobie, James Frank. *The Ben Lilly Legend*. Boston: Little, Brown, 1950.

———. "Juan Oso, Bear Nights in Mexico." *Southwest Review* 19 (1933): 34–64.

Dorson, Richard M. *Blood Stoppers and Bear Walkers*. Cambridge, Mass.: Harvard University Press, 1952.

Downs, Robert Bingham, ed. *The Bear Went Over the Mountain: Tall Tales of American Animals*. New York: Macmillan, 1964.

DuBartas, Guillaume. *The Complete Works*. New York: AMS Press, 1967.

Ehle, John. *The Winter People*. New York: Harper & Row, 1982.

Eliade, Mircea. *Shamanism: Archaic Techniques of Ecstasy*. Translated by Willard R. Trask. Bollingen Series LXXVI. Princeton: Princeton University Press, 1964.

Engel, Marian. *Bear*. New York: Atheneum, 1976.

Faulkner, William. *The Portable Faulkner*. Edited by Malcolm Cowley. New York: Viking, 1967.

Ferguson, George Wells. *Signs and Symbols in Christian Art*. New York: Oxford University Press, 1954.

Freeman, Rosemary. *English Emblem Books*. London: Chatto and Windus, 1948.

Friedman, Albert B., ed. *The Viking Book of Folk Ballads of the English-Speaking World*. New York: Viking, 1982.

Frost, John. *Wild Scenes of a Hunter's Life*. Boston: Lee and Shepard, 1871.

Fulghum, W. B. *A Dictionary of Biblical Allusions in English Literature*. New York: Holt, Rinehart and Winston, 1965.

Gaignebet, Claude. *Le Carnaval*. Paris: Payot, 1974.

Gardner, John. *Mickelsson's Ghosts*. New York: Knopf, 1982.

———. *October Light*. New York: Knopf, 1976.

Greene, Graham. *The Bear Fell Free*. London: Grayson and Grayson, 1935.

Grimm, Jacob. *The Complete Grimms' Fairy Tales*. Introduction by Padraic Colum. New York: Pantheon, 1972.

Grinnell, George Bird. *The Punishment of the Stingy*. New York: Harper and Brothers, 1901.

———. *The Story of the Indian*. New York: D. Appleton and Company, 1895.

Grinnell, George Bird, and Theodore Roosevelt, eds. "Bear Traits." In *Trail and Campfire: The Book of the Boone and Crockett Club*. New York: Forest and Stream Publishing Company, 1897.

Hair, D. S. "Marian Engel's Bear Story." *Canadian Literature* 92 (1982): 34–35.

Harding, Mary Esther. *The I and the Not I: A Study in the Development of Consciousness*. Bollingen Series LXXIX. Princeton: Princeton University Press, 1973.

Harris, Joel Chandler. *The Complete Tales of Uncle Remus*. Edited by Richard Chase. Boston: Houghton Mifflin, 1955.

Harte, Bret. *The Works of Bret Harte*. 25 vols. Boston: Houghton Mifflin, 1889.

Hasley, R. "Origins of the Shakespearean Playhouse." *Shakespeare Quarterly* 15 (1964): 29–39.

Hittell, Theodore H. *The Adventures of James Capen Adams, Mountaineer and Bear Hunter*. San Francisco: Towne and Bacon, 1860.

Holmes, Urban Tigner. *Daily Living in the Twelfth Century*. Madison: University of Wisconsin Press, 1952.

Hudson, W. M. "Another Mexican Version of Bear's Son." *Southern Folklore Quarterly* 15 (1957): 152–58.

Irving, John. *The Hotel New Hampshire*. New York: Dutton, 1981.

———. *Setting Free the Bears*. New York: Random House, 1968.

———. *The World According to Garp*. New York: Dutton, 1978.

Irving, Washington. *Astoria*. Philadelphia: Lippincott, 1961.

Jacobs, Joseph, ed. *The Most Delectable History of Reynard the Fox*. New York: Schocken, 1967.

Jung, Carl Gustav. "On the Psychology of the Trickster." *Spring* (1955): 1–14.

———. *Psychology and Alchemy*. Bollingen Series XX. Princeton: Princeton University Press, 1968.

———. *Symbols of Transformation: An Analysis of the Prelude to a Case of Schizophrenia*. Translated by R. F. C. Hull. Bollingen Series XX. Princeton: Princeton University Press, 1956.

Keller, M. "Big Bear of Maine: Toward the Development of American Humor." *New England Quarterly* 51 (1978): 565–74.

Kinnell, Galway. *Body Rags*. Boston: Houghton Mifflin, 1968.

———. *The Book of Nightmares*. Boston: Houghton Mifflin, 1971.

Kipling, Rudyard. *Collected Verse of Rudyard Kipling*. New York: Doubleday, 1925.

———. *The Writings in Prose and Verse of Rudyard Kipling*. New York: Doubleday, 1892–1937.

Kirby, W. F., trans. *Kalevala: The Land of Heroes*. 2 vols. New York: Everyman Library, 1907.

Klingender, Francis. *Animals in Art and Thought to the End of the Middle Ages*. Cambridge: Massachusetts Institute of Technology Press, 1971.

Lang, Andrew, ed. "East of the Sun and West of the Moon." In *The Blue Fairy Book*. Harmondsworth, Middlesex, England: Penguin, 1975.

Lankford, G. E. "Pleistocene Animals in Folk Memory." *Journal of American Folklore* 93 (1980): 293–304.

Lathem, Edward Connery, ed. *The Poetry of Robert Frost*. New York: Holt, 1928.

Leake, Jane Acomb. *The Geats of Beowulf, A Study of the Middle Ages*. Madison: University of Wisconsin Press, 1967.

Lemay, J. A. Leo. "The Text, Tradition, and Themes of *Big Bear of Arkansas*." *American Literature* 47 (1975): 321–42.

Levertov, Denise. *Relearning the Alphabet*. New York: New Directions, 1967.

Lévi-Strauss, Claude. *The Savage Mind.* Chicago: University of Chicago Press, 1966.

Longfellow, Henry David. *Poetical Works.* London: Oxford University Press, 1979.

Loomis, Roger Sherman. *A Mirror of Chaucer's World.* Princeton: Princeton University Press, 1965.

Macbeth, George, ed. *The Penguin Book of Animal Verse.* Harmondsworth, Middlesex, England: Penguin, 1965.

McClintock, Walter. *Old Indian Trails.* Boston: Houghton Mifflin, 1923.

McCracken, Harold. *Alaska Bear Trails.* Garden City, N.Y.: Doubleday, Doran and Company, 1931.

———. *The Biggest Bear on Earth.* Philadelphia: Lippincott, 1943.

McCulloch, Florence. *Medieval Latin and French Bestiaries.* Chapel Hill: University of North Carolina Press, 1960.

Mailer, Norman. *Why Are We in Vietnam?* New York: Putnam, 1967.

Matthews, Washington. *Navaho Legends.* Vol. 5. New York: American Folk-Lore Society, 1897.

Meine, Franklin, ed. *Tall Tales of the Southwest.* New York: Knopf, 1930.

Miller, Joaquin. *True Bear Stories.* Chicago and New York: Rand McNally, 1900.

Milne, A. A. *The House at Pooh Corner.* New York: Dutton, 1928.

———. *Winnie-the-Pooh.* New York: Dutton, 1926.

Moore, Marianne, trans. *The Fables of La Fontaine.* New York: The Viking Press, 1964.

Morris, William. *The Collected Works of William Morris.* Vol. 7, *The Story of Grettir the Strong, the Story of the Volsungs, and Nibelungs.* London: Longmans, Greene, 1910–15.

Neumann, Erich. *The Great Mother: An Analysis of the Archetype.* Translated by Ralph Manheim. Bollingen Series XLVII. Princeton: Princeton University Press, 1955.

Newman, Anne, and Julie Sak, eds. *Bear Crossings: An Anthology of North American Poets.* Newport Beach, Calif.: New South, 1978.

Opie, Iona, and Peter Opie. *The Classic Fairy Tales.* London: Oxford University Press, 1974.

———. *The Oxford Dictionary of Nursery Rhymes.* London: Oxford University Press, 1951.

Paine, Albert Bigelow. *The Arkansaw Bear.* New York: Harper, 1925.

Porter, J. R., and W. M. S. Russell. *Animals in Folklore.* Cambridge, England: Cambridge University Press, 1978.

Prokhorov, A. M., ed. *Great Soviet Encyclopedia.* New York and London: Macmillan, 1970.

Radin, Paul. *The Trickster: A Study in American Indian Mythology.* London: Routledge and Kegan Paul, 1956.

Ralston, W. R. S. "Beauty and the Beast." *The Nineteenth Century* 4 (1878): 990–1012.

Rawson, Jessica. *Animals in Art*. London: British Museum, 1977.

Read, A. W. "*Bear* in American Speech." *American Speech* 10 (1935): 195–202.

Rich, Adrienne. *The Diamond Cutters and Other Poems*. New York: Harper & Row, 1955.

Ritchie, W. A. "Another Probable Case of Bear Ceremonialism in New York." *American Antiquity* 15 (1950): 247–49.

Rose, H. J. *A Handbook of Greek Mythology*. New York: Dutton, 1959.

Rothenberg, Jerome, ed. *Shaking the Pumpkin: Traditional Poetry of the Indian North Americans*. Garden City, N.Y.: Doubleday, 1972.

Rowland, Beryl. *Animals with Human Faces: A Guide to Animal Symbolism*. Knoxville: University of Tennessee Press, 1973.

———. *Blind Beasts: Chaucer's Animal World*. Kent, Ohio: Kent State University Press, 1971.

Schwartz, Delmore. *Selected Poems: Summer Knowledge*. Garden City, N.Y.: Doubleday, 1938.

Sells, A. Lytton. *Animal Poetry in French and English Literature and the Greek Tradition*. Bloomington: Indiana University Press, 1955.

Skinner, Charles M. *American Myths and Legends*. Philadelphia: Lippincott, 1943.

Snyder, Gary. *Earth House Hold*. New York: New Directions, 1957.

———. *Myths and Texts*. New York: New Directions, 1960.

Thompson, Lawrance. *Robert Frost: The Years of Triumph, 1915–1938*. New York: Holt, Rinehart and Winston, 1970.

Thompson, Stith. *The Folktale, Stories Men Tell: From Egyptian Myth to Uncle Remus*. New York: Holt, Rinehart and Winston, 1946.

———. *One Hundred Favorite Folktales*. Bloomington: Indiana University Press, 1968.

———. *Tales of the North American Indians*. Bloomington: Indiana University Press, 1929.

Thorpe, T. B. "The Big Bear of Maine." *Spirit of the Times* 11 (1841): 43–44.

Thurston, Edgar. *Omens and Superstitions of Southern India*. New York: McBride, 1912.

Toynbee, Jocelyn M. C. *Animals in Roman Life and Art*. London: Thames and Hudson, 1967.

Tyner, Troi. "The Function of the Bear Ritual in Faulkner's *Go Down Moses*." *Journal of the Ohio Folklore Society* 3 (1968): 19–40.

Utley, Francis Lee, Lynn Z. Bloom, and Arthur F. Kinney, eds. *Bear, Man and God: Seven Approaches to William Faulkner's The Bear*. New York: Random House, 1964.

Von Franz, Marie Louise. *Individuation in Fairy Tales*. Zurich: Spring, 1977.

———. *Interpretation of Fairy Tales*. Zurich: Spring, 1973.

White, T. H. *The Bestiary: A Book of Beasts*. New York: Putnam, 1954.

Williams, William Carlos. *Pictures from Brueghel and Other Poems*. New York: New Directions, 1962.

Wimberly, Lowry Charles. *Folklore in the English and Scottish Ballads*. Chicago: University of Chicago Press, 1928.

Wright, William H. *The Grizzly Bear*. New York: Scribner, 1909.

Index

Grateful acknowledgment is made to the following for permission to reprint copyrighted material:

Columbia University Press: *Religion of the Kwakiutl Indians*, by Franz Boas, from the Columbia University Contributions to Anthropology Series, Vol. X. New York: Columbia University Press, 1930. By permission.

Doubleday & Company, Inc.: "The Heavy Bear Who Goes with Me." Copyright 1938 by Delmore Schwartz. From *Summer Knowledge*, by Delmore Schwartz. Reprinted by permission of Doubleday & Company, Inc.

Holt, Rinehart and Winston, Publishers: "The Bear," from *The Poetry of Robert Frost*, edited by Edward Connery Lathem. Copyright 1928, © 1969 by Holt, Rinehart and Winston. Copyright © 1956 by Robert Frost. Reprinted by permission of Holt, Rinehart and Winston, Publishers.

Houghton Mifflin Company: "The Bear," from *Body Rags*, by Galway Kinnell. Copyright © 1967 by Galway Kinnell. "Grizzly Bear," from *The Children Sing in the Far West*, by Mary Austin. Copyright 1928 by Mary Austin. Copyright © renewed 1956 by Kenneth M. Chapman and Mary C. Wheelright. "The Spirit of the Bear Walking," from *One Smoke Stories*, by Mary Austin. Copyright 1934 by Mary Austin. Copyright © renewed 1962 by Kenneth M. Chapman and Mary C. Wheelwright. Reprinted by permission of Houghton Mifflin Company.

James Koller: "Sioux Metamorphosis," from *Working*, by James Koller, from Frances Densmore. Copyright © 1967 by Coyote Books.

New Directions Publishing Corporation: "An Embroidery I," Denise Levertov, *Relearning the Alphabet*. Copyright © 1969 by Denise Levertov Goodman. First published in *The Partisan Review* in 1967. "This poem is for bear," Gary Snyder, *Myths & Texts*. Copyright © 1978 by Gary Snyder. "The Polar Bear," William Carlos Williams, *Pictures from Brueghel*. Copyright © 1962 by William Carlos Williams. Reprinted by permission of New Directions Publishing Corporation.

The New Yorker: "In Love with the Bear," by Greg Kuzma. Reprinted by permission; © 1969 The New Yorker Magazine, Inc.

W. W. Norton & Company, Inc.: "Bears" is reprinted from *The Fact of a Doorframe, Poems Selected and New, 1950–1984*, by Adrienne Rich, by permission of the author and W. W. Norton & Company, Inc. Copyright © 1981 by Adrienne Rich. Copyright © 1975, 1978, by W. W. Norton & Company, Inc. Copyright © 1981 by Adrienne Rich.

Gary Snyder: "Fear of Bears." © 1985 by Gary Snyder. An earlier version of this essay was translated into Japanese by Hisao Kanaseki and was published in Chuo Koron, December 1972.

University of California Press: A selection from *Saint Francis: Nature and Mystic*, by Edward A. Armstrong, 1976.

Viking Penguin Inc.: "The Bear and the Two Schemers," from *The Fables of La Fontaine*, translated by Marianne Moore. Copyright 1952, 1953, 1954, © 1964, by Marianne Moore. Copyright renewed © 1980, 1981, 1982, by Lawrence E. Brinn and Louise Crane, Executors of the Estate of Marianne Moore. Reprinted by permission of Viking Penguin Inc.

A. P. Watt Ltd.: An extract from "The Truce of the Bear," by Rudyard Kipling, from *The Definitive Edition of Rudyard Kipling's Verse*. By permission of The National Trust for Places of Historic Interest or Natural Beauty, and Macmillan London Ltd.

Wesleyan University Press: "The Turning," by John Haines. Copyright © 1966 by John Haines. Reprinted from *The Stone Harp*, by permission of Wesleyan University Press.

PLAY IT AGAIN

PLAY IT AGAIN

HISTORIC BOARD GAMES
YOU CAN MAKE AND PLAY.

ASTERIE BAKER PROVENZO
EUGENE F. PROVENZO, JR.

*Illustrations and Playing-Board Adaptations
by Peter A. Zorn, Jr.*

A SPECTRUM BOOK

PRENTICE-HALL, INC., *Englewood Cliffs, New Jersey 07632.*

Library of Congress Cataloging in Publication Data

PROVENZO, ASTERIE BAKER.
    Play it again.

    (A Spectrum Book)
    Bibliography: p.
    Includes index.
    1. Board games.   2. Board games—History.
    I. Provenzo, Eugene F., joint author.   II. Zorn,
    Peter A.   III. Title.
    GV1312.P76   794   80-17026
    ISBN 0-13-683367-5
    ISBN 0-13-683359-4 (pbk.)

10   9   8   7   6   5   4   3   2   1

Editorial/Production Supervision
and Interior Design by ERIC NEWMAN.
Page Layout by MARIE ALEXANDER.
Cover by AL PISANO.
Manufacturing Buyer: CATHIE LENARD.

PRENTICE-HALL INTERNATIONAL, INC., *London.*
PRENTICE-HALL OF AUSTRALIA PTY. LIMITED, *Sydney.*
PRENTICE-HALL OF CANADA, LTD., *Toronto.*
PRENTICE-HALL OF INDIA PRIVATE LIMITED, *New Delhi.*
PRENTICE-HALL OF JAPAN, INC., *Tokyo.*
PRENTICE-HALL OF SOUTHEAST ASIA PTE. LTD., *Singapore.*
WHITEHALL BOOKS LIMITED, *Wellington, New Zealand.*

To the memory of our grandfathers,
Bill Sprow, Morris Kutner, and June Baker,
who always found the time to play it again.

CONTENTS

CONTENTS.

STEEPLECHASE.
119

QUEEN'S GUARD.
129

CHIVALRY.
137

GO-BANG.
147

SEEGA.
161

FOX AND GEESE.
167

NYOUT.
189

DRAUGHTS.
195

BACKGAMMON.
219

ACKNOWLEDGMENTS

Our thanks go to the many people whose interest and help have contributed to the writing of this book. Important assistance in collecting visual materials and the histories of many of the board games was provided by the librarians and staff of the Newberry Library, Chicago; the Regenstein Library, University of Chicago; Olin Library, Washington University in St. Louis; Sterling and Beinecke Libraries, Yale University; and the United States Patent Office.

Our special thanks go to Bernard Reilly, Library of Congress; Patricia Pardo, Interlibrary Loan Office, Richter Library, University of Miami; Julanne Good and R. David Weaver, St. Louis Public Library; Susan Heintzelman, Teachers College Library, Columbia University; John Thomas, Yale Center for British Art; Wanda Slayton, Ft. Lauderdale, Florida; Lee Dennis, Peterborough, New Hampshire; Herb Siegel, Wyncote, Pennsylvania; and Eric Newman, Prentice-Hall, Inc.

Asterie Baker, Ann and Steven Freedman, and Shep Sporel, as always, were generous with their hospitality and their interest in our project.

INTRODUCTION

Play It Again is a book about some of the most popular board games from both ancient and modern times. It is a book about their history, how to play them, and how to make their boards and playing pieces. As you turn the pages of this book, the historical illustrations, the rules, the boards themselves, and the descriptions of the games will give you the opportunity to explore more than just the world of games—you will become familiar with the history of different cultures and peoples and with the art of gamesmanship.

Almost all board games are imitations of situations in real life. Some depict moral themes; one example of this is the Royal Game of Goose, a race game in which fortunes change suddenly as you land on different squares representing the trials and rewards of life. The role of good luck and bad luck is even more dramatic in Snakes and Ladders. By simply landing on the head of the snake on square 97, your piece must slip all the way back down the snake's body to square eight! Both of these games reflect beliefs about luck and life and were often used to teach children moral lessons about the relationships between good and evil.

Board games have also been used to teach children basic facts and information about the world in which they live. Numerous games from the eighteenth and nineteenth centuries, such as The Mansion of Happiness or An Eccentric Excursion to the Chinese Empire, were used to teach morals, geography, the natural sciences, mathematics, and history. Sometimes the names of board games or even the playing pieces themselves reflected a specific historical event or personage. For

I

example, during the Indian Mutiny of 1857–58, a variation of Fox and Geese known as Asalto was updated to "Officers and Sepoys."

Other board games involve the strategic maneuvers most closely associated with warfare. Chess is a classic example of a game that imitates the basic elements of the battlefield in which players are equally matched. Although Chess is excluded from this book because of its complexity, many other battle games, such as Draughts, Alquerque, and Nine Men's Morris, are included that recreate the excitement of out-maneuvering and out-witting your opponent.

Fox and Geese and the Chinese Rebel Game are examples of another type of battle game or "hunt" in which unequal forces with different capabilities are pitted against each other. Some games, like Reversi or Go-Bang, stress the strategic positioning of your playing pieces. In these games, based solely on skill, it is the placement of pieces and the manipulation of your opponent that determine the winner.

Luck often plays a role in many board games. Steeplechase, which mimics a real horse race, is played out entirely according to the throw of the dice. Other games, such as Pachisi, combine strategy with luck. In fact, Pachisi is an example of a game that can at first be played as one in which chance is more important than strategy. But as you play it again and again and begin to master the game, you will see that it is possible to influence the role of luck by strategically positioning your pieces to out-maneuver and block your opponents. The same opportunity is found in Backgammon. In most of the board games in this book, you can set out to out-wit not only your opponents but chance as well and determine your own fate!

Play It Again is a book for everyone. Whether you want to read the historical information or simply check the rules and play the games, you have the opportunity to discover an extraordinary variety of board games that have been played by children and adults for thousands of years. Easy-to-copy patterns are included for all of the boards and pieces needed to play these games. All you need are paper, cardboard, scissors, pens, pencils, and a ruler to make these simple boards and playing pieces.

Some of the games are very simple to make and easy to learn and can be enjoyed by children under the age of ten. Others are more complicated to learn and master. But the fun of *Play It Again* is that all these games are in one book and you can decide for yourself which ones you want to make and learn to play. Once you have made the boards, started playing the games, and become involved in the strategies necessary to win, you will probably find that the more you play, the more fun they are and that no challenge is too complicated. So, have fun and play it again!

LEXICON.

Some of the most common terms, moves, and rules of gamesmanship used throughout *Play It Again* are explained in this section so that you can get right on with playing the games and testing your luck as well as your skill in out-maneuvering your opponents.

PLAYERS.—The suggested number of players or best combinations of players are listed for each game described in *Play It Again* along with the directions and rules for the games.

PLAYING PIECES or COUNTERS.—Traditionally, stones; seeds; wooden, ivory, and bone pegs; carved wood pyramids; coins; buttons; and marbles are among the many objects that have been used as playing pieces in board games throughout the world. All of the playing-board patterns in *Play It Again* have been designed so that pennies fit easily onto spaces and points. Therefore, we have included instructions on making playing pieces out of pennies in the section "Suggestions for Making Playing Pieces."

DIE (plural, DICE).—A die is usually a small six-sided cube, made of bone, ivory, or plastic, that is marked with one to six dots on its sides. Cubic dice have the advantage of being balanced so that any side should have an equal chance of landing face up. Some of the games in *Play It Again* use a die to determine moves, whereas others use a pair of dice.

The oldest-known dice were probably divining sticks made from twigs. They were rounded on one side and flat on the other, just like more modern carved versions and used in the same way to determine your future. Pyramid-shaped dice, inlaid with ivory and lapis lazulis, were buried in the royal tombs of Ur more than 5,000 years ago. Both four-sided stick dice and cubic ivory and bone dice have also been found in Egyptian tombs.

3

Casting dice to see how they will land has intrigued people for thousands of years. In some countries, such as India, cowrie shells are used to determine the future. Knuckle-bones (from legs of mutton) and divining sticks have also been used as dice in many different countries throughout history by people who believed that the gods would reveal the future to those who understood how to interpret their signs.

Sometimes, in Medieval England, dice were thrown on a dice board. The board was divided into six spaces. A funnel was suspended above the board and the dice were tossed through this cup. Actually, the cast depended not upon the markings of the dice that landed up but upon the value of the space they landed upon.

Otherwise, dice were usually shaken in a wooden cup and tossed out together upon the table. Dice cups are still used today, especially in games like Backgammon, where they are even padded to muffle the sound.

ILLUSTRATION FROM THE SEVENTEENTH CENTURY
OF A DICE-CASTING BOARD AND GAME BOARDS.

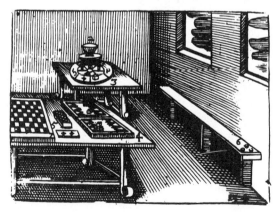

DOUBLET or PAIR.—When a pair of dice is thrown and the same number of dots appears on the upper faces of both dice, a "doublet" has been thrown. In most board games, a pair or doublet entitles a player to another throw and turn.

Throwing a doublet may also mean that two playing pieces are joined as a team and moved together as one piece, as in Pachisi.

COCKED DICE.—If one or both of the dice land on top of a piece on the board or are tilted against something, they are "cocked" and should be tossed again.

TEETOTUM.—A teetotum is a four- or six-sided top that is spun with the fingers. The sides are marked with numbers or dots so that the number that lands down when the top stops spinning determines the player's move.

The teetotum probably originated in Germany during the Middle Ages. Originally, teetotums were inscribed with letters and were used to predict the future. Jewish children often play a game with a four-sided top called a *dreidel* that is marked with Hebrew initials. Both dreidels and teetotums can be made of wood, lead, or even fine silver. During the nineteenth century, American children often made teetotums out of cardboard to use to determine the moves in their board games.

THE FIRST MOVE.—Since the first move often gives a player a great advantage in games involving strategy, it is very important to fairly determine who will make the first move. One way is to roll a die or a pair of dice. Each player rolls and the one with the highest throw takes the first turn.

Another method is to flip a coin. One player flips the coin and if the opponent guesses correctly whether heads or tails is up, the opponent begins the game. If the opponent guesses incorrectly, the player makes the first move.

Two players normally alternate turns. If more than two people are playing, turns may be taken either according to the highest numbers thrown or in a clockwise direction around the board.

Further restrictions on the first move, such as special throws or starting squares, are described when they apply to the games in *Play It Again*.

HOME BASE.—The side of the board or space from which a player begins to move his pieces, as in Draughts or Pachisi, is the "home base" of that player. In Pachisi and Ludo, there is also a home space that is really the finishing line, or the final space to be reached by a playing piece in order to win the game.

MOVES.—Playing pieces on the games described in *Play It Again* may be moved in any one of four directions as described in the rules for the individual games. When a piece is moved to an adjacent space or point, it is the square or point next to or adjoining the position of the playing piece.

> *Forward:* Away from a player's home base.
> *Backward:* Back, toward a player's home base.
> *Sideways:* Right or left across the board.
> *Diagonally:* From one corner of a square to another or toward the corner of the board.

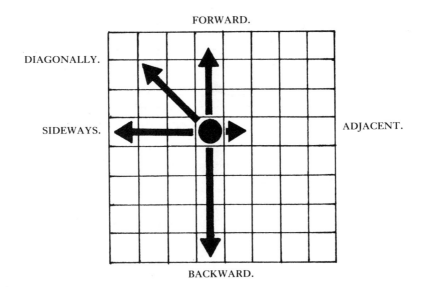

STEP MOVE.—A piece is moved into an adjoining or adjacent space forward, backward, sideways, or diagonally.

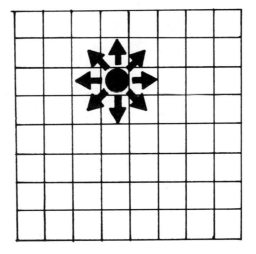

Hop or Jump Move.—A piece is moved over a piece on an adjacent space, onto a vacant space or point directly next to the jumped piece.

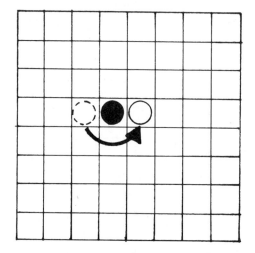

Multiple jumps are allowed in many of the board games in *Play It Again,* as long as the piece making the jump is able to land on a vacant space directly after each jump.

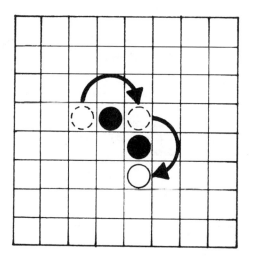

Flank or Out-Flank Move.—When two pieces of one player surround one of the opponent's pieces on both the right and left sides in a straight line, the opponent's piece is out-flanked, and it is usually considered captured and is removed from the board.

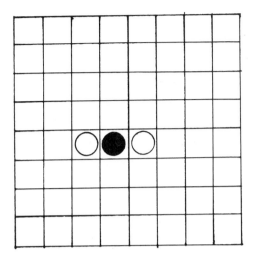

HUFF.—To "huff" a piece is to remove from the board a piece that has been moved wrongly. In some board games, a player's piece may also be huffed by another player if she fails to make a capturing move.

CROWN.—When one playing piece is placed on another one of the same color that has reached the opponent's home base, as in Draughts, the piece is "crowned."

MILL.—Three or more playing pieces placed on adjacent spaces or points in a line form a "mill."

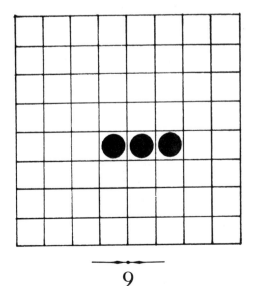

DRAW.—When a board game ends in a "draw," as when neither player is able to make a move, it ends in a tie with neither player winning.

RULES OF GAMESMANSHIP.

In any of the board games in *Play It Again* in which pieces are moved and dice are thrown, there are some rules and penalties that should be remembered. Players should always decide if they are going to observe these rules before they begin to play the games:

Once a player has removed his hand after moving a piece, he may not change the move.

When a player has made an incorrect move, the opponent may insist that the error be corrected if the opponent has not begun her own turn. Some rules state that if a player makes an incorrect move and the opponent catches it, the player automatically forfeits or loses that turn.

If a mistake has been made in setting up the playing pieces on the board, either one of the players may correct it before the first turn is completed.

USEFUL STRATEGIES.

A move that serves several purposes is always better than one that only opens up one option.

Always use the smallest number of pieces necessary to complete a move.

Always decide ahead whether a move will lose or maintain the offensive advantage in a game.

In many games, disconnected pieces are often easier to attack than pieces lined up together.

TOOLS AND SUPPLIES.

The following is a list of suggested tools and supplies that are needed to make the game boards and playing pieces in *Play It Again*. Illustrations and explanations are included to make your job easier in getting together all of the materials that you will need.

Scissors.

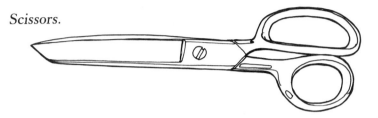

X-acto Knife.

Ruler.

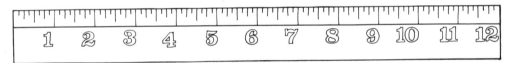

Pencils.

Felt-tip Pens and Markers.

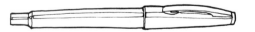

Glue.—Rubber cement or spray adhesive glues will enable you to glue the game-board patterns to the cardboard or posterboard smoothly. White glue may be used to glue heavier-weight cardboard.

Tape.

Paper Fasteners.—Use paper fasteners to assemble the game boards for Pachisi and Ludo and to fasten the spinner pointer to the spinner board.

Tacks.—You may also use tacks to attach the spinner pointer to the spinner board.

Paper.—Plain white paper is best to use for copying most of the boards and playing-piece patterns in this book.

Cardboard and Posterboard.—Medium-weight cardboard can be cut from gift boxes or cardboard packing boxes. Posterboard can be purchased at art-supply stores, stationery stores, college bookstores, and some hobby stores. Heavier cardboard can also be cut from cardboard packing boxes.

SUGGESTIONS FOR COPYING AND ASSEMBLING PLAYING BOARDS.

Game boards and playing pieces have provided an opportunity for craftsmen and artists to create works of art for thousands of years. Boards of inlaid woods, intricately carved ivory, and beautiful colored lithographs, as well as carved and cast playing pieces, are an important part of the tradition and excitement of historic and contemporary board games.

At the same time, many of the board games have been inscribed on stone or drawn on the ground. All over the world and throughout

history, people have drawn simple combinations of lines and spaces that make up many of the boards for the games in this book.

All of the board-game patterns in *Play It Again* can easily be traced over with a sheet of lightweight white paper or tracing paper. If you do not want to spend time tracing or copying the patterns, photocopy machines will help you reproduce them quickly and conveniently. After copying the boards and cutting them out, you should assemble and mount them with spray mount or rubber cement onto medium-weight cardboard or posterboard.

You may find it easier to assemble the playing boards by working on a piece of waxed paper so that any extra glue can be easily wiped up.

Some of the playing patterns in *Play It Again* are in one piece and will be very easy to copy and mount. Other patterns have more than one piece and are slightly more complicated to assemble. The more complex patterns are presented in the order in which they should be assembled.

The spaces on boards for such games as the Game of Goose, Snakes and Ladders, and Steeplechase are numbered so that the first number on the second board-pattern piece should follow the last number on the first piece of the pattern. On the Game of Goose board, for example, the second pattern piece connects up with the 3rd space and the 40th space on the first pattern piece; the third pattern piece connects up to the 12th space, and space 46 follows the 45th space on the second pattern piece; and the fourth piece of the pattern connects both the 22nd and 52nd spaces and the 59th and the 32nd spaces on the third pattern piece.

Other playing boards, such as those for the versions of Draughts, Nyout, and Fox and Geese, have more than one identical pattern piece. On the patterns such as these, a flap is included that indicates where to glue the pieces together. Place one pattern piece down, put glue on the flap, and position the second piece on the flap and so on until the complete board is assembled, as shown on page 15.

COLORING THE PLAYING-BOARD PATTERNS.—The boards in *Play It Again* can be left plain or may be colored with felt-tip pens. Pachisi and Ludo boards, for example, are traditionally colored red, green, blue, and yellow. Some of the board patterns have been drawn to look like inlaid wood and could be carefully shaded to give the feeling of a

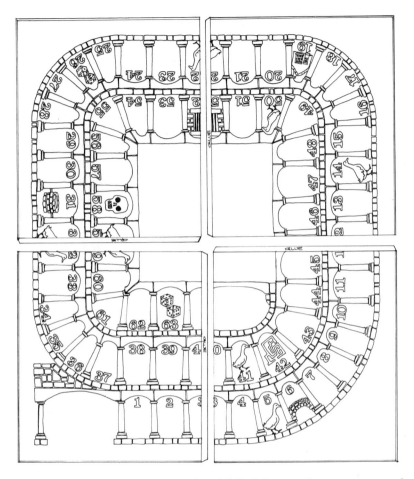

wooden playing board. So, you should feel free to decorate your playing boards in any way that pleases you!

MAKING MORE-ELABORATE PLAYING BOARDS.—All of the board-game patterns included in *Play It Again* can be used to make more-elaborate and carefully crafted game boards. Games using pits, such as Mancala and Wari, can be made out of clay. Press a slab of clay with a rolling pin until it becomes flat. Trim the piece of clay into the shape of a rectangle and make a depression in the clay for each of the pits. Designs can be inscribed into the board before the clay is fired in a kiln. Different glazes will not only add color to the board but will also provide it with a resilient surface.

Games like Pachisi have traditionally been made of cloth so that they could easily be rolled up and carried around. The Pachisi-board pattern included in *Play It Again* can be used as a guide for cutting strips of cloth to make a board. Once the strips are sewn together to form the cross-shaped board, brightly colored yarn or embroidery thread can be used to decorate the board.

Wooden boards provide a particularly interesting challenge for the craftsman. Lightweight plywood provides an excellent surface for making many of the boards in *Play It Again*. Wood stains, varnishes, and paint can be used to decorate the surfaces of the playing boards. Strips of molding or plastic colored tape can be used to finish and frame the edges of the boards.

Lines in the playing surfaces of wooden boards can be made by inscribing them with an awl and then filling in the indentations with paint or colored tapes.

More elaborate wooden boards, such as those for Backgammon and Draughts, may be inlaid with pieces of different types of wood. Holes or spaces can be carved out of solid boards for games played with marbles, such as Solitaire or Chinese Checkers.

DICE, TEETOTUMS, AND SPINNERS.

Since making accurate dice is extremely difficult, we suggest that you either buy a set of dice from a toy, hobby, or dime store or that you use a pair from another game you may already own.

A simple teetotum can be made to use in games that only use one die. Simply copy one of the patterns shown below and glue it onto a

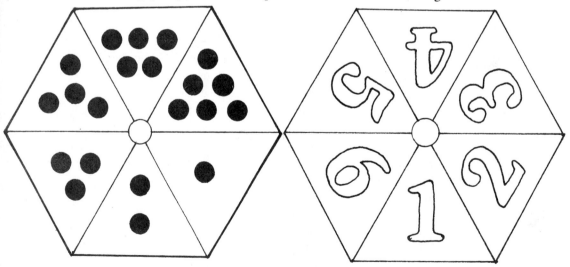

piece of posterboard. Cut it out and then punch a sharpened pencil stub through the center. Spin the teetotum with your fingers by twirling the eraser end of the pencil.

You may also make a simple spinner to be used in games that require only one die. Copy the patterns shown below and glue them onto lightweight cardboard. Cut out the spinner board and pointer. You can attach the pointer to the board with a paper fastener. A tack can also be used to attach the pointer to the spinner board if the board is mounted on a piece of thick cardboard or a piece of wood.

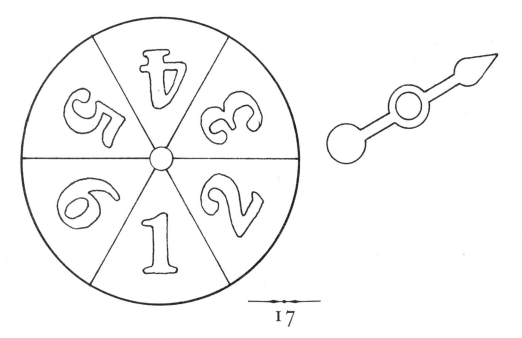

SUGGESTIONS FOR MAKING
PLAYING PIECES.

Throughout history, people have used all sorts of materials and objects as playing pieces for board games. Nearly all of the games in *Play It Again* will require at least two different colors of pieces. You may use such simple objects as pennies, nickels and dimes, buttons, or even seeds to play the games. Pennies and other coins may be painted different colors (spray paint works best) for different players.

You can also place the number of pennies required for each game on pieces of white or black paper. Draw around them, and cut the circles out and glue them onto the pennies. Three-quarter-inch adhesive marker dots, which come in many different colors and may be purchased at most stationery stores, can also be applied to the pennies to make different-colored playing pieces.

Playing-piece patterns are included with each game. All of the patterns are designed so that they can be copied and taped or glued onto a penny or piece of lightweight cardboard or posterboard. Special patterns are included for special pieces: "K" patterns for knights or kings; "Q" patterns for queens; and even horses for the Steeplechase game. Whenever more than two colors of playing pieces are needed, as in Pachisi or Halma, patterns are provided for a black and a white piece and an additional two white pieces that can be colored any color you want.

GAME OF GOOSE

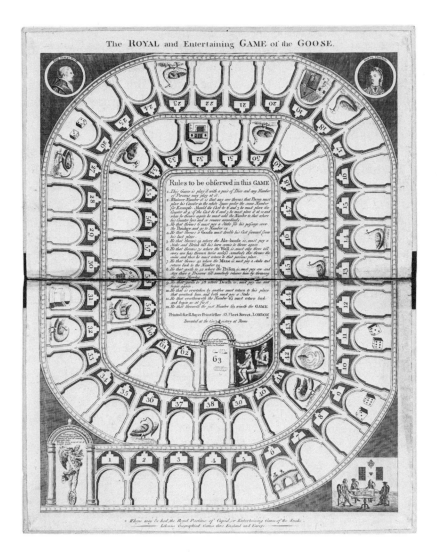

THE GAME OF GOOSE is often called the "Royal Game of Goose" because it is said that the first Goose game (*Giuoco dell'Oca*) was sent by Francesco de Medici of Florence, Italy, to King Phillip II of Spain in the sixteenth century. By 1597, this game of luck had been introduced into England, where it became just as popular as it was on the European continent.

The earliest Goose games consisted of simple journeys and adventures that depended upon chance and the roll of the dice to finish and be the winner. Good luck was rewarded, but bad luck was punished! The early boards were decorated with elaborate spiral courses that often depicted religious, mythological, political, or historical themes. By the eighteenth century, many of these games, such as those based upon Aesop's Fables, were used to teach children moral lessons.

Boards for the Game of Goose are often very dramatic. Different images, such as a death's head or a bridge, representing the trials and rewards of life, make up the 63 squares of the spiral board. Each square of the board is numbered from one to 63, beginning at the farthest outside point of the spiral. As players roll their dice and move their pieces along the squares, they experience sudden changes in fortune

NINETEENTH-CENTURY FRENCH
GAME OF GOOSE BOARD.

REGLE DU JEU DE L'OIE

CHILDREN PLAYING THE GAME OF GOOSE.

involving various penalties and bonus moves. Squares decorated with a Goose appear at regular intervals (5, 14, 22, 32, 41, 50, and 59) that allow the players an extra turn. The first player to complete the course and triumph over bad luck wins the game.

HOW TO PLAY THE GAME OF GOOSE.

NUMBER OF PLAYERS.—At least two.

OBJECTIVE.—To be the first player to reach the 63rd square on the playing board and win the game.

MATERIALS.—Spiral playing board of 63 squares, a set of dice, and a playing piece of a different color for each player.

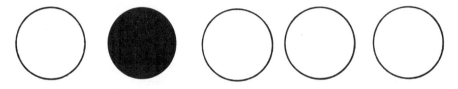

TO BEGIN PLAY.—Each player throws the dice, and the player with the highest number takes the first turn. Players in turn throw the dice and move their pieces the number of squares equal to the sum thrown.

TO PLAY.—Players will come upon good luck and bad luck as they progress along the spiral board. If one player lands on a square occupied by another player's piece, the player who first landed on the square must return to the square just left by the second player.

A player must land exactly on the 63rd square to win. If a higher number is thrown, the player is penalized and must move backwards a number of squares equal to the number of those in excess of 63. If this brings him to a square with a Goose, he must move backwards a number equal to twice the excess number!

REWARDS AND PUNISHMENTS
IN THE GAME OF GOOSE.

Number 6.—BRIDGE.

If a player's piece lands on Number 6, she advances over the Bridge to Number 12.

Number 19.—INN.

A player must remain at the Inn until all the other players have each had two turns.

Number 31.—WELL.

The player must pay a fine by losing two turns.

Number 42.—MAZE.

When a player lands on square Number 42, he must return to square Number 30.

Number 52.—PRISON.

A player landing on this square must remain here until freed by another player landing on the same square.

Number 58.—DEATH'S
HEAD.

If a player lands on this square, she is severely punished by having to return to square Number 1 and begin the game all over.

Numbers 26 and 63.—
DICE.

When a player lands on square Number 26 or 63, he may throw the dice again in the same turn and take another turn.

Numbers 5, 14, 22, 32,
41, 50, 59.—GOOSE.

When a player lands on a square with a Goose, she gets a second throw of the dice.

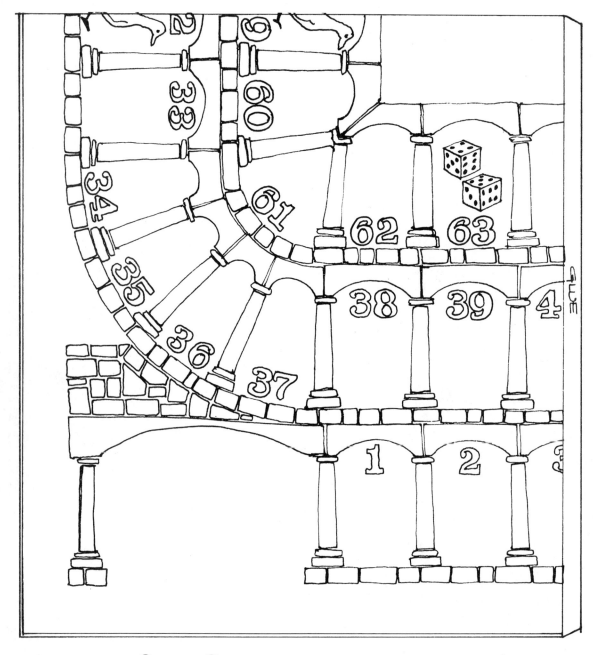

GAME OF GOOSE PLAYING-BOARD PATTERN.—I.

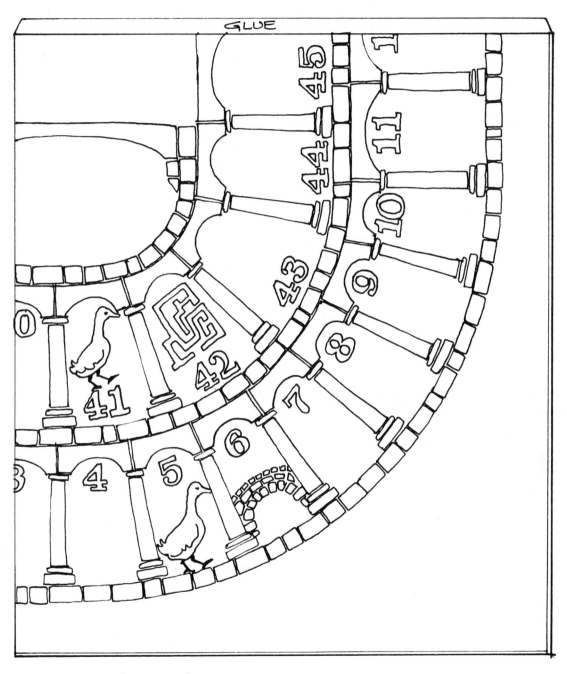

GAME OF GOOSE PLAYING-BOARD PATTERN.—2.

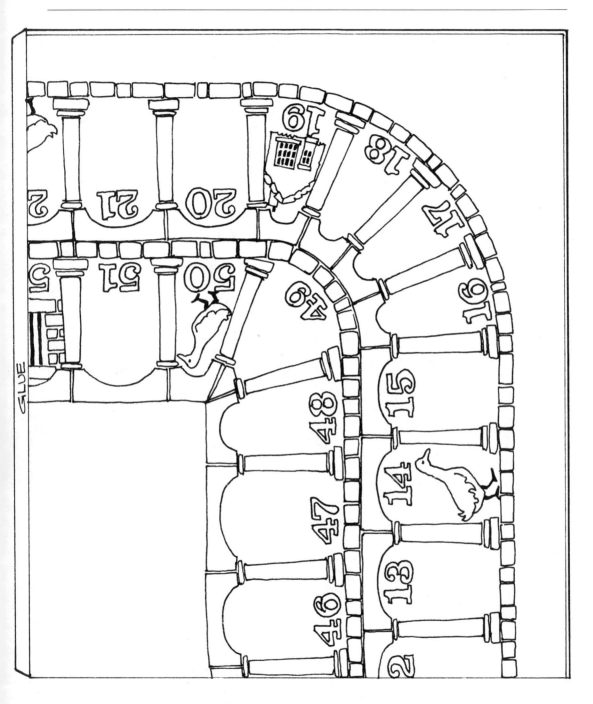

GAME OF GOOSE PLAYING-BOARD PATTERN.—3.

GAME OF GOOSE PLAYING-BOARD PATTERN.—4.

NINE MEN'S MORRIS

SIX MEN'S MORRIS
THREE MEN'S MORRIS
ACHI

NINE MEN'S MORRIS is not only one of the world's most exciting strategy games, but it is also one of its oldest. Boards for the game have been found carved into the roof of the Egyptian temple of Kurna, dating from 1400 B.C., and they are illustrated in fifteenth-century Medieval manuscripts as well.

The board for Nine Men's Morris consists of concentric squares connected with one another by lines. By strategically placing and maneuvering their nine pieces, each player tries to capture or block at least seven of the opponent's pieces.

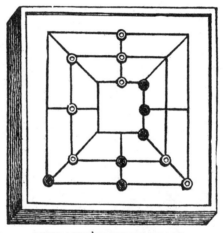

NINE MEN'S MORRIS BOARD.

Nine Men's Morris boards have been scratched on the ground with a stick all over the world. Evidence has been found that the game was played in Bronze-Age Ireland, ancient Troy, and Viking Norway, as well as in the Southwestern United States, where Kere, Tigua, Tewa, and Zuni Indians played versions of the game known as *paritariya*, *picarva*, and *pedreria*. In France, the game was originally called *merelles* and today is known as *jeu de moulin* (Game of Mill), whereas in Germany it has always been called *muhle* (mill).

New versions of Nine Men's Morris are always being invented. For example, several war games, such as "Trencho," inspired by trench fighting, appeared during World War I. In many of these battle games, a Morris board was superimposed upon a map and decorated with battle scenes and military equipment.

30

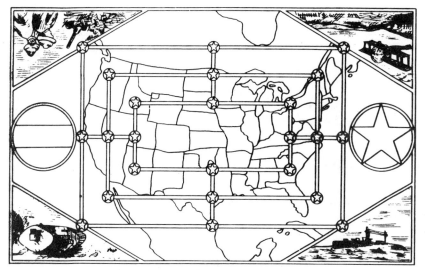

A GAME BOARD PATENTED IN THE
UNITED STATES IN 1918.

HOW TO PLAY
NINE MEN'S MORRIS.

NUMBER OF PLAYERS.—Two.

OBJECTIVE.—To be the first player to reduce the opponent to only two pieces or to block the opponent so that further moves are impossible.

MATERIALS.—A playing board marked with three concentric squares connected with lines. Each player has nine playing pieces of his or her own color.

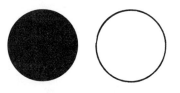

TO BEGIN PLAY.—The game is played on the 24 points of intersection of the lines on the board. The players decide who is to go first and then the first player places one of her pieces on the board at one of the points of intersection. The players continue alternating turns.

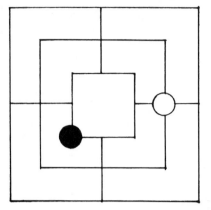

To Play.—The players take turns placing one of their pieces on an empty point on the board wherever two lines intersect, trying to get three of their pieces in a row in order to form a "mill."

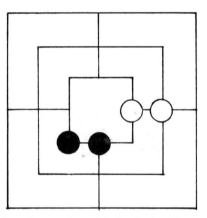

Once a player has formed a mill, he is entitled to "pound" the opponent by removing one of her pieces from the board.

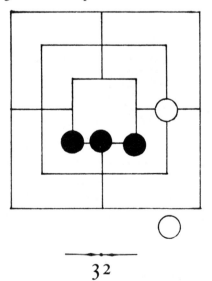

A player may not remove an opponent's piece if it is part of a mill unless there are no other pieces available on the board. Once a piece is removed from the board, it cannot be used again.

When all of the pieces have been laid down (nine turns for each player), the players then attempt to create new mills by maneuvering their pieces. A player may move each of her pieces from its existing

NINE MEN'S MORRIS PLAYING-BOARD PATTERN.

position on one of the points of intersection to any adjacent point that is free. Mills may be broken and re-formed any number of times by moving one of the pieces off the line and then returning it to its former position. Each time a mill is re-formed or a new one is created, a player is entitled to pound his opponent and remove one of her pieces.

The game continues until one player is reduced by successive poundings to only two pieces on the board or until one player's pieces are blocked by the opponent's pieces so that the player is unable to make a move.

SIX MEN'S MORRIS

SIX MEN'S MORRIS is a version of Nine Men's Morris that is played on a board marked with two concentric squares. Each player has six playing pieces of his or her own color to place on the board, one at a time in alternating turns. The purpose of the game is to form a mill and pound the opponent.

As in Nine Men's Morris, once all 12 of the pieces have been placed on the board, the game is continued by the players' moving pieces to adjacent free points in order to form new mills. Both placing the pieces on the board and moving them are equally important in the one-on-one strategy of the game.

When one player has only two pieces left, or cannot move because her pieces are blocked, the game is over.

THREE MEN'S MORRIS

THREE MEN'S MORRIS is played on such a simple board that it looks quite easy. But don't be deceived, for this game can be one of the most fast-paced of all board games! The board is marked with a square divided into four equal squares. Each player has four pieces of his or her own color. Players alternate turns, placing their pieces on points of intersecting lines until one completes a mill and is the winner.

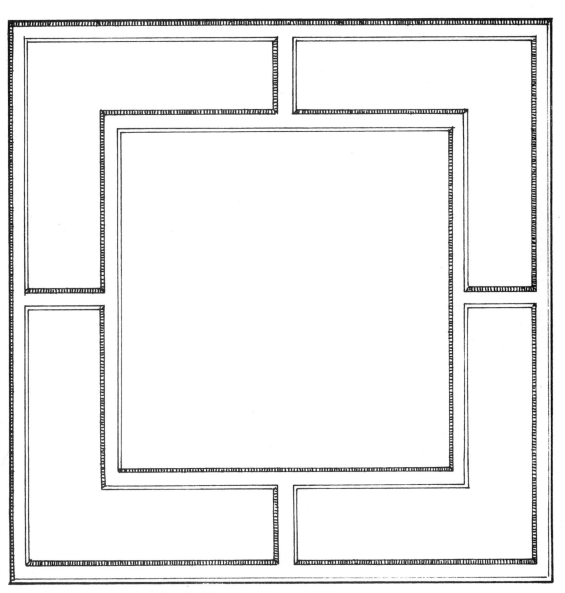

SIX MEN'S MORRIS PLAYING-BOARD PATTERN.

THREE MEN'S MORRIS PLAYING-BOARD PATTERN.

ACHI

ACHI, a Central African variation of Nine Men's Morris, is often played by children on a board drawn in the dirt. Stones are used as playing pieces. With easy-to-learn rules, Achi is played simply and quickly and is another example of why the Morris-type games are some of the most popular board games throughout the world.

DESIGN.

J. J. DONAHUE & J. H. SULLIVAN.
GAME BOARD.

No. 25,349.   Patented Apr. 7, 1896.

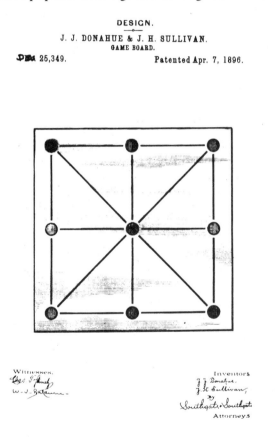

Witnesses.   Inventors
                                     J. J. Donahue,
                                     J. H. Sullivan,
                                        By
                                     Southgate & Southgate
                                        Attorneys

Each player is given four pieces of his or her own color to play with. The object of the game is to be the first player to place three pieces in a row, forming a mill, as in Tic-Tac-Toe. Achi begins with both players' placing their pieces on the points of intersection of the lines on the board, in alternating turns.

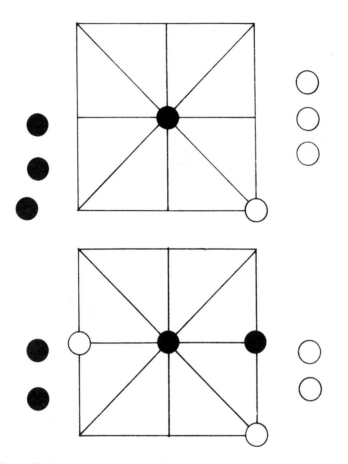

When all eight pieces are on the board, the players may move one piece each turn along the lines to a vacant point of intersection, trying to arrange three pieces in a row, in order to win the game.

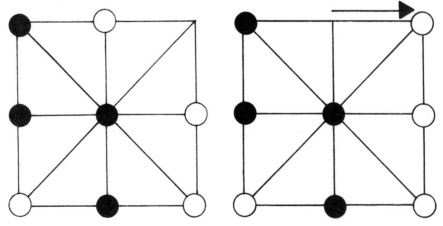

ACHI PLAYING-BOARD PATTERN.

PACHISI

LUDO

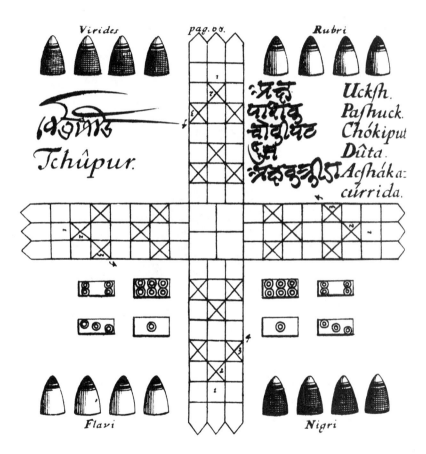

Virides · pag. 00. · Rubri

Tchûpur.

Ucksh.
Pashuck.
Chókiput
Dûta.
Acsháka-
cúrrida.

Flavi · Nigri

41

Pachisi, a game with equal measures of luck and skill, has been played in India for more than 1,200 years. Some Indian rulers liked the game so much that they built giant marble Pachisi boards in their palace courtyards. Akbar the Great, a Mogul Emperor who ruled from 1556–1605, played on a huge board of red and white squares. In the center was an enormous stone platform where Akbar sat. He and his friends actually played the game with young slaves from his harem as playing pieces! Each player had 16 girls, dressed in different colors, who moved along the squares on the board according to the numbers thrown on the cowrie-shells used to play the game.

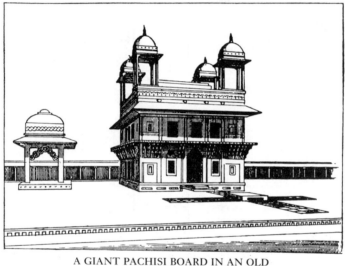

A GIANT PACHISI BOARD IN AN OLD
INDIAN-PALACE COURTYARD.

The name "Pachisi" comes from the Indian word for twenty-five, which is the highest number that could be thrown on the cowrie-shell dice. Today, Pachisi is also played in Indian homes and cafes, usually on boards made of decorated cloth that can be rolled up and carried about.

Eventually, Pachisi became known in Europe, where it was mentioned as early as 1694 by the Englishman Thomas Hyde in his famous book *De Ludis Orientalibus* (Games of the Orient), which is one of the first books ever written about games.

By the late 1800s, Pachisi had also become a very popular game in the United States, where it was called Pachisi, Parchesi, Parcheesi, or even Chessindia. All of these variations of Pachisi combine judgment and skill as the players try to make the best possible moves. In this way, Pachisi is a lot like the game of Backgammon.

A 1908 SEARS, ROEBUCK & CO. CATALOGUE
ADVERTISEMENT FOR PACHISI.

HOW TO PLAY PACHISI.

NUMBER OF PLAYERS.—Two people can play, or four players can compete in teams of two.

OBJECTIVE.—Each player tries to move his or her four playing pieces around the board and back into the central starting space before their opponents.

MATERIALS.—A cross-shaped playing board divided into 96 smaller squares and a central space called the *charikoni*, or home space. Twelve of the smaller squares are designated as safe resting spaces. In the English versions of Pachisi, these spaces were often called castles.

Playing pieces are free from capture here and if a castle is occupied, a partner's piece may also rest here, but it is off limits to an opponent's piece.

Each player has four playing pieces of his or her own color.

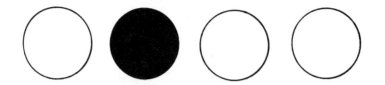

A die is needed to play the game, or you can use six pennies in place of the cowrie-shells that are traditionally used as dice. The pennies are scored as follows:

2 heads up ——— 2
3 heads up ——— 3
4 heads up ——— 4
5 heads up ——— 5
6 heads up ——— 6 and another throw
1 head up ——— 10 and another throw
0 heads up ——— 25 and another throw

To Begin Play.—Each player places his or her four pieces in the center of the board. If four people are playing, those sitting opposite each other are partners. Each player throws the six pennies (or die cowrie-shells, if you have them) to determine who begins the game. The player with the highest throw throws again and begins. Turns are then taken by the players, counterclockwise around the board.

Each piece is moved from the *charikoni* down the center of the player's side of the cross and then around the board, counterclockwise, and back up the center of his or her own side to the *charikoni*. Once a piece has made it around the board and into the *charikoni*, it should be removed from the board so that it will not be mistaken for captured pieces or pieces that haven't yet left the *charikoni*.

A player's first piece may enter the board on any throw, but the other three pieces (or the first piece if it has been captured and has to repeat the trip) can only enter on a throw of 6, 10, or 25. Pieces can only reenter the *charikoni* after completing their trip around the board, on an exact throw.

44

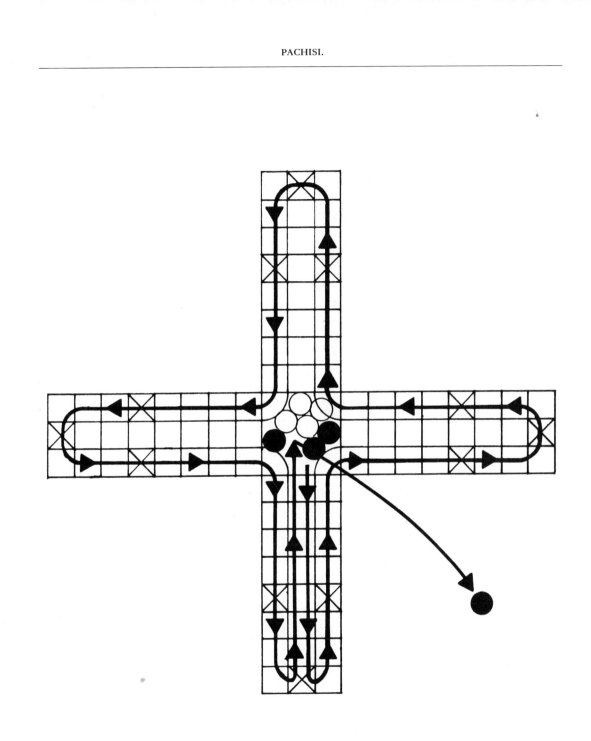

45

To Play.—Each player moves a piece the number of spaces indicated by the throw of the pennies or cowrie-shells. If a player gets to throw again in the same turn (by throwing 0, 1, or 6 heads up), the second throw may be used to move a different piece. A single throw may not be split between more than one piece. After having had at least one turn, a player may refuse to throw or to move in order to prevent being captured or to help his partner.

As the pieces are moved around the board, they may be captured unless they are on a castle square. These are marked with an *x*. A player captures an opponent's piece by landing on the same square occupied by the opponent. The opponent's piece is removed from the square and placed in the *charikoni*, and it must re-enter the board again. The player making the capture gets another turn. When a piece makes its way back to the center row of its own arm of the cross, it is safe and may not be captured.

A player, or partners, may double pieces to create a blockade by moving two pieces to the same square. An opponent or the same player cannot move a single piece past this blockade, and the blockade can only be captured by two or more of the opponent's pieces landing on the blockade at once. If the blockade is on a castle square, it may not be captured. Two or more pieces making up a blockade may be moved around the board together on a single throw.

When a player reaches her own arm of the cross, she may decide to continue on a second trip around the board instead of moving up the center of the *charikoni* in order to help out her partner. The player or partners who manage to move all of their pieces around the board and back into the *charikoni* first win the game.

NOTE ON ASSEMBLING THE PACHISI PLAYING BOARD.

The Pachisi playing board may be assembled in two ways: You may copy the four pattern pieces and cut them out and mount them on a piece of posterboard so that the four center rings match up, one on top of the other; or, you may copy the pieces and mount them and cut them out and then fasten them together by punching a paper fastener or tack through the center rings of each piece, one after another, so that all four pieces are connected at the center.

PACHISI PLAYING-BOARD PATTERNS.—1 and 2.

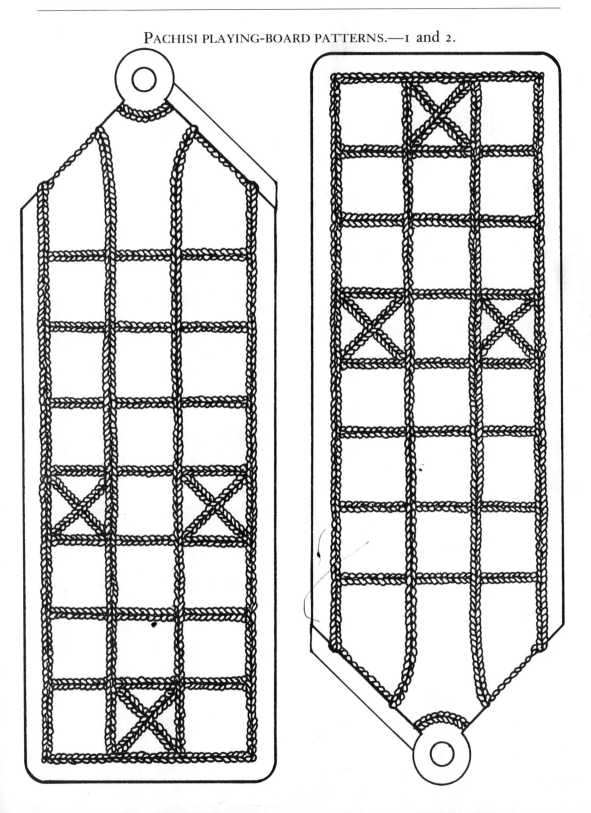

PACHISI PLAYING-BOARD PATTERNS.—3 and 4.

LUDO

LUDO, a much simpler version of Pachisi for children, was popular in England and the United States at the end of the nineteenth century. It is played with one die instead of six pennies or cowrie shells.

HOW TO PLAY LUDO.

NUMBER OF PLAYERS.—Two, three, or four.

OBJECTIVE.—To be the first player to move all four of his pieces safely into his home space.

MATERIALS.—A square board with four arms of a cross leading to the central home space. In each corner of the board are the home bases for each player's four pieces, all of a different color from their opponent's pieces. Traditionally, the Ludo board and playing pieces are colored red, blue, green, and yellow. There are no safe squares on the board as in Pachisi, but once a player's pieces have reached the central row of the arm leading to her home space, they are safe from capture. A die is used to determine the moves.

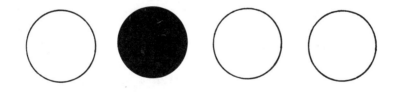

TO BEGIN PLAY.—Each player chooses which color of home base and pieces he or she wants to play with, and then the die is thrown to see who gets the highest number and will take the first turn. The pieces are moved around the board from each player's starting point in a clockwise direction, as shown at the top of page 50.

Each player must roll a 6 in order to place a piece on the starting space. Throughout the game, whenever a player rolls a 6, he is allowed another throw of the die. The number thrown on the die cannot be divided between two or more pieces, unless a player rolls a 6, when a different piece may be moved for the second throw.

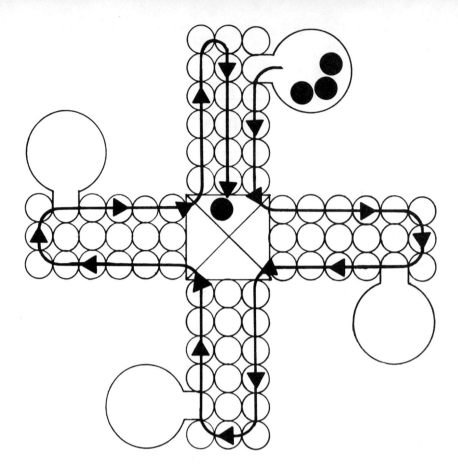

To Play.—If a player's piece lands on a space already occupied by an opponent's piece, the opponent's piece is captured and sent back to its home base, where it can only re-enter the board when a 6 is thrown on the die.

Once a piece has entered the last five spaces before its home space, it is safe from capture by an opponent's pieces.

A piece may be moved into the home space only when the exact number needed is thrown on the die. The game is over when one player has all four of her pieces moved into her home space.

NOTE ON ASSEMBLING THE LUDO PLAYING BOARD.

The Ludo playing board is assembled in the same way as the Pachisi board. After copying, mounting, and cutting out the four separate pieces of the board, connect all four through their centers with a paper fastener or a tack.

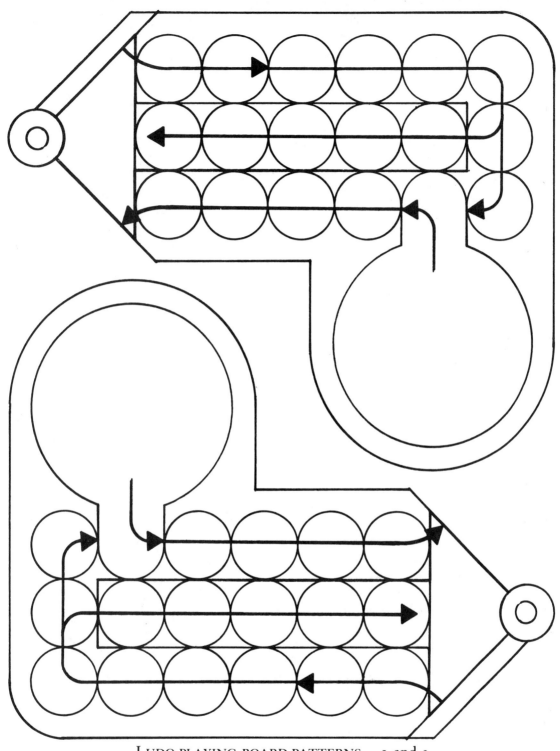

LUDO PLAYING-BOARD PATTERNS.—1 and 2.

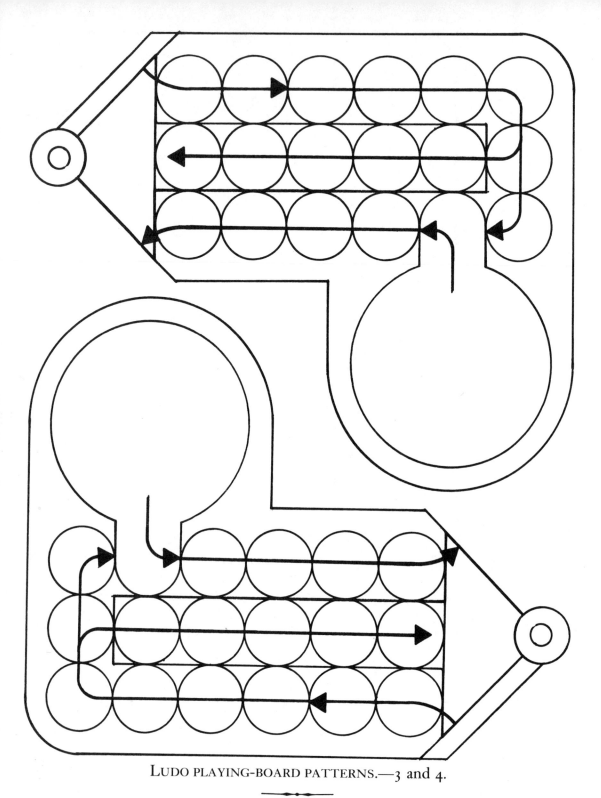

LUDO PLAYING-BOARD PATTERNS.—3 and 4.

SNAKES AND LADDERS

Snakes and Ladders has been a favorite race game with children in England and America for nearly one hundred years. Even though it is a simple game of chance, it becomes exciting when good luck is dramatically rewarded and bad luck is disastrously punished! Imagine landing on the head of a snake on square 97 and having to slip all the way back down the snake to square 8! But you can also have the good luck to land on square 19 and climb up the ladder all the way to square 91.

As you can see, winning in race games such as Snakes and Ladders is entirely dependent upon the luck of your throw of the die, so all players are really equals.

Snakes and Ladders is probably based upon a very old Indian game called *moksha-patamu*, in which good and evil exist side by side. The game teaches that virtuous acts, which are represented by the ladders, will shorten the journey across the board, just as the Hindus believe that these acts aid the soul's journey to perfection in real life. Evil deeds and bad luck are represented by the snakes. Just as bad luck or an evil deed will set you back in real life, landing on a snake means that your playing piece must be moved back down the snake's body to the square at its tail.

HOW TO PLAY SNAKES AND LADDERS.

NUMBER OF PLAYERS.—Any number.

OBJECTIVE.—To be the first player to escape as many of the evil snakes as possible and safely reach the 100th square at the end of the board.

MATERIALS.—A playing board consisting of 100 squares. Varying numbers of snakes and ladders, representing good and bad luck, are depicted on the board. The heads of the snakes are always at a higher-numbered square than their tails. Each player uses a playing piece of a different color from the opponent's piece. Moves are determined by the throw of one die.

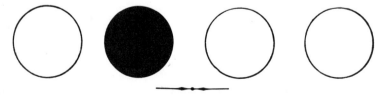

To Begin Play.—As in many other race games, there are different rules for playing Snakes and Ladders. The following rules are only one way to play the game.

Each player rolls the die to see who goes first. The player with the highest roll takes the first turn. The other players take their turns depending upon the number they rolled.

Each player throws the die and moves his or her piece the number of squares indicated by the throw. However, a player must throw a 6 in order to enter a piece on the number one square on the board. That player then gets to throw again and move the piece the number rolled. Throughout the game, whenever a player throws a 6, a second throw is awarded that player.

To Play.—If a player's piece lands on a square already occupied by an opponent's piece, the opponent's piece is knocked back to the number one square.

Whenever a piece lands on a square marked with the bottom of a ladder, the piece is automatically moved up the ladder to the square at the top.

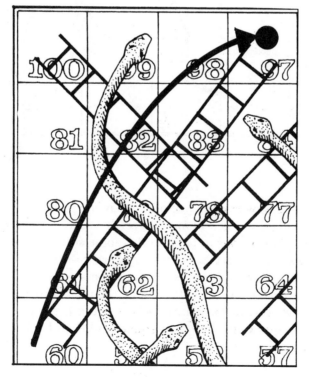

If the player's piece lands on a square marked with a snake's head, the piece must be moved all the way down the snake's body to the square at its tail.

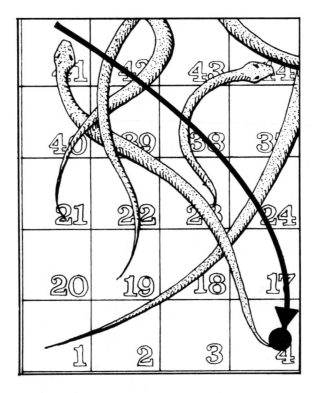

The game is over when one of the player's pieces lands exactly on the 100th square, or the "home" space. If a player's throw is higher than the number needed to land on the home square, then he is penalized and his piece must be moved forward to the 100th square and then back the number of moves remaining in the throw. For example, if a player's piece is on the 98th square, then a 2 throw is required to win the game. But if the player rolls a 3, the piece must be moved forward two squares to the 100th square and then back one square to the 99th square.

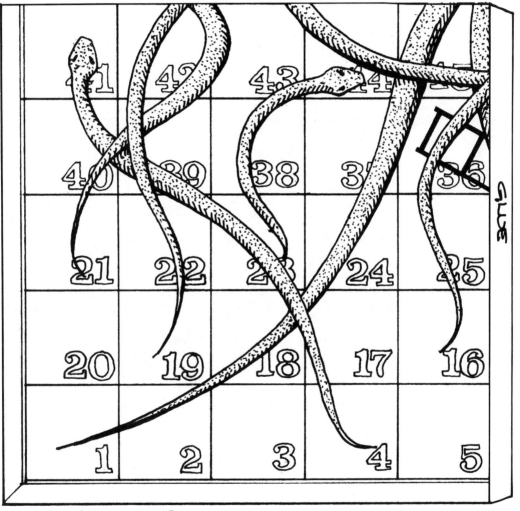

SNAKES AND LADDERS PLAYING-BOARD PATTERN.—I.

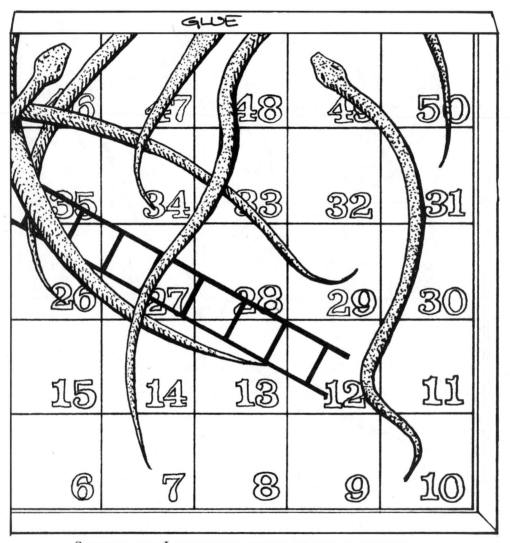

SNAKES AND LADDERS PLAYING-BOARD PATTERN.—2.

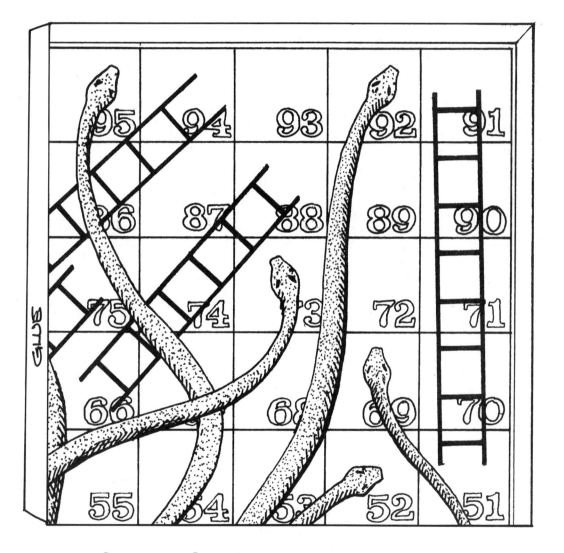

SNAKES AND LADDERS PLAYING-BOARD PATTERN.—3.

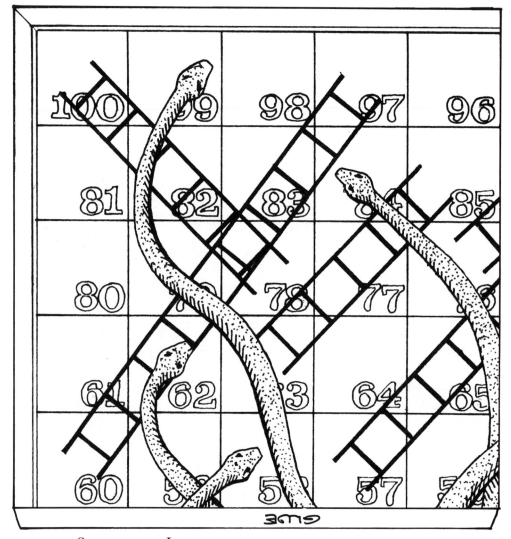

SNAKES AND LADDERS PLAYING-BOARD PATTERN.—4.

ALQUERQUE

FANORONA
FIGHTING SERPENTS
PERALIKATUMA

ALQUERQUE is among the oldest of all board games. Examples of the game have been found dating from 1400 B.C., carved into the roof of the temple of Kurna in Egypt. During the Middle Ages, Alquerque was introduced by the Moors into Spain. Called *el-quirkat* in Arabic, the game and its rules are mentioned in the tenth-century Arabic work *Kitab-al Aghami.* Several different versions of the game also were included in the *Libro de Juegos* (Book of Games) of Alfonso X (A.D. 1251–1282), King of Castile.

Alquerque was brought to the New World by the Spanish and became popular among the Kere and Hopi Indians in the southwestern part of the United States, where it is known as *aiyawatstani* or *tuknanavuhpi.*

Twelve-man Alquerque ("Alquerque de Doce") has probably always been the most popular version of the game. In many respects, the game is similar to Checkers and Chess. It is played on a square board containing 16 smaller squares, each of which is divided by a diagonal line. Each player attempts to jump and capture his or her opponent's pieces. The game remains popular in Spain today.

HOW TO PLAY ALQUERQUE.

NUMBER OF PLAYERS.—Two.

OBJECTIVE.—To capture all of the opponent's pieces.

MATERIALS.—A square playing board divided into 16 smaller squares and 24 playing pieces, 12 of one color for one player and 12 of another color for the second player.

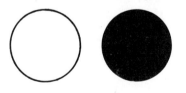

TO BEGIN PLAY.—Place each player's pieces on the board as shown at the top of page 63 and determine who is to take the first move.

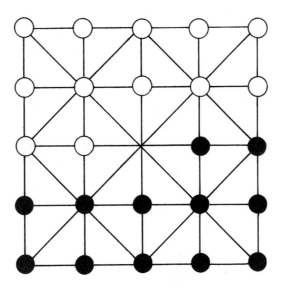

TO PLAY.—The game is played by one's moving a piece from its original place on the board to an empty place adjacent to it.

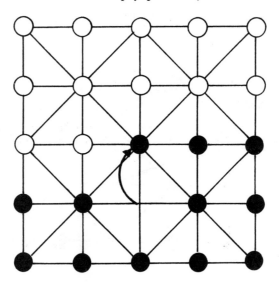

When a player's piece meets an opponent's piece, it may jump over it if the space beyond the piece is vacant. The opponent's piece is then captured and removed from the board for the remainder of the game.

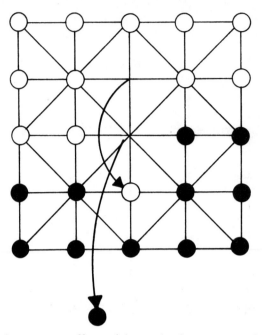

Multiple jumps are allowed in a single move and can include a change in direction.

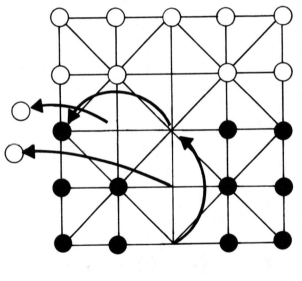

When one player has the opportunity to jump an opponent's piece and does not jump it, her piece is removed from the board and considered captured by the opponent.

A player can win the game of Alquerque by capturing all of his opponent's pieces or by blocking them so that the opponent cannot move. If neither player can move, then the game ends in a draw.

ALQUERQUE PLAYING-BOARD PATTERN.—I.

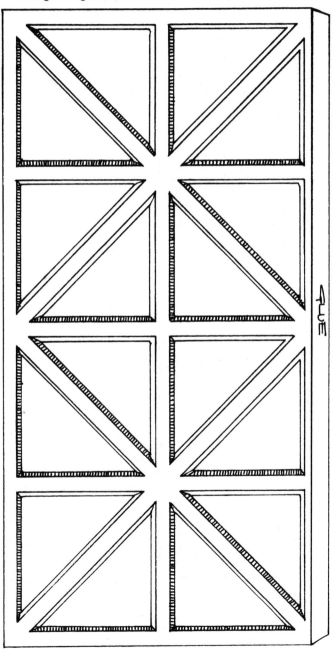

ALQUERQUE PLAYING-BOARD PATTERN:—2.

FANORONA

FANORONA is an Alquerque game from Madagascar (now the Malagasy Republic) that is said to have magical powers that enable it to predict the future. Invented during the seventeenth century, the game was played on a double Alquerque board inscribed on flat stones or drawn on the ground. Captures in Fanorona are not made by jumping over an opponent's piece as in most of the other versions of Alquerque. Instead, a whole row of the opponent's pieces can be captured by simply maneuvering one of your own pieces next to their row of pieces! This unique capturing move makes Fanorona a fascinating challenge to anyone who has mastered Alquerque.

It was during the storming of the capital of Madagascar by the French in 1895 that the game was supposedly played by the Queen of Madagascar and her advisors, who believed that the outcome of the game would predict who would win the forthcoming battle.

HOW TO PLAY
FANORONA.

NUMBER OF PLAYERS.—Two.

OBJECTIVE.—To capture all of the opponent's pieces.

MATERIALS.—A double Alquerque playing board and 22 playing pieces. Each player uses a different color.

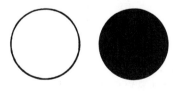

TO BEGIN PLAY.—Place each player's pieces on the board as shown at the top of page 68. One space is left vacant in the center of the board.

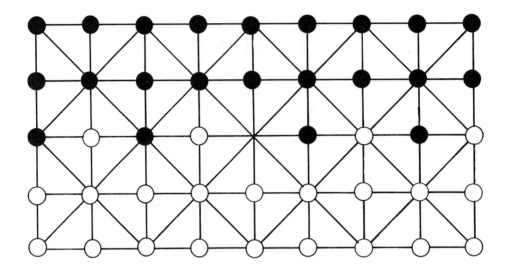

Decide which player will play with the white pieces. That player takes the first turn. Playing pieces may be moved along the lines—diagonally, forward, backwards, or sideways—to a vacant intersection, as shown below.

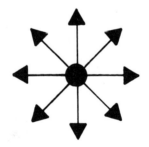

If a player moves a piece next to an opponent's piece without a vacant point in between, then all the opponent's pieces that extend in an unbroken line from that player's piece *in the direction of the attack* are captured and removed from the board.

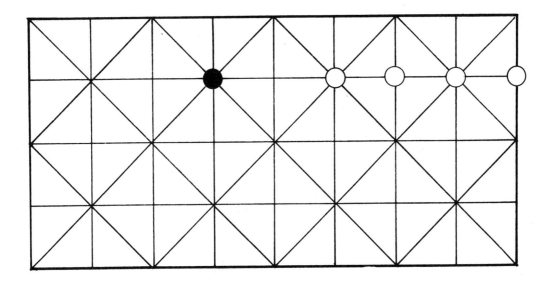

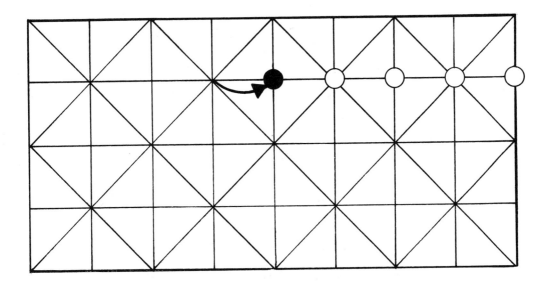

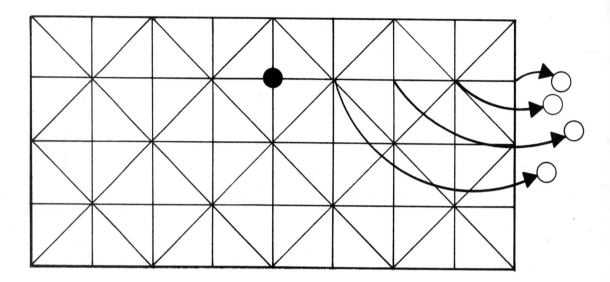

If the line of the opponent's pieces is broken by a vacant point or by one of the player's own pieces, then the opponent's pieces are captured up to that point or piece only, as shown below and opposite.

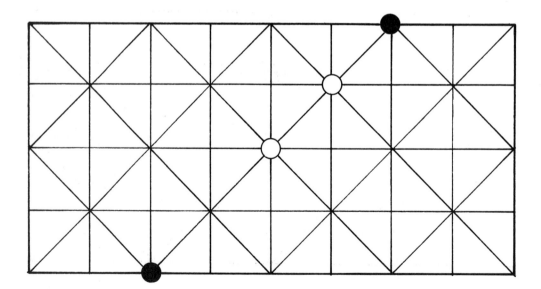

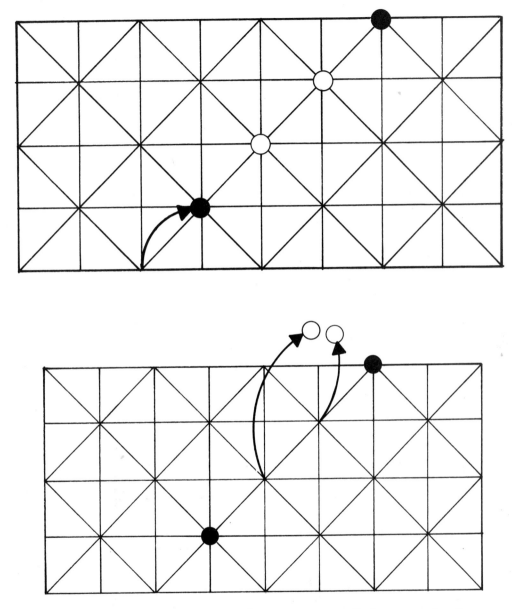

All three of these types of captures are called capture by "approach." Captures may also be made by "withdrawal." If a player moves a piece *away* from a line of the opponent's pieces, then the opponent's pieces in the line of the withdrawal move are captured and removed from the board.

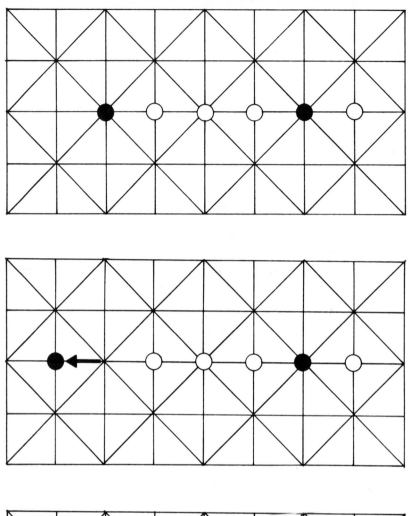

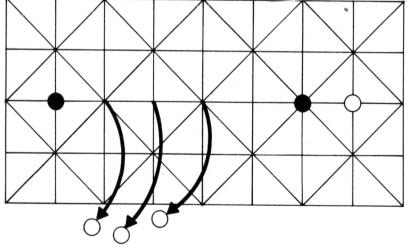

If a player's move threatens two or more rows of the opponent's pieces, the player may decide which row to capture. The player is not required to choose the longest row for capture.

To Play.—The first player is allowed only one move. From then on, each player may continue taking moves until it is no longer possible to capture any of the opponent's pieces. But each move must be along a different line on the board, so that even if the same piece is being moved, it must be moved in different directions.

FANORONA PLAYING-BOARD PATTERN.—I.

FANORONA PLAYING-BOARD PATTERN.—2.

FIGHTING SERPENTS

FIGHTING SERPENTS is an Alquerque-type game invented by the Zuni Indians of New Mexico. Called *kolowis awithlaknannai*, after the mythical serpent the *kolowisi*, the game tests your ability to out-

74

maneuver your opponent within the tight confines of a narrow board crisscrossed with lines and to capture all of her pieces. The game appears to be based on a quadruple version of Alquerque that was introduced into Mexico by the Spanish Conquistadors in the sixteenth century. The Zuni version of the game is often inscribed on long oval stone slabs or even into the clay roofs of houses.

HOW TO PLAY FIGHTING SERPENTS.

NUMBER OF PLAYERS.—Two.

OBJECTIVE.—To be the first player to capture all of the opponent's playing pieces.

MATERIALS.—A narrow playing board crisscrossed with lines, and 46 playing pieces, 23 for one player and 23 of a different color for the other player.

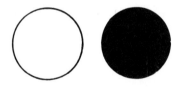

TO BEGIN PLAY.—Place each player's pieces on the board as illustrated below so that only three spaces are left vacant. Decide who will take the first turn.

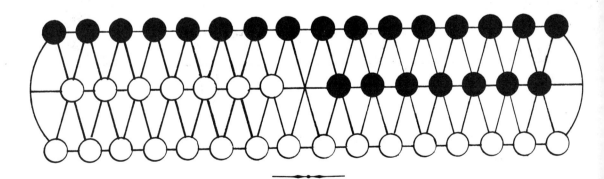

To Play.—The first player moves one of his pieces along the lines to one of the three vacant spaces on the board.

A player must capture an opponent's piece whenever possible. This is done by jumping over one of the opponent's pieces into an empty space next to it. Pieces are removed from the board when they are captured.

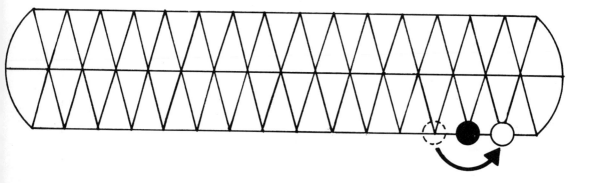

Multiple jumps are allowed and can involve a change in direction, but jumping must be in a straight line. Going around the end of the board is not allowed, as it requires moving in a curved line.

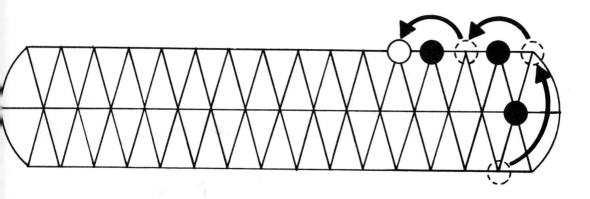

The game ends when all of one player's pieces have been captured.

FIGHTING SERPENTS PLAYING-BOARD PATTERN.—1.

FIGHTING SERPENTS PLAYING-BOARD PATTERN.—2.

FIGHTING SERPENTS PLAYING-BOARD PATTERN.—3.

PERALIKATUMA

PERALIKATUMA is an interesting variation of Alquerque that is played in Ceylon. The rules and strategies are the same as in Alquerque, but the board is quite different. Each player has 23 pieces instead of 12. They are placed on the board as illustrated below.

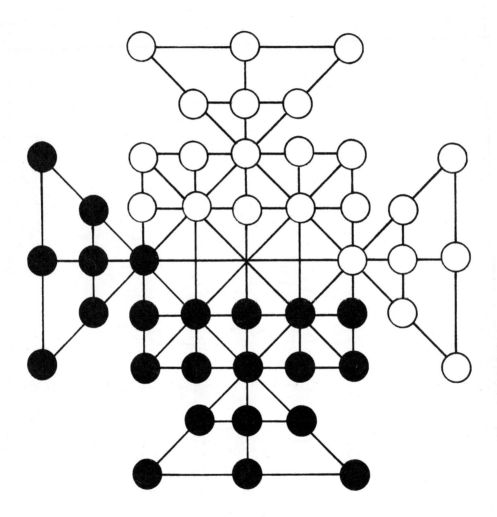

PERALIKATUMA PLAYING-BOARD PATTERN.—1.

PERALIKATUMA PLAYING-BOARD PATTERN.—2.

PERALIKATUMA PLAYING-BOARD PATTERN.—3.

PERALIKATUMA PLAYING-BOARD PATTERN.—4.

SOLITAIRE

THE CROSS

SOLITAIRE is said to have been invented by a French aristocrat to help him pass the time while he was imprisoned in solitary confinement in the Bastille. Played by only one person, Solitaire is a fast-paced game that tests your ability to plot the strategy of each successive move.

Introduced into England at the end of the 1700s, Solitaire continued to be very popular into the Victorian period. In Germany, the game was known as the "hermit's game." It is usually played on a square wooden or plastic board having 33 holes that hold a set of pegs or marbles. More-elaborate boards, including the traditional octagonal French versions with 37 holes, were often made of carved ivory or inlaid woods with ivory or bone pegs.

In the most popular version of Solitaire, the pieces are arranged so that the center hole is vacant. The objective is to clear the board of all but one of the pieces by jumping, horizontally or vertically, over an adjacent piece and removing it from the board. Even though Solitaire is easy to learn, it presents you with an ongoing challenge to master and has become an especially popular board game in recent years.

HOW TO PLAY SOLITAIRE.

NUMBER OF PLAYERS.—One.

OBJECTIVE.—To remove as many pieces as you can from the playing board. The real challenge of Solitaire is to be able to remove all but one piece from the board.

MATERIALS.—A playing board with 33 holes and 32 playing pieces.

TO BEGIN PLAY.—Place a piece over each of the holes in the board, except for the center hole, which is marked with a star.

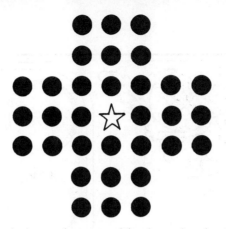

TO PLAY.—Each piece can be moved by jumping backward, forward, or sideways, but not diagonally. When a piece is jumped over by another, it is removed from the board.

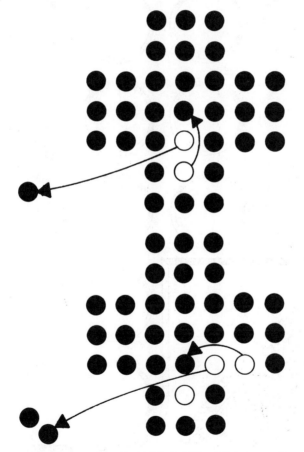

If the game is played correctly, it should end with the last piece left in the center hole marked with the star.

SOLITAIRE PLAYING-BOARD PATTERN.—I.

SOLITAIRE PLAYING-BOARD PATTERN.—2.

THE CROSS

THE CROSS is a variation of Solitaire in which nine pieces are used, positioned on the board as shown below.

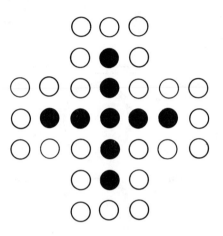

The object of the game is to remove eight of the nine pieces from the board, leaving only one piece left in the center.

You can devise your own versions of Solitaire by setting up new patterns of pieces and attempting to play the game so that only one piece remains at the center of the board.

HALMA

CHINESE CHECKERS

H ALMA, a battle game in which
your only weapon is your ability to plan ahead, was an extremely popular board game invented during the second half of the nineteenth
century. Its name is derived from a Greek word meaning "to jump."
Played by both children and adults, Halma has the advantage of combining very simple rules that can be learned in a few minutes with the
strategic possibilities of moves found in Checkers and Chess.

In the game, each player tries to block, out-maneuver, and outwit
his or her opponents and capture the opponent's side of the board by
occupying it with all of his or her own pieces. An early advertisement
for Halma claimed:

> It has, as a game, the advantage which Dr. Holmes attributes to
> rowing, as an athletic exercise—you can put into it just as much or
> as little strength as you choose. Children of eight or ten like it, and
> the most intellectual people of my acquaintance are delighted with it.

In the United States, Halma was published by the Milton Brad-
ley Company until 1889, when the Halma Company took over its production and sale.

HOW TO PLAY HALMA.

NUMBER OF PLAYERS.—Two, three, or four. The game is best played
with either two or four players, each player playing for him- or herself.
Four players can also play as partners, but three players must play
separately, although in such a case a balanced game is difficult.

OBJECTIVE.—To move all of one's own pieces into the "yard" diagonally across the board from one's starting position. The first player or
pair of players to achieve this objective wins the game.

MATERIALS.—A square board divided into 256 squares, 16 by 16.
Each corner of the board is separated by a line into a "yard" of 13
squares. Two of the yards, diagonally opposite each other, contain an
additional six squares, marked off by another line. These two yards
with 19 squares are used when two players play the game. When three
or four players play, only the original 13 squares in each yard are used.

Four sets of playing pieces, each set a different color, are used for the game. Two sets must have 19 pieces, whereas the other two sets need only 13 pieces.

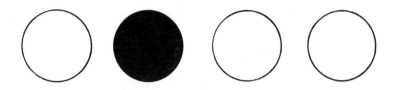

To BEGIN PLAY.—In order to play Halma with two players, place 19 pieces in two yards opposite one another, as shown below.

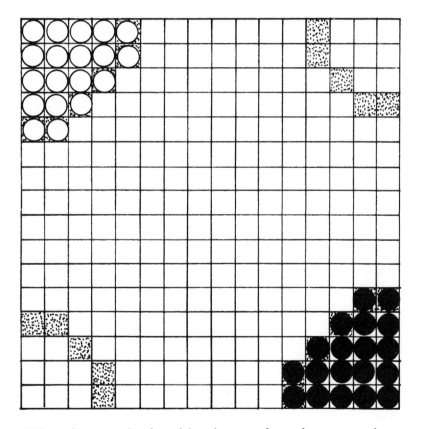

When the game is played by three or four players, 13 pieces are placed on the board, as shown at the top of page 94.

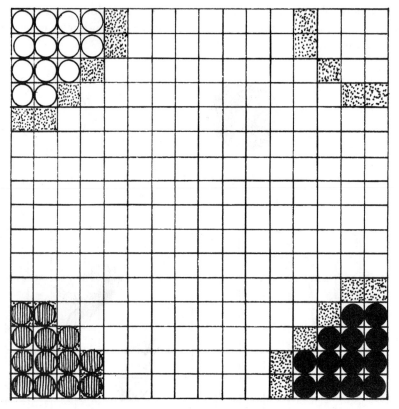

Decide which player will move first. Only one piece may be moved at each turn. Players continue taking turns counterclockwise around the board.

To Play.—The basic move for Halma is to move one piece one space in any direction.

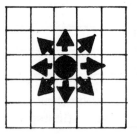

Jumping moves are also allowed. A player may jump one piece over an opponent's piece or over one's own piece. Jumps may also be made in any direction, as long as there is a vacant square to land on after each jump. Pieces are not removed from the board when they have been jumped. A player may not combine the basic move or "step" with a jump or "hop" move in the same turn.

The most effective stategy for Halma is to set up a "chain" of pieces across the board that can rapidly be jumped with one's piece, as in Checkers or Draughts.

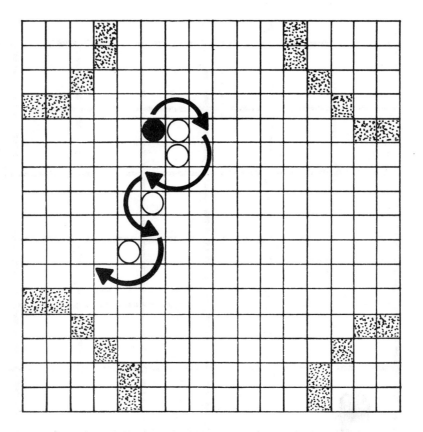

Blocking the opponent's ability to move and jump is also an important element in successfully playing the game of Halma.

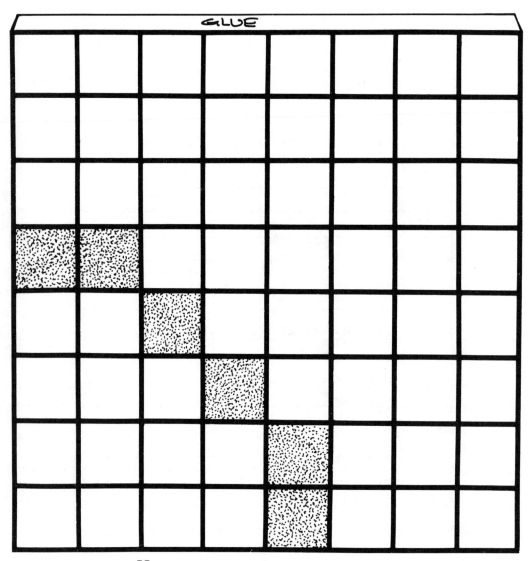

HALMA PLAYING-BOARD PATTERN.—1.

HALMA PLAYING-BOARD PATTERN.—2.

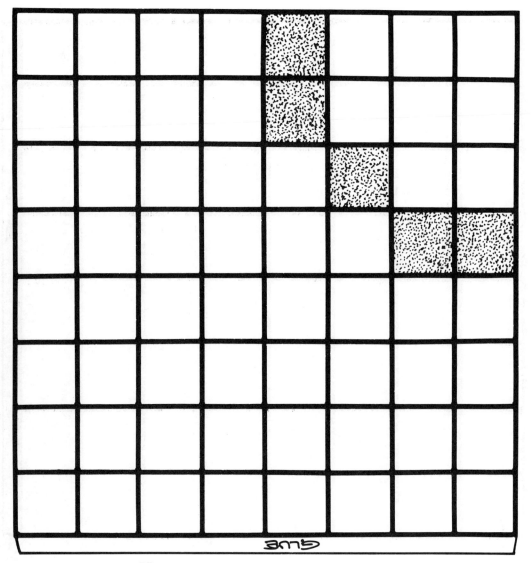

HALMA PLAYING-BOARD PATTERN.—3.

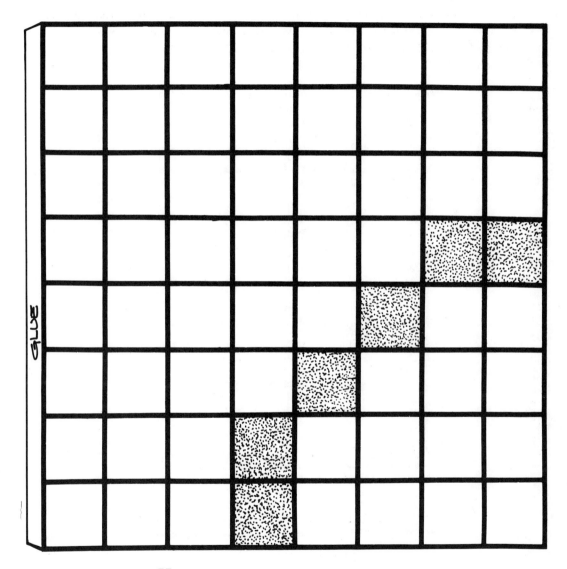

HALMA PLAYING-BOARD PATTERN.—4.

CHINESE CHECKERS

CHINESE CHECKERS is a simplified, faster version of Halma that became popular during the 1880s. Whether or not it was invented in China is not known, but it is played in the People's Republic of China today as well as in Europe and the United States.

March 18, 1941.   J. E. HUFFAKER   2,235,615

GAME BOARD

Filed March 28, 1940   2 Sheets—Sheet 1

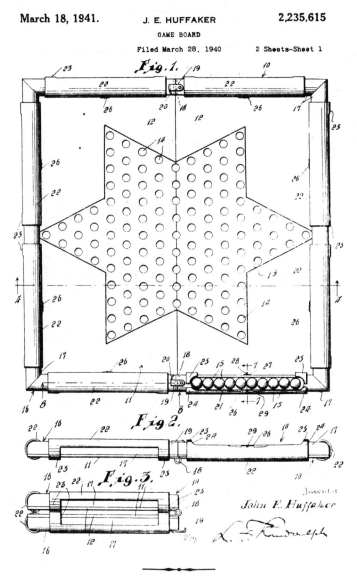

Fig.1.

Fig.2.

Fig.3.

Inventor

John E. Huffaker

HOW TO PLAY CHINESE CHECKERS.

NUMBER OF PLAYERS.—Two, three, four, or six. When four or six people play, they may form partnerships.

OBJECTIVE.—To be the first player to move all of one's pieces into the opposite corner of the star board. When partners play, they both must move all of their pieces to the other's starting corner of the board.

MATERIALS.—A star-shaped playing board of six points, and sets of ten or 15 playing pieces, each set a different color.

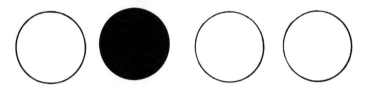

TO BEGIN PLAY.—Determine which player is to go first. If only two people are playing, they each place 15 pieces in opposite home bases, as shown below.

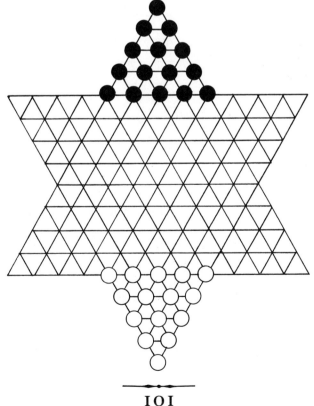

If three or more people play, set up the board with ten pieces for each player at alternate points of the star. If four or six play, each player places his or her pieces opposite an opponent or partner.

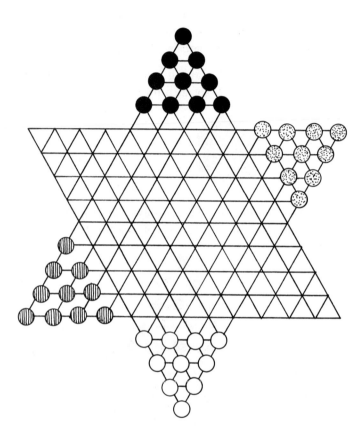

To Play.—Pieces are moved in much the same way as in Halma— either one step at a time in any direction along the connecting lines, or by jumping over one's own pieces and/or those of an opponent, as long as there is a vacant point to land on after each jump. As in Halma, a step move and a jump move may not be combined within the same turn. Pieces that are jumped are not removed from the board.

You may try to block or slow down your opponent's moves as in Halma, but be careful not to leave a piece off by itself where it can only make a single step move and slow down your own chances of winning the game.

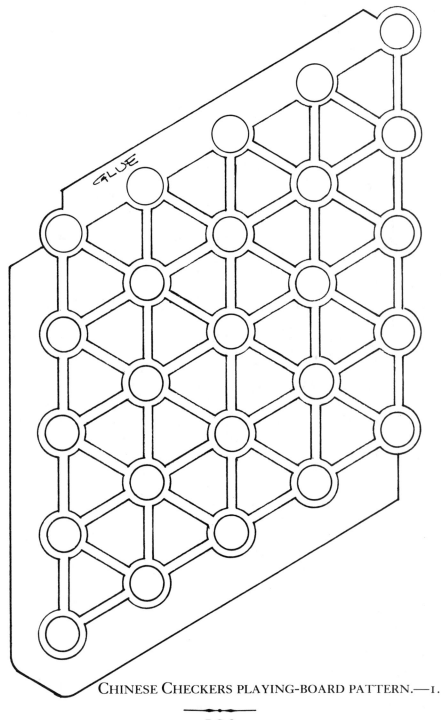

CHINESE CHECKERS PLAYING-BOARD PATTERN.—I.

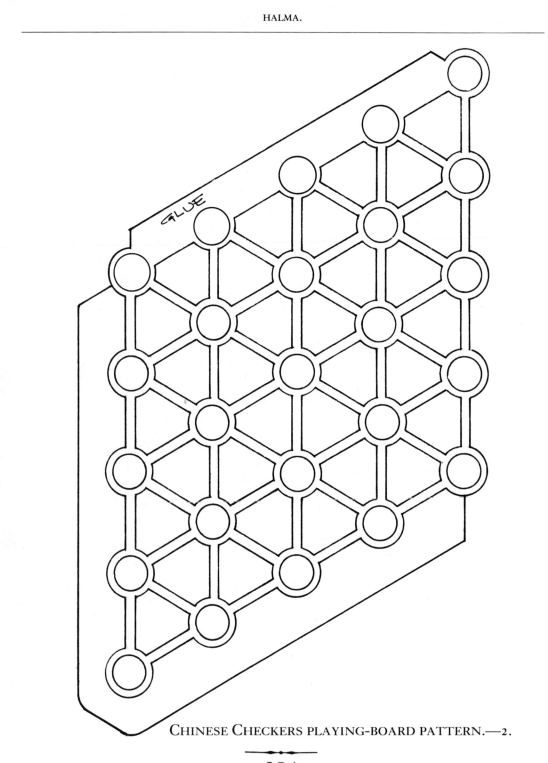

CHINESE CHECKERS PLAYING-BOARD PATTERN.—2.

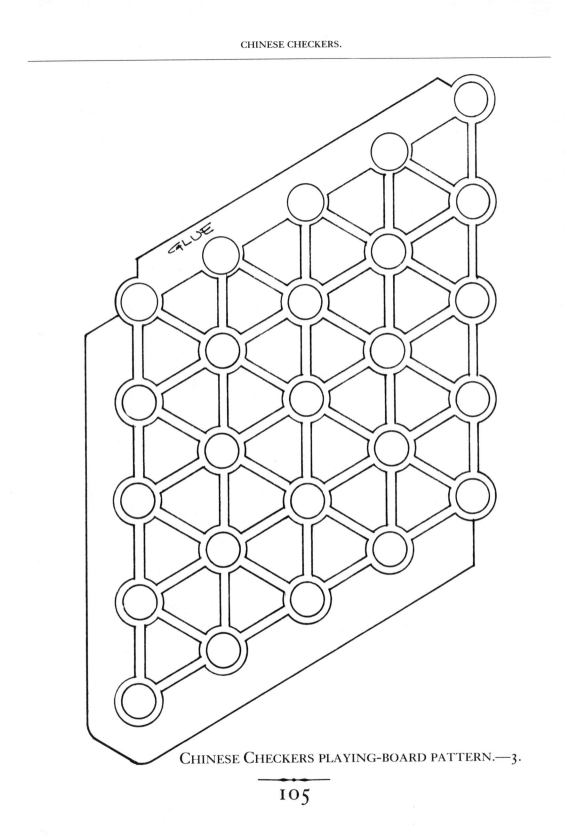

CHINESE CHECKERS PLAYING-BOARD PATTERN.—3.

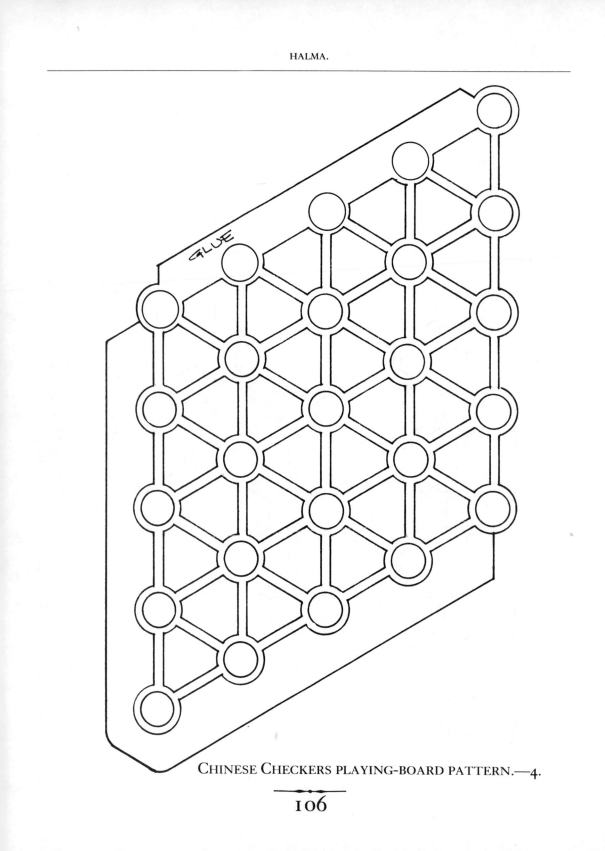

GLUE

CHINESE CHECKERS PLAYING-BOARD PATTERN.—4.

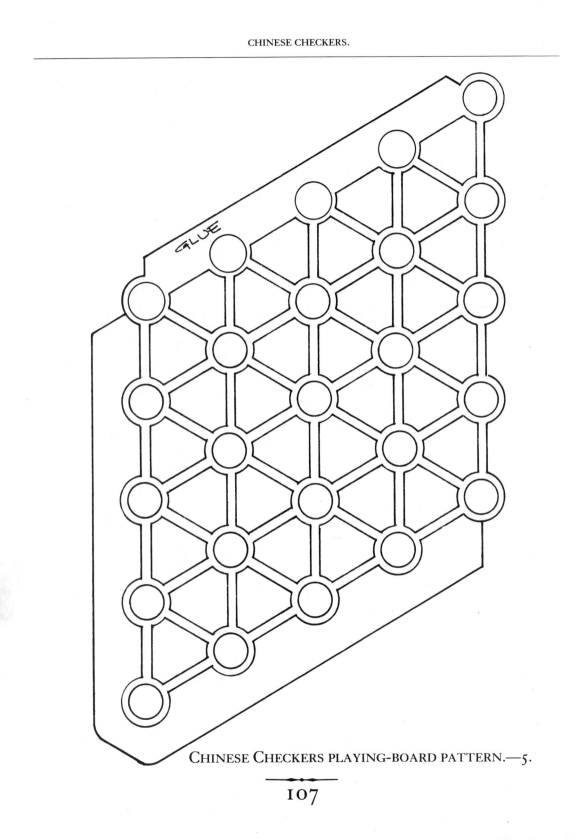

GLUE

CHINESE CHECKERS PLAYING-BOARD PATTERN.—5.

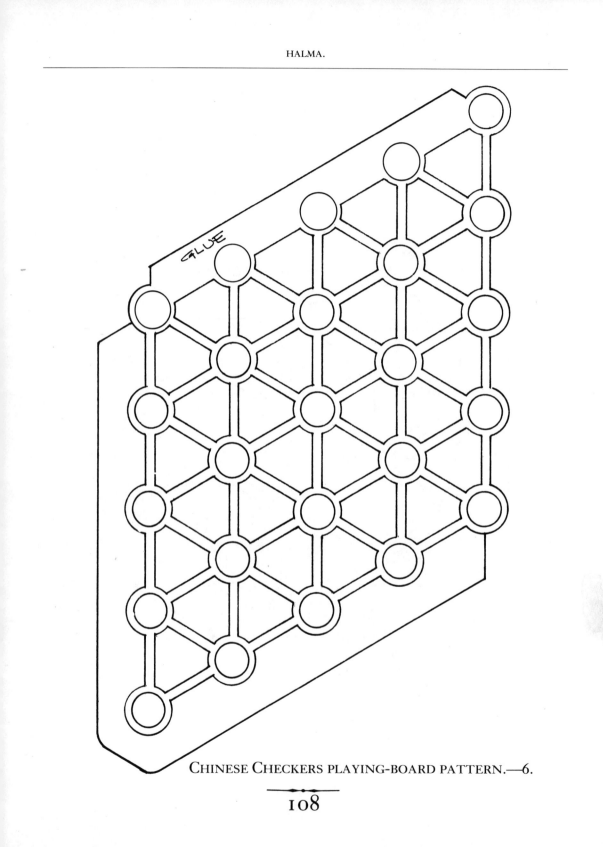

GLUE

CHINESE CHECKERS PLAYING-BOARD PATTERN.—6.

MANCALA

WARI

MANCALA games are some of the most intriguing and oldest two-player strategy games in the world. One version of these games, Kalaha, was played more than 7,000 years ago throughout Asia and Africa. Ancient boards for Kalaha can be found carved on the base of the columns of the Amon Temple at Karnak in Egypt and in the rock ledges along the ancient caravan routes. This provides clues as to how the game probably spread throughout the world.

Although the name and rules may vary from country to country, the boards and the strategy of the various Mancala games are closely related. All have simple rules to learn, but the strategies involved in winning the games are quite challenging!

Traditionally, Mancala games are played on a board carved out of wood with two rows of six playing cups each and two scoring cups. But the game is still played in some rural areas of the world by children and adults with simple pits scooped out of the ground. Perhaps the simplicity of Mancala boards partially explains why these games are so universally popular.

A MANCALA BOARD FROM THE MALDIVE
ISLANDS IN THE INDIAN OCEAN.

HOW TO PLAY MANCALA.

NUMBER OF PLAYERS.—Two.

OBJECTIVE.—Each player attempts to capture as many of the "seeds" or playing pieces as possible.

MATERIALS.—A playing board of two rows of six pits, two larger bins (*Kalahas*) at each end of the board, and 36 playing pieces or seeds.

To Begin Play.—Place three pieces or seeds in each pit and decide which player will take the first turn.

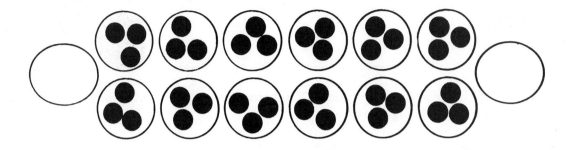

To Play.—The first player picks up all the pieces from any one of her six pits and sows the pieces, one in each pit, around the board counter-clockwise, including in her own *Kalaha*. If there are enough pieces, the player continues sowing into the pits on the opponent's side of the board.

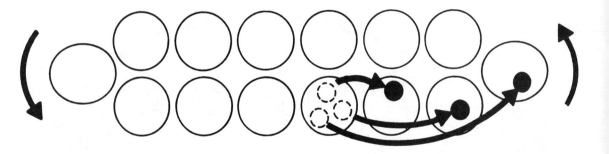

If a player's last piece lands in his own *Kalaha*, he gets another turn.

A player may capture the pieces in her opponent's pit if her last piece is sown in an empty pit on her own side of the board. The player then gets to capture all of the pieces in the opposite pit (her opponent's) and store them in her own *Kalaha* along with the capturing piece (her own).

III

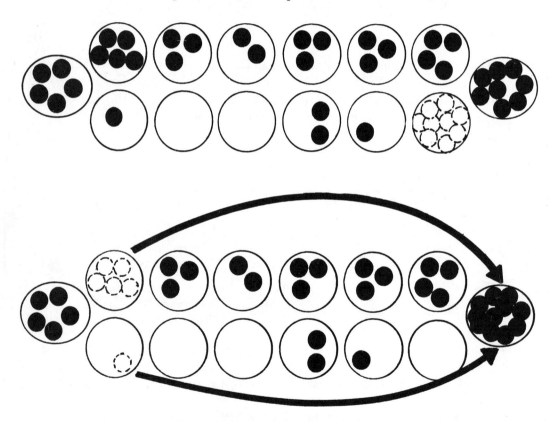

The dotted circles (below) indicate where nine playing pieces were before being moved into new pits.

When all six pits on one side of the board are empty, the game is over. The player who still has playing pieces in his own pits gets to put them in his own *Kalaha*. The winner is the player with the most "seeds" or pieces in his or her own *Kalaha*.

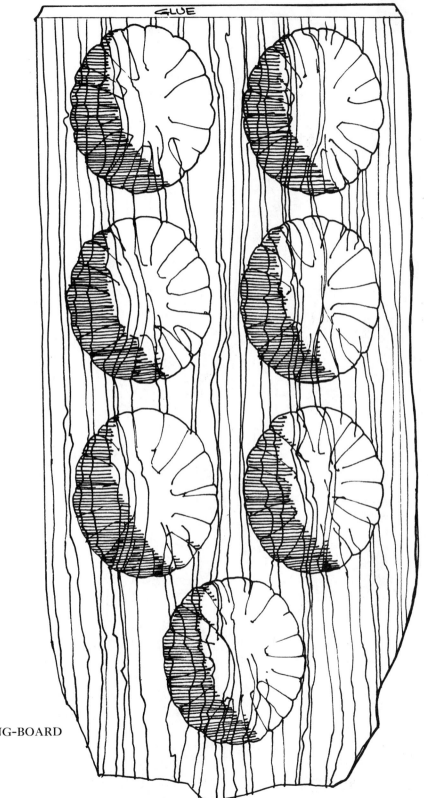

MANCALA PLAYING-BOARD
PATTERN.—I.

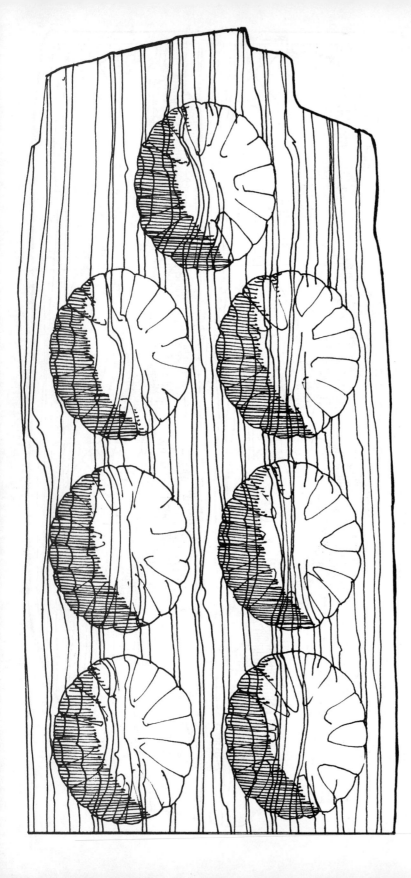

MANCALA
PLAYING-BOARD
PATTERN.—2.

WARI

WARI, another Mancala Game, is especially popular in Egypt and West Africa. Since each player has six more playing pieces than in Mancala and the rules are a bit more complicated, the possibilities for out-maneuvering your opponent are even more exciting.

April 3, 1951   M. B. LORENZANA ET AL   **Des. 162,742**

GAME BOARD

Filed Nov. 9, 1949

Fig. 1.

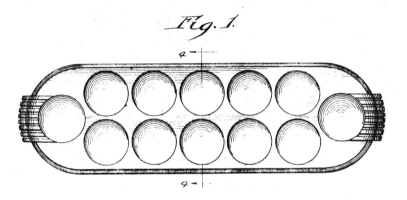

Fig. 2.

Fig. 3.   *Fig. 4.*

Inventors.
Moises B. Lorenzana.
Francisco B. Lemi.
By. Schroeder, Merriam
Hofgren & Brady.
Attorneys.

HOW TO PLAY WARI.

NUMBER OF PLAYERS.—Two.

OBJECTIVE.—Each player tries to capture as many "seeds" or playing pieces as possible.

MATERIALS.—A Mancala playing board (identical to the Mancala board) and 48 playing pieces or seeds.

TO BEGIN PLAY.—Place four pieces in each pit and decide which player will take the first turn.

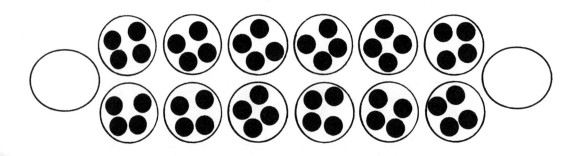

TO PLAY.—The first player picks up all of the pieces in one of her pits and sows them, one in each pit, around the board counterclockwise. Unlike in Mancala, no pieces are placed in the large pits, or *Kalahas*, at each end of the board. These bins are used only to store captured pieces.

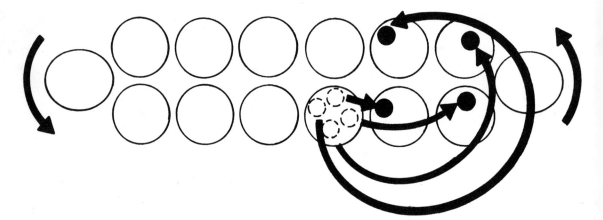

If there are more than 12 pieces in a player's pit, then she will have to sow the pieces from that pit completely around the board. In this case, the emptied pit is passed over when completing the sowing.

When an opponent's pits are empty, a player must, if possible, make a move that provides the opponent with a piece to play with. If the player fails to do so, he forfeits all of his pieces to the opponent. If it is impossible to provide the opponent with a piece, then the game ends and all of the pieces left on the board go into the player's *Kalaha*.

A player may capture pieces in her opponent's pits by placing the last piece of a move into an opponent's pit that already holds one or two pieces. If the pits that precede this pit also contain two or three pieces in an unbroken sequence, then the pieces in these pits are also captured.

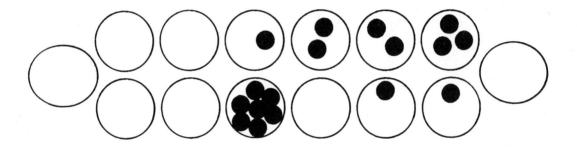

The dotted circles (below) indicate where seven pieces were before being moved into new pits.

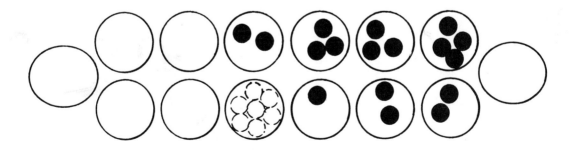

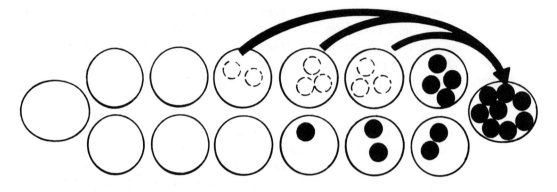

A player cannot capture all of the opponent's pieces, since this would make it impossible for each player to alternate turns.

The game ends when it is no longer possible for either player to capture any of the opponent's pieces. Each player adds the pieces left in the pits on his or her side of the board to his or her own store (*Kalaha*), and the player with the largest number of pieces is the winner.

STEEPLECHASE

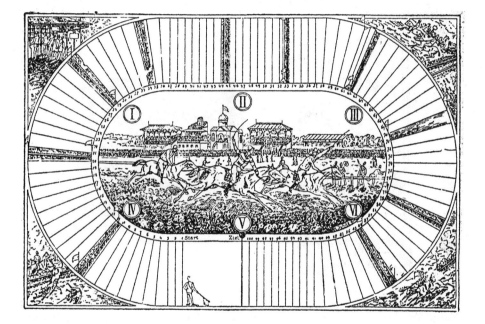

STEEPLECHASE was one of the most popular nineteenth-century versions of the Royal Game of Goose. The game first appeared in England about 1850, where it was played on an oval race course with cardboard horses and riders mounted on stands. But instead of death's heads and bridges representing bad luck, obstacles such as jumps, hurdles, ditches, fences, and hedges appeared along the race course. The horses and riders were moved around the track according to the spin of a teetotum or the roll of a six-sided die. The player who moved his horse around the track to the finish line first, dodging and overcoming all obstacles, was the winner. Bets were often placed on the outcome of the race, just like in real horse racing.

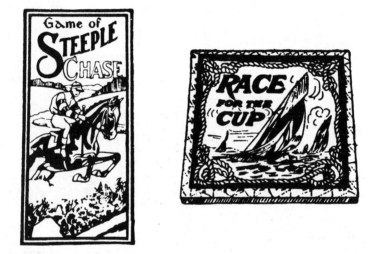

The popularity of Steeplechase undoubtedly encouraged the development of other types of racing games during the second half of the nineteenth century. Since many of the early race games were printed by map makers, their journeys often wove their way over boards that were actually maps. The board for "An Eccentric Excursion to the Chinese Empire," one of the most popular early race games published by the William Spooner Company in England in the 1840s, was decorated with all sorts of exciting mishaps and adventures, including a flight in Henson's steam-powered airplane! More-modern versions of the game included automobiles, boats, and even airplanes racing one another.

HOW TO PLAY
STEEPLECHASE.

NUMBER OF PLAYERS.—Two to six.

OBJECTIVE.—To be the first player to complete the race by passing the last square on the board, which is the finish line.

MATERIALS.—A round or oval playing-board race course divided into playing spaces, some of which are designated as obstacles. A six-sided teetotum or die and a playing piece of a different color for each player are also needed.

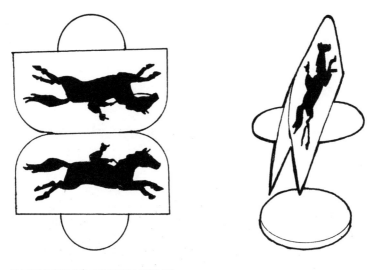

PATTERN FOR STEEPLECHASE
PLAYING PIECE.

TO BEGIN PLAY.—Each player spins the teetotum or throws the die to see who gets the highest number and goes first. The other players take their turns according to the number they threw, with the highest going second and so on.

TO PLAY.—Each player's piece is moved according to the number shown on the teetotum or die. If a player lands on a square marked with a fence or hurdle, which appear at intervals along the race course (squares 3, 9, 15, 28, 33, 40, and 54), then she loses her next turn. The first player to pass the final square or finish line wins the race.

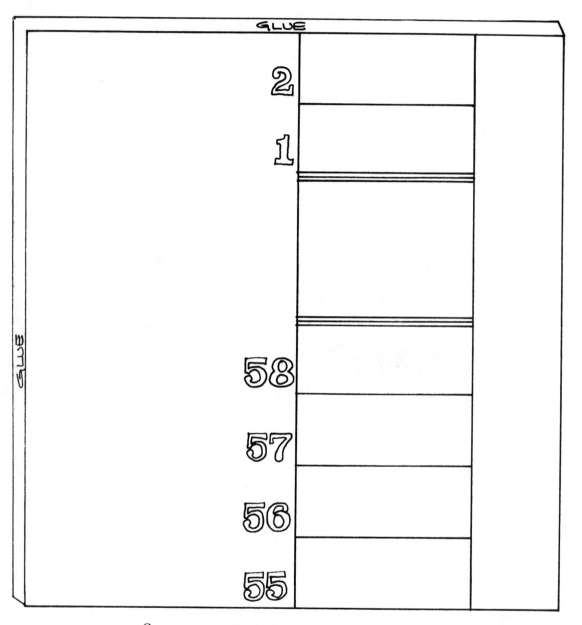

STEEPLECHASE PLAYING-BOARD PATTERN.—I.

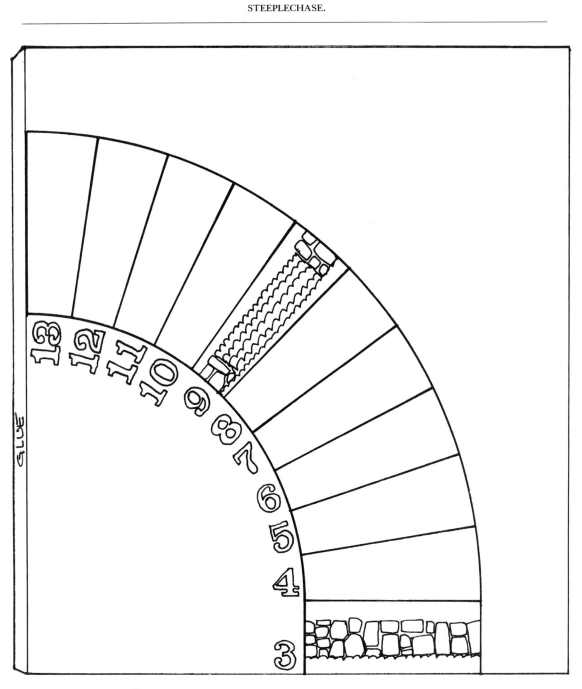

STEEPLECHASE PLAYING-BOARD PATTERN.—2.

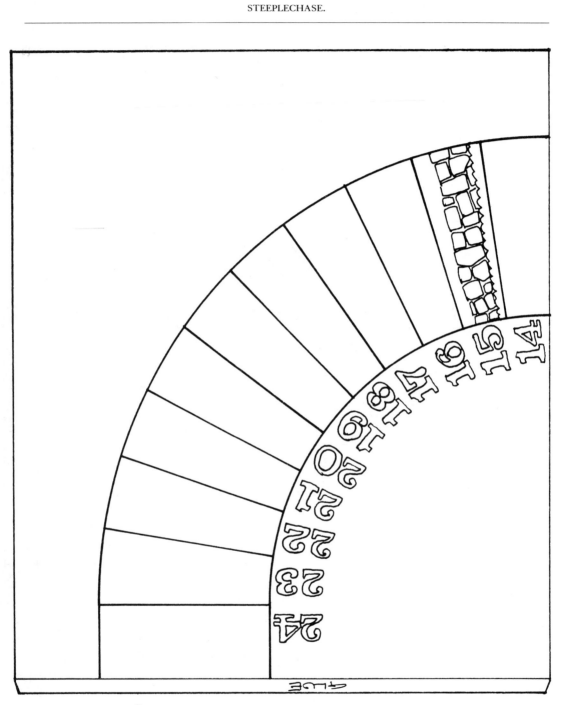

STEEPLECHASE PLAYING-BOARD PATTERN.—3.

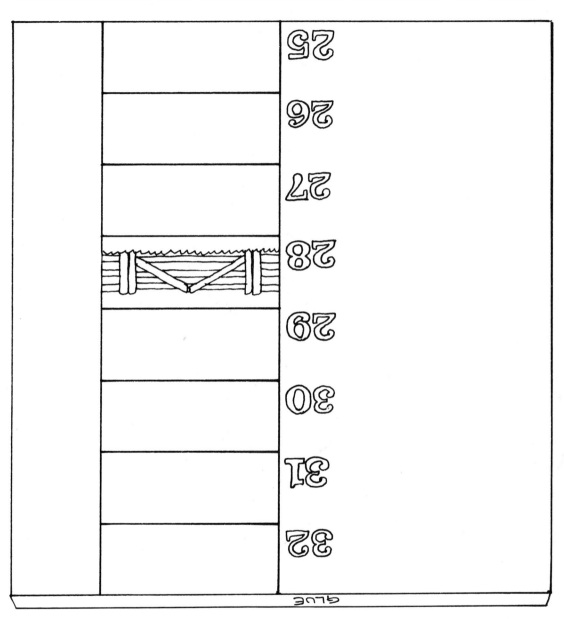

STEEPLECHASE PLAYING-BOARD PATTERN.—4.

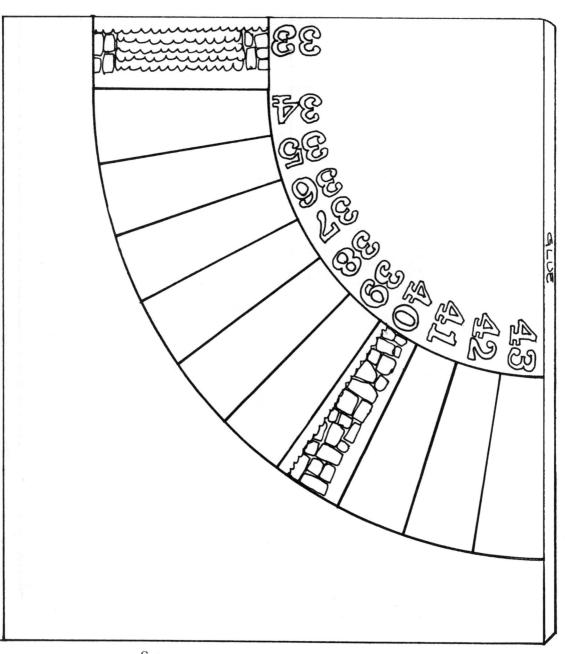

S<small>TEEPLECHASE</small> PLAYING-BOARD PATTERN.—5.

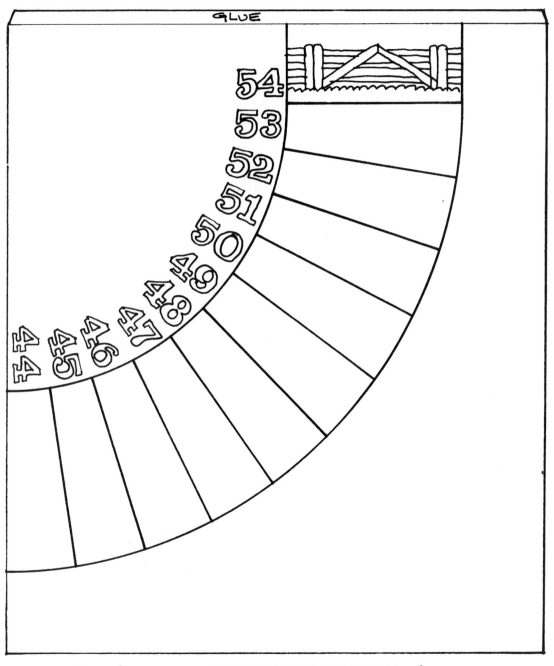

GLUE

54
53
52
51
50
49
48
47
46
45
44

STEEPLECHASE PLAYING-BOARD PATTERN.—6.

QUEEN'S GUARD

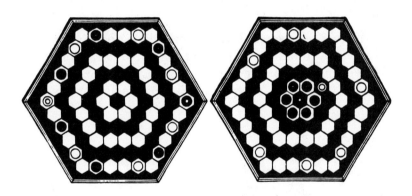

QUEEN'S GUARD, also known as *Agon*, was a popular board game during the Victorian Era that combined the complexity of the strategy in Chess with the simplicity of the moves in Checkers. The game is won when one of the players positions his Queen in the center of the board surrounded by her attending guard of six pieces.

HOW TO PLAY
QUEEN'S GUARD.

NUMBER OF PLAYERS.—Two.

OBJECTIVE.—To be the first player to place your Queen in the board's central space and surround her by your other six pieces (the Queen's guards).

MATERIALS.—A hexagonal playing board made up of 91 smaller hexagons. Each player has seven playing pieces whose color is distinct from those of their opponent's pieces. One of these pieces is specially designated as a Queen. The remaining six pieces are guards.

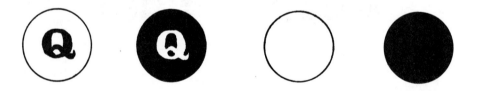

TO BEGIN PLAY.—After determining which player is to go first, you can begin the game in two different ways. In the first, the Queens (represented in the following illustration by square pieces) are placed in opposite corners, with each player's guards taking alternating positions around the outer rim of the board, as shown at the top of page 131.

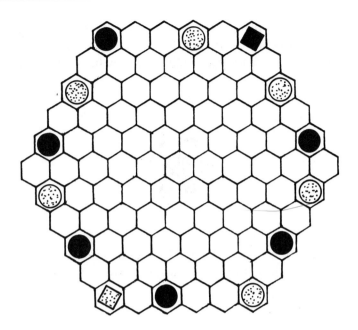

In the second version, each player takes alternate turns placing his or her pieces wherever they like on the outer rim of the board.

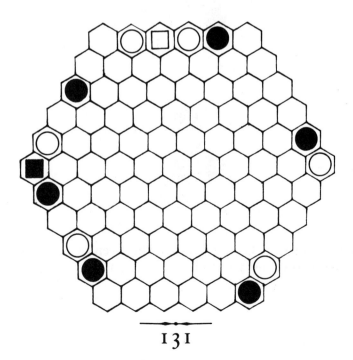

Pieces are moved one space forward or sideways. Once a piece has been moved toward the center, it may not be moved backwards toward the outer rim. If a player touches a piece, he must move it or forfeit his turn.

To Play.—When a guard is trapped between an opponent's pieces, its player must move it to any vacant space on the outer rim of the board in her next turn.

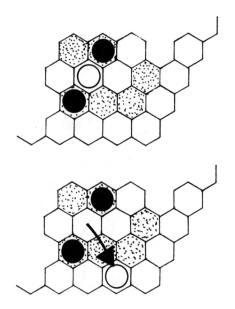

When a player's Queen is trapped between two of the opponent's pieces, the player must move his Queen to any vacant hexagon chosen by the opponent for his next turn.

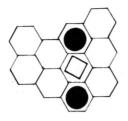

If more than one piece is trapped in a single turn, the player must continue to use her turns until all of the trapped pieces have been returned to the outermost ring of the board. Guards may be returned to the outer ring in any order, but if a Queen and a guard are captured together, the Queen must be moved first.

Only a Queen can be placed in the central hexagon. The game is forefeited by a player if the central hexagon is empty and he encloses it with six of his guards, as shown below.

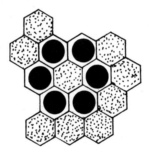

The game is won when a player places her Queen in the central hexagon on the board and surrounds her with her six guards.

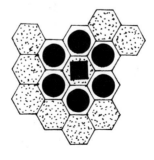

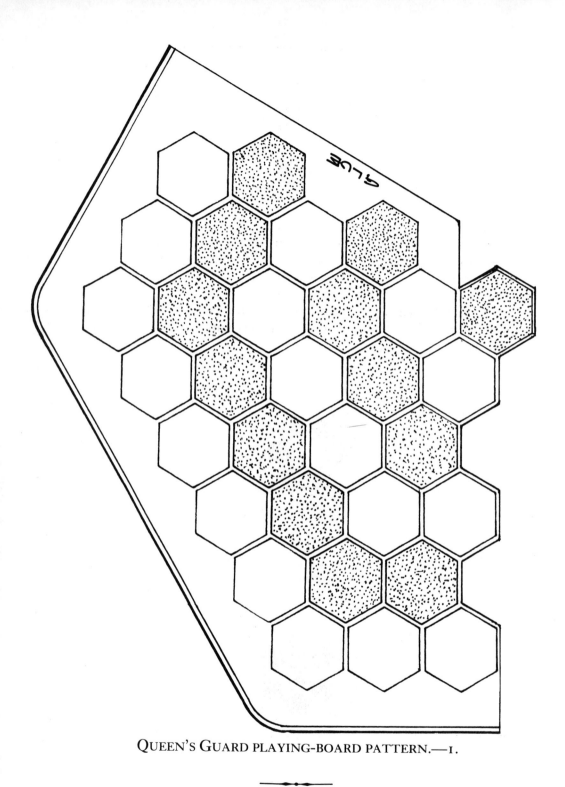

QUEEN'S GUARD PLAYING-BOARD PATTERN.—I.

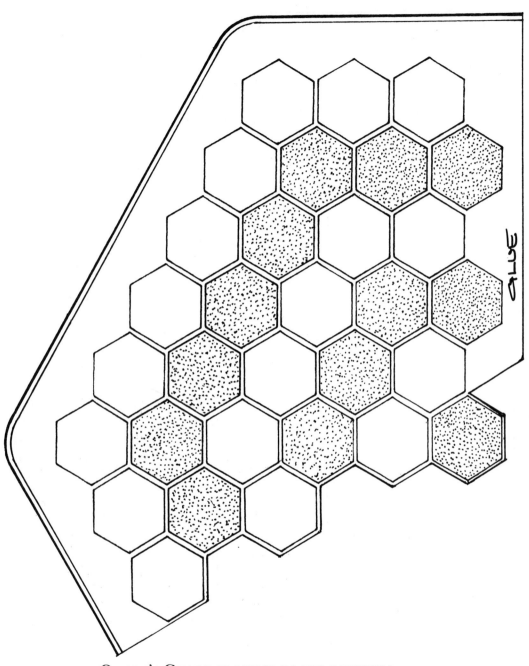

QUEEN'S GUARD PLAYING-BOARD PATTERN.—2.

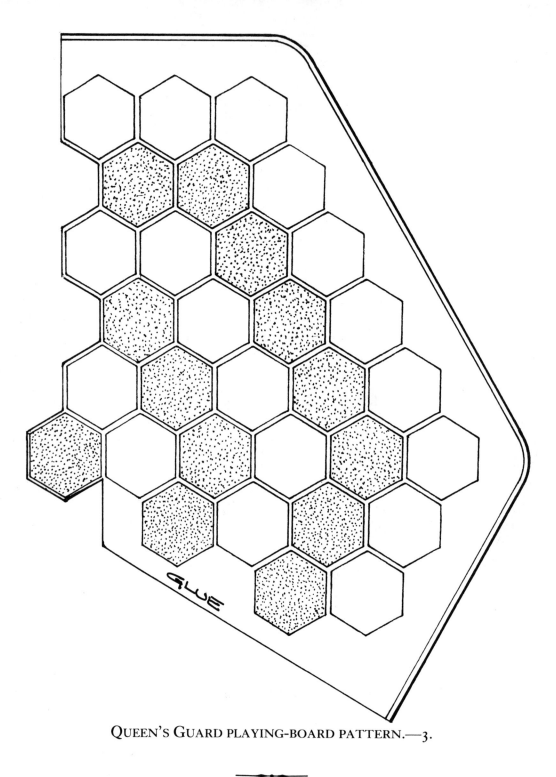

GLUE

QUEEN'S GUARD PLAYING-BOARD PATTERN.—3.

CHIVALRY

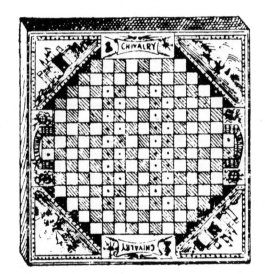

Chivalry was one of the many battle games manufactured by Parker Brothers of Salem, Massachusetts, during the late 1880s. Included among these games were such titles as the "Battle of Manila," "Waterloo," "Trafalgar," and "Roosevelt's Charge." But it was Chivalry that the Parker Brothers Catalogue described as the best board game invented in 2,000 years!

THE 1930 PATENT FOR CAMELOT, A SIMPLIFIED VERSION OF CHIVALRY.

Oct. 28, 1930.   G. S. PARKER   1,780,038

GAME

Filed Jan. 28, 1930   3 Sheets—Sheet 2

Fig. 2.

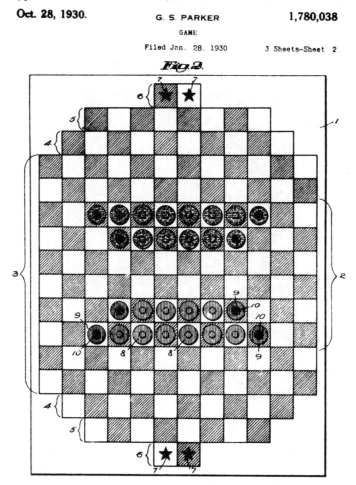

Inventor:
George S. Parker
by Emery, Booth, Varney & Townsend
Attys

138

In Chivalry, each one of the players has an army of eight knights and 12 pawns with which they try to capture the opponent's pieces and occupy his stronghold to win the game. Although the knights and pawns can make different moves, as in Chess, Chivalry is a much simpler game to learn. Despite its simplicity, the number of tactical possibilities in the one-to-one battle between players in Chivalry makes it as exciting and stimulating as the most complicated board games.

Parker Brothers introduced a simplified version of Chivalry known as Camelot in 1930. But neither Chivalry nor this new version of the game was able to attain the original game's popularity, for both were superseded by a revived interest in the even older game of Backgammon.

HOW TO PLAY CHIVALRY.

NUMBER OF PLAYERS.—Two.

OBJECTIVE.—To be the first player to occupy the stronghold spaces on your opponent's side of the board with any two of your own pieces.

MATERIALS.—An irregularly shaped playing board of 176 squares. Both player's stronghold spaces are marked with stars or *xs* on opposite sides of the playing board. Each player has 12 playing pieces that are pawns and eight pieces designated as knights. All the pieces are of a different color from their opponent's pieces.

TO BEGIN PLAY.—Place each player's pieces on the board as illustrated at the top of page 140 and decide which player will take the first turn.

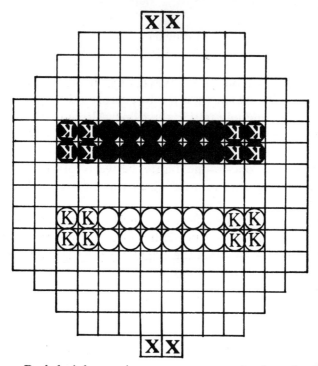

To Play.—Both knights and pawns can move in three basic ways:

- By moving one space in any direction, but not diagonally.

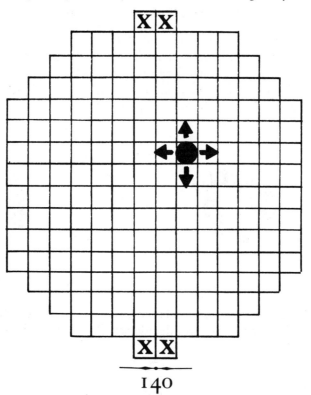

140

○ By "cantoring," or leaping over, one of your own pieces to a vacant space on the other side. Players may leap over as many of their own pieces as possible within one turn. A player does not have to make a cantor move if one is possible.

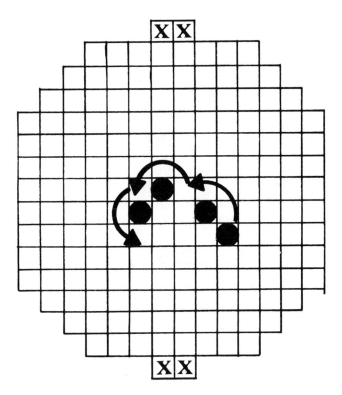

● Or, by jumping over an opponent's piece in any direction to a vacant space on the other side (see next page). When an opponent's piece is jumped, it is removed from the board. A player must make a jump move whenever possible and must continue jumping all the pieces possible within one turn.

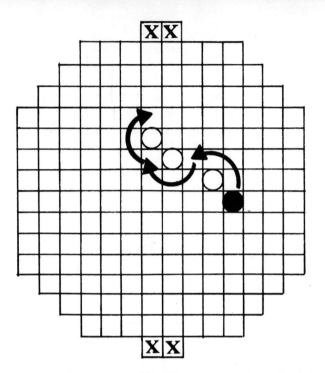

Pawns can make any of the three moves described but cannot combine any of them within one turn. Knights can combine cantoring over one of their own pieces with jumping an opponent's piece or pieces, but all of the cantor moves must be made before the jumps.

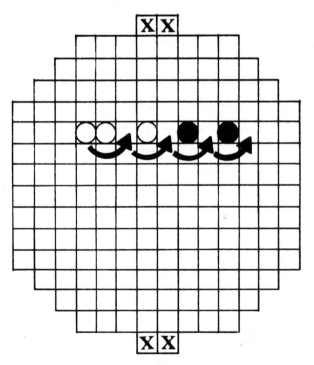

A knight cannot combine the basic move of advancing one space in any direction with a cantor or jump move.

The first player to succeed in placing any two of her pieces in her opponent's two stronghold spaces on the opposite side of the board wins the game.

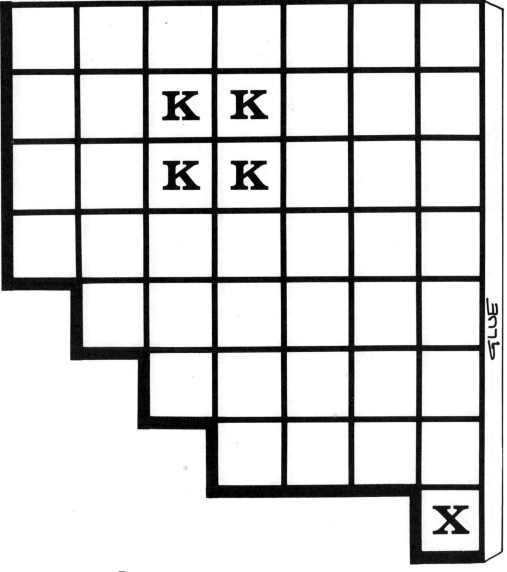

CHIVALRY PLAYING-BOARD PATTERN.—I.

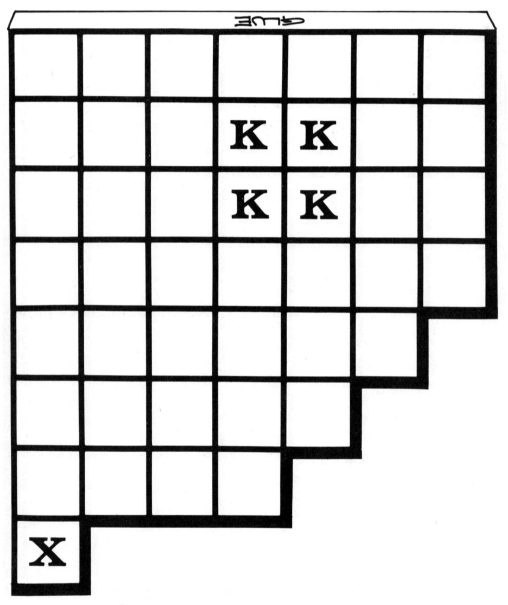

CHIVALRY PLAYING-BOARD PATTERN.—2.

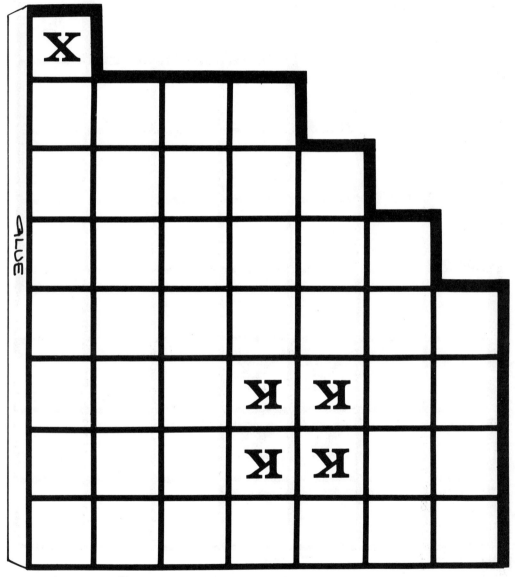

CHIVALRY PLAYING-BOARD PATTERN.—3.

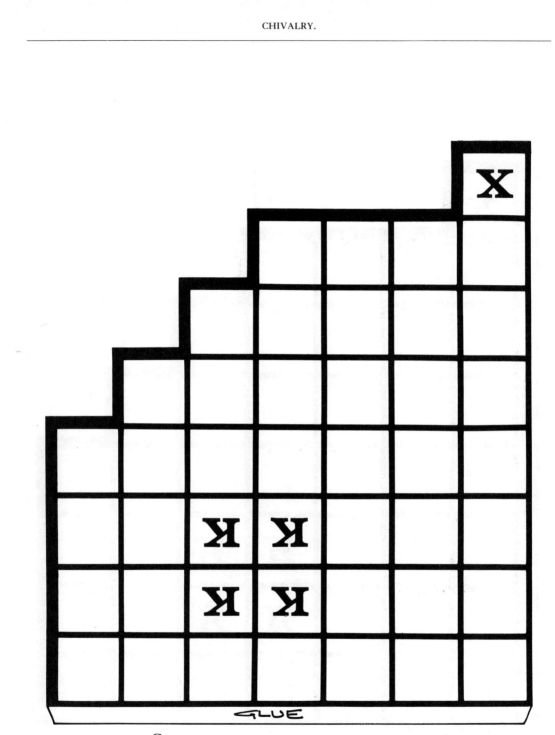

CHIVALRY PLAYING-BOARD PATTERN.—4.

GO-BANG

HASAMI SHOGI
DARA

W. B. SILVER.
GAME BOARD.

No. 255,892. Patented Apr. 4, 1882.

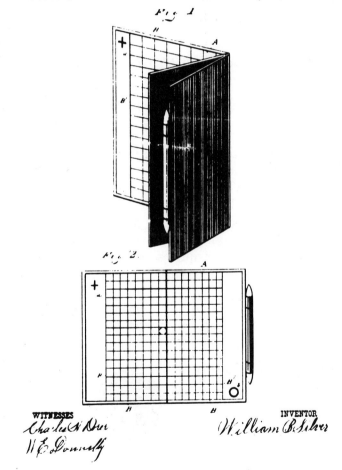

WITNESSES
Charles N. Dun
W. E. Donnelly

INVENTOR
William B. Silver

GO-BANG, a great strategy game for two players, originated in Japan, where it is called *Go-Moku.* The game is played on the same board as *Go,* which is believed to be one of the oldest games in the world, having been invented in China more than three thousand years ago. Since both players are constantly attacking and defending their positions all over the board, the game can be very exciting and complicated. As seen in the patent by W. B. Silver (page 147), Go-Bang was not only a popular board game in America during the nineteenth century, but it was also commonly played on slates such as the one invented by Mr. Silver, which could be folded and carried in a pocket.

HOW TO PLAY GO-BANG.

NUMBER OF PLAYERS.—Two.

OBJECTIVE.—To form a straight line of five playing pieces, either vertically, horizontally, or diagonally.

MATERIALS.—The traditional Japanese Go table ("Go-ban"), a large square marked off in a grid of 18 squares on each side, is made of wood and is stained yellow. There are 361 points of intersecting lines on which the game is played.

Go-Bang can also be played on a simpler board of 100 squares, ten on each side. When playing on a board of 100 squares, each player places his or her pieces on the squares instead of on the points of intersecting lines. This is the version that will be explained on the following pages.

Each player has a set of 50 playing pieces, with each player's set being of a different color from his opponent's.

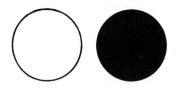

To Begin Play.—The players decide who will play with which color of pieces. The dark pieces always take the first turn. The playing pieces are placed anywhere on the board, one each turn in alternating turns.

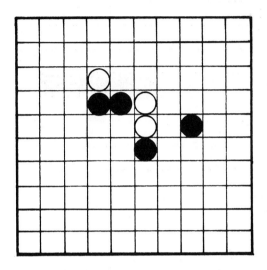

To Play.—Once a piece has been placed on a square on the board, it cannot be moved until the end of the game. In order to win, players must place five pieces in a row, vertically, horizontally, or diagonally.

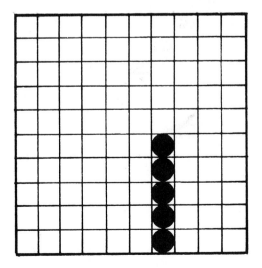

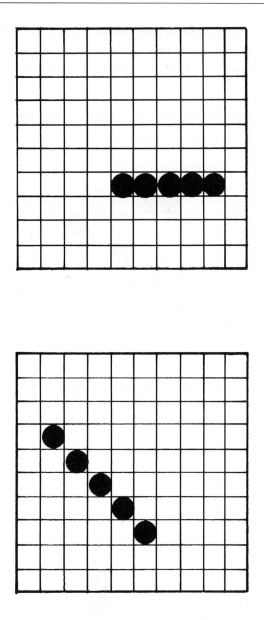

If neither player has succeeded in forming a "five" before all the pieces are placed on the board, then the game ends in a draw.

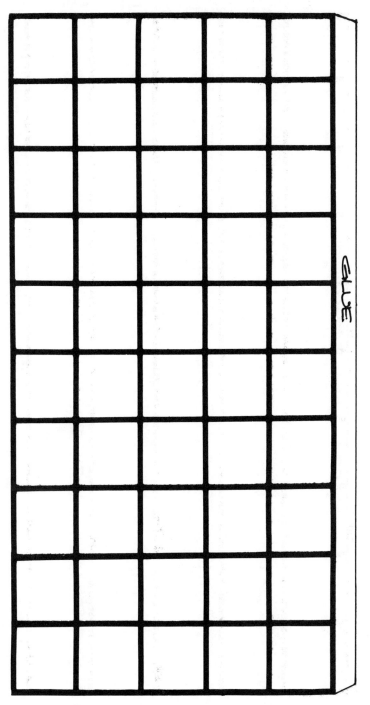

GO-BANG PLAYING-BOARD PATTERN.—I.

GO-BANG PLAYING-BOARD PATTERN.—2.

HASAMI SHOGI

HASAMI SHOGI, another variation of Go-Bang, is a very popular children's game in Japan. Played on a board similar to a Go board, the game quickly becomes exciting as both players not only try to capture their opponent's pieces, but also try to prevent their opponent from forming a row of nine pieces. At the same time, they are trying to form their own row of nine pieces. This makes the game a fast-paced combination of blocking, attacking, and out-witting your opponent.

HOW TO PLAY
HASAMI SHOGI.

NUMBER OF PLAYERS.—Two.

OBJECTIVE.—To be the first player to complete a row of nine pieces in any direction anywhere on the board, except the two rows designated as your own home base. At the same time, each player tries to capture as many of the opponent's pieces as possible to prevent the opponent from completing a row of nine pieces.

MATERIALS.—A square playing board divided into 81 squares, nine on each side. Each player has 18 playing pieces with one player's set being a different color from the opponents'.

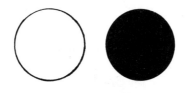

TO BEGIN PLAY.—Each player places his or her 18 pieces on the board, as illustrated at the top of page 154, and decides which player will take the first turn.

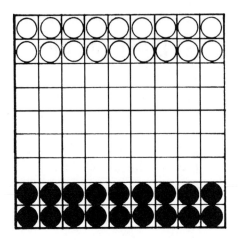

To Play.—Each player may move one piece per turn in any direction, expect diagonally.

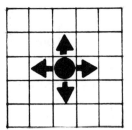

A piece may be moved to a vacant adjacent square or may jump over a piece, either the player's or the opponent's, to a vacant square next to it.

Jumped pieces are not removed from the board. No more than one jump is permitted per turn.

An opponent's piece may be captured and removed from the board if a player's piece can be moved so that it traps the opponent's piece between two of the player's pieces, or traps the opponent's piece in one of the corners of the board. A piece is not captured if it is diagonally flanked by two of the opponent's pieces.

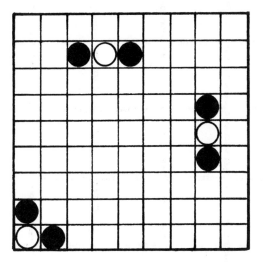

A player's piece is not considered captured if the player moves it onto a vacant square between two of the opponent's pieces.

The game is won by a player's either capturing all of his or her opponent's pieces, or by successfully moving nine pieces into a row, horizontally or vertically, anywhere on the board except along the player's own two home base rows. If a player captures at least ten of the opponent's pieces, it is impossible for the opponent to form a row of nine pieces. But even if ten or more of your pieces are captured, you may still prevent your opponent from forming a row of nine pieces or you may even capture all of your opponent's pieces and win the game!

HASAMI SHOGI PLAYING-BOARD PATTERN.—I.

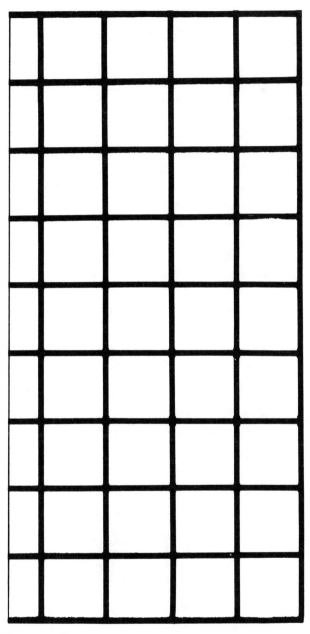

Hᴀꜱᴀᴍɪ Sʜᴏɢɪ ᴘʟᴀʏɪɴɢ-ʙᴏᴀʀᴅ ᴘᴀᴛᴛᴇʀɴ.—2.

DARA

DARA (or Derrah), a popular North African version of Go-Bang, is usually played on a wooden board with thirty pits. Pebbles, beans, or marbles are used as playing pieces. Since the game is played in two phases, it involves both strategic planning and the concentration necessary to both block and out-maneuver your opponent.

In the first phase, the players place their twelve playing pieces on the board wherever they choose; however, no more than two pieces of the same color may be next to each other. In the second phase, players take turns moving their pieces, trying to get three in a row. This gives them the right to remove one of their opponent's pieces from the board.

Dara can be played on a board with pits, on a board marked with 30 squares, or even on the ground in hollows dug out of the earth.

HOW TO PLAY DARA.

NUMBER OF PLAYERS.—Two.

OBJECTIVE.—Each player tries to move his or her pieces so that they form a row of three, which entitles them to remove one of the opponent's pieces. When one player is no longer able to form a row of three pieces or when all of one player's pieces have been removed from the board, the game ends and the other player is the winner.

MATERIALS.—A rectangular playing board divided into 30 squares, six on one side and five on the other. Each player has 12 playing pieces; one player has one color and the other player has another color.

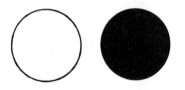

TO BEGIN PLAY.—After deciding which player will take the first turn, the players alternate placing their pieces on any square of the board. No more than two pieces may be placed next to each other by the same player during the first phase of the game.

Since the placement of pieces during this part of the game will determine which moves will be possible during the second phase, it is important to plan carefully where to place the pieces.

TO PLAY.—After all of the 24 pieces are on the board, each player may move one piece one square per turn, backward, forward, or sideways, but not diagonally.

Neither player may set more than three pieces in a row. Rows of four pieces do not count or allow a player to remove the opponent's piece from the board.

DARA PLAYING-BOARD PATTERN.

SEEGA

Seega is the modern version of Senat, one of the most ancient games of skill. As in many other very old board games, pieces are captured by being confined on two sides. But in Seega, the pieces are not arranged on the board at the beginning of play. Instead, they are placed on the board alternatively by each player, so great foresight and planning are required to be sure that your pieces occupy the most strategic positions to complete the game and win.

Although the rules for Senat have not survived, we know that it was played in Egypt nearly 5,000 years ago. In fact, four different Senat boards were found in the tomb of the Pharoah Tutankhamon (c. 1347–1339 B.C.) when it was discovered in 1922. Seega is played on a smaller board than Senat, and with fewer pieces.

Today, the modern game of Seega is popular in Egypt and North Africa, where it is often played on a board drawn on and scooped out of the sand. Pebbles, beans, or small pieces of wood are used as playing pieces. They are called *kelbs*, or "dogs."

HOW TO PLAY SEEGA.

NUMBER OF PLAYERS.—Two.

OBJECTIVE.—To capture all of the opponent's pieces or to block them so that they cannot move.

MATERIALS.—A square playing board divided into 25 squares, and 12 playing pieces. Each player uses a different color. The game may also be played on a board of 49 or 81 squares. In each case, the number of playing pieces is increased to total one less than the total number of squares on the board.

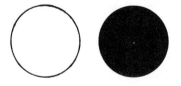

TO BEGIN PLAY.—The players decide who will take the first turn. The first player places two pieces on any squares of the board, except

on the center square. The second player then does the same, and they continue placing two pieces per turn until all of the pieces are on the board. The center square is always left vacant.

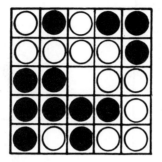

To Play.—The last player to place two pieces on the board makes the first move, moving one piece forward or backward, but never diagonally. Obviously, the first move must be made into the center square. But if the first player to move a piece is unable to do so because the opponent's pieces are blocking the center square, then one of the opponent's pieces is removed.

A player may capture an opponent's piece by flanking or confining it on both sides with two of their own pieces, horizontally or vertically, but not diagonally.

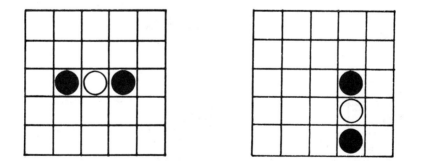

Captures can only be made after all of the playing pieces have been placed on the board. A player may capture more than one of the opponent's pieces if by continuing to move *the same piece*, the player can again flank one of the opponent's pieces, as shown on page 164.

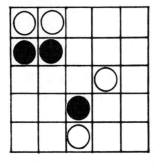

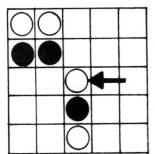

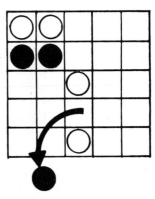

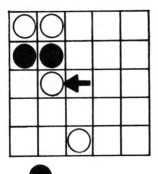

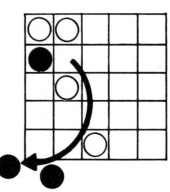

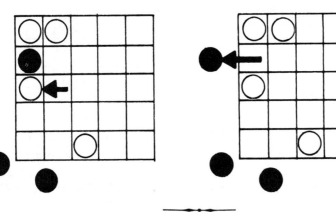

Likewise, a player may capture more than one of the opponent's pieces by moving into the position shown below.

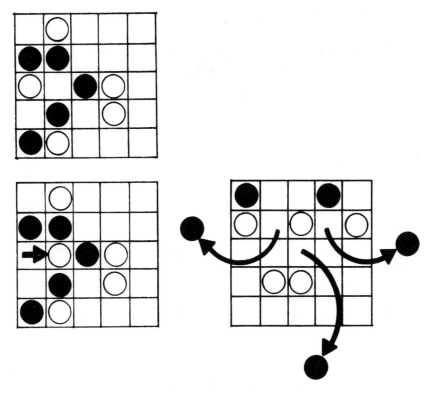

A player can move his or her own piece into a square between two of the opponent's pieces without being captured.

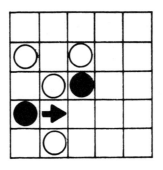

If a player becomes blocked and cannot move a piece, the opponent takes another turn.

The game is over when one player captures all the other player's pieces or when one player's pieces are completely blocked and unable to move. If both players are blocked, the game ends in a draw.

SEEGA PLAYING-BOARD PATTERN.

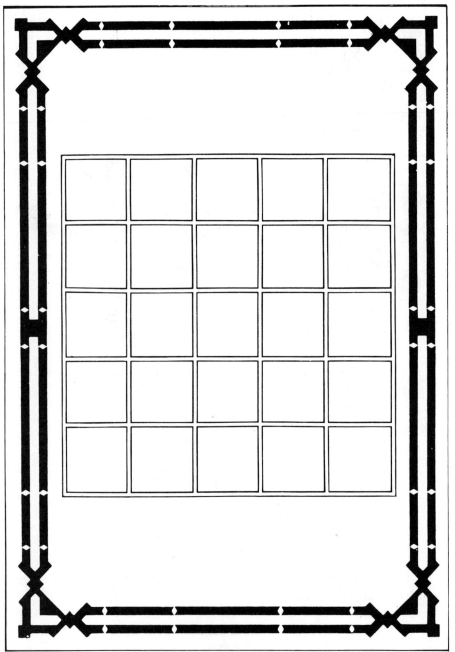

FOX AND GEESE

ASALTO
THE CHINESE REBEL GAME
HARE AND HOUNDS

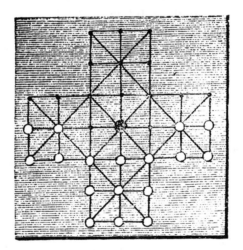

Fox AND GEESE, an intriguing contest between two unequal opponents, has been a favorite game throughout Europe since the Middle Ages. Even though the Geese outnumber the Fox in this hunt game, they are more restricted in the moves they can make and must try to capture the Fox by crowding it into a corner where it cannot move. But the Fox has a different objective. It tries to capture as many of the Geese as possible to prevent its own capture. If careful in their strategic chasing of the Fox, the Geese should always win the game.

Not only does a description of Fox and Geese appear in the *Grettis Saga*, an Icelandic poem written about A.D. 1300, but also in the household accounts of Edward IV of England (1461–83), who purchased two Fox and Geese sets made of silver. English royalty was still playing the game during the nineteenth century, and it is known to have been a favorite of Queen Victoria and Prince Albert.

The tactical possibilities in Fox and Geese make it a popular game not only in Europe but in the Orient and North America as well. Japanese call the game *juroku musashi*, or "sixteen soldiers." In their version, 16 soldiers try to surround their general. Among the Indians of the Southwestern United States, a coyote tries to outwit the chickens, or a jack rabbit attempts to escape Indian hunters. The Cree and Chippewa Indians of Canada also played Fox and Geese but called it *musinaykahwhan–metowaywin*.

Fox and Geese is one of the many board games included in this book that were often played outdoors with their board inscribed on stone or in clay, or drawn on the ground. It is also a popular game often played by children on playgrounds or in the snow, where a number of concentric circles, crisscrossed with straight lines, are drawn.

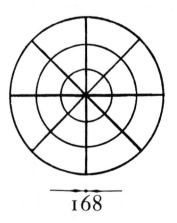

Just as in the board game, the Geese have greater flexibility. The player who is picked to be the Fox can only run along the straight lines, but the Geese can run along any of the paths. On the playground, the game is really tag, for if the Fox touches a Goose, that Goose must become the Fox.

HOW TO PLAY FOX AND GEESE.

NUMBER OF PLAYERS.—Two.

OBJECTIVE.—The Geese try to trap the Fox so that it cannot move, and the Fox tries to capture as many of the Geese as possible so that they cannot surround it.

MATERIALS.—A cross-shaped board with 33 holes or spaces connected by straight and diagonal lines. Seventeen playing pieces of one color for the Geese and one piece of another color for the Fox are used.

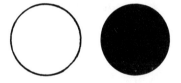

TO BEGIN PLAY.—Place the pieces on the board as illustrated below. The Fox is usually placed in the center, as shown, but it may be placed on any vacant spot the player chooses.

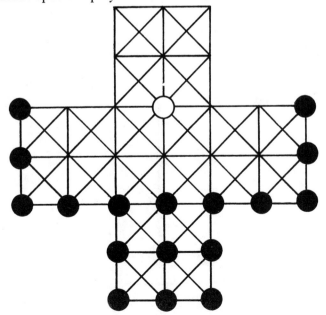

To Play.—The Fox always takes the first turn. It is able to move in any direction: forward, backward, diagonally, or sideways, along the connecting lines.

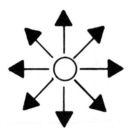

The Fox tries to capture the Geese by jumping over them into a free space on the board. It may capture more than one Goose in one move as long as there is an empty space for it to land on next to each Goose that is captured. The captured Geese are all removed from the board.

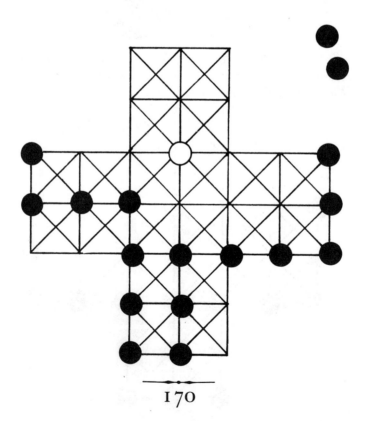

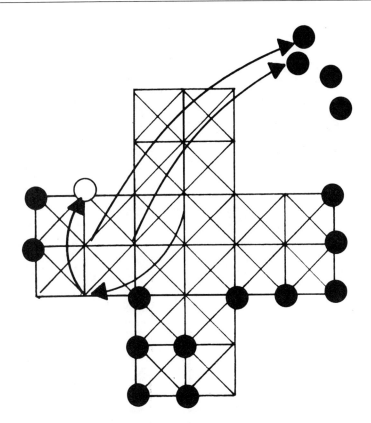

If it has no other move, the Fox must jump a Goose even if it lands on a vulnerable spot.

The Geese may move forward, to the side, or diagonally along the connecting lines, but never backward.

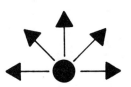

Geese may not jump over the Fox but must try to surround or trap it instead.

The Fox and Geese alternate turns. The Geese try to win by crowding the Fox into a corner so that it cannot move. The Fox can win by capturing so many of the Geese that they cannot surround it or by forcing all the Geese to move forward to the other side of the board so that they no longer have a move and can't chase it.

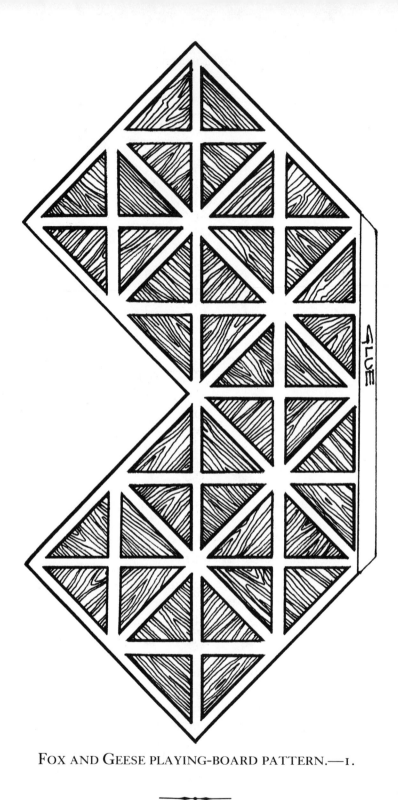

Fox and Geese playing-board pattern.—1.

FOX AND GEESE PLAYING-BOARD PATTERN.—2.

ASALTO

ASALTO ("Assault"), one of the variations of Fox and Geese, is also a contest between two unequal opponents who try to block, out-maneuver, and outwit each other. In this game, a large but poorly armed force attacks a small but powerful fortress. Asalto is played on a board that is the same as the Fox and Geese board, but nine points are separated from the others and designated as the fortress.

One player occupies the fortress with two playing pieces—the officers (or sharpshooters). The other player has 24 pieces, or the foot soldiers, which occupy the surrounding points on the board, which are the battlefield. In order to win the game, these soldiers try to trap the two officers in the fortress, pen them anywhere on the battlefield so that they cannot move, or occupy every point within the fortress. If the officers capture so many foot soldiers that these maneuvers are impossible, they win the game.

An exciting variation of Asalto is Siege, which is played on a larger board that makes the game even more challenging.

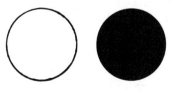

HOW TO PLAY ASALTO.

NUMBER OF PLAYERS.—Two.

OBJECTIVE.—The 24 foot soldiers try to trap the officers inside the fortress or on the battlefield or try to occupy every point in the fortress. The officers try to capture so many of the foot soldiers (at least 15) that they cannot possibly trap them in the fortress or on the battlefield.

MATERIALS.—A cross-shaped playing board with 33 holes or spaces that are connected by straight and diagonal lines. Nine of these holes, all in one arm of the cross, are separated and designated as the fortress. Twenty-four playing pieces of one color for the foot soldiers and two pieces of another color for the officers or sharpshooters are used for the game.

To Begin Play.—Arrange the pieces on the board as illustrated below. The sharpshooters or officers may stand anywhere within the fort at the beginning of the game.

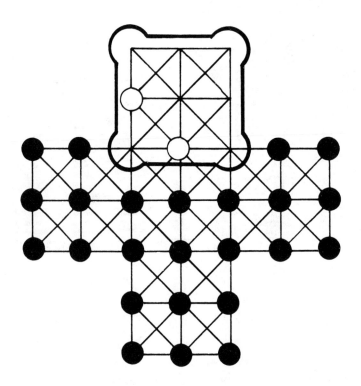

After you decide which player will play the foot soldiers and which will be the sharpshooters, the sharpshooters move first.

To Play.—As in Fox and Geese, the officers may move in any direction along the connecting lines, one space at a time. An officer or sharpshooter may capture a foot soldier by jumping over it to the next space, if it is vacant. The sharpshooters may make as many jumps and captures as they can in one turn, as long as they land on vacant spaces after capturing each soldier. The captured soldiers are removed from the board. If one of the officers fails to make a possible jump and capture, it is removed from the board.

The foot soldiers may only move forward, diagonally, and sideways, but never backward. They may not jump officers but must try to trap them in the fortress or on the battlefield to win the game.

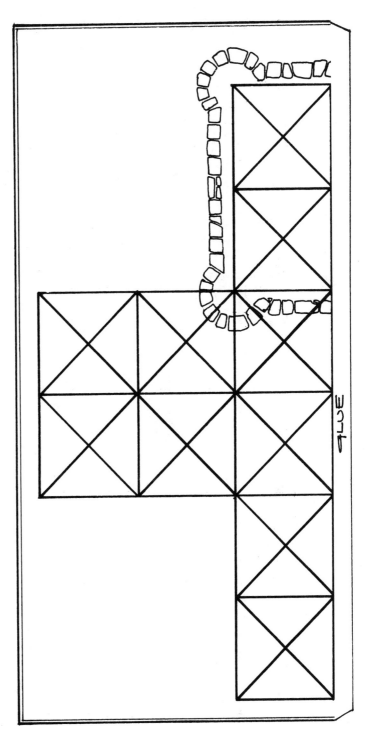

ASALTO PLAYING-
BOARD PATTERN.—I.

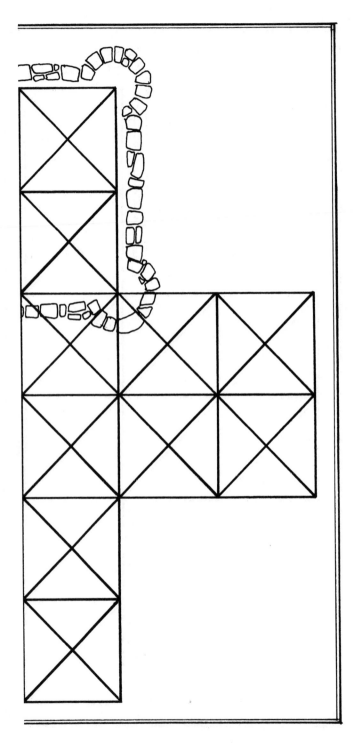

ASALTO PLAYING-
BOARD PATTERN.—2.

THE CHINESE REBEL GAME

THE CHINESE REBEL GAME, another battle game related to Fox and Geese, is played on a board like the one illustrated below. A Commander, who corresponds to the Fox, is placed in the center of the board. He attempts to evade the 20 Soldiers who surround him. Although he is outnumbered and heavily surrounded, the Commander may capture the Soldiers by jumping over them as in Fox and Geese.

CHINESE REBEL GAME BOARD FROM
THOMAS HYDE'S *DE LUDUS ORIENTALIBUS* (1694).

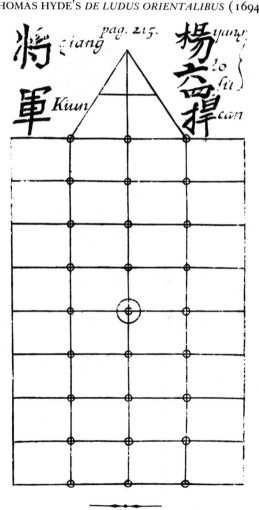

HOW TO PLAY THE CHINESE REBEL GAME.

NUMBER OF PLAYERS.—Two.

OBJECTIVE.—The Soldiers try to trap the Commander by surrounding him or penning him into a corner. The Commander may win by capturing so many Soldiers that it is impossible for them to surround him or by returning to his camp, which is marked by the *x* on the playing board.

MATERIALS.—A rectangular playing board of 39 spaces with a triangular area that surrounds the specially marked camp of the Commander at one end of the board, and 20 playing pieces of one color for the Soldiers and one piece of another color for the Commander.

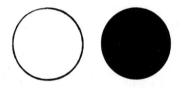

TO BEGIN PLAY.—The pieces are arranged as illustrated below.

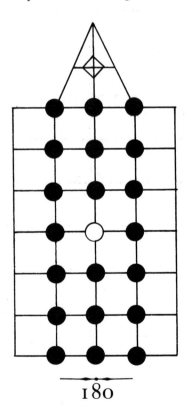

The players decide who is the Commander. The Commander takes the first turn and the players continue alternating turns.

To Play.—Both the Soldiers and the Commander may move forward, sideways, and backward into a vacant spot where the lines intersect, but neither can move diagonally. The Commander may capture a Soldier by jumping over it into the adjacent vacant spot. He may jump only one Soldier at a time. That Soldier is removed from the board when captured. The Commander will always capture a Soldier on his first move.

Since the Soldiers almost always win, unless the Commander is particularly cunning, it is suggested that the players alternate being the Commander and play a set of games to see who can trap the Commander the most number of times.

CHINESE REBEL GAME PLAYING-BOARD PATTERN.—I.

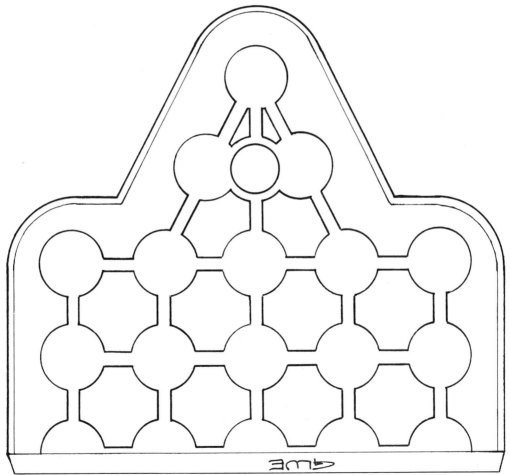

CHINESE REBEL GAME PLAYING-BOARD PATTERN.—2.

HARE AND HOUNDS

HARE AND HOUNDS is a modern variation of Fox and Geese that was first manufactured in England by the Chad Valley Game Company in 1922. As in Fox and Geese, a highly mobile player, the Hare, attempts to avoid capture by a pack of less mobile Hounds.

HOW TO PLAY
HARE AND HOUNDS.

NUMBER OF PLAYERS.—Two to six. One player is the Hare and the other players are the Hounds.

OBJECTIVE.—The Hare attempts to escape the Hounds and reach one of the two spaces marked with an *x* at one side of the board, while the Hounds attempt to capture the Hare by surrounding it so that it cannot move.

MATERIALS.—A square playing board that is marked with many circular spaces that are connected by lines. Five playing pieces of one color represent the Hounds and one piece of another color represents the Hare.

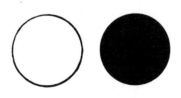

TO BEGIN PLAY.—The Hare is placed in the center space on the side of the board that has five playing spaces. The Hounds are placed in any five of the six playing spaces on the opposite side of the board.

TO PLAY.—The Hare always has the first move and may move one space in any direction in each turn.

The Hounds also move one space per turn and can move in any direction except backwards.

The five Hounds may be moved in any order. If more than one player is moving the Hounds, these players must agree on which Hound is to be moved each turn.

The five Hounds try to win the game by surrounding and trapping the Hare so that it cannot move, as illustrated below.

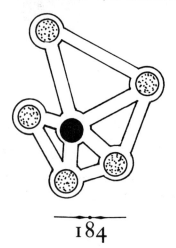

For the Hare to win the game, it must evade the Hounds and reach one of the spaces on the board marked with an *x*.

HARE AND HOUNDS PLAYING-BOARD PATTERN.—I.

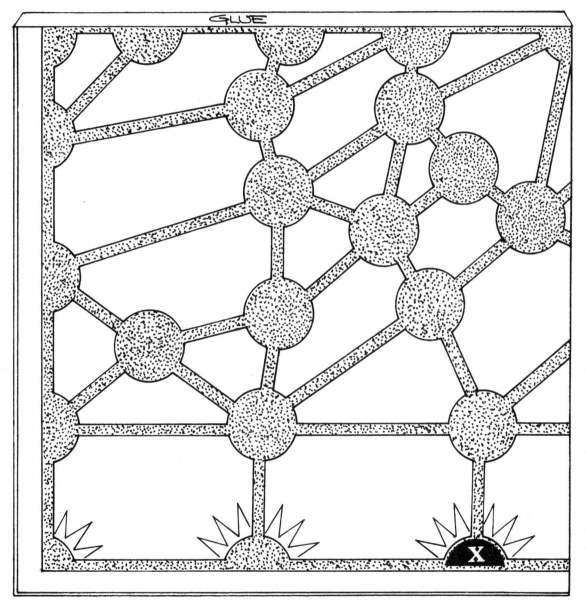

Hare and Hounds playing-board pattern.—2.

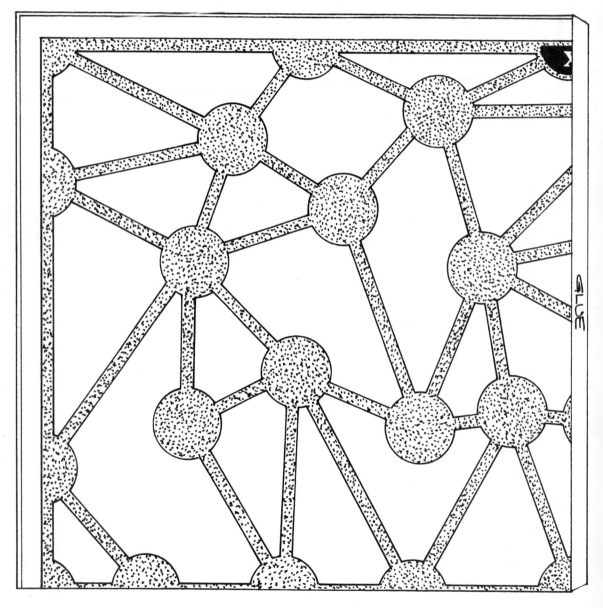

HARE AND HOUNDS PLAYING-BOARD PATTERN.—3.

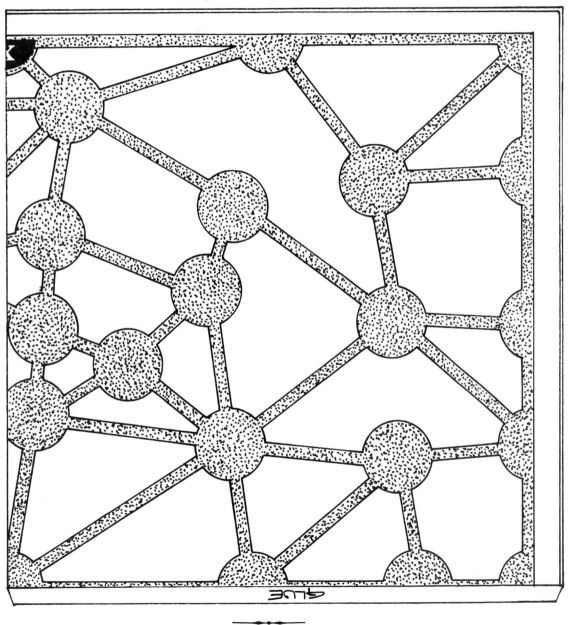

HARE AND HOUNDS PLAYING-BOARD PATTERN.—4.

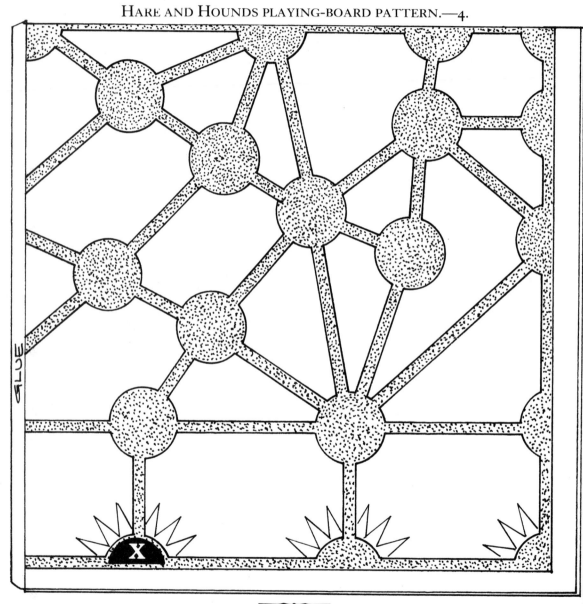

NYOVT

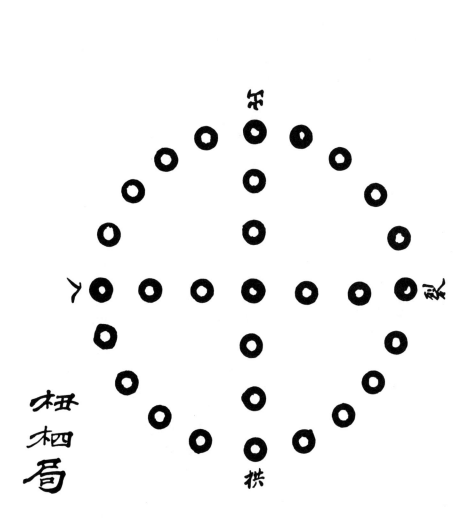

Nyout, a cross-and-circle race game that has been played in Korea for hundreds of years, combines luck with unique possibilities to out-maneuver your opponent. The playing pieces are traditionally carved out of wood or ivory and are known as *mal*, or horse. The boards are often decorated with symbolic images in place of the circles commonly used today.

By the late nineteenth century, Nyout had also become a popular parlor game in the United States that was manufactured by Parker Brothers.

HOW TO PLAY NYOUT.

NUMBER OF PLAYERS.—Any number may play individually or in teams.

OBJECTIVE.—To be the first player to get all of your pieces, or "horses," around the board.

MATERIALS.—Nyout is played on a board marked with 20 colored circles forming a larger circle. Nine more circles form a cross in the interior of the larger circle. The circles at the center of the cross and at the North, South, East, and West points on the outer circle are larger than the others.

Each player has two, three, or four playing pieces of a different color from their opponent's pieces. It is up to the players to decide how many pieces they will play with.

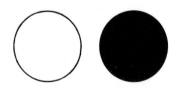

Traditionally, the game is played with flat strips of wood to determine moves up to a score of five, but a die may also be used.

TO BEGIN PLAY.—The players each throw the die, and the one throwing the highest number takes the first turn. Whenever a six is thrown, the player cannot use it and must roll again.

Each player enters his or her piece or pieces according to the number thrown. Horses are entered on the starting circle, which counts as one, and are moved around the board in a counterclockwise direction.

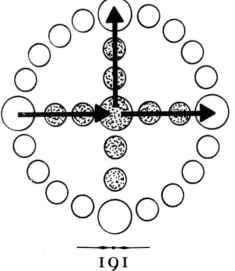

A player may have more than one piece on the ring at a time, and if partners are playing, each partner may move either his own pieces or the partner's pieces.

TO PLAY.—Whenever a horse lands exactly on one of the larger circles, the player may move it on an alternate route along either the horizontal or vertical arms of the interior cross. These routes provide shortcuts to the exit circle or may allow a piece to evade an opponent's horse.

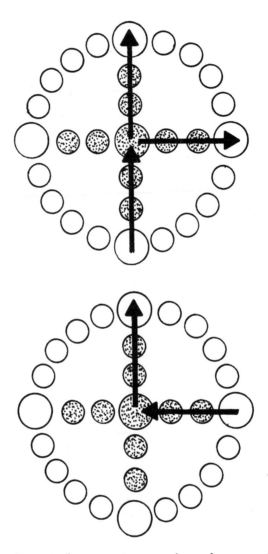

A player does not have to move a piece along an alternate route but may decide to continue along the outer ring of circles.

If a player's horse lands on a circle already occupied by an opponent's horse, the opponent's piece is captured and returned to the starting circle. The player is then allowed another roll of the die.

When a player's piece lands on a circle already occupied by one of that player's horses or one of the player's partner's horses, the two horses may be moved together as a "double piece" in any subsequent turn by the player or the partner.

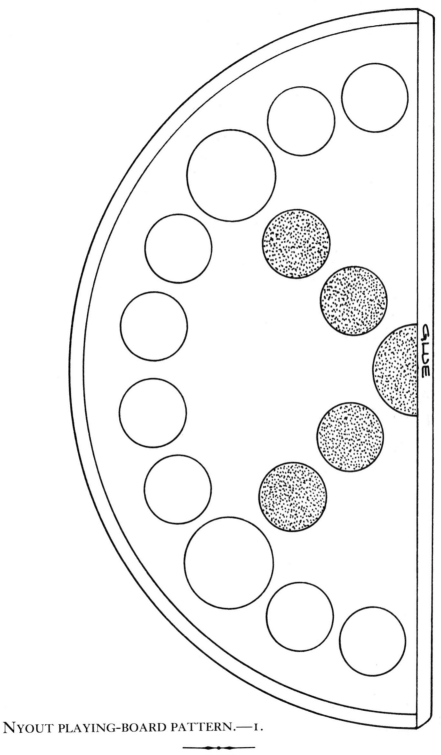

NYOUT PLAYING-BOARD PATTERN.—I.

193

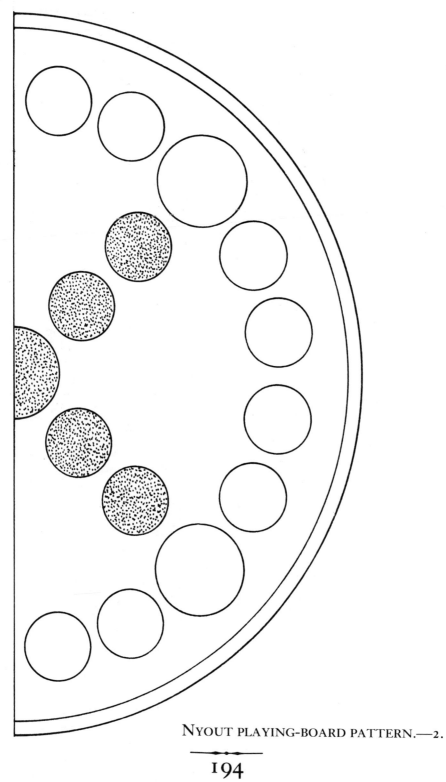

NYOUT PLAYING-BOARD PATTERN.—2.

194

DRAUGHTS

LOSER DRAUGHTS
DIAGONAL DRAUGHTS
CONTINENTAL DRAUGHTS
DRAUGHTS FOR THREE
REVERSI

Draughts, one of the all-time favorite two-player board games, combines a Chess board of 64 black and white squares with the pieces of medieval Backgammon and the moves of Alquerque. The simple rules can be learned in minutes, but the fast-moving game always provides exciting opportunities to block and out-maneuver your opponent.

Draughts originated about A.D. 1100 in southern France, where the pieces were called *Ferses*, after the name of the queen in the medieval game of Chess. The game itself was known as *Fierges*. But when the name of the Chess queen was changed to *Dame*, each piece in Draughts also became known as a *Dame* and the game as *Dames*.

When a rule making it compulsory to capture an opponent's piece became popular in France around 1535, two versions of the game emerged. The capturing game was known as *Jeu Forcé*, and the non-capturing game or non-huffing game as *Le Jeu Plaisant de Dames*, later simplified to *Plaisant*. The capturing game made its way in the sixteenth century to England, where it was called Draughts, and on to North America, where it is called Checkers.

Draughts was such a popular game during the nineteenth century that 27 different books on it were published in England alone between 1800 and 1895! One of the most famous of these books, the *Guide to the Game of Draughts, Containing 500 Select Games*, published by Joseph Sturges in 1800, summed up the universal fascination of Draughts:

> To ascertain, distinctly, consequences in their causes—to calculate with promptitude the result of intricate variety, to elude by vigilant caution the snares of stratagem, are lessons the game of Draughts strongly inculcates, and uniformly explains.

HOW TO PLAY DRAUGHTS.

NUMBER OF PLAYERS.—Two.

OBJECTIVE.—Each player tries to either: move the pieces so that the opponent is unable to make a move; or capture all of the opponent's pieces and remove them from the playing board.

MATERIALS.—A square playing board of 64 dark and light squares. Both players have 12 playing pieces, each player having a different color.

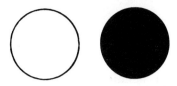

To Begin Play.—The game is played on the dark squares. The player with the dark pieces always takes the first turn, so the players must decide who will play with the dark pieces. Each player arranges the 12 pieces on the 12 dark squares in the first three rows on their side of the board.

Each player may move only one piece per turn. Once a player has touched a piece, it must be moved in that turn. The pieces are moved one square at a time, diagonally only. Pieces may not be moved backwards.

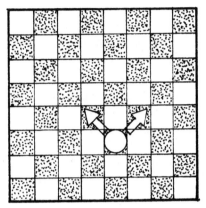

To Play.—An opponent's piece is captured when a piece jumps over it to a vacant square next to it. More than one piece may be captured each turn, as long as there is a vacant square to land on after each successive jump, as illustrated below, but a piece may not be jumped more than once.

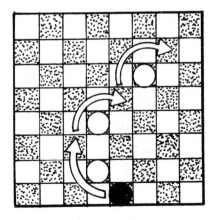

A player may have a choice of whether to capture a small or large number of pieces. But if the player decides to make the larger capture, all the possible jumps and captures must be completed. If a player has a choice between a non-capturing move and a capturing move, the capturing move must be taken. Failure to make a capturing move or to complete a capturing move can result in one of the following penalties:

● The opponent may request that the piece that has just made the move be returned to its original position and that the correct and complete move be made.

○ The opponent may let the move remain as made, but the piece that failed to make a capturing move must make that move in the player's next turn.

● Or, the opponent may choose to remove, or huff, the player's piece that has just made an incorrect move. This huff does not count as a turn, so the opponent gets to then make a move.

(In modern Checkers, these penalties have been revised to rule that the opponent should correct a wrong move and force the player to make it correctly before the game continues.)

Once a piece reaches the last row on the opponent's side of the board, it becomes a "king." The player's turn ends as the piece becomes a king, even if other jumps are possible. A king is "crowned" by a player's placing another piece of the same color on top of it. Once a piece becomes a king, it may be moved either forward or backward along the diagonal squares to a vacant square.

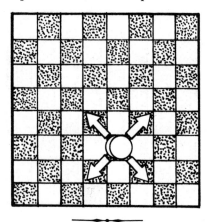

A king may be captured by either a regular piece or by another king piece.

If neither player can remove all the opponent's pieces or prevent the opponent from moving, then the game ends in a draw.

DRAUGHTS PLAYING-BOARD PATTERN.—I.

DRAUGHTS PLAYING-BOARD PATTERN.—2.

LOSER DRAUGHTS

LOSER DRAUGHTS is Draughts with a twist. The object is to lose the game! If a player can successfully place his or her pieces so that the opponent must jump them all and thus loses all of his or her pieces, then that player is the winner. You can also win by positioning your pieces so that it is impossible to move anywhere on the board.

Loser Draughts is played on a regular Draughts or Checkers board of 64 squares. Each player has 12 playing pieces of his or her own color that are placed on the board as in Draughts.

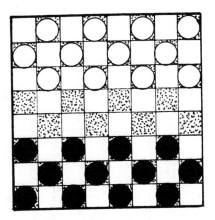

The same rules apply to Loser Draughts as do in Draughts except when a player fails to jump an opponent's piece. Instead of the player's piece being "huffed," or removed from the board, the opponent should request that the player make the jump and remove one or more of his (the opponent's) pieces. Likewise, if a player has several possible jump moves, the opponent may insist that the move that captures the most pieces is made since the opponent wants to lose as many pieces as possible in order to win the game.

DIAGONAL DRAUGHTS

DIAGONAL DRAUGHTS, one variation of Draughts, is played with the same board and rules as Draughts, but the playing pieces are positioned on diagonally opposite corners of the board. The game may be

played with nine pieces for each player, which are placed on the board as illustrated below.

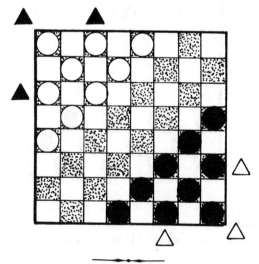

The squares marked with the triangles indicate the squares that must be reached by a piece from the opposite side of the board in order to be crowned a king.

The game may also be played with 12 pieces per player; they are placed on the board as illustrated below. The squares that must be reached in order to be crowned are also marked with triangles.

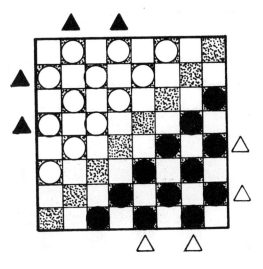

CONTINENTAL DRAUGHTS

CONTINENTAL or POLISH DRAUGHTS, considered one of the greatest two-player board games in the world, was first played in Paris in the 1720s. Various modifications in the rules for the game, which is played with 20 pieces for each player on a board of 100 squares, have made it a fast-moving battle that tests your ability to plan your moves in advance. The unique maneuverability of the king pieces, which can be moved diagonally any number of vacant squares, is especially exciting in this version of Draughts.

As in other Draughts games, the objective of Continental Draughts is to capture all of your opponent's pieces or to trap his or her pieces so that it is impossible for them to move.

TO BEGIN PLAY.—Each player's 20 pieces are positioned on the board as illustrated below.

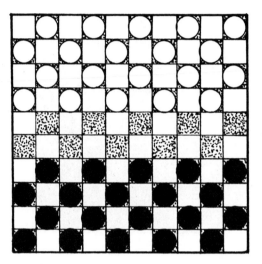

Each piece may be moved diagonally forward one square—except when jumping to capture, when a piece may jump both diagonally forward and backward, as illustrated below.

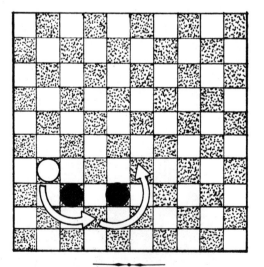

If a player has the choice of a small capture or a large capture, the larger capture must be made. If more than one capture of equal quantity is possible, the most damaging capture (one that includes a king, for instance) must be made.

A player's piece may be crowned a king when it reaches the opponent's back row and remains there at the end of a turn. If a piece reaches the back row but must continue moving on to complete captures, it cannot be crowned. It must wait until it lands on a square on the opponent's back row and remains there at the end of the move.

A piece that has been made a king has much more power than in regular Draughts, Checkers, or Diagonal Draughts. A king may be moved diagonally any number of vacant squares in one move, as illustrated below (left).

A king may also land on any diagonally vacant square, after capturing a piece, as illustrated below (right). An opponent's piece may be jumped only once within a capturing move.

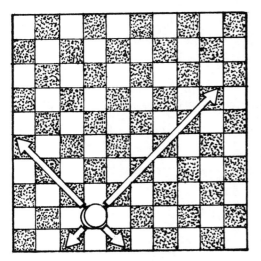

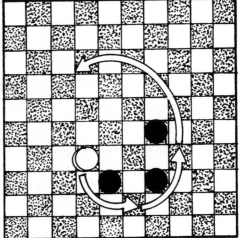

CONTINENTAL DRAUGHTS PLAYING-BOARD PATTERN.—I.

CONTINENTAL DRAUGHTS PLAYING-BOARD PATTERN.—2.

DRAUGHTS FOR THREE

DRAUGHTS FOR THREE was invented by an Englishman, John Hyde, and patented in the United States in 1888. Played by three people on a triangular board, the game requires even more concentration and strategy than Draughts because both the rules and the game are much more complicated.

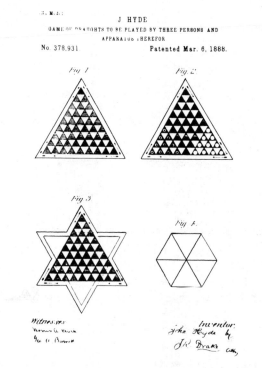

HOW TO PLAY DRAUGHTS FOR THREE.

NUMBER OF PLAYERS.—Three.

OBJECTIVE.—Each player tries to capture as many of the other two players' pieces as possible so that only one player is left in the game, becoming the winner.

MATERIALS.—A triangular-shaped playing board divided into 81 equilateral triangles, alternately dark and light. Each player uses ten playing pieces of his or her own color.

TO BEGIN PLAY.—Each player places his or her ten pieces in the corners of the board on the dark triangles. The players decide who will take the first turn. All subsequent moves are taken in rotation

TO PLAY.—Each player may move one piece one triangle (one space) per turn, toward either opponent's home base, as indicated by the arrows in the above illustration. The game is played on only the dark triangles.

A player crowns a piece once it reaches the last line of triangles (except for the triangle forming the corner of the board) of either of the opponent's home bases. Once a piece is crowned it may also move

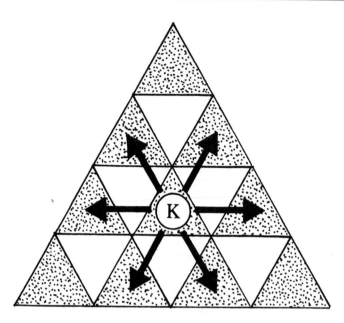

horizontally. The horizontal can be determined as being parallel to the base of the triangular board farthest from the piece's home base.

When a piece is crowned and becomes a king, it cannot be moved along the outer rows of the board until it has been moved in at least one space from the outer row. After being brought in, it may be moved back to an outer row, but each time it moves to the outer row, the king must be brought back to an inside row again.

As in Draughts, a piece may be captured by regular pieces and kings by being jumped. More than one piece may be jumped and captured in the same turn. If a player has a choice of jumping and capturing one or more pieces of either opponent, the choice is the player's. If a player fails to make a capturing jump, her piece may be "huffed," or removed from the board, as in regular Draughts.

After one player is out of the game, the player who succeeds in capturing the remaining opponent's last piece is the winner. If the two remaining players both have only a king left and they are unable to force each other into a position in which a king can be captured, the game is considered a draw. Likewise, if all three players are left with only a king and are unable to force the capture of their opponent's pieces, the game ends in a draw.

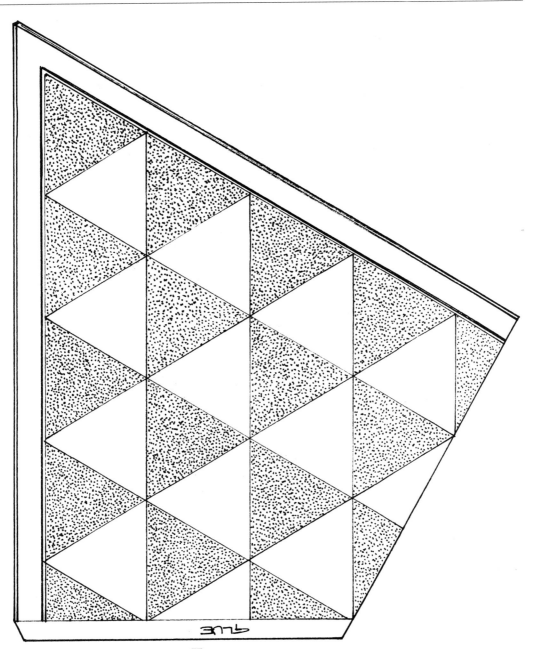

DRAUGHTS FOR THREE PLAYING-BOARD PATTERN.—1.

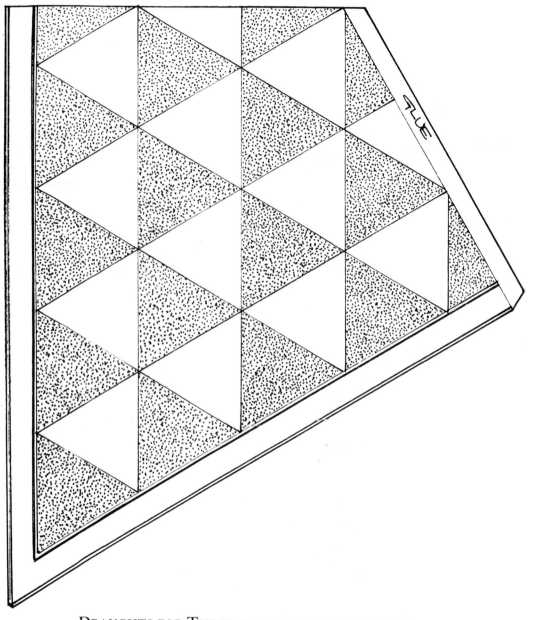

DRAUGHTS FOR THREE PLAYING-BOARD PATTERN.—2.

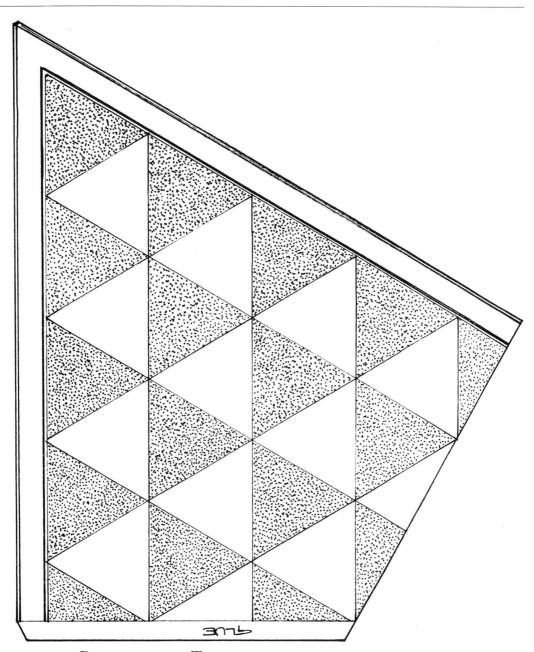

DRAUGHTS FOR THREE PLAYING-BOARD PATTERN.—3.

REVERSI

REVERSI, a board game for two that was invented in England in the late nineteenth century, is played on the Draughts or Checkers board of 64 squares. Even though the rules are as simple as in Draughts and take just a minute to learn, Reversi can take a lifetime to master!

Throughout Reversi, the players strategically place their pieces on the squares until the entire board is covered. But whenever one player outflanks one or more of the opponent's pieces, those pieces are reversed to the player's colors. Thus, Reversi is especially exciting as fortunes change and the colors of pieces are dramatically reversed throughout the game.

HOW TO PLAY REVERSI.

NUMBER OF PLAYERS.—Two.

OBJECTIVE.—To have more pieces of your own color on the board at the end of the game than your opponent does.

MATERIALS.—A Draughts board of 64 squares. Since the contrasting colors of the squares on a Draughts board have no significance in Reversi, you may find it less confusing to play the game on a grid of 64 plain squares and decide to make a board especially for Reversi, using the patterns provided. Sixty-four playing pieces, black on one side and white on the other, are used to play the game.

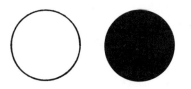

TO BEGIN PLAY.—Each player takes 32 pieces to use throughout the game. Determine which player is to take the first turn. Black always moves first. Each player places two pieces on the board in either of the two arrangements shown at the top of page 215.

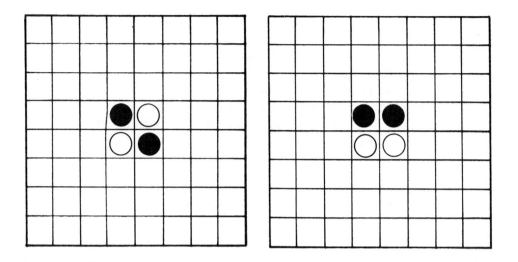

To Play.—Each player places one piece on the board at a time so that one or more of the opponent's pieces are bordered at each end, or "outflanked" by two of the player's own pieces. When one or more pieces are trapped by their being outflanked, they are reversed to show the color of their captor, as illustrated below.

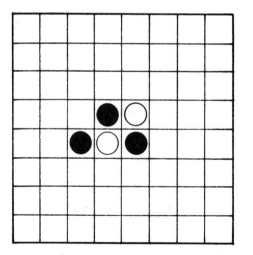
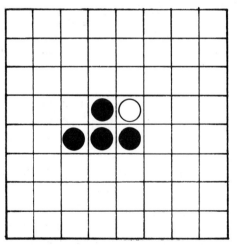

A player's piece may outflank any number of pieces in one turn. Any of the opponent's pieces that are in a row or continuous straight line may be outflanked. If the line is broken by one of the player's own

215

pieces or by a vacant square, it does not qualify as a continuous row and is not a correct move.

A player may outflank an opponent's pieces in any direction (diagonally, vertically, and horizontally) and in any number of directions in one turn, as shown in the following illustrations. In the first diagram, the white piece marked with the black square is the last piece placed on the board. Its position enables the player to outflank every one of the opponent's pieces and to reverse them to the player's own color!

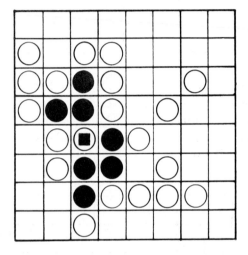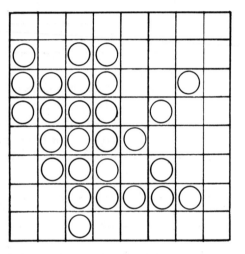

All the pieces that are outflanked in any move must be reversed even if not to the player's advantage. If a player mistakenly reverses a piece, or fails to reverse an outflanked piece, the mistake may be corrected if the opponent has not already moved. Otherwise, the pieces cannot be reversed and the mistake stands.

When a player cannot outflank at least one piece, his turn is forfeited. But if a player runs out of pieces and has the opportunity to outflank one of the opponent's pieces, the opponent must give the player a piece to make the move.

When all 64 pieces are on the board or when neither player can make a move, the game is over. The player with the most pieces on the board is the winner.

REVERSI PLAYING-BOARD PATTERN.—I.

REVERSI PLAYING-BOARD PATTERN.—2.

BACKGAMMON

THE POINTS GAME
THE DOUBLING GAME

Backgammon, a one-to-one battle, is one of the world's oldest games. In fact, Backgammon has been exciting and challenging board-game players for thousands of years. This intriguing game combines the luck of the dice with the calculating strategy of moving and positioning one's playing pieces. The rules are simple to learn—but the possibilities of combinations of moves are astounding!

The oldest known Backgammon board was one of five gaming boards found by Sir Leonard Woolley in the royal tombs at Ur in Iraq, which date from about 3000 B.C. Another version of the game, known in Persia and the Near East as *Nard*, is more than 1,600 years old. It is believed that Nard was introduced into Europe by the Arabs. Their game included a board with 24 points, 30 playing pieces, and a pair of dice.

Not only has Backgammon been played throughout history, but it has been popular all over the world as well. By the sixth century, the game was well known in China, where it was called *t'shu-p'u*. Both the Chinese and Japanese versions, *sunoroko*, are played on a circular board. Fifteen variations of the game are illustrated in the *Libro de Juegos* of King Alfonso X (1251–1282) of Castille. In fact, Backgammon appears in all sorts of writings from Plato and Sophocles to Chaucer's *Canterbury Tales*.

Originally, Backgammon was known by the Latin name *tabula*, which became "tables" when the game was introduced into England. Many other games that were played on a table, such as Chess, were at one time known as Tables. In Spain, Backgammon is called *tablas reales*, and in Italy, *tavole reale*, both references to "royal tables." Germans call the game *puff*, and the French game is known as *trictrac*.

LE TRICTRAC.

In the seventeenth century, the game became known as Back-gammon, since pieces are often required to go "back" and re-enter the board, or "gamen."

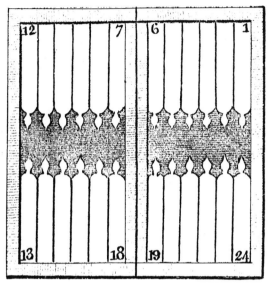

THE BACKGAMMON BOARD.

Since the Middle Ages, the Backgammon board has given crafts-men the opportunity to express their skill by making boards and pieces that are beautiful works of art, made out of inlaid woods, polished stones, silver, and gold leaf. As the game has experienced periodic re-vivals in popularity, improvements have been made in the board and dice. For example, in 1873, a folding Backgammon board was patented in the United States. In 1884, another American patented a Backgam-mon board and dice cup lined with soft material to muffle the rattling noise usually associated with the game.

Perhaps the greatest contribution Americans made to the game was the addition of the doubling cube during the 1920s, when Back-gammon was experiencing another surge in popularity. Not only is the cube a lethal weapon with which to bluff an opponent, but it also en-hances the gambling possibilities of the game. This associaton of Backgammon with gambling is not new. In the seventh century the game was declared illegal by Emperor Jito of Japan, and throughout the Middle Ages, the Catholic church also tried to prohibit it. Today, the doubling cube remains an important part of modern Backgammon sets, which are usually portable sets that can be carried around and played anywhere, just as the game was carried by the Crusaders more than 800 years ago!

(No Model.)

A. A. JACKSON.

GAME BOARD, DICE BOX, &c.

No. 296,012.

Patented Apr. 1, 1884.

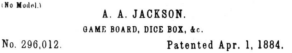

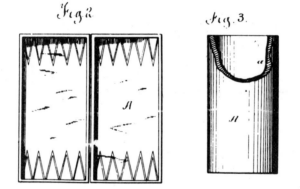

Witnesses:
Tom. A. Rosenbaum
Wm M. Stockbridge.

Inventor
A. Amelia Jackson
by V.D. Stockbridge
atty

HOW TO PLAY
BACKGAMMON.

NUMBER OF PLAYERS.—Two.

OBJECTIVE.—To be the first player to move all of your pieces to your inner table, where they can be removed (borne off) from the board. The first player to "bear off" all his or her pieces from the board wins.

MATERIALS.—A rectangular board consisting of 24 points, or elongated triangles of alternating colors. A "bar" divides the board down the middle. Players sit on opposite sides of the board. Their first six points are called their "inner table." Points seven through 12 are the player's "outer table."

Each player has 15 pieces of a different color from their opponent's pieces. Two pairs of dice are used to determine moves, and sometimes dicing cups are also used to throw the dice.

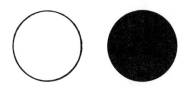

To BEGIN PLAY.—Pieces are placed on the board as illustrated below. Traditionally, the inner tables are always nearer the source of light.

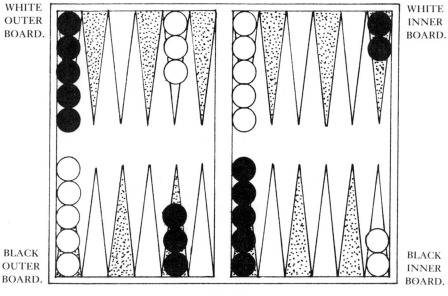

WHITE OUTER BOARD.

WHITE INNER BOARD.

BLACK OUTER BOARD.

BLACK INNER BOARD.

Each player rolls a single die. The player rolling the highest number goes first, choosing which side of the board and color of pieces to play with. This player moves first, combining the two single throws of the players as her first move. Throughout the rest of the game, each player both throws the die and moves accordingly in alternating turns.

The two numbers of the two dice thrown each turn may be used separately to move two pieces or combined to move one piece. For example, with a throw of "four" and "two," a player may move: one piece two points and then move the same piece another four points; one piece four points and then the same piece two more points; or two pieces, one for two points and one for four points in either of the possible combinations.

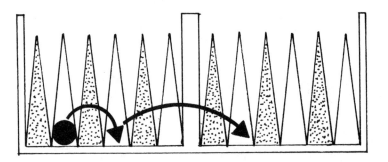

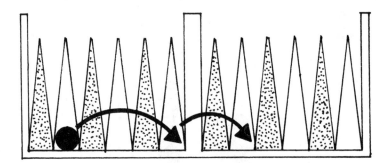

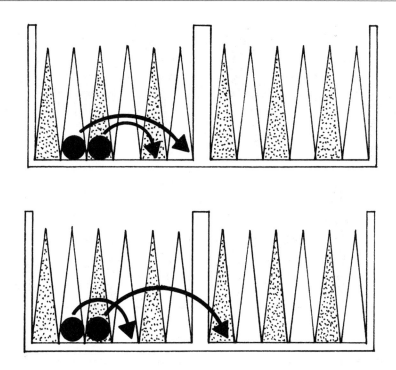

A player's pieces may be moved to any point except one already occupied by two or more of the opponent's pieces. When a player has two or more pieces on a point, this is called "making a point," and the opponent is barred from landing on that point. If one piece is being moved both the numbers thrown, neither count may land on a point "made" by the opponent's pieces.

If a player throws a pair, this throw is known as a "doublet," and the player is allowed to move double the number thrown. For example, if a "five" and a "five" are thrown, the player is allowed to move five, five, five, and five. The player may use the four fives in any combination.

A player must always use both numbers thrown whenever possible, but if a player can use only one of the numbers on the pair of dice, and there is a choice, the highest number must always be used. Any part of the throw that cannot be used is lost.

The two players move their pieces in opposite directions. For example, white would move from black's inner board to black's outer board, then on to white's outer board and, at last, to white's inner board or home.

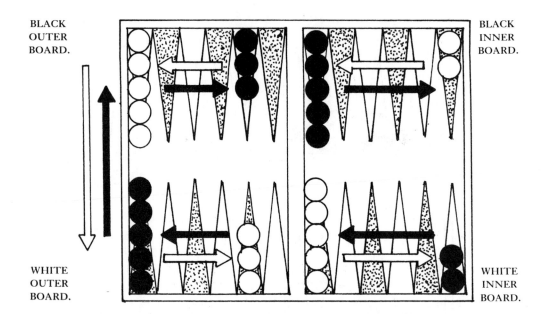

When all of a player's pieces are in his or her inner board, or home, then this player may begin to "bear off."

To Play.—When a single piece occupies a point, this is known as a "blot." If the opponent lands on this blot, the piece is removed from the board and placed on the "bar," where it must remain until it can be entered into the opponent's inner board.

A player must re-enter any pieces from the bar before any other moves may be made. A piece may enter the board on points of the same number as shown on the dice. For example, if a "five" and "three" are thrown, a piece may be entered on a five point or a three

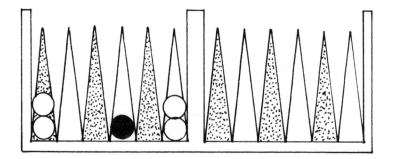

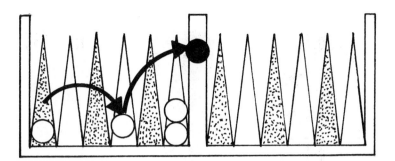

point in the opponent's inner board. If a point is made by two or more of the opponent's pieces, a player may not enter on that point. If all six of an opponent's inner-board points are made, the player forfeits that turn until the opponent's plays open up the inner board and make entry possible.

A player may land on two or more blots in the same throw. Likewise, a player has the choice of landing on a blot or not landing on it unless no other move is possible.

A player may begin to bear off pieces when all 15 pieces are on points in that player's inner board area. The numbers thrown on the dice may be used to bear off a piece or to move it forward, or both. If a number higher than any point occupied by the player's pieces is thrown, a piece from the highest point is borne off. If a number is thrown for any points not covered by pieces and it is not sufficient to bear off a piece, then a piece from the highest point (farthest point) may be moved forward. Four pieces may be borne off at the same time with a doublet.

If a player's blot is hit by the opponent while the player is bearing off, the piece must be entered from the bar and moved around the board to the player's inner board before any more pieces may be borne off.

Traditionally, the winner of a game of Backgammon may "score" the victory in the following manner:

A "single game"—if the opponent has borne off at least one piece and has no pieces in the winner's inner board.

A "double game" or "gammon"—if the opponent has not borne off any pieces.

A "triple game" or "backgammon"—if the opponent has not borne off any pieces and has at least one piece still on the bar or in the winner's inner board.

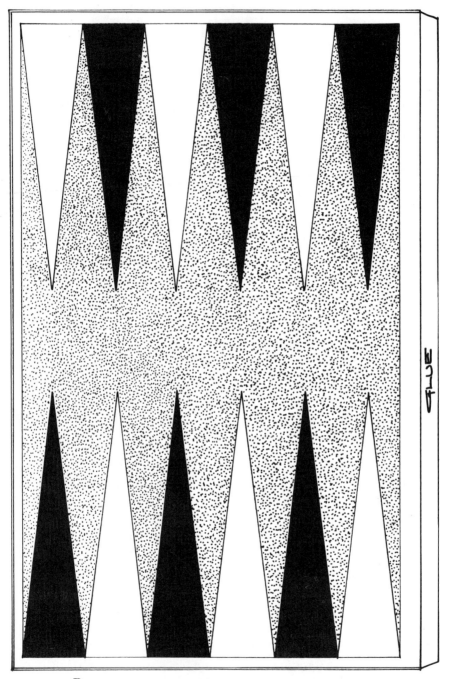

BACKGAMMON PLAYING-BOARD PATTERN.—I.

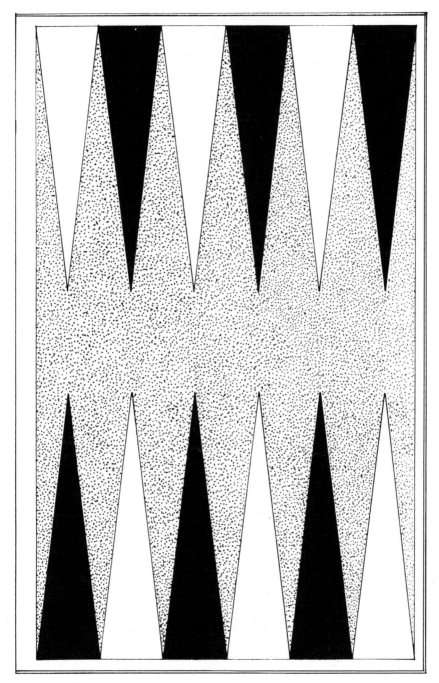

BACKGAMMON PLAYING-BOARD PATTERN—2.

THE POINTS GAME

THE POINTS GAME of Backgammon is another way to play the game with degrees of victory. The winner gets four points for each of the opponent's pieces still in the winner's inner board or on the bar, three points for each of the opponent's pieces in the winner's outer board, two points for each of the opponent's pieces in the opponent's outer board, and one point for each of the opponent's pieces in the opponent's inner board. If the opponent has not borne off any pieces, the score is doubled for a gammon. If the opponent has not borne off any pieces and has at least one piece still on the bar or in the winner's inner board, the score is tripled for a backgammon.

THE DOUBLING GAME

THE DOUBLING GAME is another way to play Backgammon, and it was invented in the United States during the 1920s. The doubling cube is a large die with the numbers 2:4:8:16:32:64 on its sides.

Throughout the game, the stakes may be doubled and redoubled in addition to the traditional double for a gammon and a triple score for a backgammon.

At the beginning of the game, the doubling cube is placed with the number "64" up to denote a value of one. If matching numbers are thrown by the two players when they are throwing the die to determine who is the first player, the cube is usually automatically doubled to "2." It is up to the players to decide if they will allow only one such automatic doubling of the cube or how many times they want this to happen.

Throughout the game, each player has the right to offer the first voluntary doubling of the cube to the opponent. If the opponent accepts, the cube is doubled. If not, the opponent forfeits the game at the stakes represented by the present number on the cube. A player must offer the doubling cube to an opponent before the dice are thrown for his turn.

After the first voluntary doubling of the cube, a player may only offer the doubling cube if the opponent made the previous doubling offer. Thus it is possible for a player to win a game with stakes as high as "192"—if the doubling cube has been doubled to "64" and then the player wins a Backgammon, which automatically triples the "64" to "192"!

HISTORICAL ILLUSTRATIONS (SOURCES)

The historical illustrations used in *Play It Again* are drawn primarily from works published during the nineteenth century. In addition to children's magazines and books, sources for the illustrations include patents, rule books, and classic works on board games, as well as the board games themselves. The following references will, we hope, be of use to those interested in doing further research on the history of board games.

ii ⊖ Board games. Hermann Wagner, *Speilbuch für Knaben* (Leipzig and Berlin: Otto Spamer, 1885), figs. 208–212.

4 ● Dice. Jacques Stella, *Games and Pastimes of Childhood* (Facsimile of the 1657 edition reprinted by Dover Books: New York, 1969), pl. 37.

4 ⊖ Dice-Play. Charles Hoole (trans.), *Orbis Sensualium Pictus*, Jan Amos Comenius (London: F. Kirton, 1659), p. 272, pl. cxxxiv.

5 ● Dice and Dicing Cup. *Backgammon: Its History and Practice*, "By the Author of 'Whist'" (London: D. Bogue, 1844), title page.

5 ⊖ Le Toton. L. Harquevaux and L. Pelletier, *200 Jeux D'Enfants* (Paris: Librairie Larousse, n.d.), p. 161.

10 ● Checkers. (William Clarke), *Boy's Own Book* (New York: C. S. Francis & Co., 1855), n.p.

233

13 ☉ Game Boards, Dice, and Dicing Cups. *Harrod's Catalogue*, 1895, p. 1302.

19 ● "The Royal and Entertaining Game of Goose," Courtesy of the Yale Center for British Art, folio A, G1.

20 ☉ Nineteenth-century Game of Goose board. L. Harquevaux and L. Pelletier, *200 Jeux D'Enfants* (Paris: Librairie Larousse, n.d.), p. 166.

21 ● Children playing the Game of Goose. L. Harquevaux and L. Pelletier, *200 Jeux D'Enfants* (Paris: Librairie Larousse, n.d.), p. 167.

29 ☉ Le Merelle and Le Cerf Volant. Jacques Stella, *Games and Pastimes of Childhood* (Facsimile of the 1657 edition reprinted by Dover Books: New York, 1969), pl. 17.

30 ● Morrice Board. Miss Leslie (Eliza), *The American Girl's Book* (New York: James Miller, 1851), p. 148.

31 ☉ Game board. R. Creifelds, U.S. Patent No. 52,784. Patented December 24, 1918.

37 ● Game board. J. J. Donahue and J. H. Sullivan, U.S. Patent No. 25,349. Patented April 7, 1896.

41 ☉ De Indorum Ludo Tchupur. Thomas Hyde, *De Ludis Orientalibus* (London: 1694), p. 68. Courtesy of the Beinecke Library, Yale University.

42 ● Pachisi board in the courtyard of Futteypore Sikri Palace. Edward Falkener, *Games Ancient and Oriental* (London: Longmans, Green & Co., 1892), p. 257.

43 ☉ Pachisi. Sears, Roebuck & Co. Catalogue, 1908, p. 1046.

53 ● Box lid for Snakes and Ladders game, manufactured in 1911 by the Chad Valley Company, England. From the Brian Love collection, as reproduced in *Play the Game* (Los Angeles: Reed Books, 1978), p. 91.

61 ☉ Knights playing Alquerque. Alfonso X, *Das spanische schachzabelbuch des königs Alfons des Weisen vom jahre 1283* (Leipzig: K. W. Hiersemann, 1913), 91 Verso, pl. CLXXXII.

85 ● Solitaire. Gaston Tissandier, *Popular Scientific Recreations*, trans. Henry Frith (New York: Ward, Lock and Co., 1890[?]), p. 739.

91 ◒ Halma advertisement from the early 1890s.

100 ● Game board. J. E. Huffaker, U.S. Patent No. 2,235,615. Patented March 18, 1941.

109 ◒ Turkish Girls Playing Mancala. Stewart Culin, "Mancala, The National Game of Africa," *United States National Museum Report*, 1894, pl. 1.

110 ● Mancala Board, Maldive Islands. Stewart Culin, "Mancala, The National Game of Africa," *United States National Museum Report*, 1894, p. 599, fig. 5.

115 ◒ Game board. M. B. Lorenzana, et al., U.S. Patent No. 162,-742. Patented April 3, 1951.

119 ● Das Wettrennspiel. Hugo Elm, *Speil und Beihaftigung* (Dresden: Verlag von A. Müller-Fröbelhaus, 1892), p. 283, fig. 371.

120 ◒ Game of Steeple Chase. In the *Butler Brothers Catalogue*, 1914, p. 189.

120 ● Race for the Cup, *Butler Brothers Catalogue*, 1914, p. 189.

129 ◒ Queen's Guard boards. John D. Champlin and Arthur E. Bostwick, *The Young Folks Cyclopedia of Games and Sports* (New York: Henry Holt & Co., 1899), p. 1.

137 ● Game of Chivalry. *Butler Brothers Catalogue*, 1895, p. 99.

138 ◒ Game. G. S. Parker, U.S. Patent No. 1,780,038. Patented October 28, 1930.

147 ● Game board. W. B. Silver, U.S. Patent No. 255,892. Patented April 4, 1882.

161 ◒ Seega—the Modern Egyptian Game. Edward Falkener, *Games Ancient and Oriental* (London: Longmans, Green and Co., 1892), p. 63.

167 ● Sedentary Games. Joseph Strutt, *The Sports and Pastimes of the People of England*. Revision of the 1801 edition by J. Charles Cox (London: Methuen & Co., 1903), pl. XXXIII.

168 ⊜ Playground Fox and Geese. John D. Champlin and Arthur E. Bostwick, *The Young Folks Cyclopedia of Games and Sports* (New York: Henry Holt & Co., 1899), p. 363, fig. 5.

174 ● Asalto. Hermann Wagner, *Speilbuch für Knaben* (Leipzig and Berlin: Otto Spamer, 1885), p. 255.

175 ⊜ Siege. *Gamages Christmas Bazaar Catalogue*, 1913, p. 216.

179 ● Subjugatio Rebellium. Thomas Hyde, *De Ludis Orientalibus* (London: 1694), p. 215. Courtesy of the Beinecke Library, Yale University.

189 ⊜ Nyout Playing Board. Stewart Culin, *Korean Games with Notes on the Corresponding Games of China and Japan* (Philadelphia: University of Pennsylvania, 1895), p. 67, fig. 75.

195 ● Draughts. *Every Boy's Book* (London and New York: George Routledge & Sons, 1868), p. 689.

201 ⊜ Draughts. *The Boy's Own Book*. Seventh Edition (London: Vizetelly, Branston and Co., 1831), p. 305.

202 ● Draughts. *The Boy's Treasury of Sports, Pastimes and Recreations* (Philadelphia: Lea and Blanchard, 1847), p. 275.

203 ⊜ Draughts. Miss Leslie (Eliza), *The American Girl's Book* (New York: James Miller, 1851), p. 142.

208 ● Game of Draughts to Be Played by Three Persons. J. Hyde, U.S. Patent No. 378,931. Patented March 6, 1888.

219 ⊜ Backgammon table from fourteenth-century manuscript. Joseph Strutt, *The Sports and Pastimes of the People of England*. Revision of the 1801 edition by J. Charles Cox (London: Methuen & Co., 1903), pl. XXXIV.

220 ● Le Trictrac. Fréderic Dillaye, *Les Jeux de La Jeunesse* (Paris: Librairie Hackette et Cie, 1885), p. 325.

221 ⊜ Sedentary Games. Joseph Strutt, *The Sports and Pastimes of the People of England*. Revision of the 1801 edition by J. Charles Cox (London: Methuen & Co., 1903), pl. XXXIII.

222 ● Game Board, Dice Box, etc.   A. A. Jackson, U.S. Patent No. 296,012. Patented April 1, 1884.

230 ⊖ Backgammon. *Backgammon: Its History and Practice.* "By the Author of 'Whist' " (London: D. Bogue, 1844), p. B.

INDEX